Photo by Five Petals Photography

Abigail Owen is an award-winning author who writes romantasy and paranormal romance. She is obsessed with big worlds, fast plots, couples that spark, a dash of snark and oodles of HEAs! Other titles include: wife, mother, Star Wars geek, ex–competitive skydiver, AuDHD, spreadsheet lover, Jeopardy! fanatic, organizational guru, true classic movie buff, linguaphile, wishful world traveller and chocoholic. Abigail currently resides in Austin, Texas, with her own swoon-worthy hero, their (mostly) angelic teenagers, and two adorable fur babies.

abigailowen.com

FICTION

ALSO BY ABIGAIL OWEN

THE CRUCIBLE
The Games Gods Play

DOMINIONS

The Liar's Crown
The Stolen Throne
The Shadows Rule All

INFERNO RISING

The Rogue King
The Blood King
The Warrior King
The Cursed King

FIRE'S EDGE

The Mate
The Boss
The Rookie
The Enforcer
The Protector
The Traitor

BRIMSTONE INC.
The Demigod Complex
Shift Out of Luck
A Ghost of a Chance
Bait N' Witch
Try As I Smite
Hit by the Cupid Stick
An Accident Waiting to Dragon

THE CURSED KING

INFERNO
RISING

ABIGAIL OWEN

The Cursed King
© 2021 by Abigail Owen
ISBN 9781038945044

First published in the USA by Entangled Publishing, LLC.
First Australian edition published 2024
by HQ Fiction
an imprint of HQBooks (ABN 47 001 180 918), a subsidiary of
HarperCollins Publishers Australia Pty Limited (ABN 36 009 913 517).

HarperCollins acknowledges the Traditional Custodians of the lands upon which
we live and work, and pays respect to Elders past and present.

Edited by Heather Howland
Cover art and design by LJ Anderson, Mayhem Cover Creations and Bree Archer
Stock art by Photo2008/GettyImages, draco77/GettyImages, getgg/Depositphotos,
and PHOTOGraphicss/GettyImages
Interior design by Britt Marczak

A catalogue record for this book is available from the National Library of Australia
www.librariesaustralia.nla.gov.au

Printed and bound in Australia by McPherson's Printing Group

To Alyssa – friend, mentor, and all round beautiful and amazing woman.

The Cursed King is a high-heat fantasy romance—and not just from the dragon fire. As such, the story contains elements that might not be suitable for all readers, including war, battle, blood and gore, PTSD, torture, violence, death, gang violence, murder, burning, injury, hospitalization, imprisonment, perilous situations, graphic language, alcohol use, loss of family, grief, and sex on the page—on *a lot* of pages. Readers who may be sensitive to these elements, please take note and get ready to enter a spicy new world of dragon shifters!

THE DRAGON CLANS

GOLD
King: Brand Astarot
Location: North Europe
Based in: Store Skagastølstind, Norway

BLUE
King: Ladon Ormarr
Location: Western Europe
Based in: Ben Nevis, Scotland

BLACK
King: Samael Veles
Location: Western Asia/Northern Africa
Based in: Mount Ararat, Turkey

GREEN
King: Fraener Luu
Location: Eastern/Southern Asia
Based in: Yulong Xueshan, China

WHITE
King: Volos Ajdaho
Location: Eastern Europe/Northern Asia
Based in: Kamen, Russia

RED
King: Pytheios Chandali
Location: Central Asia
Based in: Everest, Nepal/China

Nor shall this peace sleep with her; but as when
The bird of wonder dies, the maiden phoenix,
Her ashes new create another heir
As great in admiration as herself;
So shall she leave her blessedness to one,
When heaven shall call her from this cloud of darkness,
Who from the sacred ashes of her honour
Shall star-like rise, as great in fame as she was,
And so stand fix'd.

~Shakespeare, Henry VIII

PROLOGUE

Three months ago…

Angelika Amon stuck to the perimeter of the large training room in the mountain stronghold of Ben Nevis in Scotland, headed for the smaller, human-sized door that led to the platform outside. Jedd would kill her if he knew she was planning to go out there at all, let alone without him.

Then again, he was supposed to be her bodyguard.

The night her mother died, she had sent each of her daughters to different protectors— Kasia to their faithful hellhound Maul in Alaska, Meira to gargoyles in some still unknown place, Skylar to a rogue dragon shifter in South America, and Angelika to a pack of wolf shifters in the Pyrenees. The same pack that was with her now, living inside a dragon shifter mountain just to give her a cover story. If she hadn't believed in miracles before, that would have convinced her.

Jedd, one of the best fighters of the pack, was her best friend more than bodyguard these days. She hated to worry him. Even so, she *had* to get out. Alone. The cave walls felt as though they were closing in on her.

Not claustrophobia. Not exactly. Worries piled so high she couldn't see her way around them.

The Kings' War had set dragon shifters on opposite sides. The Black, Blue, and Gold Clans had risen up against the corrupt regime in place for five hundred years: the Red, Green, and White Clans that supported Pytheios, the no-longer-rotting King of the Red Clan. The same king who'd murdered both of Angelika's parents as well as her grandparents and many others in power in order to secure the Red throne for himself and declare himself High King. A position that had always been held by the king mated to the phoenix.

Only he hadn't had a phoenix.

She and her sisters had been in hiding with their mother—the best-kept secret in history for five centuries—thought to be extinct.

Until recently.

Now their mother was dead, her sisters were outed, and Angelika was the only one still a secret, hiding in plain sight while her world fell apart around her.

Kasia and her mate, Brand, were barely holding on to the Gold Clan he ruled. Skylar and Ladon ruled the Blue Clan here. They were fine by comparison but losing their allies in rapid succession. Meira was supposed to have mated the King of the Black Clan, but that had gone sideways in a hurry. She was out there right now, running from one danger to the next in search of her missing king.

And Angelika...well, she hadn't inherited any of her mother's phoenix powers or the ability to shift like her dragon father, so she'd been rendered obsolete in this war. No one seemed to know what to do with her.

Worse, Pytheios claimed to have found another phoenix, which was impossible. Four was already unheard of. There had only ever been one at a time.

What else could go wrong?

She needed to get out. Fresh air and a moment to herself would center her just so she could keep going.

She had taken precautions, at least. White-blond hair bundled under a black beanie—check. All black clothing, like a badass black dragon—check. One of Jedd's jackets, making her person smell even more of wolf and less like the phoenix she technically wasn't—check,

check, check.

See. Precautions appropriately taken.

As usual, a shifter was guarding the massive dragonsteel door that shut the mountain off from the outside world—open during the day, it remained sealed shut at night. Ignoring the grumpy face, she gave him a cheerful wave where he sat inside a glassed-in control room. Except the door didn't click. She turned back to face him, eyebrows raised, then flashed a thumbs-up, gestured at the door, and another thumbs-up. Rolling his eyes, the guard reluctantly pressed whatever combination of buttons needed to be pressed to automatically unlock the smaller, human-sized door leading outside to the flattened ledge used as a landing pad.

Outside, she paused and closed her eyes and breathed, letting the tension drain away as she stood under the clear, open sky.

"It is not good for you to be out here unaccompanied."

Angelika stiffened, her eyes shooting open. She *knew* that voice, though only from afar. Like dark silk or smooth bourbon, low and even. Measured. From a man impossible to overlook. Turning her head, she found Airk Azdajah standing at the precipice, the white dragon shifter's toes practically hanging over the edge to the canyon below.

"I can take care of myself," she said. Knee-jerk response. Everyone seemed determined that she was in need of protection.

"You did not even know I was out here until I spoke."

Unlike most shifters, whose speech changed slowly over time, the same way humans' did, this dragon still spoke more...formally. She liked it. It made him sound old-fashioned, or chivalrous, even, which was why she smiled a little.

He shook his head in obvious disgust. "Return to the mountain, little wolf."

Angelika ignored the imperious order. Besides, she was curious. "For someone still struggling to shift, you're taking an awfully big risk, standing there."

Though she'd spoken the words with kindness, Airk's shoulders drew back, his spine going steel-rod straight.

Before he could snap back, she crossed the distance between them. "What are you doing? Trying to force your dragon to emerge? Isn't that dangerous?"

He turned ice blue eyes on her, quietly intense in a way no man she'd met before came close to. That was saying something, given the natures of shifters, whether wolf and dragon. Probably Airk's way was a holdover from centuries kept in captivity with few to talk to. The thought of him alone and caged like that made her heart ache.

She expected him to dismiss her again—that or dismiss the danger. Instead, his expression eased. "I am less concerned with falling to my death than I am with releasing a feral dragon."

He had never released the animal within, according to Skylar, who knew him best, though that wasn't by much. Not long ago, her sister had been captured by Pytheios and locked in the Red Clan's prison in Everest...with Airk. He was the one who'd helped Skylar escape, or, more accurately, they'd helped each other.

"Then what are you doing out here?" she asked.

Airk looked down into the deep ravine below before he raised his gaze to the stars, the cool light of the waning moon illuminating his face and setting his white hair aglow. His lips twitched as though a smile was beyond him, unused, stiff and almost shaky. "After centuries inside a mountain..."

He left off the rest, but she caught his meaning.

"I don't blame you." Without thinking, Angelika reached over and took his hand, giving it a squeeze.

His fingers twitched in her grasp, and he stared at their clasped hands. "You dare touch me?"

The question came out not angry or offended but almost... bewildered. She got it. She'd seen how all the dragons in this mountain avoided Airk.

She shrugged. "I'm a hugger."

He cocked his head and studied her, seeming to be as confused by the words as by her simple act of reaching out. "Most are afraid of me. Or disgusted."

"They don't know you."

He slipped his hand out of hers. "*You* do not know me."

Angelika sighed as he stepped back, putting more space between them. "I would offer to be friends, but I don't think hanging out with a wolf shifter will help you integrate into dragon society any better."

"This is true."

Disappointment shot through her, but that was nothing new in Angelika's world. As always, she shook it off. She had sort of been hoping he would ignore that truth and want to be friends. Because the fact was, she found this man fascinating. Gorgeous. Distant. Lonely.

And she was drawn to him in a way she'd never felt drawn to another.

He gestured to the door she'd come out. "Allow me to escort you to your chambers."

As much as she would like to stay out here with him, even if they simply sat in silence, she could tell by the tightness in his jaw that Airk would prefer things this way.

Maybe next time he'd be inclined to linger.

Together, they walked through the human-sized tunnels, which were rarely accessed in the daytime and abandoned at night. The wolf pack had been given suites that had clearly not been used in years and were a good distance into the mountain and up.

About halfway there, Angelika couldn't help herself. "Tell me, Airk Azdajah, what do you want?"

Hands clasped behind his back, he leveled her with a look. "You have much to say."

Angelika almost laughed at the irritation that flickered in his eyes. Clearly, he was ready to hand her off to the wolves. "I mean, for a long time, I'm guessing you've only had two goals in mind. Survival and escape."

After a second, he gave a jerking nod.

"Well then...now that you've accomplished both, what is next for you?"

"Next?"

"You had to have pictured in your mind what you would do

once you got out, right?"

Wariness stared back at her from a harshly beautiful face. "Why do you ask me this?"

She tried not to take offense at the suspicion in that question. "Because I get the impression that you're...floundering a bit. I know what that's like."

Boy did she ever. Running her entire life, never feeling as though she had roots, no matter how long they'd spent in any one location. Now she was the only sister with no powers. She'd hadn't figured out how, exactly, but she wasn't going to let that stand in the way of her being part of taking Pytheios down.

"Floundering." Airk stopped and frowned, mouthing the word as if tasting it. Then he scowled so harshly, a lesser person might've backed off. He reminded her of a wild thing in pain, bunching its muscles to lash out, even if it meant striking the person who had come to help.

He jerked his gaze to her, mouth open as if to tell her off, then paused, seeming to search her expression. Such guardedness. If she thought he would have let her, Angelika would've hugged him, penetrating that icy outer shell with the warmth of kindness. He was a dragon shifter, damn it. Ice shouldn't be part of his makeup.

Slowly, he closed his mouth. "If you were me, what would you do?"

She didn't even have to think about it. "I would find a way to kill the monster who did that to me."

After a beat of shock, Airk's gaze intensified, and his presence filled the space around them, power and purpose clotting the air.

Alpha. The word whispered through her mind.

Not that she should be surprised. His father had been her own father's Beta once upon a time. Airk had more claim to the throne of the White Clan than anyone except her and her sisters. A king destined by the fates. A king that, maybe, might have been destined for her.

If things had been different.

Her body heated at the thought.

"I shall consider your words," he said.

Then he waved her to continue on. Again, they walked side by side in silence. Only this time, the vibes that continued to pulse from him filled the space, surrounding her, penetrating her. Angelika practically wanted to crawl out of her skin. But to do what? Help him? Hug him? Fuck him?

Oh, Gods, do not *think about fucking the hot, lonely,* dangerous *dragon shifter.*

Finally, they reached her door, and she paused. "This is me."

He gazed at her, unspeaking.

Not wanting to close a door between them yet, she looked back. "Do you think you'll ever try to shift?"

He gave an almost negligent shrug, though she got the impression that he cared about this a thousand times more than he wanted to let on. "The bonds with loved ones that I would need to tether me to my humanity died with my parents the same day you lost your father."

Airk had been there. A child witnessing Pytheios's coup by murder. Part of her wanted to ask him for those memories. A part she didn't indulge.

Angelika just nodded. "I guess you'd better make friends faster, then."

Airk ducked his head, but not before she caught a hint of a smile that fairly knocked the breath from her lungs. The man was attractive in a harsh sort of way, but when he smiled... *Oh. My.*

"Perhaps I have made one tonight."

Angelika stilled. *Well, knock me over with a feather.*

Given the course of their conversation, she'd been under the impression that he would rather get rid of her than consider her a friend.

"I would like that." She swallowed because the truth of those words struck her harder than expected. "But I suggest you start with dragon shifter friends." Because, for all he knew, she was a wolf shifter.

Gaze trained on her face, he gave a sharp nod. "Allies."

"Friends," she corrected. "Particularly the kings mated to the phoenixes."

That sounded odd to say, since those phoenixes were her sisters and those kings her brothers-by-blood. But no one else was supposed to know that.

"I will consider your suggestion." He clasped his hands behind his back, as though he had to contain himself, then pivoted on his heel and walked away without another word.

"I hope you'll try it eventually," she called after his retreating form. "Shifting, I mean. A dragon in captivity is a true shame."

Airk paused and glanced over his shoulder. "Perhaps one day. Though not even your sister can see what lies ahead for me."

As he disappeared around the corner, Angelika gasped, the meaning of his words sinking in. Kasia had inherited their mother's ability to see the future. And he'd called Kasia her sister.

He knows who I am.

That realization triggered a landslide of another one. One that might let her contribute to this war.

If there was anyone who wanted Pytheios dead as much as she did—but was semi-powerless to do anything about that—it was Airk. Maybe combining forces was an idea worth looking at closer. Her sisters had mated for political leverage or protection. Why couldn't she?

Together, a phoenix and the rightful heir to the throne of the White Clan could be very...strategic.

The fact she'd recently been thinking about him in a very *non*strategic manner wasn't important.

She almost ran after Airk to toss the offer around but forced herself to wait. Better to think this through and work the pros and cons before she pitched it. Mating wasn't something to go into lightly. And who even knew if it'd work with a dormant phoenix and a dragon shifter who might go feral at any second?

"Where have you been?"

Jedd's rasping, rumbling voice made her jump. She spun around to find him standing in the doorway of the room next to hers.

"Nowhere."

The wolf shifter glowered. "No more going nowhere without me."

Angelika offered him a conciliatory smile but made no promises...not when she couldn't keep them. She hated that she couldn't give him that. "Night, Jedd."

As she closed the door of her room behind her, she couldn't resist one last peek down the hall.

Airk was long gone.

Would he even want to mate her?

CHAPTER ONE

Present day...

Motherfucking dragon shifters.

Hampered by the limp body slung over one shoulder like a bag of bones, and dripping into one of his eyes, Airk slipped and slid his way down the ice and rock of a Siberian mountain peak. He picked his way between abandoned "buildings" that made up this particular dragon-shifter colony. Inside him, his dragon was going berserk, a constant roar in his head, clawing to be released so it could fight off their attackers.

Nothing new.

The animal side of him was always an unceasing barrage of violence within, trying to get out. But Airk would *never* release that side of himself. He shut it down. Ignored it, dead focused on getting himself out of this situation.

Keep moving.

If he could get to the next entrance and find a mirror, he'd get himself and his passenger both out of here.

His boot-clad feet skidded on loose shale, but he recovered quickly. Instead of burrowing deep into this peak, the dragon shifters who made a home here had gone shallow, using naturally occurring caverns as individual homes, like a village dotting the mountainside. After a week of sneaking around like a damned demented ghost and observing this smaller community, he'd finally shown his face to a woman he'd recognized from childhood. One who he'd remembered was a friend of his mother's.

Colossal mistake.

She'd run away screaming and brought the whole damn community down on top of him. Not the best result for what was supposed to be a diplomatic mission to convince his fellow White Clan dragon shifters to switch sides in the Kings' War. How the blue and black kings had convinced him he could be successful at anything that required persuading others to follow him was a fucking mystery. Being around anyone—especially other dragon shifters—only set off the beast inside him more.

Especially when they went for his throat before he'd gotten five words out.

The unmistakable bellow of an enraged dragon above him set small rocks tumbling down the side of the mountain. His own dragon blasted an answering challenge in his head, one so loud pain echoed off the inside of his skull. Airk only held on harder to that empty, emotionless place he'd learned to go to inside him. Emotions were messy and forced mistakes.

Better to shut them off.

He ran faster, gaze darting here and there. One of these homes had to have a mirror. The one he'd planned to use to leave had been shattered before he got to it.

The limp body he carried suddenly twitched, his passenger waking up, then kicked out and upset his balance. Airk's boot lodged between two rocks as he tipped sideways and came down hard. Pain tore through his calf.

What in the seven hells? Had he landed on a dragon's tooth? Meanwhile, the woman over his shoulder shoved at his back. "What—"

His dragon snapped his teeth that another dared touch them. In the same instant, a shadow passed overhead, and the woman Airk was attempting to rescue gasped in terror.

The other dragon was too high up to get to them fast. Its first mistake. "If you want to get out of here, stay still," Airk snarled.

She immediately went motionless against him, and he shot to his feet and took off, now trying to hide a limp and ignore the burn ripping through his flesh with each movement.

"Airk."

The sound of his name was barely a whisper on the wind. His enhanced hearing picked it up, and everything inside him went stock-still with recognition even as he kept moving.

He was immediately slammed with a memory. Angelika Amon standing before him, gorgeous in a figure-hugging gown for her sister Meira's mating ceremony celebrations. Her frosty white-blue eyes had searched his as she'd asked him a question. "Have you decided what's next yet?"

That's how she'd started it.

Then she'd gone on about how she wanted to help him reach out to the White Clan and maybe turn them away from Pytheios, make them allies of her sisters' clans. How his people needed a new king to lead them to the other side of the war.

He'd been stupid enough to ask how, and then she'd said the words. Words that pierced the usual numb he kept wrapped around himself.

"If we were to mate…"

Hells. Airk had done the only thing he could. It had taken everything in him to do it, but he'd said no, unequivocally, and then he'd walked away.

He'd been avoiding her ever since.

What the fuck was Angelika doing here? And where was she?

He searched the mountainside for a glimpse of her. Was he hearing things now?

At a tiny movement, he jerked his gaze to the right, and he damn near tumbled ass over head at the sight of her—long, white-blond hair tossed in the winds whipping at the mountain, framing her perfectly heart-shaped face.

She stood hunkered down in a doorway, beckoning him like

the siren she was with a tiny wave of her hands, no doubt trying to not also attract the attention of the dragon overhead.

Through the emotionless numb where he usually existed, a gut punch of fury swept through him in a scorching wave at her recklessness showing herself here like that, risking her preciously rare phoenix neck.

Airk didn't have time to argue with her methods right now, though.

Shoving the emotions down deep where they couldn't touch him, he kept moving. Five more steps and he ran past her through a rotting wooden door disguised to blend with the rock face and into what had once been a home.

"What in the seven hells are you doing here?" he demanded. No emotions, only logic now.

"Helping." She shot him a patient smile, though it quickly disappeared behind urgency. "Follow me."

He stared at her back…then did as she asked. They had one minute. Two at most.

Limping hard by now, he picked his way around toppled furniture and over shredded pieces of wood covered in layers of dust and grime. The air smelled dingy. This residence hadn't been used in a century at least.

He kept close as Angelika rushed to a back room. One that happened to have an intact mirror, though spotted with age and exposure to the elements.

He skidded to a stop in front of it beside her and blinked at the sight of his reflection staring back. Always a shock, after five hundred years in Pytheios's prison, to see himself. He looked like hell. Even more than usual.

Taking out the guard in the small dungeon in order to rescue the woman he now hefted had left him with a decent gash above his eye, already closing thanks to a shifter's accelerated healing abilities. His starkly white hair—that he'd shorn short as soon as he'd had a chance after escaping captivity—was spattered with blood. His, he was fairly certain. More blood dripped at a rapid pace onto the stone floor from whatever he'd just done to his leg, pooling under the heel of his boot.

"What are you doing?" the woman over his shoulder asked, starting to squirm again.

"Waiting." He glanced a question at Angelika, who kept her gaze on the mirror but nodded an affirmation.

The shouts outside were growing louder. Closer.

"What for? They're coming." His passenger was starting to panic, nails biting into his back.

Airk started to plan in his head what he'd do if he had to fight.

The unmistakable *thud* of a dragon landing nearby set his own dragon slashing inside him even more frantically. The creature half of him had never been this uncontrollable inside their prison cell, maybe because, strangely, there Airk had never been under direct threat. He fisted his hands against the raging push to shift, and he waited, the effort tightening his muscles to the point of pain.

He glanced at his watch—a handy invention he'd been introduced to at the time of its making several hundred years ago, while he'd still been held captive in the Red Clan's high dungeons in Everest. Back when he'd still had hope of escape. He'd had no idea it would take another three hundred years before he would succeed.

His heart thumped with each movement of the second hand, and he found himself urging what came next to happen faster, counting down to the arranged moment the portal was supposed to be opened with each tiny tick. "Four. Three. Two…"

He dropped his hand and looked up as the image in the mirror changed abruptly, with no warning or sound, now no longer showing his reflection. Instead, a couple stood in a cavernous bedroom framed by the tarnished edges of his own mirror.

Samael Veles—black hair, black eyes, a bred warrior, and the King of the Black Clan—watched from beside his mate, Meira, his fiery gaze on whatever threat might come through the mirror.

Meira's strawberry blond curls, so at odds with her more angular face and serious mind, lifted around her head in a halo of black-tipped flames as she used her power to teleport through reflective surfaces to manipulate both sides of the portal she'd created.

"Perfect timing," Angelika said, except her voice was tight. She clearly knew the hells were about to rain down on them and jumped through quickly. Then she turned and faced him, head cocked as though to ask what he was waiting for.

His dragon went eerily still, and the roaring in Airk's head went dead silent, as if seeing her safe on the other side of the mirror settled them both.

Her scent—sunlight and summer and fresh air, all things he'd missed—wafted toward him.

Fuck.

The beast inside him lunged for Angelika. A patch of skin on his arm shimmered like a desert mirage, white scales showing hazily through. Airk slammed down every mental cage he'd built in his head to contain both his own emotions and the instinct-driven animal inside him.

The woman he carried screamed as men burst into the room in the same instant, and Airk finally forced his legs to move. He threw himself and his female passenger through the gateway opened in the mirror. His injured leg collapsed as soon as he was on the other side, and they both went sprawling across the hard rock floor.

"What happened—" Meira started to gasp.

"Close the mirror!" Angelika shouted and shoved her sister.

Immediately Meira's fire was doused. The angry expressions of the people coming at them from the other side turned to shock, especially the man closest who'd reached an arm through. Because the "doorway" slammed shut, becoming a mirror again. The man's arm severed cleanly and dropped to the floor to twitch there like a crushed cockroach.

They all stared at it for a second.

Airk, chest heaving from the effort of escape, and even more from the effort to hold his dragon in check, dropped his head back against the cool stone floor, reminding him incongruously of the slab he'd used as a bed in his prison cell for so long. Only this wasn't Everest anymore; this was Meira's bedroom in the black dragon stronghold of Mount Ararat.

He flung an arm over his eyes with a grunt.

"*That* was a close one," Angelika murmured.

Even with his eyes closed, he could picture her smile, deliberately casual. Did others catch how forced those smiles had become lately? Or would they only see what she wanted them to?

Still, what the hells had she been thinking, putting herself at risk like that? Had she been afraid for him? She shouldn't be. He was expendable.

Curling up inside him, his dragon damn near purred at her nearness, even as it snarled at Airk. Airk didn't trust it not to try for her again, but at least he could shut back down now.

The way he functioned best. The *only* way.

"How did you know where I would be?" he asked, dropping his arm, gaze on the ceiling.

"Kasia had a vision," Angelika said simply.

"That did not mean you needed to come in person." He shouldn't care that she had, or even be grateful, but he was still getting over the unaccustomed fear that had struck him like a damn thunderbolt the instant he'd heard her voice.

Emotions were dangerous. His control only worked when he could shut everything else down—and control was the only reason he was still alive.

"I take it negotiations to convince those dragon shifters to join our side didn't go well?" Samael asked, ignoring his jab at Angelika.

He grunted again.

A tiny, thrilled meow sounded half a second before a runt of a cat jumped on Airk, and he barely stopped himself from growling, especially when Angelika's muffled chuckle followed. The foolish animal curled up in a ball right in the center of his chest and set to purring.

"Meira." That was all he said.

The tiny cat—Meira and Samael had rescued her somewhere in the journey that resulted in their mating not that long ago—seemed determined to make him her friend. Much like Angelika that way.

But unlike the cat, Angelika wants a mate.

He shoved the thought down deep where it couldn't touch him.

"Sorry." Meira's voice shook suspiciously as she lifted the animal off him.

Airk dropped his arm to his side and glared at the ceiling.

Clearing her throat, Angelika squatted down not in front of him but before the female he'd saved. "Who is this?"

The woman—almost a girl, really, and probably no older than nineteen—opened and closed her mouth several times, not even a squeak of sound emerging.

"A human who is showing dragon sign," Airk answered, carefully pushing himself to sitting, gritting his teeth against the pain in his leg. "They had her trapped in their dungeon. I gathered that she refused to mate the dragon they...assigned her."

Samael let out a rumble of anger at that. Mates were not supposed to be assigned.

"Look." The woman he'd saved seemed to have found her voice. "I don't know who you people are, but—"

"We're people who won't hurt you," Meira assured her, crouching beside Angelika. In that position, her simple dress stretched and pulled, revealing the beginning swell of the baby growing in her womb.

"I know this must be confusing and scary," the newly crowned Queen of the Black Clan said. "But...we're here to help."

The female glanced from her to Airk, who nodded. "I guess anything is better than a dungeon," she said.

"You know you're bleeding pretty badly, right?"

Angelika's question was directed at him, despite the fact he still wasn't looking at her.

He glanced over, only to collide with blue eyes so pale they were near white, like the deepest part of a glacier, and yet still filled with impossible...warmth. Warmth that was purely *her*. The death of her parents, her grandparents—all slaughtered at Pytheios's hands—that alone should have taught her the cruelty of life. Instead, the woman was a creature of silver linings, imbued with the kind of faith in others that would only get her killed.

He just hoped he wasn't there when it happened.

Just to give himself anywhere else to look, he peeled back the leg of his black pants. They'd suggested he wear a suit to make him appear more official. He'd gone a different way, choosing combat pants with pockets for weapons, food, and other provisions, and a snug-fitting long-sleeved black shirt in a modern material that was soft against his skin.

He grimaced at the deep gash already starting to close up. That fast, he made a decision never to walk into another dragon-shifter community unless he was armed to the teeth and there to kill.

No more diplomatic missions. This was his last failed attempt. Time for a new strategy.

Suddenly Angelika was kneeling beside him, soft hands pressing at the flesh around the wound. Airk gritted his teeth as his entire body responded with a rush of lust that, if he wasn't already on the ground, would have taken his knees out from under him.

He always reacted like this to her, and that was damn dangerous. Being around her was both heaven and hell.

Meira winced. "That's a lot of blood."

"I'll take him to the infirmary." Angelika stood and held out a hand to help Airk up. "Let's go, tough guy."

He scowled. She was the only person, other than the damn cat, brave enough to get this close. After all, everyone knew his dragon was feral. He could snap at any second.

So damn tempting to reach for her hand. Or her waist. Or—

No. Physical contact would be akin to setting off a spark in the middle of a forest of dead trees. He avoided touching her. Always. Ever since the first night she'd spoken to him. He'd gone so rock hard from her voice alone, her scent, that as soon as he'd made it to his room he'd had to flog his cock to keep his dragon contained. Three times. All to images of Angelika—her mouth on him, hands on him, his dick buried inside her.

Airk levered to his feet, ignoring the frustrated snort of his dragon, careful to keep his weight off his injured leg. "Describe to me the way."

"These days we say, 'Show me the way.' And I'm going with you whether you like it or not."

His nostrils flared. How did she not get offended? Wasn't it obvious that he was trying to keep her at a distance? And why did his dragon like her stubbornness so much? If they weren't careful, the creature would get out and kill her.

When he didn't speak, she raised her eyebrows, and that was when he caught it.

Disappointment shadowed her eyes.

His irritation took on a whole new direction—at himself.

"Follow me," she said and didn't wait for him, leaving the room.

Gritting his teeth, he trailed after her.

Avoiding her had become an exercise in futility. Especially that gentle smile that perpetually hovered about her lips, ready to shine into the darkest corners of a heart. He'd only once been able to rid her of that smile and replace it with an emotion he didn't want to identify since he'd known her.

The day he'd said no to something he wanted so much he'd ached every day since.

CHAPTER TWO

I t took a lot to get Angelika angry, but she would cheerfully throttle the dragon shifters in this mountain. Every single one of them.

Starting with the one walking behind her, but now, also everyone else. Each person she and Airk happened across on the way to the infirmary practically glued themselves to the walls of the hollowed-out tunnels carved throughout Mount Ararat. Not to scoot their cowardly ways around *her*. She was a curiosity.

Now that her secret was out and everyone knew she was a phoenix and not a wolf shifter, they all watched her with a different light in their eyes. She didn't have the company of the wolf pack to hide behind anymore—they'd gone to seek safety among the Federation of Packs. Jedd hadn't even said goodbye, still angry and hurt that she hadn't accepted his mating proposal not long before they left. That still made her heart pinch when she thought about it.

But right now she wasn't the one these shifters were avoiding— Airk was.

All the fire breathers anywhere she'd seen so far—didn't matter what clan or creed they hailed from—avoided the man like he was a rat on a ship come to inflict his brand of curse upon them. Even her sisters' mates, each a powerful, badass king in his own right, were visibly wary around Airk.

Granted, despite being a closed off, unemotional robot, the man still managed to give off an aura of threat, more than the usual that came with these incredibly dangerous shifters.

But it seemed to Angelika that any creature tortured with the kind of isolation he'd endured for centuries deserved to be surrounded by care. Not pity. She found it impossible to pity the kind of strength he'd shown to survive that. But to continue to isolate him by making him a social pariah…that was just cruel.

The disappointment from a moment ago when he refused to touch her wrapped a tighter fist around her heart. She could have been the one to care for him—as a friend—but she'd gone and ruined it with that damn suggestion to mate. He hadn't even let her get out a single reason or tell him all the ways it would benefit them both. She'd only wanted to open a…discussion. But he'd shut her down hard, and no amount of persistence or cheer on her part had been able to break through the walls he'd slammed up between them.

Another black dragon shifter skittered by like a frightened rabbit, pewter-eyed gaze darting between her and Airk, and she hissed through bared teeth, which only made him duck his head and scurry faster.

Airk said nothing. No reaction, as usual. Though, in small moments when he thought he went unwatched, she sensed he wasn't oblivious. He noticed. Even so, the man seemed to feed into the fear, if anything, doing nothing to make friends or influence people to his side, generally keeping to himself.

Why anyone believed he'd be a good ambassador to other white dragons was beyond her.

Her back to the man limping along behind her in stone-cold silence, Angelika swung into the medical room. Everything in this room screamed infirmary from the bright lights, to the sterile stainless steel appliances, white-sheeted hospital beds, and glass-fronted cases showing a multitude of medical tools and items.

"Sit," she said, pointing at one bed.

She grabbed blunt-tipped scissors, then turned and froze at the sight of a bare male chest. Impressions hit her all at once—the breadth of his shoulders and the ridges of his muscles, but also a series of scars crisscrossing his abdomen. As though he'd been flayed open so many times, his dragon healing eventually couldn't prevent the scarring. Gods, the things this man had been through.

Awareness slid through her like melted butter.

Logic had driven her mating proposal. Or so she'd told herself. But the way she had to tamp down the lust swamping her now, maybe it had been a bigger part than she'd let herself believe.

His hands went to the button of his pants.

Holy shit. "I didn't say strip!" she squeaked.

He jumped, then stopped moving, watching her closely.

Heat flooded her face. Helping him with his wound was her priority—or should be. Only, given the way her body had come to buzzing life thanks to what he'd bared so far, she was struggling mightily not to forget herself. What would he do if she'd let him strip naked and she wrapped her hand around his cock? Maybe tasted him? Had any woman gifted him that kind of pleasure before?

Given his treatment of her so far, he'd probably sit back, arms crossed, and glare at her until she got it over with.

Get your mind on the task.

His expression went from wary to blank in a flash. "I offer my apologies. Any time they cared for me in…" A muscle in his shoulder twitched as though he couldn't speak the name of Everest. "They didn't let me out of my cell when tending to my person. Instead, I was made to remove my clothes in order for them to inspect me from afar."

Angelika cleared her throat. Forget a blow job. The man clearly needed a long, strings-free cuddle. Except the last thing he'd want from her was a hug, even though she desperately wanted to wrap her arms around him and press her lips to his temple. "You're in a better place now."

He stared back, unmoved. Airk did that a lot around everyone. She didn't take it personally.

Instead, she snagged a rolling stool and pulled it up to sit in front of him, then proceeded to cut away the material of the black combat pants he wore. Apparently Airk had taken modern clothing tips from her sisters' mates, all three warriors first and foremost. Each a reluctant king.

Seeing that the wound was on the back of his leg, she stood. "Flip to your stomach and scoot up on the bed, please."

He did as she asked, resting his chin on his crossed arms, the muscles playing across his back. Her nipples tightened.

Gah.

Forcing herself to focus, Angelika inspected the wound a long gash from the back of his knee almost to his Achilles, which was closing slowly. Whatever he'd hit had cut deep, ripping into the flesh. "What did this?"

"Rock. I think."

No wonder the rending appeared so jagged. "Hmmm. If you weren't a shifter, I'd say you need stitches. Instead, I'll bandage it so you don't trail blood everywhere until it heals properly."

Silence.

She wrinkled her nose at his back and took that as agreement, then left him lying there to gather the things she'd need. She didn't speak again until she was rolling a bandage around the leg, covering the non-stick gauze she'd taped over the wound. "Don't do anything too strenuous the next hour or two."

"I heard you had been educated in the medical profession." He kept his head turned away, talking to the wall.

Her eyebrows lifted. Airk instigating conversation was a rare thing. "I'm a trained nurse," she confirmed. "I have a degree and experience working in several hospitals and everything." Her hands slowed as unbidden memories washed over her. "Mama had each of us learn different skills that would serve us in the modern world both in terms of supporting ourselves and as possible skills that would be needed on the run. Meira has her computers. Skylar is a pilot. Kasia was getting an engineering degree when Pytheios found us."

"Meanwhile, you chose to heal people."

She shrugged, not that he saw it. "Given that dragon shifters were after us, I figured medical skills would come in handy."

"No. You like to take care of people."

Angelika's hands paused, and she glanced at the back of his head. Even though she knew he did, she was often surprised by the way Airk observed things others did not.

Airk's observant nature must've come from years of trying to piece together what was happening in the outside world through the small and random contact he had with other prisoners who had come and gone where he was kept.

"I do," she agreed. "At least it makes me..."

"Caring?"

Airk still wasn't looking, but she shook her head anyway. "No. Useful."

He did glance over his shoulder at that, bright eyes so like hers taking in her expression and maybe more than she wanted him to see. "You do not see yourself as useful?" he asked.

She glanced at the door she'd closed behind them. "A dormant phoenix with no powers?" she said in a low voice, because the dormant part was still a secret. "I'm no more helpful than a human. Fragile and in the way."

He stiffened as though he didn't like that description. "Power does not always come from a physical ability."

"It doesn't come from physical weakness, either," she pointed out. Then shook herself out of what could become a big funk if she let it. "But I refuse to be sidelined."

"Sidelined?" he asked.

"It's a phrase from modern sports that means not allowed to play or removed from the game and left to the side to merely observe but not participate."

"I see. You wish to be helpful."

"More than helpful." She blew out a breath, wanting to explain but sure he didn't really want to hear it. "You were there when Pytheios killed my father."

Airk nodded slowly, almost reluctantly.

"My parents' mating bond hadn't solidified, so my mother didn't die him. She was pregnant and ran to save us. She taught us to survive even while she grieved every single day for him. Kept us a secret. Until Pytheios found her and killed her, too."

Angelika swallowed. In her dreams every night, she still saw her mother the last night they were all together, lying in that burning field dying.

"I thought that was the worst that could happen, but then Maul—" She cut herself off before her voice broke.

"They told me," Airk said quietly. "The legend about hellhounds being reincarnated souls of warriors with unfinished business is true."

True, and a huge revelation.

"Did they tell you how Maul turned out to be the soul of our father? Pytheios killed him, too. Again."

But Angelika hadn't been there that day.

Pain speared her through the heart, and she gasped silently, breathing through it. Something that had happened out of the blue at least once a day since she'd learned of how Maul had died.

"I should have been there. I should have had a chance to say goodbye to him." Her sisters had. She shook her head. She wanted to rail at the fates who, for some unknown reason, had prevented her from taking her place beside Meira, Kasia, and Skylar in this war. "I might have no fire, no power like my sisters, but I *am* going to make a difference in this war."

"Healing people is a way to be helpful." Airk seemed to be offering the option to her, and she would love to have kissed him for the effort. A sweet kiss this time.

"It is," she agreed. "But with the accelerated healing shifters have, I'm rarely needed in any capacity that way. Never in a lifesaving one. A Healer with a universal blood type is the one who makes a real difference around here."

Airk said nothing. Not that he could. She wasn't wrong.

"That's why I wanted to discuss our mating that night," she said. "It seemed like the only thing I could do to make a difference."

He shot upright, rolling over and swinging his legs to dangle off the high bed, to stare at her with that inscrutable, immovable expression of his.

"I refuse to discuss mating with you." The words came out flat.

Well, hells. He didn't have to be *mean* about it. "I wasn't going to propose or anything," she snapped. She hadn't actually proposed the last time. She'd only wanted to bring the option up. She couldn't help a muttered, "Even if rejecting me wasn't very forward-thinking of you."

Silence.

She ducked her head, pretending to be focused on fixing the bandage now dangling and loose. They sat quietly, the room thick with unspoken words as she continued to work.

"Why do you wish to mate me?" The words sounded almost offhand, as though he was asking the time of day.

Her hands stilled in their work, and she blinked at his leg. "Like I said…to make a difference," she repeated. "For my family and for our people."

"Is that all?"

Angelika's eyebrows tried to crawl into her hair. Did he sound… disappointed? "I mean, physically, I think we'd—"

"No."

He clapped his hand over his wrist, but not before she caught the shimmer of a shift.

Yikes. His dragon was way closer to the surface than she'd realized. She *should* be nervous of that. Unnervingly, she wasn't. Instead, that visible display only gave her another arguing point.

"You know, a mate would give your dragon an anchor," she pointed out. "You could try to shift—"

"The time for that passed long ago." He was speaking slowly and quietly now. Not a good sign, given that the way he appeared to keep control was to never lose it. "If I shift, I go feral, and your sisters' mates will have to put me down. Are we finished here?"

She glanced at the bandage, which had started to unravel again with how tense he'd gone, then pulled the stool closer and started rewrapping it. Again.

"Okay. Then maybe I can travel with you to help reach out to dragons from the White Clan. I'm a people person. Plus, they might be more willing to listen to both a phoenix *and* one of their royals. Maybe I'd have...er...a little more success in convincing others to our side."

"As opposed to my lack of success, I take you to mean?"

She cleared her throat. "I believe that's the third settlement that"—how to word this to avoid discouraging him—"wasn't interested?"

"That chased me out violently is what you meant to say." He was back to that unshakable calm.

"What if—"

"I refuse to negotiate this with you further."

She shouldn't have pushed. "I didn't think we were negotiating. I was just—"

"Angelika."

What would it be like to hear him say her name like that, growl it, if they came together?

Good grief, girl, get your mind on the problem and not...sex. Maybe she needed a few rounds with her vibrator. It *had* been a while.

"Then what's your plan?" She secured the end of the bandage and scooted back to look up at him.

"My plan does not concern you."

Ouch. She hid a wince, heart pinching even harder than when Jedd left without saying goodbye. Which was ridiculous, since she'd only known Airk a short time.

She shot to her feet, and, almost defensively, he did the same... which brought them very, very close. He'd have to touch her to move her, and she'd seen how he avoided that, but she'd stood up first, damn it. She wouldn't move aside to cater to whatever stick he had up his ass.

She lifted her chin. "Not mating you doesn't mean I don't care what happens to you. We once talked about being friends, and I would like that—"

"No."

Gods, did the man ever feel anything? What would he do if she pressed against him right now?

Heat blanketed the room, like a roaring fire on a cold winter's night. Was it coming from him? Or her? A muscle in his jaw ticked, but no flame entered his eyes. The man was locked down as tight as a submarine underwater. And yet, she couldn't look away. Couldn't step away.

"I want you." The whispered words tore from her.

Her eyes flared wide on the realization that she actually said that out loud. Oh hells. She was tempted to flee, but that required scooting around him, which involved touching, and...no. She was too on edge for that.

His eyes narrowed. "Is this a new idiom I have yet to encounter?" he asked slowly, carefully.

Yep. She definitely needed to flee. "Er...I hope not."

He stared at her, mind working through who the hells knew what. "What do you want me for?"

This really was getting lost in translation. "Pleasure."

"Pleasure." He sort of rolled the word around in his mouth as though it were a foreign concept.

Heat that was definitely *not* hers rioted between them. And, oh gods, it was delicious. Her muscles trembled with need.

"Yes." She tried her best not to squirm because this wasn't at all where she'd intended the conversation to go, and her body was reacting in a highly inappropriate way, given his stance on their... non-relationship.

"You wish me to pleasure you?" Doubt layered the words.

Seven hells. Just the words coming from his mouth had her knees going weak and far more sensitive parts of her body perking up. "Yes."

He jerked as though he wanted to take a step back—not that he could. But he also didn't look away.

She took a deep breath. If they were going to go there, she might as well go the rest of the way. "And I want to pleasure *you*. And make you laugh. And show you things about the world today and—"

His expression went blank, and his arms dropped to his sides.

"You pity the pathetic creature from the dungeons of Everest. Is that it?"

"No." She grabbed his hand, driven by her need to make sure that he didn't believe his own words. "This isn't pity, *dammit*. It's companionship. And...and..."

"And?"

"Chemistry." She flung the word at him, frustration driving her now.

He frowned. "I do not—"

Angelika went up on her tiptoes and pressed her lips to his. A soft, sweet, barely there touch.

Airk went utterly still at the contact for half a heartbeat, and in that blip of a moment, despair snuck in as she anticipated another rejection. And why wouldn't he reject her? It would be just one more way she'd failed. She started to pull away. To give up—

He groaned as though in pain, then slipped his hand under the heavy fall of her hair to cup the back of her neck and urge her closer.

Of their own volition, her arms crept up around his neck, and Angelika pressed herself to him as their lips collided, but with such desperate need, it took them a second to line everything up right. The kiss took off from there. They melded and meshed, pressed and released, and came back together with a shocking desperation that overwhelmed her and flooded her senses.

Where did he learn to kiss like this in captivity? Her mind paused at that as he gripped her hips, pulling her harder against him. *Who cares, because...damn.*

He took over, kissing her the same way a drowning man might hold on to a rope in a storm, as though she might anchor him to this world by her touch alone. She moaned into his mouth at the taste of him, smoke and bourbon and cherries, like his scent. The velvet sweep of his tongue—questing and yet commanding—sent every pulse point into fluttering overdrive while at the same time blending with a sincere jolt of shock.

She'd kissed other men. Humans she'd been around when she'd been in hiding, and a wolf shifter, just the once. None of those experiences had gone like this. *Felt* like this. Unexpected and so immediately consuming, shutting out the rest of the world and cocooning them together in what could have been a different universe for all she cared.

All she wanted was…more.

"*No*." Airk thrust her away hard enough that she stumbled back. "This cannot happen. No kissing, or mating, or friendship," he said. "Especially not with you."

A jolt of spiky hurt knocked her to the side, and she said nothing as he stalked from the room. As soon as the door closed behind him, she slumped against the cool wall, tipping her head back to stare blindly at the stone ceiling.

That could have gone better.

CHAPTER THREE

Airk stalked the mostly empty human-sized halls up to the level where he'd been given a room any time he stayed in Ararat. Most dragons preferred to fly up to their chambers in these larger mountains via an atrium built at the center that allowed for their size. With perches to land on outside each individual room or suite, he could see how that would be more convenient.

He couldn't do that. Fly. Never would. Besides, this way, he avoided bumping into most people. Alone was what he needed to be right now.

Gods above, Angelika Amon knew how to kiss.

Granted, he didn't have any experience. He'd been too young when he'd been imprisoned to know that kind of touch. A few red female-born dragons had risked their lives trying to offer their bodies to the prisoner trapped in Everest. Not that he would have hurt them. If anything, those women fell even lower on Pytheios's personal hierarchy ladder than Airk did. Hurting one wouldn't gain Airk his freedom. But despite his own physical needs, he'd said no. He couldn't give Pytheios anything to hold over him. Ever.

But touching Angelika...

Sheer terror.

Twice in the last hour his dragon had moved so close to the surface that Airk had had to fight to keep the beast inside him caged, his control suddenly tenuous in a way it hadn't been through all the long years. But she brought the beast within him forward in a different way. Instead of rage and roaring and thrashing to be released, his dragon turned...something else. Not happy, exactly, but eager. Content.

Dangerously so.

The animal side of him would press toward her, like Meira's cat rubbing against Airk's leg like he was one of her favorite humans. Harder for Airk to contain because the problem wasn't about caging his animal. It was about fighting himself and the dragon at the same time.

"If you're finished being bandaged up," a familiar male voice sounded in his head via the telepathic method with which all shifters were able to communicate when in their animal forms. Meira's mate, Samael Veles. *"We need to talk."*

Not able to shift, Airk couldn't answer in the same way. Samael damn well knew that. Airk stopped in the middle of the stone hallway, arms crossed, and waited.

"Meet me in my chambers," came the direction.

Perhaps better than going to his room alone with too much time to think. Turning on his heel, Airk made his way back through the same halls. Given the labyrinthine passages, it took him a solid ten minutes to reach his destination. One would not know, gazing at the nondescript, heavy dragonsteel door, that this was the chamber of royalty. His knock was answered almost immediately by Samael himself, rather than servants.

The king ushered Airk inside and didn't bother with niceties. "So this last attempt to recruit others didn't go well."

"I believe you witnessed the results," Airk answered.

"Tell me about what happened before that." An order. Samael, like Ladon and Brand, wasn't entirely sure how to handle Airk. As a peer of royal blood? An ally? An added danger to their people? Consequently they tended to lean toward treating him like a soldier.

He could handle that. "This last attempt definitely showed me to be unsuitable for this endeavor." The sarcasm he did not bother to hide. A rare luxury he was getting used to. Letting it show as a captive had often gotten him beaten—or worse—for the effort.

Samael ran a hand through his black hair. "Damn. I was hoping you wouldn't say that."

Airk paused. Had the allied kings been relying so heavily on his ability to sway more dragons of his clan to their side? Fewer to fight, Angelika had said.

Only this was an ineffective use of him as a tool.

"I have a better idea." Airk had been thinking on this since his pitiful first attempt and had worked it all out in his head.

Samael lifted thick black brows in vague interest. "Oh?"

"I would make a much better assassin."

To give the other man credit, he didn't hesitate or question. Instead, he took his time thinking through it. "Not a bad idea. In and out with Meira's help. Start with the White Clan and take out leaders identified as intractable in which side they come down on."

His thoughts exactly. "In addition...I am expendable."

Samael didn't quibble. Airk didn't expect him to because they both knew his words were truth. A dragon no one trusted because he couldn't shift, or, if he did, risked killing many, was of no use to anyone. Usually feral dragons were put down, the brutal action seen as a mercy. By all rights and laws, the kings should have turned him loose as a rogue the second he showed up at the very least.

However, an assassin who, if they lost him, cost them nothing... that was another situation entirely.

"I'll talk with Brand and Ladon, and we'll draw up a list of targets."

Airk pulled a folded piece of paper out from one of the many pockets of his pants. Modern fashions had a few decent new developments. Combat pants and socks that stayed up on their own were two of his favorites. "Start with these. Tell me if I am wrong about any of them or the order in which I have listed them."

Samael unfolded the paper, and this time his brows did go up slowly with each name he came across, then he raised a gaze full of questions to Airk.

"I have had a long time to think about who might be traitors within my clan."

Samael nodded slowly. "I'll inform the other kings, but they won't have a problem with this list."

"I will start with the lower-ranked names first."

"Why them?"

"Because unless the way clans work has altered, the lower ranked do most of the dirty work at the orders of those higher up."

Also, starting with them would put the fear of the gods that he was coming into those leaders who'd abandoned his parents and Angelika's parents when Pytheios took over. He wanted to see terror in those traitors' eyes when he slit their throats, their warm blood pooling around them as they watched in horror. Some wounds even dragon shifters couldn't recover from. He intended a slow death for each and every person who'd done nothing when the time came.

"Remind me not to piss you off," Samael muttered, smoothing a hand over his jaw, his stubble scratching roughly in the silence of the room.

"You have nothing to worry about from me," Airk said. "My dragon is another matter and merely another reason to send me away."

Samael didn't argue, and Airk appreciated that from the other man. A good leader could face hard truths head-on.

"When do you plan to go?" Samael asked.

"As soon as I determine the location of my first kill—"

"Mark," Samael corrected.

Airk paused, then realized he was being given a more modern term. "My first mark," he adjusted with a nod of thanks, "and a plan to get to him, I will go. Hopefully no longer than a few days."

"It's probably best if we don't advertise your new mission. The High King has his spies."

"As do we," Airk agreed.

A hard glint entered the king's black eyes. "Yes, we do. I'll reach out to my network rather than have you do it."

"Has Meira infiltrated their financial systems yet?" She was a computer whiz, whatever that meant. He'd heard how she had been spending most of her hours trying to track Pytheios's money. Airk didn't understand the way money was real but not tangible, stored in something called the cloud along with all sorts of other things, but if it crippled Pytheios in any way, he was all for it. Only a select few were aware of that mission as well.

"Not yet." Samael's lips flattened, his gaze sliding to a doorway. Probably to the room where Meira was working. "She's been putting in long hours."

The man clearly was not thrilled with that state of affairs. Airk wouldn't be, either, if his mate put any part of herself, including her health, at risk. But women of this time period were different than what he remembered as a boy. More independent. More involved. Fighters in their own right. A state of affairs to which he would need to accustom himself.

"I offer my hopes that she…what is the term? Cracks the code? Shortly."

"Thanks." Samael frowned. "Speaking of which, I would prefer she didn't know about this change of plans. She's stressing herself out over what she's trying to do with Pytheios's finances, and with the pregnancy…any additional worry I could shield her from…"

"I understand." Newly mated dragon shifters were already highly protective of their mates, but add pregnancy to that, and the way Pytheios was coming for them, Samael had to be struggling not to fly Meira off somewhere secret and force her seclusion.

Assuming their conversation was concluded, Airk performed a quarter bow, appropriate for a king in these circumstances.

Samael waved him off. "Not necessary."

Airk paused midway to rising. "You had better adapt yourself to such gestures."

"Yes, but not from friends."

Airk stilled. There was that word again.

Given what he and Angelika had just been doing, the night they'd first met popped into his head.

In the dead of night, she had appeared outdoors on the open-air landing platform of Ben Nevis. He had often spied her out there.

That night, for some reason, he had made his presence known. He'd figured out who she was almost the first time he'd seen her, but no one else had seemed to come to the same realization.

He honestly did not understand how all the other dragon shifters had missed the similarity of her face to her sisters'—same eyes, same lips, same stubborn chin—despite the white-blond hair, no doubt inherited from her white dragon father. But they obviously desired to keep her identity a secret, and so he had not approached her.

Not that he was in the habit of approaching anyone.

Especially not her. Something about this waif of a woman with her gently inviting smiles and a clear, sweet laugh easily shared with others unnerved him, even then. But she'd tipped her head to the sky as though being trapped inside was a weight she could finally shed, and he knew that feeling better than anyone.

So he'd spoken.

And they'd talked. And she'd dared to get near him. The summer-and-sunshine scent of her, slightly marred by the muddy odor of wolves, had wound around him, through him, and his dragon had…settled. Quieting inside him.

And then she'd offered to be friends, sort of. Mostly she'd talked about how he needed to befriend the dragon kings who gave him asylum. More shocking, though, he'd tried to take her up on her part of the offer.

"Perhaps I have made one tonight," he'd said. But even as he'd smiled, his facial muscles stiff and unused to the motion, he'd known… He could *never* be friends with her. Not with who she was, and who he was, and the way his dragon was behaving in her presence.

Through the numb, an ache had wrapped around his heart like barbed wire that squeezed and pierced at the same time. He shouldn't have let her think friendship was possible, not without risking hurting her.

Now, yanking his mind almost violently from the memory—one he'd gone over almost daily since that night—he stared at Samael.

"A good friend is something of which I have been informed I am in need."

He watched for any sign of humor at such a confession, but Samael didn't laugh. "We're going to bring down the son of a bitch that did unspeakable things to all of us."

Airk nodded his thanks at that, then turned and walked away. Friends with Samael. She would be pleased.

Not that he held any intention of telling her.

CHAPTER FOUR

Angelika stared at the string of one-sided texts on her phone. The unanswered words were a beacon to how she'd failed in one of her closest friendships. She'd texted Jedd every day since he'd left with the rest of the pack, but he never replied. Never even read the texts, as far as she could tell.

The problem was he'd fallen in love with her. Only, she hadn't seen it until it was too late...the day he'd proposed to mate her.

That day, he'd escorted her back to her room after lunch. As soon as the door closed behind them, he had blurted out, "Will you mate me, Angelika?"

She'd had her back to him, and the shock that had coursed through her was just as sharp now as it had been then. She knew now just as she'd known then that it was her fault. That she should have seen his feelings sooner. Maybe she could have spared him pain.

"I asked you a question," Jedd had said. He put a hand on her arm and turned her to face him. "Will you mate me?"

Had there been anything she might have said to let him down easily? She'd thought about it countless times since that night. "I can't."

A muscle at the corner of Jedd's jaw had twitched in a steady rhythm. "Because of some warped sense of belonging to those arrogant, asshole fire breathers?"

"To them? No. To my sisters? Yes. To my family's legacy? Yes. To my murdered mother and father? Even more, yes."

"But you can't—"

She'd put a hand out, stopping him. "I can't offer much, but I know I can make a difference. The gods blessed my mother with four daughters for a reason."

His dark eyes had been intent and achingly hopeful when he grabbed her by the shoulders. "You can do that as effectively at my side. You feel something for me. I know you do."

She'd cupped his face. Even now, she remembered the sadness that squeezed her heart. "You have become one of the most important people in my life. My best friend."

"Then why not—"

"Because that's *all* I feel for you. Friendship."

Jedd's hope had visibly died a quick, agonizing death, and her faithful wolf shifter's eyes darkened with pain even as his expression contorted with anger, turning ugly. He'd accused her of having a fascination with Airk.

Had it been that obvious? She hadn't even known at the time.

"I don't know what part he has to play yet," she'd answered.

Jedd jerked from her touch and paced the room. "I've seen the way you watch him. Like you're studying him. I guess it makes sense in a warped way. Another phoenix mated to another dragon shifter, and four out of six clans with one of the Amon sisters at the helm if you put him on the throne. No way will the other two clans stand against you after that."

Jedd had been hurting, and, because he was her friend, she'd hoped he would understand. "It's not about our family ruling all the clans, Jedd. It's about taking out the man who destroyed things in the first place."

He hadn't understood. Not at all.

Instead, Jedd had whirled on her, urgency in the taut line of his shoulders. "That's not fate. It's politics and strategy."

He was talking about fated mates, but she wasn't a dragon mate. Phoenixes were the ones who did the choosing, which was why she could never mate him.

Whatever he'd seen in her face that night must've convinced him, because his head dropped forward, a sign of total defeat. If he'd been in his wolf form, he might've dropped to his belly, nosing at her ankles, which broke her heart just thinking about it now.

But then he'd pulled his lips back, baring his teeth. "If you think I'm going to stand by and watch you make the biggest mistake of both our lives, then you aren't the woman I thought you were."

That had been the last time they'd spoken alone.

Gods, what a mess she'd made. In her selfish need to have a friend, she'd hurt him. Badly. Their relationship had remained strained after that, and when his pack left the dragon stronghold, Jedd had left without a word to her.

She stared at her phone, disappointment and regret turning heavier by the second.

Unanswered texts, almost a hundred of them, stared back at her from the screen as she waited, hoping he might reply to this one.

But no reply came.

A knock on the door had her jerking her head up, pulling herself out of her own thoughts. "Yes?"

A familiar dark head, one of Samael's men, popped in. "Urgent video call for you."

She was on her feet and out the door almost before he'd finished delivering the message. Angelika ran through the halls as quickly as she could. Each time she had to slow down as she passed another person—granted, that didn't happen often—she gritted her teeth at the need to present an unhurried, calm demeanor. Now that the dragon shifters knew who she was, all eyes were on her and her sisters and their king mates for guidance.

Urgency could be misconstrued as panic, and that would cause its own problems.

Not a situation she'd ever found herself in. Their life in hiding with their mother had been conducted as simply and quietly as possible among humans. Nothing to draw attention. Ever.

Angelika nodded at an older gentleman—or she assumed older,

given the gray peppering his jet-black hair, though that wasn't always an indication—and received a suspicion-lined stare in return. One she'd repaid with a deliberate smile, hiding the flare of hurt.

How would he look at her if he knew she was useless?

Still, addressing suspicion or even hatred with the same clearly hadn't made anything better for dragon shifters over the centuries. Maybe it was time to fight fire with kindness. She didn't see that as weakness or letting the hatred stand. She saw it as addressing the true heart of the situation.

Knowing a person, being treated well by that person, would make it harder to doubt or hate that person.

See? Women really should rule the world.

She slipped around the corner and into a room with an entire wall of monitors. This room was for communications only—unlike the war room, dedicated to tracking dragon fires, which burned hotter than human-made flames, with the screens showing heat maps of the local regions. There were also cameras on the mountain itself in the event of an attack. Currently, most of the wall showed Kasia's and Skylar's faces, along with their mates, in blown-up high-def.

Ladon stood out the most, his black hair and the grim slash to his mouth, when added to the scar that ran down the left side of his face, making him look scary as shit. But his remarkably blue eyes were kind, and Angelika had never feared him. He might be the Blood King, but he would never harm Skylar or her sisters. His expression right now was probably more about bad news than anything.

Meira and Samael already stood in the room waiting for her. In addition, in the room with her, two representatives from the Gold Clan and two others, Reid and Arden, sent by Ladon to represent the Blue Clan, had gathered. Likewise, representatives of the Black Clan, among others, reflected in the monitors standing behind her sisters. A new addition to help with clan-to-clan relations as well as witnesses there to be part of all decisions made as allies.

Airk, surprisingly, stood with those in the room. She glanced at him, then at Meira, who wasn't looking back. He must be needed for a specific reason to be included on such a call.

She closed the door behind her, trying to breathe a little less heavily after hurrying so hard. "Sorry it took me so long—"

"Pytheios is coming for you," Skylar stated baldly.

It took Angelika a second to get out of her own head, because that had been the furthest thing from what she'd expected to hear. An attack, maybe, or an uncovered plot to take down the kings standing against Pytheios. But...

"Me?" She nearly looked around for a different "you" her sister could be referring to, but logic settled in before she embarrassed herself that way. Of course he'd be coming for her. She was the last unmated phoenix, and he didn't know about her being dormant. They were still keeping that bugaboo a secret.

She blew out through her nose. "I wondered when that would be coming."

A cough from Airk had her glancing in his direction. Not that he showed any emotion to go with the sound. Probably disapproval.

"This is bad, Angelika," Skylar snapped.

She pursed her lips, swallowing back a sarcastic retort. "I'm well aware," she answered quietly instead. "How do we know this is true?"

Skylar and Kasia both hesitated.

"One of my early visions was of a man—tall and wearing an ornately embroidered collarless suit. Skinny to the point of appearing emaciated, with his cheekbones and bones jutting out from under his skin, and pale almost to the point of being albino, though his hair was reddish."

To her right, out of the corner of her eye, Angelika caught how Airk stiffened at the description, but he didn't question Kasia, who continued.

"He was speaking. He said, 'I can save your sister, my queen, but you must act fast.'"

She paused.

"You describe the Stoat," Airk said. No inflection, as usual, and yet Angelika got the sense that his personal feelings about the man were anything but steady.

"Stoat?" Kasia asked.

"For the weasel he is," Airk stated. "The man is one of Pytheios's closest advisors. I saw little of him where I was held. Usually only when he was bringing in one of Pytheios's latest prisoners."

"His name is Jakkobah," Ladon supplied in his gravel-and-smoke voice. Most supernaturals didn't have discernable accents. They lived too long and spoke too many languages to hang on to them. But Ladon still had a trace of the British Isles in his.

Why was this important? "Why are you bringing up this old vision now?" Angelika asked.

"Because I heard those words from Jakkobah's lips myself," Skylar said. "Verbatim. Just now."

"She was with me when I received the call," Ladon said. "Jakkobah asked to speak to her directly."

Silence settled over the room, thick and uncomfortable. A dragon high in Pytheios's leadership wanted to help Skylar save one of her sisters?

"We cannot trust this man," Airk stated. Still controlled, and yet she felt his anger like a lash.

No one else appeared to notice that anger, though, given that no one was giving him extra space or watching him like a grenade with the pin pulled. How did they not see the roil of emotions behind the mask?

"He is my spy within Pytheios's organization," Ladon dropped into the conversation.

Airk may as well have been carved of ice he went so cold. "He is *your* spy?" he asked slowly. "How do you know he is not playing you into Pytheios's traps?"

"I don't," Ladon admitted. "But he has yet to steer me false."

"What else did he say?" Angelika pressed. There had to be more. How did they know *she* was the sister he referenced?

Through the screen, Skylar's gaze landed smack on her. "He said Pytheios has set his eyes on you, little sister, and that he already has several dragons loyal to him placed within Ararat. They are positioned to come for you in days, a week at most. He wasn't sure exactly when."

"Do we trust him?" Angelika asked.

"About this?" Ladon flicked Airk a quick glance. "My experience with Jakkobah's information in the past has always been proven true. Combined with Kasia's vision, I don't think we have a choice."

"So do I come back to you?" Angelika asked.

She refused, this time, to look at the man beside her. Returning to Ben Nevis meant leaving Airk.

"No." Skylar shook her head. "According to Jakkobah, Pytheios has men positioned with all three of our clans in case you disappear from one and show up in another."

Well…damn.

"Let me contact the gargoyles," Meira offered. "They are probably the best option to keep you safe."

Keep her cloistered was what they meant. An option that would exclude her from everything. Out of the war. Out of avenging their parents' deaths. Out of helping her sisters, though she was limited in the ways she could.

"You want to keep me from the fight?" She'd already missed so much, hiding among the wolves, dammit. Angelika closed her eyes, thinking of her father. "Those were my parents he killed, too, you know," she whispered.

None of her sisters said anything, though beside her Meira flinched. They didn't need to speak, though. When she opened her eyes again, their expressions told her everything. They would do whatever it took to keep one another safe, and she, of all of them, needed the most protecting. As she was youngest of the quadruplets by only minutes, they'd always underestimated her. Now the fates had heaped coals onto the fire and betrayed her by giving her nothing. Not a smidgeon of power, no way to defend herself or be helpful or act as anything but a problem.

A problem they now wanted to hide.

The hells with this.

She'd find a different way. One that would be difficult for

Pytheios to pin down but still allow her to be involved, even if in a small way. She slid a glance in Airk's direction, an idea stirring.

He was really going to hate it.

. . .

Angelika had to time approaching Meira with her plan exactly right, because she couldn't even get started without her sister on her side.

Almost two days she'd had to wait, because Airk had disappeared the first night after they'd received Jakkobah's message. Two days that Angelika had held her breath through every agonizingly slow second, worried that the gargoyles would finally respond to Meira reaching out to them. Her sister had promised the notoriously private and secretive creatures that she would no longer come to them via reflection, which meant a slower form of communication.

Angelika had no idea where Airk had gone during that time. Meira hadn't had more information beyond another smaller settlement within the White Clan's boundaries. But she'd managed to winnow out information of his return, which had been late last night. Not only that, she'd learned he was leaving again today…and she intended to be part of that plan.

Which meant getting Meira to agree.

This conversation would take privacy and major begging. Knees on the floor might be involved, maybe tears and hand-wringing as well. The timing was the critical part because she'd also need to get to her sister before Meira was in front of her computers. Once her focus involved a screen, Meira didn't tend to absorb anything else. She also got pissy about interruptions.

Like a cave troll.

Which was why Angelika was lurking in the damp stone hallway outside her sister's chambers, just around the bend with a massive vase as her cover. She was not an expert on antiquities, but this one was no doubt priceless.

She shifted, trying to keep her foot out of a puddle. The constant dripping in this area of the mountain was due to the fact that a natural cavern, versus dragon-made, formed a small pool nearby. If one followed the water all the way down the natural flow of the mountain, eventually you ended up in a thermally heated lake at the bottom. The dragons here used that as a source for hot water for their showers, which meant most of the time her hair smelled of sulfur. Not her favorite thing.

Angelika peeked around the vase, then slowly withdrew and leaned against the wall. Nothing. Samael usually left about now. What was keeping them?

Actually...strike that question. The fact that she didn't have shifter hearing was probably a good thing right this moment, given the way Meira and Samael could hardly keep from touching each other. All her sisters and their mates were like that, actually. Still... without having the proof shoved down her ears, she could pretend that Meira and Samael were sleeping, or brushing their teeth, or something equally mundane.

Then the sound she'd been waiting for reached her ears—the soft click of a lock followed by the handle turning and the swoosh of the door opening.

"Airk won't need you until tonight," Samael was saying. Which meant Meira wasn't working yet if he was talking to her at all.

Angelika took advantage of her opening and scooted around the vase, casually strolling down the hall toward her brother-by-blood. Although, given how mating worked, calling him her brother-by-fire would probably be more accurate. "Hi, Sam."

He cocked his head—only Meira was allowed to call him that—and she chuckled. "Sorry. King Samael Veles." She executed an overly frilly bow with lots of toe pointing and hand twirling.

He snorted a laugh, dark eyes amused and the white of his teeth stark against his bronzed skin. "That's worse."

She grinned, and he shook his head.

"Do you need Meira?" he asked.

"Just coming by for a chat." She tossed in a shrug for good

measure. *No big deal happening here. Only escaping being cloistered with a bunch of stone people and a goat. That's all.*

He nodded, but his gaze was directed over her shoulder, searching the passageway behind her. "Where's Alim?"

The bodyguard they'd assigned to "keep her safe" until she went to the gargoyles? She'd hoped Samael would miss the fact that she'd given the man the slip. Skylar wasn't the only sneaky phoenix in the family who could make herself difficult to follow or find when she wished.

When Angelika merely stared back with wide eyes, Samael's lips flattened. "I see."

A smidge of guilt at getting Alim in trouble with his king pricked. But this conversation was important.

"I'll be fine with Meira in your room," she insisted. "No one can get in there, and she can always get us out. Send Alim up, and I won't leave the room without him. Promise."

"Gods save us from the Amon sisters," Samael muttered, then opened the door wider to usher her inside.

She didn't miss the fact that he locked it from the outside when he left. Untrusting ass. But that didn't matter as far as plans went. "Mir?" she called out.

"Back here."

Uh-oh. Her sister was already in her office. Angelika hurried across the sunken living area—decorated more casually than one would expect for royalty, if you discounted the massive royal seal in the floor made of onyx stone—to the open door leading into the office. "Have you already gotten started?"

Meira was sitting at a wall of monitors, not unlike the war rooms in all the dragon shifter mountains Angelika had seen so far. Only way fancier. A mating present from King Gorgon, Samael's predecessor, before his death.

"Not yet. I was about to." Her sister smiled even as her gaze drifted toward the monitors on her setup.

Angelika silently gave herself a pat on the back for timing this so well. Did she know her sibling or what?

"Oh good." She scooted the deep leather desk chair, squeaky wheel protesting loudly all the way, around Samael's big oak desk and across the room to where Meira sat, then plopped herself down.

"So…what do you need?" Meira asked.

"Can't a girl just want to spend time with her sister?"

Meira shot a glance at the clock in the corner of the center screen. "At six in the morning? Nope."

"Maybe I had trouble sleeping and knew you'd be up," Angelika pointed out.

Only Meira frowned, concern lining the pucker between her brows. "Is that true?"

Half true. "I can't go stay with the gargoyles, Mir."

Her sister, curls escaping the loose bun she'd shoved her hair up into, only frowned harder, her eyes darkening to a deeper blue with her concern by the second. "I wondered when you'd say something."

Because of her empathic abilities? Or because she knew Angelika?

Of the four of them, Angelika had always been closest to Meira. Though they were quadruplets, born over the course of roughly an hour, according to Mama, they acted more like sisters born years apart. As the oldest, Kasia and Skylar were close, leaving Meira and Angelika to form their own unique bond. She adored all her sisters and would do anything for them. But Meira…they understood each other.

Just because Angelika went through life with a smile and could find the silver lining in the darkest of thunderstorms didn't mean she was naive or always happy. What tended to upset her the most was being left out. Being coddled or overprotected or shut away "for her own sake."

Ironic, given her current situation. The fates had a terrible sense of humor.

Mama had done it to all of them—secreting them away from the world. Skylar, who acted bound and determined to take Mama's place now that she was gone, would try to do the same if Angelika let her. Kasia, too. But Meira would understand. She had to.

"Where will you go instead?" Meira asked slowly, and relief soothed Angelika's wrought nerves because her sister didn't say no or try to block her from this. "The colonies, maybe?" Meira mused. "I don't think you'll be any safer there. The wolves?"

Angelika had debated that option but discarded it just as rapidly. The problem was Jedd.

She couldn't do that to him. Not the way he felt and the way she…didn't feel. It would be cruel. Angelika shook her head. "No. I don't want to put other communities at risk. I also think it's a bad idea to stay in one place where it would be easier to find me after enough time passed."

"So, what—"

"I intend to go with Airk." The words came out in a tumble.

Meira's eyes shot wide, and she stared and stared as she digested that information. "He said he'd let you?"

"Not exactly."

Meira frowned. "Then what?"

"I don't think he'd agree initially, but I would be terrific at helping convince others to join us. I know I would. Better than him probably. Plus, it would keep me on the move and in unlikely places."

"I suppose that's true. But if he doesn't agree, then—"

"Help me show up where he's going next. He won't be able to say no until it's too late. I'll get a chance to prove myself, and if he still doesn't want me along after that, I'll go to the gargoyles."

Meira let out a low whistle. "And I thought Skylar could be reckless."

"It's not *that* bad." Angelika pulled a face. Yes, it was. "I could pass as a white dragon if I need to. We don't have to tell people who I really am unless it's necessary."

"I mean about Airk." Meira gave an exaggerated shiver. "He's not a shifter I would want to cross…or tempt his dragon, for that matter."

"He won't hurt me." How did no one else see that about him? His iron control was entirely about leashing the beast within. Sure, he was an unusual case, but someone had to have faith in the man.

"You know him well enough to say that for certain?" Meira pressed.

Maybe not, but gut instinct told her she was right, and she was rarely wrong about people. Besides, she had to do this. Going back to hiding wasn't an option.

"Please, Mir." She reached out and took both her sister's hands in hers, needing her to understand how important this was. "I have to do something to help. I can do *this*."

Meira's troubled expression didn't ease, though. "And if you're caught? He can't shift, so he can't protect you that way."

Angelika stood up and showed her sister the gun holstered at her hip, hidden by a fleece jacket. She'd always been a better shot than anything else to do with weapons. As arrogant as dragons could be, they wouldn't expect her to be armed. That would give her an advantage.

"I'm not defenseless. None of us ever truly was, thanks to Mama."

Meira's smile turned small and sad, but she still shook her head. "How can you ask me to do this? Kasia and Skylar will be furious."

"They'll understand when you explain it to them."

Meira scoffed.

"Please." Begging was not beneath Angelika. "How can you ask me to hide away? Like I'm not strong enough to face this with you or Kas or Sky."

"But—"

"How is this any different than you disappearing with Samael a few months ago?"

Meira raised an eyebrow. "I can escape easily through any reflective surface."

Angelika threw her hands in the air. "Assuming there's something shiny *around*. Come on, Mir. Powers don't make you invincible, and all of you have risked yourselves in some way or another. Skylar broke into Ladon's mountain to rescue Kasia with no way to get herself out. And Kasia went to that two-faced doctor when she kept going up in flames and couldn't control anything about her powers. Even you decided not to stay hidden with the gargoyles where you'd be safe."

Meira twisted her lips, gaze skittering off the to the side. A sure sign she was about to cave. Angelika tried not to sit forward and made sure to arrange her expression in a worried pinch. Or she hoped that's what her face was doing.

"Don't sideline me," she pleaded when her sister still held back. What she was about to say would hurt her sister, but it would also help her understand. "I never got to see our father. You did—"

She choked off the words as unaccustomed tears clogged her throat.

"What do you need from me?" Meira finally asked.

Angelika shot out of her chair and flung her arms around her sister's neck. "Thank you."

Meira clutched her tightly. "Don't make me regret it," she whispered. "Losing you would break me."

CHAPTER FIVE

Angelika slammed her fist into the heavy bag she was working, careful to keep her knuckles flat, thumb out of the way, hitting straight on and moving from her core, not her arm. It felt so good she did it again. And again, moving her body with the bag as though she was working over an opponent, focused and intent.

Airk was going tonight, and she needed something to calm her nerves before then.

The sounds of Samael's fighters training all around her in the large cavern faded away as she pictured Pytheios's face—rotten, as it had been before he recently mated.

By the time she finished, she was drenched in sweat and sucking wind. Like a damn human. She steadied the swinging bag, then dropped forward, hands on her knees, breathing hard. She was no Skylar when it came to fighting skills, but now that she was no longer pretending to be a wolf shifter, she'd gone back to her regular training and workouts.

Even more important now, given what she was about to do. The ability to defend herself was going to be critical. Probably.

"My, my." Beside her, Arden, Ladon's sister and one of his reps here in the Black Clan, raised her thick, dark brows and grinned. Dressed in pink and with glitter lining her eyes, the impression she gave off was total princess, but Angelika knew for certain this woman was a badass. *Not* to be underestimated. Skylar said Arden liked to use her femininity and male dragons' ingrained perceptions to keep the upper hand. And good for her.

"So do all you Amon sisters know how to fight?" she teased.

Still breathing hard, Angelika swiped her T-shirt-covered shoulder over her face and grinned back. "Our mother made sure we were never going to be helpless. Even when we were human." *Or still are.*

Arden sobered at that, turquoise eyes, which reflected the color of her scales when she was dragon, turning serious.

Angelika held up a hand. "Sorry. I didn't mean to drag the conversation down."

But Arden shook her head, deep black ponytail swinging. "I was thinking that I wish my mother had done the same for me."

Angelika straightened and crossed to the other woman's side. She hadn't had much opportunity to talk with Arden. "You seem to have done okay for yourself." She glanced at the heavy bag the other girl had been working.

Arden lifted a single shoulder. "My ability to fight is all thanks to my brother. Ladon taught me in secret." She made a face. "Then acted all shocked and shaken when I wanted to be one of his guards."

With a snorted laugh, Angelika shook her head. "Dragon shifters. What are you going to do?"

Arden's eye roll was directed not at her absent brother, but over her shoulder at the man who'd come here as the other representative of the Blue Clan. Reid, the Captain of Ladon's guard as well as his Viceroy of War, stood across the room, speaking with Samael and Airk. "Mate them," Arden murmured. "It's the only way to tame them."

Almost as though he'd heard her, Reid glanced up, right at Arden, and stilled, visibly arrested. Then he slowly lifted a single eyebrow in teasing inquiry. Arden blew him a sarcastic kiss, which only made him laugh before turning back to his conversation.

Angelika scooted closer. "I know Ladon gave you permission

to mate, but I hadn't heard that you had yet."

"We haven't." Pursed lips hinted at hesitation.

"Why not? If you don't mind me being nosy. It's clear there's a connection."

"Because mating me would mean he can't mate anyone else, and I'm female-born." Arden winced. "I'm sterile. I'm a fighter. How could I do that to him?"

Reid was suddenly right there with them, wrapping his arms around Arden's waist. "Because I'll haunt you and never look at another woman anyway."

The way Arden melted against Reid sent a twang of longing through Angelika. Samael looked at Meira the same way. Total and utter adoration.

"Take it from me," she said. "I watched my mother pine for my father all her life. Love is precious. A gift from the gods and the fates. Not perfect. Not easy. But don't turn your back on it just because of a few *'what if*s.'"

She slid a quick peek in Airk's direction, not wanting him to think she was saying this for him. He'd said no. She respected that. But he wasn't paying her any attention, anyway.

Returning her gaze to the couple, she tipped her head. "Not for all the *what if*s in the world would I walk away if I'd found someone who looked at me the way that he looks at you."

Not even Jedd, who thought himself desperately in love with her, had ever had that light in his eyes. Yet another reason she'd known that mating him hadn't been right.

Two pairs of stunned blue eyes gazed back at her, and Angelika laughed. "Sorry. According to my sisters, I have a tendency to butt in with advice."

"No. That was…" Arden swallowed. "That was good advice."

"I got it!" Meira's euphoric call had everyone in the room turning.

The patter of running feet sounded down the human tunnel a few seconds before she came hurrying into sight. Meira sprinted straight to Samael, who caught his mate as she threw her arms around his neck.

"Got what?" he asked, humor and love lighting up his face.

"That bastard's hidden stash of treasure."

Holy smokes. Meira had done it? Found Pytheios's wealth, taken from all the clans. Stolen or taxed. They'd suspected—in actual fact, the previous King of the Black Clan, Gorgon, had suspected shortly before his death—that the red king would hide it using modern technology, and Meira had been tracking it for months with no luck.

"You found it?" Samael asked, as though he couldn't quite believe it.

Meira nodded, as giddy as her serious sister got, her curls bouncing with the motion. "Found it and took it back. Every damn penny."

The rotting king wasn't going to like that. Angelika grinned, even as in the back of her mind she knew that would only escalate Pytheios's plans against them. Still, it was harder to wage a war without funding.

With a burst of laughter that had every warrior in the room gaping at their king, Samael lifted Meira right off her feet. "Thank the gods. Maybe now you can get more sleep."

. . .

Meira snuggled into Samael's arms, drifting to sleep knowing she was safe and loved. But they had to get up soon. At a soft brush of his fingertips over the nape of her neck, her eyes fluttered open to find her mate watching her with a smile both tender and possessive.

"Gods, you're the most beautiful thing I've ever seen," he murmured. "No wonder all it took was one look in that mirror. I was yours before I even knew you were real."

Meira grinned, an effervescent sort of happiness bubbling through her. Not just hers but his, too—she could sense it through that magical link that bound mates together. She propped herself up on one elbow to look him in the eyes. "I didn't think it possible, but I love you more every day."

He hummed in his throat. "Well, I am damn lovable."

She pinched his pec, and he yelped but laughed, wrapping an arm around her waist. Instead of tugging her closer, though, he flipped her to her back, then scooted down to lay his ear against her barely rounded belly covered by her softest nightgown. A little more than three months along, and thank the gods the nonstop nausea had finally ceased, but her breasts were still terribly sensitive. Samael hadn't liked the nausea part at all. She'd never seen her big, strong dragon warrior so…helpless. Kind of adorable, actually.

"Hello, little one," Sam murmured to her belly, as he did each morning and each night.

As happened every time, her heart swelled with love for them both. No scan had told them for sure yet that they were having a boy, but she'd seen him in a vision the night they'd conceived him.

Samael was still cooing to her belly, and Meira buttoned her lips around a grin because no way would she take away Sam's joy in this moment by giggling at his antics. He was going to be an amazing father. He would need to be, raising the first boy a phoenix had ever given birth to.

One who would be next in line for the Black Dragon Clan's throne and, possibly, for the position of High King, depending on what these next hours and days and maybe years revealed. Maybe not, though. High King was for the dragon shifter king mated to the phoenix. Rumor held that he had to claim her like a prize, but in actual fact, he needed to claim her heart. But that was before, when there'd only been one phoenix at a time. Not four. And always women.

This war wasn't over, and the absolute dread of losing this wonderful thing they'd found together hung over every decision they made, and only darkened with terror of losing their child.

An alarm went off on the phone she'd left on the bedside table, telling her it was time to send Airk to his next destination. She'd already sent Angelika in ahead of him an hour ago.

She hadn't shared Angelika's new mission with Samael. She'd promised her sister to wait so that he wouldn't feel obligated to tell Airk. But as soon as Airk was in, she would tell him.

"We'd better go," she said.

...

Airk made his way to Samael and Meira's personal chambers. The queen had had a massive wall of mirrors installed in what was essentially a guest suite. The reflections were what Meira used to move individuals between the Black, Blue, and Gold Clans' mountains. The same one he'd come through a day ago after his first assassination.

He had a new target now—Belyy Zver.

Once the man had been a member of Zilant Amon's Curia Regis, the king's council members—a trusted friend and advisor to the phoenixes' father.

None of Zilant's original council members remained on that body of advisors now, a fact that Airk had discovered with careful research and speaking with those white dragons who'd already switched sides and joined the rebel kings' cause. Most council members had "disappeared" shortly after Zilant's death, when Pytheios had encouraged the clan to place King Volos on the throne. The few still alive had been given different positions of power elsewhere.

Belyy was now the Tribune of the second biggest base established by the White Clan, in charge of all that happened within his mountain. Mönkh Saridag—a peak in the Sayan Mountain Range, located on the current human border between the countries of Russia and Mongolia—was perhaps the most strategic location for the White Clan, given its proximity to both the Red and Green Clans to the south and east, as well as the Blue, Gold, and Black Clans farther west in various directions.

Any leader who had been in power when Zilant and Airk's parents were killed could never be trusted. At the very least, they were cowards too afraid for their own lives to speak up against evil. Belyy's death would perhaps put a small piece of Airk's soul back for the killing.

Forget diplomacy. This is what he should have been doing all along.

Killing the man who'd once been Zilant's personal bodyguard yesterday had not assuaged anything, but that had to be because of how it had happened. He'd found that asshole hiding in a small village in the most northern part of Siberia. The Unnamed Mountain, where most dragons preferred not to live. Hells, it even remained unnamed because it was insignificant, so why bother. Even with their fire…too cold.

The ex-guard—a coward who'd stood outside the room the day Pytheios killed his king, never once coming inside to find out what all the ruckus was about—hadn't even defended himself, almost as though waiting for his life to end this way all this time. If Airk licked his lips, he could still taste the blood that had splattered his face.

A knock at the door was answered by Samael, who glanced down the hall before ushering Airk inside.

"Do you have everything you need?" he asked.

Each trip, he took with him easy-to-travel food and an extra set of clothes, all packed in a modern backpack, in which he'd stuffed various other items—a knife, water bottle, toilet paper, poison. Plus other items in the pockets of his utility pants. One never knew, and it was best to be prepared. "I am ready."

Meira was already in the mirrored room. Black-tipped flames— the color of her mate—danced across her fingertips as she stared into the reflection.

An enticing image of Angelika covered in white fire filled his mind.

Not real, because she'd never lit on fire. This was pushed at him by his dragon and wishful thinking. He knocked the picture from his head as fast as it showed. He'd seen the image of her face in the midst of taking a knife to that ex-guard's throat, too. His dragon was determined to make him think of her all the fucking time.

A distraction he couldn't afford.

Samael clapped him on the shoulder, and Airk had to swallow a snarl before it could rip out of his throat. Touching was still a trigger after so long without. Only Angelika's touch didn't set him off. Or…not in that way, at least.

Samael lifted his hand immediately, though he didn't comment. "Are you still sure this is what you want to do?"

"Mrrrow." The small cat appeared out of nowhere, winding around his ankles.

Samael cleared his throat and picked the creature up, holding it against his chest.

"I have proven effective at it already," Airk answered the question still hanging out there.

"That doesn't make it easy for you. Killing your own kind."

"Traitors who let all this happen?" Airk stuffed the small twinge left over, the image of that guard's eyes right before he killed him, down in the same hole with his dragon and emotions. "It is what I should have done to start with."

Samael nodded slowly, then looked to Meira, who placed her hand on the mirror. She didn't have to, but Airk had noticed that she did when she wanted to be pinpoint accurate in the location she sent him to.

Which she would need to be. This time she was placing him directly inside a mountain rather than on the outskirts.

As soon as she connected with the glass, the image changed, revealing a beautifully luxurious room beyond. Not unlike Meira and Samael's suite within Ararat but more opulent. Marble floors covered by fur rugs, gilded light fixtures…and was that a dragon carved from alabaster in the corner?

"Where is he?" Airk asked, referring to his mark.

"Currently in his lover's chambers."

Airk nodded. Samael's contacts had come through with information, including the fact that Belyy kept a human lover inside his mountain. Not one who showed dragon sign, either. The human remained in a clandestine chamber, never emerging, but that's where the white dragon spent much of his time.

Their information also told them that Belyy would return to his own suite in the middle of the night to wash away her scent before sleeping. He would not expect Airk to be waiting.

Deadly purpose settled into him, and he leaned into the emotion. He would look this traitor in the eye while he slid his dagger between his ribs, then twist and twist until Belyy was too weak from blood loss to heal himself. Then, and only then, would he snap the man's neck.

Even dragon healing couldn't do anything about that.

Raising a hand in farewell to both Meira and Samael, he stepped through the open mirror, then turned to face them. "I will see you in a week."

Several corrupted leaders cowered inside this mountain, and he intended to take the life of each and every one. Enough, hopefully, to cause chaos within the ancient halls. It would be up to the three allied kings to take it while it lay exposed as soon as he gave the signal. Then he planned to move on to the next man on his list.

"Be careful," Meira cautioned.

She lifted her hand from the mirror, and suddenly he was staring at a hideous mirror edged in gilded bones. Those of other creatures. Airk had seen enough of them in the dungeons of Everest to know, but he couldn't do anything for those poor souls. Then or now.

He could only punish those responsible.

The first thing Airk did was check every room. He trusted Meira, but he had to be sure he was truly alone. Belyy had certainly appointed himself the best of the suites within the mountain, greedy fuck.

He frowned over the oddly familiar scent inside the common living area at the center of the suite. Who had Belyy been hosting?

Airk narrowed his focus. Based on a vague memory of visiting this mountain with his father as a boy, he was fairly certain this had been the king's chambers when the royal family visited. Not that they did often. The Unnamed Mountain was more of an outpost…or a punishment. What did Belyy do when King Volos would come to visit this mountain? Although perhaps Volos, the recently deceased puppet king, loyal to Pytheios before his clan, hadn't bothered to inspect his mountains or visit the people he ruled.

Did that mean Belyy's power was even more than a typical Tribune?

Assured that he was alone and that no recording devices existed inside the suite, he determined the best place to lay his trap.

The last thing he could allow to happen was to have Belyy run to the perch outside the large window in the living area. From there, the man could shift, call for help from his guards, or fly away, and Airk would have no way to defend against shifted dragons, or even multiple in their human form, if they came to take him.

Likely, however, that the man would come in from that direction, being the fastest way to reach these levels.

With that in mind, Airk decided to tuck himself into a small room, one of several family or guest bedrooms, at the opposite end of the suite from the bedchamber Belyy used. By the stale smell, the spaces went unused. From the doorway, he had a view down a dark hallway of the living area Belyy would have to pass through to get to his bedroom on the other side, regardless of which entrance he used to access the suite. Once the man was inside and had gone to bathe, Airk would corner him there.

Likely hours from now.

Best if he spent the night in here, containing his own scent to a space that his mark shouldn't need to visit. He took three steps toward the small hallway, then paused as a stronger, now entirely familiar perfume drifted through the open window.

One whose presence here was impossible—sunlight and summer and fresh air.

Angelika.

Was he descending into madness, scenting her everywhere now? Sheer white curtains covering the windowed door out to the dragon's perch in the atrium suddenly blew in a wisp of breeze, and he caught the outline of a woman. She stood on the other side of the glass, looking inside. Watching him.

Airk's dragon roared to the fore, and he clenched his jaw, holding himself together, but a spike of unaccustomed fear—for her—managed to break through. "Angelika?"

She parted the curtains and stepped through, white hair braided in a crown across the top of her head, moving cautiously, gaze wary. Of him.

She lifted her determined little chin in the air. "Don't be mad."

CHAPTER SIX

Pytheios strode at a clip his previously rotting body had not allowed. The oldest of all living dragons, his body had been deteriorating until his recent mating to Tisiphone—with the help of his witch. Perhaps he should have mated and extended his life sooner. The freedom of simple movement filled him with relish, the power coursing through his veins unstoppable. Soon he'd live forever. Though, right now, that pleasure was eclipsed by a fury he planned to take out on the traitors in his mountain.

His money was *gone*. All of it.

Disappeared into thin fucking air. He'd been so smart, hiding it within human banking systems behind smoke screens of human conglomerates and companies. But someone had found his secret accounts and emptied them.

He needed to take those fucking phoenixes out before he couldn't afford this war any longer.

But first, he had to deal with a traitor.

With purpose in his stride, he made his way through one of the more populated centers of Everest, nodding at his people, who bowed and scraped as he went.

The mountain commons were unique to his mountain. The early designers had deliberately brought nature inside. Everest, usually ice and snow and cold on the outside, could have been so inside as well. But once the early dragons figured out how to bring sunlight and air to the interior and warm it, they'd constructed a flourishing garden in the center of the massive mountain.

Green rolling hills were dotted with lush trees with pops of color thanks to beds of flowers. The landscape spread up the sides of the cave walls, like a valley. They'd even designed it to rain. The mountain was eternally spring with a stone ceiling for the sky, illuminated by strips of lighting that reflected the daylight outside. This was usually a place of peace inside Everest—one where his people came together. But with a single order, Pytheios was about to turn a corner of this untouchable land into a warning to all.

He nodded at the two guards standing shoulder to shoulder, keeping the gathering crowd at bay, and the rumble of angry voices dimmed as they realized who was in their midst.

Pytheios knew exactly who waited behind the guards. He'd left the fucker here for several days, both as part of the warning and because in his own initial anger he would have killed the man too quickly. He needed information. After that, the traitor could suffer.

One of the guards stepped aside, almost like a living door swinging open, and Pytheios's gaze landed on the captive chained to a chair. Not any chair. Humans were rarely good for anything, but during the years of their so-called Middle Ages, they'd shown some imagination when it came to torture. This particular device he'd had modeled after one of those.

Made of dragonsteel, it included a stiff seat with the back that didn't come up to the captive's neck. Spikes were placed to stick onto the flesh along the spine, at the back of the knees, and along the undersides of the arms.

The mistaken soul who deserved this punishment was chained— naked, of course—not only by wrists and ankles. A collar had been locked around his neck, and another larger one around his middle. If Jakkobah dared to shift forms, the dragonsteel metal wouldn't break. Instead, it would decapitate him, as well as slicing the man in half and severing his hands and feet.

Blood dripped over the edges of the chair's arms and seat, pooling in the lush green grass beneath. His pale red hair, typically pulled back in a neat ponytail, hung around his face in greasy strands, and his previously perfectly manicured nails were missing entirely, only bloody, raw sockets where they had been until recently. Jakkobah's head lolled forward, hanging between his shoulders limply, as though he were either asleep or could no longer hold it up. But his heartbeat told Pytheios the man was awake.

"Look at me," Pytheios commanded quietly.

Jakkobah slowly lifted his head. For once, his pale eyes didn't seem to take in the room or even Pytheios himself. Almost as though he was no longer aware of what was being done to him.

Perhaps I have left him too long.

Pytheios waited.

As he did, he allowed his gaze to skate over the liar he had considered his most loyal advisor until a few days ago. Bony to the point of being emaciated, the man was all angles. Unusually pale for a dragon shifter, Jakkobah's only nod to the fact that he came from the Red Clan was his hair, technically red but really more orange. Even his eyes were milky imitations of what they should be.

I should have known the man they call the Stoat was not to be trusted.

Everyone knew weasels were liars. Thieves, all of them. Jakkobah had proved this truth when he'd stolen from Pytheios. Stolen his secrets and his trust. Caught passing information to Ladon Ormarr. This man had taken from Pytheios more than anyone except Serefina Amon and now her fucking phoenix daughters.

"Ah." Jakkobah blinked and seemed to return to the here and now, his gaze suddenly sharpening, focusing on Pytheios. "Our ever benevolent, ever wise, ever true *High King*," he croaked in that nasal voice that had always been an irritant to Pytheios.

"Take his head!" someone from the crowd held at bay by the guards shouted.

Loyal dogs. Pytheios allowed himself a satisfied smile. "More true, it seems, than you."

"You lost your way long ago," Jakkobah stated, almost unhurried.

All reports indicated he'd taken his punishment thus far with not a word or sound. Not for much longer, though. Usually, this man loved to play to the crowd, but he wasn't doing so now, only addressing Pytheios. Perhaps the urge for those mind games had been beaten out of him.

Good.

"My loyalty is to dragon shifters," Jakkobah said. "You'll ruin us all if left to rule."

Pytheios examined the backs of his hands. He found himself looking at his unmarred, youthful hands often lately. So strange to look down and see young skin rather than age spots, gaping sores, and the flesh falling away from his bones.

He fisted his hands, reveling in the energy, the capability, then bent a bored look on Jakkobah. "Before we get started…a small demonstration."

A nod over his shoulder, and two of his men escorted Nathair up to where they stood together.

His younger brother—a late-in-life oops on his parents' part—did not meet his eyes. Not from guilt. Nathair had difficulty looking anyone in the eyes, a condition of his brilliant mind. His dark hair flopped over his forehead and into his eyes, and despite the hold the two guards had on his elbows, his brother's fingers moved in midair in unison, as though he still held the cube toy puzzle that usually kept his mind from overwhelming him with information.

A toy that had disappeared the same day Airk Azdajah and Skylar Amon had escaped Everest.

Turning to the crowd, Pytheios shared a little story…

"When Skylar Amon escaped, at first I assumed she'd had help or somehow had a power that aided her." After all, he'd figured out centuries ago how to contain Airk. "But then my own brother's behavior drew suspicion."

Nathair's fingers didn't pause in their movement over an invisible cube he no longer held. If anything, they sped up in a sign of agitation.

"After reviewing footage of the cameras in the room, I now have proof that Nathair Chandali is directly responsible for her escape."

And Airk's. But that wasn't for his people to know.

"You wouldn't dare execute your own brother," Jakkobah sneered behind him. "His mind is too valuable to you."

True. But then again, he could no longer trust that mind to work for his good. Jakkobah's betrayal, while a surprise, hadn't hurt, only enraged. But his own brother...

Even now, the razor's lance of pain ate at him.

Pytheios slowly turned to face the Stoat, cocking his head in curiosity. At the same time, the guards backed away from his brother on cue. "*All* traitors are subject to judgment," he said to Jakkobah.

Before anyone could so much as take a breath, Pytheios shifted a single part of his body. His dragon's tail whipped out and slammed down on his brother, the mace-like spike driving through bone and flesh with a slurping crunch and a finality no one could deny.

In fact, Pytheios had to shake the corpse off himself before reversing the shift and tucking the tail away.

Jakkobah's pale skin turned a sickly green as he stared at Nathair's pulverized body, horror more than evident in his usually blank gaze.

"If you tell me what I need to know," Pytheios said, not even bothering to glance over as the guards dragged his brother's body away—Nathair was nothing to him now. "I will make your death as quick. But if not..." He shrugged.

Jakkobah's horror remained etched in his eyes as he turned them away from the bloody trail the body left behind. "You are so hungry for power, you'd murder your own kin—"

"I judged a traitor. And my rule is not about my power. It never was."

Jakkobah shook his head, unbelieving.

Pytheios stepped closer, lowering his voice. "I am the *only one* ensuring that we don't have to rely on mating some flaming bird to move forward as a species."

The Stoat scoffed, though the noise brought on a fit of coughing. "By creating a false phoenix and mating her instead?"

At the murmur from those nearest them in the crowd, Jakkobah came as close to a smirk as anything. "Will you tell that to all of our kind after you take out the Amon sisters the same way you did your own brother?"

"A desperate man spreading lies," Pytheios dismissed with a wave. And silence descended behind him.

What his witch had done…Tisiphone was no longer false. Created, not birthed, she wielded the powers many phoenixes before her had. A weapon he intended to unleash at the right moment. He didn't need to explain his actions to this man, this betrayer who clearly could not see the future Pytheios pictured. "Now…what did you tell that bastard on the blue throne?"

Jakkobah's mouth thinned. Weaselly fucker.

Nothing from his former advisor, despite the continued green cast to his pallor. Still…the man had never been privy, until this moment, to the way Pytheios interrogated traitors.

Anticipation welled inside him, fizzing in his blood. He'd make this pale excuse for a dragon shifter break. And he'd enjoy doing so.

· · ·

"What the fuck, Angelika?" Airk said, sounding more like Brand suddenly. Coldly in control as always, but his anger—the first time she'd witnessed that strong of an emotion from him—edged his reaction like embers eating away at a forest floor during a controlled burn.

She held up her hands in a conciliatory gesture. "Hear me out."

"Nothing you can say could possibly make this right." He didn't move closer as he stared at her. "Have you taken leave of your wits?"

Oh, hells no. That question was always a sore spot for her. Forget convincing him. She dropped her hands, eyes narrowed. "No more than you," she snapped.

He straightened at that, holding himself almost painfully stiff. "You think me a fool?"

So *that* was his Achilles' heel? Others thinking that his long imprisonment had broken his mind?

"No more than I," she said. And maybe the adamant tone in her voice convinced him, because his stance eased marginally.

"I can *help* you here," she insisted.

There went any give in him. "I cannot do what I need to if I am worrying about *you*."

"I can handle myself. My mother trained us all to fight." She drew her gun from her holster, careful to keep her finger off the trigger and aiming at the floor as she showed him the weapon. "I'm not defenseless."

He passed a hand over his face. "Go back to your sisters, Angelika. Pytheios is after you."

"This is the last place he'd look."

"You only put both of us in more danger being here."

She crossed her arms. "People *like* me."

He snorted. "What does that indicate? That they would hesitate to kill you because you make them smile?"

She cocked her head, sizing him up. "Do I make you smile?"

"Do not change the subject."

"I'm not." She was perfectly solemn, eager, even. "I meant it. If I can make *you* smile, feel a pleasant emotion, even if only every once in a while, then I can definitely convince others to join us. Or, at the very least, keep them from killing us first and asking questions later."

"They are going to take one whiff of you and assume you are—"

"Not a phoenix," she broke in. "Exactly." She couldn't help herself, adding a teasing, "Although if we want to fool them into thinking I'm a dragon, it might be best if you rub up against me."

Yes, she was in the midst of trying to convince him to let her try this. Despite that, her lips twitched at his sour expression, and at the same time her body tightened at the mere thought, blood heating. What an inconvenient moment for awareness to strike like a hot poker.

He crossed his arms. "I am not here to negotiate," he said, expression going flat. "I am here to kill."

Angelika's jaw dropped. Killing people was *not* part of her plan.

"Since when? Meira would have said—"

"Samael didn't want to burden her with another worry."

Oh dear. No doubt her brother-by-blood would be informing her sister *now*. Angelika almost snorted a laugh at the mental image that made. Not that she wasn't taking this seriously, but Meira would be furious, and at the same time, she'd kept Angelika's role a secret as well.

Stop. Focus on the man in front of you.

Angelika quickly flipped through and discarded myriad options. Actually, this didn't change things. Not really. "So, we both do this a little differently."

"No. You go back, and I kill my mark."

Stubborn, intractable jackass. He wasn't the only bloodthirsty one in this fight, dammit.

Without thinking about it, she stepped into his space, because this had to work. "My way is better. Let me convince you—"

Airk went even colder and slowly stepped away from her. "Angelika."

Uh-oh. The growling of her name was a bad sign. "Don't you see? We start with me trying to convince people to join us." She knew she could. She'd always been blessed with that knack. "If that doesn't work, you do your...killing thing...then we leave."

Yes, she was simplifying, but still.

A dangerous glint entered his eyes, one that would've had her backing up if she wasn't so damn determined. This was the *only* way she could think of to stay in the conflict in some small way.

"Go back," he demanded.

"No."

"If I must drag you through that mirror myself—"

"I know I can do this. Just give me a chance—"

In a blink, Airk shot out an arm, hand over her mouth. With no regard for handling her roughly, he dragged her backward down a short, unlit hallway and into a room, plunging them into darkness.

"Be quiet," he hissed in her ear.

No shit.

She kept the thought to herself and at the same time did her best not to shiver in stark response to suddenly being plastered against Airk's body. When he'd arrived in Ben Nevis, he'd been gaunt. But he'd filled out since, replacing those bones and hard angles with a wall of muscle. Her body *wanted* him. The sensation was turning into an unbearable need inside her.

Hells, he smelled incredible. Like good bourbon, tart fruit, and the underlying smoke of a dragon.

But he'd been clear. He didn't want her. So she did her best to pretend her own reaction wasn't a thing, focusing on why he'd hidden them back here.

The sound of the sliding glass door leading from the dragon perch outside into the suite stole her breath. She had to consciously slow her heartbeat, in case the person entering heard her.

Hopefully, he didn't smell them, even though she and Airk had just been standing by that door.

She almost expected the boom of a giant's footfall and a deep, "Fee. Fie. Foe. Fum," like in the childhood stories that became popular some two hundred years after her birth.

Airk, meanwhile, was a statue behind her, so still she would've wondered if he still lived if his breath wasn't lightly feathering over the back of her neck. Right over the spot where, if she mated successfully with a dragon shifter, his family mark would appear. With a hand locked to her mouth and another arm locked around her stomach, she could practically feel his intensity seeping into her muscles through his touch.

Footsteps padded in the opposite direction from their hiding place, followed by the sound of running water—the shower.

Airk blew out a breath and released her, turning her to face him at the same time. "Stay here." He whispered the words, and in the dim light, she had to focus on his lips to make them out.

"Let me speak with him first."

"You risk too much. It's reckless."

She plopped her hands on her hips. "All right, John Wilkes Booth, what was your plan?"

"Who?"

"An assassin from American history—" Why was she explaining? "Never mind." She waved for him to go on.

"I attack now, while he is most vulnerable. That was always the plan."

She stared at him hard. There had to be more that he simply wasn't sharing with her, because that plan sucked. "And you call *me* witless?"

"I said reckless—"

"Let's not go down that road again."

She glowered at him, and he stared back, unmoved.

But she held out. Long enough that his lip suddenly curled. "You are not going to leave, are you?"

A small twinge of guilt pricked under her skin. "Actually, I can't. Not until your prearranged time with Meira." She frowned suddenly, as the timing struck her as off. "Wait. Why do you need a week here if you planned to kill him immediately?"

"He is not the only one on my list." His expression didn't change by one twitch, and Angelika had to suppress a shiver.

She closed her eyes, visions of what she could achieve slipping away in the face of his intractable determination. "Fine. I'll stay here while you go do whatever you have to do."

His dark brows lowered in a deep frown as she opened her eyes again, but she was through pushing.

Airk's lips pinched. "Follow me."

With that, he turned and walked out of the room, down the hall, and paused in the common room. "Stay here," he whispered. "Faster escape when I'm done."

She nodded.

Then watched him disappear down the hall that led in the opposite direction they'd come from. Angelika turned away, hoping not to hear the killing. Gods, what a mess.

Instead, she tried to distract herself, focusing on the paintings hung up in here. As she turned toward the back wall, a small movement caught her eye, and she turned, only to stumble to a halt in front of a tall man, one too lean, as though he didn't eat enough, his bronzed skin stretched over bone rather than muscle. Unusual for a white dragon, his hair was inky black. But the feature she focused on most was his eyes, filled with white fire.

"I thought I scented something sweet on my perch," he snarled.

Angelika didn't dare glance away to see where Airk was. This man clearly sensed them, but at the moment he didn't seem to realize she wasn't alone.

Brazening it out, she offered her sweetest smile. "My name is Angel, and I was hoping for a moment of your time."

"A moment of my time?" he repeated, flames in his eyes setting an eerie glow flickering across his features.

Older. Her parents' contemporary, had they lived this long, though with dragons and the way they aged, she often found it difficult to tell. Still, if he was the age she guessed, had this man been around when her father was killed and her mother ran? Was that why he was on Airk's list?

Damn. I really messed things up.

"For what, may I ask?" he prompted when she didn't speak.

The polite words didn't dispel the look of certain death in his eyes, but she refused to back down. Instead, she took a huge risk and a leap of faith that her guess was right. "Actually, my name is"—Airk was surely going to kill her for this—"Angelika Amon."

The man's head snapped back like she'd socked him in the jaw with a well-placed uppercut.

She kept going. "I am the daughter of Zilant Amon and Serefina Hanyu Amon. I am assuming by your reaction that you knew my father?"

Flames were doused, leaving his gaze smoldering in wisps of smoke. "Gods above," he rasped, voice cracked like burned wood. "You *are* the spitting image of your father."

Then his gaze skittered around the room as though searching for something. Airk or the ghosts of his past? Angelika dared to glance over her shoulder. No Airk. Where was he?

Please don't already be dead. What if this man had killed him before coming out to her?

Swallowing and trying to keep her heart from pounding, she turned back. "I am not here to harm you."

Whoops. Okay, so that was a semi-lie, because while *she* might not be there to slit his throat, Airk was, assuming he was still alive. Angelika hid a cringe. Not the best way to start negotiations.

"Then why are you here? To curse me? To—"

"I'm here to ask you to pledge your allegiance to me and my sisters." Technically, she should be asking for his allegiance to the kings, but the few white dragons who'd switched sides had done so for Skylar, and more had come later, following the way Maul had died and the revelations about who she and her sisters were had come out. Maybe they had a better chance getting these stubborn shifters to go against their clans if their change of heart wasn't for another clan but for a phoenix. Or four.

Well…three, technically.

The man—she really should learn his name—sort of stumbled backward until his ass landed on the couch. Elbows to his knees, he ran his hands through his hair in a distracted manner, gaze aimed somewhere at her feet, not really seeing anything she suspected. "I knew this day would come," he mumbled.

He had? Angelika said nothing, but she took another risk. *Sorry, Airk.* She cast the thought behind her in the dark of the hall where she hoped like hells he lurked.

Angelika crossed the room to the man who she could only describe as weighed down with a terrible burden, his shoulders stooped with the effort to bear it, head bowed. She sat beside him and took one of his hands in hers, noting how his bones felt frailer than he looked, like holding a bird.

At her touch, he lifted his head to stare at her. "Whatever your sins," she urged, "it's not too late for redemption."

Again, she was merely guessing at the reasons for his reaction.

"You are asking me to go against my king. Go rogue."

She shook her head. "Pick one of my sister's kings, and you will not be rogue. The white dragons who have joined us carry their brands instead."

He swallowed, the loose skin at his neck working with the action. "Then you are asking me to declare war within my own mountain. Setting brother against brother."

"I am asking you, as the daughter of the man who would still be your king if Pytheios hadn't murdered him, to take the stand you should have all those centuries ago. Here and now. Let the others follow as they will. Or we can get you out if we have to."

Even though she knew they were running out of room in the three mountains they had. Pytheios had taken all the other mountains of the Blue, Black, and Gold Clans, leaving each clan with only one.

He stared, gaze fathomless. Was she getting through?

"Only half will come with me," he said. "The others, I can tell you, will remain loyal to whoever takes the white throne now that Volos is gone."

Volos, the puppet king Pytheios had placed on the throne after her father's death, had disappeared weeks ago without word or contact since. All assumed he was dead.

"Volos was unmated and without child. Wouldn't his Beta take the throne?"

A nod and held a hand up to show the king's symbol on his hand was still that of Volos's house. "Mös's name has been put forward. We are waiting on approval from the High King and his...phoenix."

Angelika frowned at the way he'd paused.

Tisiphone. That's who he was talking about.

Angelika and her sisters had had no idea of another phoenix in existence or their mother having any other offspring ever. Their father died while they were still in the womb. And yet Pytheios had apparently successfully mated a woman who showed every sign of being exactly what he claimed, flaming marks of feathered wings and all.

"She is *not* a phoenix," the man whose hand she still held said heavily. Then ran his free hand through his hair. "I don't think."

Angelika suddenly realized why Airk did that stonelikeimpersonation-of-a-gargoyle thing instead of reacting. Because if she even breathed, she would show the shock ping-ponging around her insides, and that might influence the man's own reaction.

"What do you mean?" she asked slowly.

He straightened, looking her directly in the eyes. "Pytheios's new mate is the spitting image of a young woman I know well. One brought up here. Her name is also Tisiphone, but she wasn't a phoenix. She is...was...a female-born dragon shifter."

Another bolt of shock ricocheted through her even harder, and she clasped his hand in an attempt to keep hers from noticeably shaking. How was that even possible?

"You lie," a low, soft voice snarled from the darkness. Twin flames of white appeared in the dim hallway, lighting only Airk's face, the angles of his cheekbones suddenly taking on a demonic bent.

Granted, most demons didn't glow, but she'd heard of their uncommon beauty. Made more so because of that whiff of death that surrounded them. She hadn't understood the appeal until right this second. Airk was...breathtaking.

What a word, and what a moment to think it.

The man beside her on the couch stiffened, his hand gripping hers with a sudden ferocity of tension, but he didn't speak. Not at first. Instead, he stared, as though trying to make sense of the man standing before him.

"Georgei?" he whispered.

The quaver to his voice spoke volumes to Angelika. Was the old man seeing Airk's father in the younger version before him?

Airk stepped farther into the room. Prowled, more like, with the indolent, contained grace of a jaguar, pale gaze intent on his prey. Where had he learned to move like that when he'd been kept for so long in such small confinement?

And why did she want to wrap her arms around him right now?

"No," he said. The word soft, contained. "*Not* Georgei."

This wasn't going well. Angelika summoned her courage and a pleasant smile, waving a hand in Airk's direction. "May I introduce

Airk Azdajah."

"Do you not remember me, Belyy?" Airk asked, still quietly, before the man could speak. "You used to bring me exotic fruit from your travels to the other clans."

Angelika winced at the stranglehold the older man now had on her hand, even as she noted his name.

"Dragon fruit was your favorite," Belyy whispered. "Airk? Seven hells, the rumors were true for once."

Airk remained unmoved. How did he contain his emotions that way? It couldn't be healthy.

Angelika squeezed Belyy's hand, pulling his focus to her. "Airk was imprisoned by Pytheios all this time," she explained. "I won't lie. Unlike me, he is here for vengeance while helping our cause."

Belyy cast a quick, cautious look in Airk's direction and swallowed hard at the immovable wall of dragon shifter watching him. "If you are trying to gain allies, bringing him is perhaps not the best move."

"Proof of what the High King has done to this clan? A man who is still one of you—still a dragon of the White Clan?" She left out the not-shifting part. "A man who, other than myself and my sisters, holds the most legitimate claim to the throne?"

"You are mated?" Belyy asked, glancing between them as though that changed the situation. Which it would.

Tempting to toss an "I told you so" look in Airk's direction. She resisted.

"We are *not* mated," Airk stated categorically.

Belyy frowned, but Angelika bent a warning look on the mass of tightly leashed fury standing across the room. So self-contained it hurt her to witness.

Give me a chance, she urged him silently.

A hiss of frustration ripped from his throat.

She turned to a confused and frowning Belyy. "I posed the idea. He turned me down. I believe honor had something to do with it."

See? she was trying to say to both of them. *A man of honor would give you a second chance.*

"We are not discussing this," Airk snapped.

Apparently Airk wasn't listening to her underlying message. And she was only making the alpha-male vibes radiating through the room worse. Best to return to the topic at hand. "Airk is here to kill you, but if you swear allegiance to me and my sisters, fight for us, and bring those you can to our side, he will not."

"Angelika." The sound of her voice couched in a deadly growl lifted the hairs on the nape of her neck. Not in fright, but full-on and sudden throbbing need. If he did that when they made love…

Holy hells.

She tried her damnedest to shake it off and shot him a glare. "You will *not* harm him if he does. He is too valuable to us as an ally."

"A man who let his king and his Beta and their mates die?"

Belyy appeared to shrink in on himself with each word emotionlessly hurled at him. But Airk did not let up. "You stood by and watched your friends be murdered at the hands of that usurper."

"I witnessed nothing. None of us were there. Only rumors and lies reached me. Then I was removed from the Curia Regis."

Airk kept talking as though Belyy hadn't spoken. "Murdered by a man who then turned around and placed kings loyal to him on every throne—"

"Pytheios was High King—"

"Without a phoenix?" Angelika pressed, though gently.

The older man flicked his gaze to her. "Not a day—not *one*—goes by that I do not regret."

"You owe my father more than regret." Airk's hand moved to the hilt of the dagger still sheathed at his side. "You owe your king, *her* father, much more."

Belyy released his hold on her hand and rose to his feet, slowly so as not to trigger Airk's predatory instincts. "You ask me to choose between two different deaths."

"Exactly. How would we ever trust you?" Airk asked.

Angelika frowned as she stared at him, trying to see beneath the surface control. How was he still so bloody cold in the midst of this moment? Not a twist of a lip or a tweak of emotion, save the flames in his eyes.

"If he changes allegiances and means it, his king's mark will change," Angelika pointed out, well aware that the hope in her heart was shining through her voice. They needed this—more allies—and she needed to prove her worth.

"He carried Zilant Amon's mark right up until the moment your father was slain." His hand fisted around the dagger, though it remained sheathed.

"If that is the measure of loyalty," Belyy said, "then no dragon shifter in all the world is innocent. We *all* allowed this to happen."

"Except me." Airk went even quieter.

Because he'd been a boy, and the only reason he hadn't been killed immediately was a prophecy made that very day. That any man who killed Airk or gave the order for his death would not be long for this world. Pytheios had been too afraid to kill him outright. And that had turned Airk into the man he was, standing before them now.

What else might convince him to let go of his hate?

Angelika was wincing at what she was about to do before she did it. She got to her feet and moved to stand directly before Airk. Not touching, but close enough to absorb the heat of his skin through his clothes and hers. "We find us a witch or warlock who can perform an oath spell."

She ignored the sharp intake of breath behind her, focused on convincing the man in front of her.

A ripple of emotion that might even be called a sneer flickered over his features. "I do not want his soul bound to mine."

"Fine. Then he makes the oath to *me*." After all, Airk wasn't the only one expendable around here.

Airk finally jerked his gaze from over her shoulder to her face, eyes flaring with something that looked suspiciously like possessiveness. But she had to be mistaken.

"No."

Without thought, because she was a toucher, she laid her hand on his arm. "I'm well aware of the dangers."

Airk's gaze managed to both soften and harden at the same time. "How could you possibly be? Have you ever had that spell performed on you?"

"No, but I know that the magic is unpredictable. No one ever quite knows how the oath will be upheld."

"It could harm you as easily as it could harm him should it be broken."

"It's worth the risk. This mountain could be strategic. Turning more dragons against Pytheios could be even more so. We have to *try*."

"I'll take the oath," Belyy offered from behind her. "Whatever it takes to right my wrongs. I'll do it."

Airk searched her gaze.

"Will you trust him otherwise?" she demanded.

He struggled with the question but finally gave a tiny growl. "No."

She nodded.

Airk looked over her head at Belyy. "Both of us. If you break it and the oath doesn't kill you, I will."

CHAPTER SEVEN

Airk sat, arms crossed and feet stuck out in front of him, in the wing-backed chair in the living area with a view of both exits to the suite. Belyy had gone back to his hidden mistress to sleep, leaving him alone with temptation. Angelika, of course, had refused to go into one of the guest bedrooms to rest, lying down instead on the couch. Also directly in view.

In less than an hour, the stubborn woman had commandeered his assassination and done what he couldn't in the three other visits he'd paid to various white dragons: brought someone over to their side.

He'd seen the interest alight in Belyy's eyes at the idea of their mating, and even in the midst of trying to decide whether or not to go ahead with his plan to kill the man or wait and see if Angelika's way worked out, for a heartbeat, Airk had considered reopening that discussion.

Would white dragons be more inclined to follow them as a mated pair? The son and daughter of the two most powerful men in the clan before Pytheios's reign? Of her sisters, Angelika looked most like a white dragon, too.

He dragged a hand over his face. Of course he wasn't seriously reconsidering. Her presence tested his control to the edges of his limits. Dangerous didn't begin to cover it. Why had he even hesitated?

You know why, a small inner voice piped up.

He cast his gaze over her features, so innocently breathtaking in repose—crystal clear gaze hidden from him, her dark lashes fanned out over flushed cheeks, pretty bow of a mouth pink and slightly open.

Wanting her was never the problem...or was the heart of the problem, if he was honest.

Even without the striking white-blond hair and the angelic face that made her name more than appropriate, she was...magnetic. Almost as though the darkness inside him was curious about the light inside her. But his turgid cock was no reason to deliberately put her in danger. Neither was her smile. And his darkness was enough reason to stay away.

"I can practically hear you overthinking," Angelika mumbled without opening her eyes.

"I am merely keeping watch."

She lifted her head at that, glacial eyes sparkling at him, daring him to loosen up, at least when it was just the two of them. "You're trying to figure out how to get rid of me. Am I right?"

He refused to give her the satisfaction, not moving by so much as a twitch or a blink.

"See!" She laughed. "I am right."

"You are in danger—"

She scowled suddenly, the expression adorable the same way a baby snow leopard pouncing on its mother was, and he found himself in the unaccustomed position of having to stow away a chuckle.

Gods, she was getting to him.

"I'm in danger anywhere I go," she insisted. "A fact that has been true my entire life."

"Meira's gargoyles—"

She hopped up and padded across the room in bare feet, a fact he found eminently distracting. Toes should not be that sweet. Then she dropped suddenly to kneel between his outstretched feet, and the position that put her in—the proximity to a certain member of his anatomy already half-hard thanks to her presence—had him sitting carefully forward to wrap his hands around her arms. "Get up."

She shook her head, stubborn chin in prominent evidence. "Even with the gargoyles, I'm not fully safe. I would feel dreadful if something happened to them because someone found me there."

Unable to dislodge her without giving away what she was doing to him, Airk gentled his hold on her arms, though he didn't let go. "Why me?"

"Well—"

"Let me rephrase." He didn't need a rehash of that. If she told him she wanted him again, he'd bend her over the couch arm and bury his pulsing cock in her in a heartbeat. Couldn't have that. "I mean why did you pick me as the person to keep you safe?"

"Oh. Because…" She bit her lip, even, white teeth digging into the plump, pink flesh, and his dick jumped.

Fucking hells. The worst of it was, she was clearly unconscious of the effect she was having on him.

Her lips twisted as she glanced away. "You call yourself expendable," she said and looked back up, gaze assessing. "I disagree, but that's beside the point. I know you can handle yourself. So I feel less…guilty, I guess?…because you're already being hunted, same as me, and already putting yourself in the position we're in. So by coming with you, I'm not putting you more at risk."

There went that soft heart of hers again. Compelling him to go along.

"I can do something good, Airk. I *know* it."

Look at what she's already accomplished tonight.

Airk kept the thought to himself, staring at her.

"I need to be part of this, even if it's only in some small peripheral way."

"As if you could ever fade into the periphery," he muttered.

Angelika perked up, the innocent joy in her expression lighting her up like the heavenly creatures her name evoked. "Really?"

Damn, he shouldn't have said that. It would only encourage her. He opened his mouth to take it back, but she held up a hand, stopping him. "Forget the mating thing—"

No. The knee-jerk reaction was near violent.

Oblivious, she continued. "I think as just partners approaching them together, we could coax more white dragons to follow us—"

"They will abandon us the second they discover our—"

She flinched as though anticipating the verbal assault. And maybe that's how the word *dormant* felt to her. *Broken, twisted, rogue*—all those words were an assault to him. He understood. Maybe more than anyone else.

"Limitations," he finally said.

The way her shoulders dropped, tension easing from her, a tiny warm glow lit inside him that he'd at least navigated that quagmire without hurting her. Even so, he had to tell himself that it was *not* making her feel accepted that caused that warmth inside him.

"So we are upfront with them about those limitations from the beginning. We tell Belyy in the morning. But I still say we are more powerful as a team. Apart we are...limited...as you say. I think your previous lack of success wasn't just about you. Together, we become harder to ignore."

Why was she starting to sound more and more reasonable? Only now all this talk of doing things together just made him think about doing...other things. Carnal things. His dragon pressed outward, as though reaching for her. So did his cock.

Chemistry, she'd called this thing between them.

Technically, he knew the word, but in relation to a man and a woman, he would have used something else.

Combustion, maybe. Folly, most assuredly.

What would she do if he released his cock and threaded his hands in her hair, urging those lips around him? What would it feel like? What noises of pleasure would she make? Anything like the ones when they'd kissed, and he might unravel. He had a damn good imagination, but he suspected it didn't come near the reality.

He released her and gripped the arms of the chair to stop from doing exactly that and finding out. "We will do this your way. We will work together. Target leaders within the White Clan, and either you convince them to join, or I kill them."

Angelika breathed a visible sigh of relief. "It's a deal."

The problem was, he wanted to please her. He wanted to do the things she asked. And giving in on this...gods, he wanted to give in on the rest, too. "About the mating—"

"Hey. I did *not* bring that up."

No. He was the one doing that. Which was why, instead of doing something stupid like putting that back on the table, he said, "There are others you could mate who might give you leverage or power."

His dragon snarled a protest inside him, and his gut turned sour, twisting in on itself as she silently considered him.

"Jedd wanted to mate me," she dropped between them.

The wolf shifter that trailed her everywhere? The one she'd been pretending to be mated to before her true identity had been made known?

That darkness inside Airk grew fangs.

"Why didn't you?" he forced himself to ask. "You appeared to be quite...friendly."

"Exactly," she said. "Friends. But never more than that. Not for me. There's no—"

"Chemistry?" The word sprang unbidden from his lips, and he wanted to swallow it whole the second it was out there between them.

Angelika stilled. "I was going to say mutuality. He sees me as his to protect, not to stand beside. But chemistry is also true. Even more so. It's important." Her gaze searched his. "Don't you agree?"

. . .

Airk had asked, but Angelika knew she was pushing him too far. Could see it in the way he held himself so stiffly. The both of them had been forced into cages not of their own making all their lives. His with bars, hers with fear. Guilt swirled, eclipsing the want and even the reality of their situation. "We can talk about something else—"

Lips, warm and firm, pressed against hers, and every word she was going to say ignited like paper on fire, burning right out of her head.

This kiss was so different than the last. As though he savored every brush, every slide of their mouths. The cherry-and-bourbon scent of him all around her.

"Silk," he murmured against her lips. "This is what I always imagined silk must feel like."

What he'd imagined while alone and caged? Her heart crumpled. She swayed and surged up to her knees, chasing more, pressing into him.

He groaned, tongue darting out to slide against her lower lip as though tasting. Tentative at first, then with utter control.

Had he fantasized about this? Not about her, but still, she wanted to give him more...better than those wishes in the dark. With a needy noise she'd never heard from herself coming from the back of her throat, Angelika crawled up into his lap to straddle him.

She took his face in her hands and sank into him, absorbing everything about him. The strength that had taken him through those very long years, the patience and perseverance, but also the power underneath. Lying dormant inside him, held back. Her fingers somehow found his shirt, awkwardly tugging it from his combat pants—she'd never undressed a man before—until she reached skin.

His stomach jumped under her touch. And she stilled, lips pressed to his, and waited. Then he inhaled slowly, relaxing into her, and she trailed the tips of her fingers higher, savoring the feel of him, the warmth and hardness, pausing at the first raised ridge of scarring.

"What did they do to you?" she whispered.

He said nothing, and she pulled back enough to look him in the eye, searching his gaze. The hardness had softened, leaving only a tender sort of refusal to speak of it.

"That bad?" she whispered.

"That bad."

Her heart ached for the boy he must have been and the man he was then. Not the man he was now. Except she wished with all that aching heart she could make it better for him. Make the bad memories disappear. Heal the scars so he didn't have to be reminded.

"Don't pity me."

She smiled and raised her hand to the neck of his shirt. "Never that." She pushed the material to the side, then bent over and placed a kiss to the scar across his collarbone, a small part of her amazed at her own daring.

"Seven hells," he muttered. "You must be part witch."

"Why is that?"

He traced the lines of her neck to thread his fingers into her hair. "Because you make me want things I should not."

Then he took over, claiming her with kisses that went beyond carnal need to something deeper. Something that wrapped around her heart.

With a gasp, she pulled away, staring into his eyes, breasts heaving as she battled her own needs and what she knew was right. "Have you ever had a woman's mouth on you?" she asked.

He stilled, his lips against the skin of her shoulder, and shook his head. The need to give him that, to gift him that experience, to be his first in that way, flash flooded through her, and she slipped from his lap, undoing his pants with frantic hands.

"You do not have to—"

But she already had her hand wrapped around his cock, and he groaned long and low as she squeezed. "Do you want me to stop?" she whispered, desperately hoping he didn't say yes.

Airk shook his head, blazing eyes on her.

With a smile that felt all woman, satisfied and sexy and in charge, she leaned forward and wrapped her lips around the pulsing, hot tip.

A first for her, too. So *this* was what this felt like.

"*Gods.*" The harsh whisper tore through him, his hands tightening around her shoulders.

But he still didn't stop her, and she smiled around him before drawing as much of him into her mouth as she could. Breathing in the warm, male scent of his skin, she kept her eyes on his harshly beautiful face as she slid up and down his shaft, squeezing the base with her hand as she did, trailing her tongue up and down the backside and swirling it around the hooded crown. When he started to pump his hips, she paused, offering him a siren's smile when his head snapped up, then dragged the pointed tip of her tongue between his balls and up that straining, rigid cock.

She'd read that in a romance novel once, and damned if it didn't work.

"Fuck," he groaned.

Only to groan again as she wrapped her mouth back around him and went harder, deeper, sucking and licking and doing her best to drive his body to the brink, trying to read his reactions and repeat anything he liked.

His cock swelled inside her mouth, but Airk's hands, still at her shoulders, suddenly forced her back, as though he didn't want his essence inside her. Ignoring the sting of hurt at that, she fisted him his cock, pumping her hand until hot spurts shot from his body and his shout of release hit the roof, falling all around her.

As he shuddered, relaxing into her touch, she released him and, after he cleaned up quickly, crawled back into his lap, wrapping her arms around him, her chest expanding and contracting as his arms came around her as well. Satisfaction surged through her because, even as untutored as she was, she'd given him pleasure. His first like that.

Something for her to treasure in the secret recesses of her heart, no matter what happened next.

He let out an unsteady breath and tried to move her away. "I need you to—"

His face spasmed, and the telltale shimmer of a shift settled over him, multiple parts of his body showing white scales. He gritted his teeth, gaze suddenly faraway, or turned inwardly as he shut everything down to leash the beast inside.

Oh gods.

Needing to help somehow, Angelika did the only thing she could think of and settled her hand over his heart and leaned in to place her lips at his ear. "Breathe. With me. In...out." She inhaled and exhaled with the words.

After a beat, his chest moved. Jerking at first, then smoother, until they were breathing together, in harmony. After a few more inhalations, the scales disappeared and the shimmering left his body, but he didn't relax. Instead, he sort of settled. Then he picked her up bodily by the arms and set her on her feet, well back from him.

"Do not do that again." Back to cold and in control.

"I helped." Couldn't he see that?

The way his lips compressed, she could tell he wanted to deny it. But he didn't. "You put yourself in danger."

She shook her head. "I've experienced danger. That was not it. I do not fear you, Airk Azdajah. Any part of you."

"Dammit." The quietly uttered word actually made her jump. So this is what Airk looked like angry. Still in control but wound so tight he'd snap a spring any second. "I have never been that close to letting him out," he said.

Accused, more like.

She put her hands on her hips, not backing down. "He won't hurt me."

"A feral dragon does not care about human life. He will not know you. Will not care about you other than as food or foe. And I will not be able to stop him."

Even though her gut very definitely told her that she wasn't in danger from either half of the man in front of her, she couldn't truly be sure.

"What should I do?" she asked.

"No more kissing. No hugging, touching. None of that."

Ouch.

Airk moved away and crossed the room to look out the window into the atrium, which glowed softly with light despite still being night. "Go back to sleep, Angelika."

After staring at Airk's back for a long bit, she lay down on the couch and scooted under the sheet Belyy had brought her.

Stubborn. Overprotective. Untrusting. And despite all that, she still wanted to hitch herself to this dragon shifter. Maybe even more now.

She could have wept for the walls between them.

CHAPTER EIGHT

Airk stood behind Angelika, who sat in one of the wing-backed chairs facing what was becoming a growing room of supposed allies. Hand resting on the back of her chair as a not-so-subtle signal to the others that she was under his protection, he surveyed the men and one woman who had agreed to join them. So far.

And they observed him.

He was dressed in a white suit with a black shirt that Belyy had supplied. Cut simply, the size was slightly small on his frame, making him feel constricted. If he did have to fight one of these fuckers, he'd split a seam with the first swing. But Angelika and Belyy both insisted he "look the part" of a dragon leader.

Lies, as far as he was concerned, because he was no leader, but he understood. So he kept his mouth shut and stared right back.

Meanwhile, more than one man in the room watched Angelika closely, the light in their white-blue eyes carnal. From who the hells knew where, Belyy had procured for her a dress of a gossamer white material that floated around her slim form. Demure at first glance, it had long billowing sleeves gathered at her wrists by a shinier material, and a sash of the same tied around her waist. But when she walked...

A slit parted revealing her long legs. Legs that had been on either side of him as she'd straddled him in this very chair, as she'd kissed him. Then she'd dropped to the floor and wrapped that pretty mouth around him. *That* image, that sensation, had burned into him like a brand and brought his dragon roaring to the fore in a way nothing, not even his anger toward Pytheios, had managed to do in all his years.

From a simple pleasure.

Granted, their pleasure had not been that simple. Layered, breath-stealing, cock-straining sensuality wrapped around him. The noises she'd made…

Gods.

But what had really gotten to him was what she'd said. *I do not fear you, Airk Azdajah. Any part of you.*

Combined with the way she'd also calmed his beast with a simple touch, breathing with them. Fuck, this woman.

Now she sat like the queen she was meant to be, had the fates not done to her what they'd done to him and stolen her potential.

Belyy had invited those he considered "influenceable" to the chamber one at a time to meet Angelika and Airk together and hear them out. Or to watch Airk warily while they listened to Angelika's story.

None professed to be aware of how Pytheios had murdered Zilant Amon, though a few indicated that they'd suspected. All dragons had been led to believe their previous king had died in another way. Possibly in the mating with his phoenix, Angelika's mother, Serefina Hanyu, or in a fight with another kind of shifter. Given Pytheios's propaganda campaign, starting when he'd introduced Tisiphone to dragon-shifter kind, more than one took extra convincing.

So far, though, Airk had not needed to kill anyone.

Like his dragon had beneath Angelika's hand last night, each shifter eventually softened to her. Airk could see it in their expressions, the way stark lines of aggression eased from their bodies. The words she used didn't seem as important as the fact that with each she was entirely sincere and open. Something Airk couldn't be. Not after centuries of holding everything about himself so close.

A knock sounded, and Angelika rose to her feet, turning to face the door. As he had the seven other times, Airk moved from behind the chair and took his place at her side. And, as she'd done each of those seven times, she reached for his arm, paused, and sent him a questioning look. He nodded. Again. Hating himself for making her question her every move around him. Every single touch. But they had to present a united front. Besides, her touch soothed his dragon with each new man who entered the room. More white dragons than he'd seen all together since he was a boy.

Belyy answered the door, warning the newcomer in low, calm tones that he had been summoned for a purpose and to enter only if he could keep an open mind.

Curiosity had pulled each previous person into the room, more so than an ability to remain open, Airk was sure. With the sound of footfall in the hall and foyer, Airk's muscles tensed, readying to defend himself. Or, more accurately, defend his...*this* fragile human.

Only the moment the newcomer rounded the corner, the fight left Airk in a whoosh, shock rushing through him in its place.

"Tovar?" he questioned.

Memories flashed in his mind's eye. Moments so old, they were like faded photographs torn at the edges. Some so hazy he wasn't sure if they were his memories or things he'd been told by others through the years.

The man in front of him vaguely resembled the boy he'd once known—white hair and eyes striking against rich mink skin—though the familiarity only lingered around the seams. As if, if Airk squinted, the lines would shift into the places he remembered. Instead of a child's face, still soft and rounded, and a child's body, all bone and skinny with it, Tovar had become a man with a solid jaw covered in dark stubble and a tall, broad frame with muscles that the child version of his friend had always said he'd get. Like his father.

Tovar's eyes widened, then sparked with flame as his steps slowed.

"It cannot be," Tovar muttered more to himself than anything.

Then his lips curled into a snarl. With no warning, the man

who'd once been the best of Airk's friends lunged across the room at him, death promised in the blazing white flames of his eyes.

Airk shoved Angelika out of the way, putting himself bodily between her and a dragon shifter bent on killing. Doing so gave him barely enough time to get his arms up to ward off the first blow.

The second to his right kidney came equally as fast and hurt like a son of a bitch. Inside his head, his dragon roared a challenge, but Airk had him locked down tight. He'd spent most of his time in his cell training in his mind for just such a moment. Nathair, the only person to show him kindness in all that time, had smuggled him books on fighting techniques, and he'd practiced. Picturing each move and countermove and acting out the conflicts on his own.

His training since his escape, mostly with Ladon's men and lately with Samael's, had shown that his methods had been effective. None had yet to best him, though most didn't try hard.

Tovar was definitely trying.

His old friend swung again for that kidney, and Airk step back and knelt, one arm up to block the punch. The other, he jabbed into Tovar's stomach. That backed the man off, but only for a beat. As he had when they were kids, he came back swinging, and Airk absorbed the first punch with his palm, clamping down on Tovar's fist, and used the momentum of the second punch to flip Tovar onto the couch.

He threw himself at the man, bringing his own fists to bear on his face. Blood sprayed from Tovar's nose, satisfaction immediate and sharp inside Airk as he did it again. Only before he connected, the other man got a foot up between them and shoved him off.

"Stop," Angelika demanded from somewhere off to the side, the worry in her voice scraping over his skin.

But out of the way enough that Airk didn't focus on her.

He and Tovar went at it, moving through a series of punches, kicks, and blocks at a dizzying speed. Airk came as near to smiling as he ever did. *This* was what he'd trained for every day for hours in his solitary cell. *This* was what he was built for.

Airk miscalculated a punch, though, and Tovar had him by the hand, twisting his arm to an impossible angle, but the positioning of which also slowed all the other man's momentum. They both sort of paused and took in the situation. But then Airk simply flipped sideways, kicking his legs over his head in a midair cartwheel maneuver that untwisted his arm and allowed him to use the motion to throw Tovar across the room, smashing into a glass-faced cabinet.

With a roar, he came charging back out, a brass candlestick in his hand, which he wielded like a club. The metal *clunk* as it hit first the wall when Airk dodged, then the marble countertop when he dodged again, told him just how heavy the thing was.

He needed a shield. The closest thing to hand was a book. Snapping it up off the coffee table, he parried another of Tovar's swings, and another, then jumped in closer and rammed the book into his one-time friend's throat.

Tovar heaved over, trying to suck in air through a collapsed windpipe. Airk raised the book like a worse weapon, prepared to slam it down into the man's head, his dragon slashing his tail with lethal intent inside his mind. Except Angelika jumped between them, palms up, facing Airk, unacceptable danger at her front and back.

"Move." He clamped his lips shut around the way his voice had gone rough, all dragon.

"Just...wait," she said. Not complying, as usual.

"I do not wish to hurt you."

"You won't," she insisted. "Or you would've plowed through me by now."

Airk straightened at that, head snapping back. Was she right?

• • •

Stepping between any kind of predatory shifter and his prey was a stupid idea. It didn't take a course in *Dealing With Shifters 101* to know that, even if her mother hadn't drilled that and other rules into her daughters. Having her back to the man who went after

Airk, no questions asked, was also not the brightest move.

But she figured she was facing the bigger threat.

Airk stared at her, sparks flashing in his eyes every few seconds. No scales showing like before, but if his voice was anything to go by, he was at the threshold of his control. When he said nothing but also made no move toward her, she slowly turned so that she stood sideways to both him and the man he'd been fighting. At least he was smart enough not to get off the floor.

"My name is Angelika Amon," she said slowly. "And the man you were trying to kill *is* Airk Azdajah."

"Bullshit," he snapped, wiping his sleeve under his nose and glaring at her.

Which part? She tipped her head, giving him a pleasantly questioning look. "Are you sure about that?"

"Airk Azdajah is dead."

She gave a hard shake of her head. "Says who? Pytheios?"

That earned her a narrowed gaze glowing brighter. "If you are who you say, why would I trust you to speak the truth?"

"Why would you trust the supposed High King, who nominated himself for that title when no phoenix was available? Who seems to need to butt into the clan politics in the Blue, Black, and Gold Clans, where new kings have been accepted by their people?"

"*Forced* on their people," he spat.

"Says Pytheios," she pointed out again. "I'm waiting for any sign that you know how to look at facts for yourself."

"You bitch—"

She stepped closer, and Airk twitched in her peripheral vision. "My sister, Skylar Ormarr, now the Queen of the Blue Clan, helped Airk escape from Everest, where Pytheios held him in a cell since the day that motherfucker killed *my* father and Airk's parents. *That* is what the man you follow as High King did to him. *Centuries* of time in a cage."

The man on the floor snapped his mouth shut so hard, she felt sorry for his poor teeth. Then his gaze moved slowly from her to a spot over her shoulder. "Prove it," he demanded through clenched teeth, breathing harshly through his nose.

She turned her head in time to see Airk loosen the set of his stance and a look come into his eyes that she could only categorize as him trying to block out emotions yet again. "You hold a family secret," he said with that careful deliberation. "Or you did when we were boys. I was there the day that secret became known."

Vaguely Angelika was aware of every other person in the room shuffling or stiffening at the words, clearly all wondering what this secret was that Airk referred to.

But Tovar...he went granite still behind her, like a hole of nothing. "It can't be."

She turned his way to find him no longer glowing with anger but pale, horror reflected in the slack set of his jaw.

"We once made a vow that we would take our places together as warriors guarding the king. And when Zilant mated a phoenix, who would give birth to only one female, another phoenix..." Airk bent a look on the man that clearly expected him to finish the thought.

"You would be king one day, and I your Beta," Tovar said.

With surprisingly gentle hands on her shoulders, Airk moved Angelika aside, and she went willingly, able to see that the violence had left them both. He leaned over and held out a hand. "It is I, Tovar. You may believe your eyes."

"Fuck me," Tovar said as he grasped his old friend by the hand and got to his feet.

Airk's lips tipped up at one corner. "I would rather not." Then grunted as Tovar wrapped him up in a hug that might've crushed a lesser man.

"I thought you were dead, all these years."

"Close enough," Airk muttered.

They pulled back, inspecting each other intently. "Damn," Tovar said with a grin. "I think you're taller than me."

"You always were small for your age."

Teasing? Airk was teasing now. A smile—that lip twitch totally counted—and now teasing. Not for her, which hurt, but she was too happy for him to mind.

Finally, Tovar seemed to take in the rest of the men in the room. "I suspect a happy reunion is not top of the list."

Airk canted his head. "These men are switching sides."

His friend didn't seem surprised. "With loyalty to whom?"

Based on a grimace barely hidden, she suspected Airk hated admitting this next part. "To me and to Angelika, and our allegiance lies with her sisters and with the kings of the Black, Gold, and Blue Clans."

"You ask us to go against our king."

"Your king is dead, and whoever takes the throne will *only* show allegiance to Pytheios."

"Our High King."

"Actually," Angelika offered sweetly, leaning around Airk. "The High King should be Brand Astarot of the Gold Clan. The *first* to mate a phoenix in five hundred years."

Tovar shook his head slowly as though rejecting the thoughts in his head. "We don't know who to believe at this point."

"I'm sorry we have to push you for it now," Angelika said, harder this time. "But the time has come to see the truth for what it is."

That got her his full attention. "So you are one of the four phoenixes."

"One of the four daughters of Zilant Amon and Serefina Hanyu. Yes." She refused to claim to be a phoenix when she wasn't.

"Pytheios's phoenix showed her phoenix sign to the entire dragon-shifter population."

Angelika nodded. "She is not a sister of mine. If she is a phoenix, she may need our help."

"Help?"

"Getting her away from that monster."

Every man in the room growled, and she held up her hands, trying to soften her stance, though not well. How could they not already see this? "I didn't say dragon shifters were monsters. I said Pytheios is. His greed for position and power has turned him into one, and you know it. If you didn't suspect, you wouldn't be here."

"So show us your phoenix sign," Tovar demanded.

Airk stiffened, and she reached for his arm, only to stop herself before touching him without his permission. She'd promised.

They knew this moment would come sooner rather than later. "If you want a show of my integrity, let it be this… Something no one other than my sisters and their mates is aware of."

The room seemed to lean in toward her as she took a deep breath. "I have not inherited my sisters' powers."

"Then how do we know you are who you say?"

"At least I am giving you the truth and the option to decide for yourself," she pointed out, firmly but trying to be gentle. "Pytheios has never given dragon-shifter leadership that kind of respect."

Anger still reflected back at her in faces full of betrayal. She could feel them slipping away, when she and Airk had been so close to gaining allies within this mountain.

I can't lose them.

What could she say, though? "Let me tell you of my mother."

CHAPTER NINE

Airk watched for half an hour as Angelika wound every person in the room around her delicate little finger with each word she uttered. She spun a remarkable tale of a pregnant phoenix on the run, hiding herself and later her daughters from a madman. One who'd caught up with them eventually.

But Serefina Amon had prepared for that, too, sending her daughters to the four corners of the earth, where they each had a supernatural protector ready to keep them safe.

The dragons in the room sneered at where Serefina had sent her daughters, especially Angelika's wolf pack, which made her mother's move even more brilliant. Arrogant, dragons always assumed that among all shifters their kind was the pinnacle. Top of the food chain.

By the time she finished speaking—including Airk's story in her own—the disbelief had miraculously disappeared from every face in the room.

"How do you know you didn't receive any powers?" Tovar asked. Not suspiciously, more curious.

Angelika shrugged. "I don't smell of smoke."

Denial had several shaking their heads. "Many dragon mates do not, either."

She offered a smile, one that thanked them for the wish that things were different. "I have neither felt nor shown a smidge of ability of any kind. My mother had so many, developed through the years. My sisters' powers were immediate, though they are still developing. I think we have to face that I am dormant at best, human at least."

She straightened, having resumed her seat in the wing-backed chair at some point during the telling. Her posture was as regal as any queen, and the braid around her head may as well have been a crown. "But I am *still* my father's daughter. My mother may have run because that was the only way she could see us safely reaching adulthood, but I am only half phoenix. Dragons are my family. I *refuse* to sit to the side while that murderer remains in power."

Hells, at the force of her words, even Airk's breast stirred with the vestiges of pride in his people and hope for the future. Like a ghost of his past feathering old emotions through the void that had become his heart. All he'd felt in ages was the need for vengeance and then to disappear. And lately, to fuck a certain white-haired enchantress of a woman.

His dragon rumbled inside him, uncurling and uneasy at the emotions.

"What happens when your skin is touched with dragon fire?" the lone woman within the group asked. She was a female-born dragon younger than Airk by a century or more. Rare for one such as she to be included in anything requiring leadership, but more had changed in his time in captivity than he knew. Maybe that included the way female-borns were treated as well.

Angelika's pause brought his gaze down to find her biting her lip. Inappropriate, ill-timed desire lanced through him, tightening his body in a way that could fast become an embarrassment.

"I haven't bothered to try," she owned.

She tipped her chin, glancing up at him with wide eyes, and Airk had to hide the jerk that ripped through him at the flash of fear in those depths. There, then she blinked and looked at the others, and the emotion was gone.

As though she'd allowed him, and only him, to witness her insecurity.

"We should at least answer that question," someone toward the back said.

Angelika's tension may not have been visible to the others, but Airk could practically see the waves of it rising from her. Slowly, as though sensing the import of the moment, she looked to him yet again, this time with a question in her eyes.

His heart shriveled inside him like a dried plum sucked of its juices, knowing what she was asking. He gave his head the barest of shakes, and she nodded. Then made it a thousand times harder when she reached over and squeezed his hand. Like she was telling him it was all right.

Nothing was all right.

"Tovar," she said. "You may try."

His old friend drew back his shoulders—that pride again. How did she do that so easily? Connect with people like that?

Angelika rose to her feet and turned her back to Tovar, who stepped forward. He inhaled, the sound low and reverberating like a bellows in a smithy. An answering growl resounded inside Airk's head, low and menacing. His dragon did not like this.

Tovar pursed his lips and sucked in.

Airk's dragon snarled, baring his teeth at the male daring to even think of touching Angelika with fire. Clenching his fists, he tried to communicate to the animal side of him that this was needed. Only the dragon gnashed his teeth at Airk, and pain sliced through his mind like a lightning bolt. Sizzling, hot and immediate, an inferno inside his head.

He glanced at his hands lest he raise his fists to pound against his own temples. The beast was turning on him.

Unaware of Airk's struggles, Tovar blew white-tipped flames across the nape of Angelika's neck. He tempered them as he did to keep from burning her delicate skin. Airk had witnessed the same with Meira at her mating day, and they had all witnessed Pytheios do the same to his new mate, Tisiphone. With a phoenix, her skin would glow. Living, breathing rivers of molten lava brought to life by the blaze. Then delicate lines of illuminated flame would spread across her skin in a design of fiery feathers. When the last feather appeared, the fire would rise from the skin and form wings, fed by the lines across her skin.

The mark of a phoenix.

Through the shards of agony caused by his dragon thrashing inside him, almost blurring his vision, Airk watched closely. Waiting.

For nothing.

A small whimper escaped Angelika's throat, and without thought, he snapped out a hand and drew her out from beneath Tovar's fire, pulling her up against his chest, her back to his. Before he knew what he was about, he'd curled one arm around her waist, securing her to him.

"Don't," he snarled at his old friend in a voice so dragon he no longer recognized himself.

Tovar cut his fire off immediately, gaze wary, and slowly raised his hands in a gesture of peace. Silence blanketed the room, each dragon still, assessing the threat.

Him.

I am the threat.

Airk swallowed, then swallowed again as he worked the dragon half of him deeper into his consciousness, away from the surface. Hard to do with Angelika's touch, her summery scent, up against him, though the beast calmed at her nearness. Angelika smoothed a hand over his forearm, making him grip her more tightly. "I'm not harmed," she assured. "It's okay."

"Wait—" Tovar's serious gaze passed between the two of them, even as Airk struggled to force himself to let her go. "Is she your mate?"

"He should be so lucky," Angelika murmured, though just a gentle teasing. Probably with a grin to bely the words, because the dragons in the room relaxed enough to chuckle with her, though the looks they continued to cast him remained wary.

"She will be." The words left his mouth, and immediately his dragon settled inside him, the pain receding.

Hells. Why had he said that? He couldn't. Ever. He knew that.

Angelika twitched in his grasp, but he was holding her too tightly, which meant she couldn't turn around. Instead, she angled her head, looking up and backward awkwardly. "*Now* you decide to take me up on my idea?"

"Angelika?" A woman's voice sent every man in the room into a defensive crouch, growls ripping through the air.

Airk included, tucking his phoenix to his side.

Only she pushed against his hold. "That's my sister," she said.

He turned them to face a mirror that showed only Meira's face.

"Don't return here until you hear from me," Meira warned. She sounded calm, but Airk picked up on the tension in her voice. Her gaze skated behind him and Angelika to those gathered in the room. All white dragons. "I'll be in touch soon."

With that, the mirror returned to normal, only now reflecting shock and indecision in the faces of every newly gained ally in the room.

That was it? That one cryptic warning? What was going on?

. . .

"Make a move, dammit." Skylar prowled to the left, studying her mate as he circled her.

These early-morning sparring sessions were the highlight of her day… Well, maybe her second favorite highlight. She studied Ladon's moves, familiar with them now, and just as determined not to admire the powerful grace of his body as she had the first time they'd fought like this. The day she'd broken into his mountain to try to rescue Kasia, so sure her sister needed rescuing.

Funny how things turned out.

His eyes were his tell, giving away intention before his body language did. A spark flickered, then Ladon lunged for her, and she blocked with ease, having seen it coming, then followed with a knee to his ribs. His grunt at the contact was music to her ears, but, as usual, she'd gotten too close.

He flipped her around and got an arm around her waist, tugging her in close to his body. "Are you trying to distract me with your manliness?" She smirked, even as her own body flipped a switch to "turned on" in an instant.

An answering smile tugged at his lips. Usually Ladon's smiles made people around him edgy, nervous, because they were more ferocious than nice. Skylar found that adorable, though.

"Is it working?" His dark-as-sin voice, like rocks in a tumbler, rumbled in her ear.

Part of her wanted to melt into him and swap out sparring for fucking, right here, right now. But the competitive side decided to take advantage of his distraction. Without warning, she slammed her head backward, right into his nose.

"Fuck." His grip loosened.

In a shot, she was out of his grip and across the room, facing off against him.

Ladon glared at her over his hands, but she couldn't miss the spark in his eyes, the flames not of anger but respect and an answering need to win. Gods, her mate was gorgeous, black hair and Greek coloring making his blue eyes even bluer, the cleft in his chin masculine as hell, and the sexiest damn voice to match.

He shot across the space, using the speed most shifters could claim. But she had her full powers now and could move with the same lightning speed when she wanted. Skylar jumped back, blocking his hand. Then struck for his face, only to have him block her in return.

They went at it, setting up a rhythm, almost a dance, as they struck, blocked, and parried, trying different moves on each other in rapid succession. Ten moves in, Ladon tumbled her to the ground.

"Skylar!"

They both stilled at the sound of Meira's shout.

Sparring forgotten, together they jumped to their feet and ran into the living area, where the massive silver-edged mirror they'd had placed in here after Meira's powers had become known waited.

Skylar gasped at the sight of her sister standing in the training room in Mount Ararat. She had to be using the glass of the control booth in that space to reach them.

Behind her in the chamber where the shifters who were fighters trained, chaos reigned.

Black and green dragons filled the space, locked in deadly battle. So many of them, they blurred together, like a flock of birds scared into flight, making it impossible to track a single one's trajectory.

"Can you hear me?" Meira called.

Skylar nodded. "Yes."

"We're—"

A horrendous boom seemed to shake the very foundations of the mountain as Skylar and Ladon both watched in silent horror. A massive stalactite fell from the ceiling, shattering into the floor with another resounding blast, rock and debris and dust flinging up into the air as though a bomb had gone off.

"They're under attack," Ladon snarled.

"They're going to need our help," Skylar said.

One shared look with her mate, the connection binding their hearts allowing them to know what the other was thinking, and he nodded.

Pulling her power forward in a blazing whoosh of flame, Skylar shoved her mate right in the chest. Using her ability to teleport others—just never herself—long distances, she sent him directly to his men, who would all be doing their morning drills.

"Use the glass in the training room!" she yelled at Meira, who had struggled to her feet, covered in dust but unharmed. "I'll get Kas."

No sooner were the words out of her mouth than the mirror flickered and she was staring at a reflection of herself. Not that she waited. Skylar took off at a sprint to get down to where she'd sent Ladon, with a stop in the communications room to contact Kasia.

If Ararat was under attack, they would need all the help they could get. Last time they'd barely survived it.

But when she got to the communications room, after ten minutes of trying, the man operating the computers shook his head at her. "No one is answering, my queen."

Fear and anger curled and curdled in Skylar's stomach. Were both her sisters' clans under attack?

. . .

Angelika sat in the wing-backed chair she'd come to think of as her throne earlier today. She'd pulled it around to face the ornate mirror her sister had communicated through. Had it been a TV, she could hear her mother warning her not to sit so close or she'd ruin her eyes.

Everyone else had left the room eventually, several promising to gather information and report back. All of that was still fuzzy to her. She'd let Airk handle everything after Meira had disappeared, too shaken to function. None of their allies had returned with news, and her sister had yet to show her face again.

Airk knelt before her, taking her hands in his and chafing at them. Were they cold? She glanced down, thinking idly of how capable his hands were. Long tapered fingers and wide palms. Strength.

"Come to bed," he urged softly.

A tiny spark flared inside her at his choice of words but died just as quickly. She shook her head. "What if she needs me?"

"I'll stay out here for you. You won't miss anything. I promise."

Angelika shook her head again, then sighed. "I'm always waiting."

All her life. Waiting to be hunted down. Waiting to be killed or captured. Then the night her mother had died, she'd sent Angelika away to safety first, and she had waited again with the wolves. She'd waited for news of her sisters. Then waited while she'd been shelved through the dragon attack on the village where her pack lived. She'd waited when Skylar had been kidnapped by Pytheios. She'd waited when both sides of the Kings' War had gone against each other in the skies over Ararat.

Each time of waiting had brought worse and worse news.

Though Skylar's escape from Pytheios had also brought her Airk. She pulled her gaze from her reflection behind him to his face, searching his expression. "Did you mean it?"

"What?"

She lifted a single eyebrow. "I do believe, right before all the hells broke loose over my sister's head, that you announced we were to be mated."

Airk's grimace told her more than enough. He was already rethinking that particular declaration.

"Oh no, you don't." He couldn't take that back.

"My dragon was—"

"An excuse."

"I could kill you if he gets loose, and he comes closer to the surface around you."

She pursed her lips, thinking that over. Because telling him to suck it up or not worry about it clearly wasn't helpful or strategic. "How about we give it a trial run?"

Airk frowned, clearly not following. Maybe her phrasing was one he had yet to encounter.

"A dress rehearsal."

He shook his head, brow not easing. "I do not follow."

Oh dear. This was going to be uncomfortable to put into words. Then again, no one had ever called her a coward. "I want you. I think we've established that."

Airk leaned way back, though he didn't move from his crouch in front of her. "I—"

She placed a single finger over his lips, stopping his words, his skin warm against hers. "Just stating a simple fact. You want me, too." Not a question. His kisses had told her that much. Not to mention how he'd reacted to her mouth around his—

"Angelika." A warning.

She ignored the growl and the shiver that skittered across the nape of her neck at the sexy, dark rumble to his voice. "I propose we have sex. Without the whole fire-and-mating thing."

"Angelika."

Gods, was she a horrible person for focusing on such a thing at a moment like this? Maybe this was shock. Or her way of coping? Somehow, even just talking about it had picked her up out of her worries. Angelika had never been one to brood. If she hadn't heard from her sisters by daybreak, she'd damn well hunt them down.

But in the meantime…

"No commitment. No promise to mate. Not even a promise to have more sex tomorrow." Though, the way her body was already starting to buzz at the mere thought, she really, really hoped sex tomorrow would be on the agenda.

Airk stared directly into her eyes, the rest of him as still as a mountain and just as complicated. Because under all that granite lay hidden rivers and caves, ravines and cave-ins. There was so much more to him she wished that he would let her see. Let her in.

But he didn't.

Just squatted and stared. His gaze slowly moved, though not losing a smidge of intensity, and damn if that wasn't starting to turn her the hell on. As though his gaze were a physical touch, tracing the lines of her mouth, her jaw, down her neck. Her nipples surged as though he'd brushed the back of his hands over them.

"Airk?" she whispered.

His gaze rose back to meet hers. "You scare me. Did you know that?"

She shook her head slowly. "How?"

His mouth twitched. "A thousand different ways." He closed his eyes and breathed deeply. "Showing up here. Sitting beside a dragon you don't know. Speaking with others who could have lashed out at any second. Getting between me and Tovar. But do you know what the worst part is?"

She waited—not that he could see it with his eyes closed. But a hint of a smile feathered across his lips, so maybe he sensed it.

"The worst part is the way you do not fear me."

"I could never—"

He moved suddenly, leaning forward, and captured her words with his lips against hers. Only now his mouth was familiar. Achingly so. As though everything right about the world settled through her at his touch.

With a whimper of sound at the back of her throat, Angelika scooted forward. At the same time, he scooped her up and spun to sit down with her across his lap. They didn't so much as break contact, and her entire world narrowed to firm lips and heat and the taste of cherries and bourbon.

"This is not me agreeing to anything," Airk said against her mouth.

And she smiled. "Okay."

Hands at her shoulders, he pulled back to look at her, all serious and brooding. "I mean it. This is—"

"Scratching an itch?"

He frowned at that. "I do not itch. I incinerate."

"Oh my," she breathed. That might be the sexiest thing anyone had ever said to her.

That twitch of a smile again. "Does that mean you understand?"

Was it possible to be even more turned on? "Yes."

"Good. Because I do not wish to stop."

Then his mouth was everywhere she wanted it to be. His tongue begging hers to come out and play, even more confident now that he'd got the hang of things, nipping along her jaw, tugging at her ear, nuzzling down the sensitive side of her neck. She might come out bruised in the morning, he was holding her so tightly, and she damn well didn't care, welcoming the unconscious sign of his need.

Besides, his mouth… Gods…

The heat of him left a scorching trail in its wake, as though lighting up every nerve ending to delicious, sparking life. He wasn't even using fire on her. Just his skin against hers.

Already frantic with need, she drew slightly away to yank her top over her head, then remembered she was still in that gorgeous dress rather than her own clothes. She tugged at the tie at her waist only to have it knot up on her and made a sound of frustration in her throat.

"Did I injure you?" Her strong dragon shifter was suddenly all solicitous concern.

"No. I want this damn dress off. Your clothes, too." She tugged at his shirt, and a button popped open, which had her perking up.

And then it happened.

Airk smiled. Full-on smiled, lips drawing back to reveal surprisingly white, straight teeth, given the dentistry he'd no doubt lacked. Even his eyes lit up with it.

The breath whooshed from her lungs so hard, she would have sworn someone punched her in the stomach.

Unsmiling, Airk was one of the most harshly fascinating men she'd ever seen. But smiling...

She reached out to trace the contours of his face. Thick eyebrows, slashing cheekbones, hollows over his cheeks to a cut jawline and up to a slashing mouth still tilted at the corners as he watched her, eyes glowing, allowing her to take this liberty.

"You're so beautiful," she whispered.

"I?" His lips tipped up more. Not quite the smile but close.

But the doubt in his voice was what sent her need careening through her. Almost as though compelled to show him, prove to him, how beautiful she found him. And that stoked the desire within her hotter and higher.

Airk watched her, his chest rising and falling, each breath harsher.

"If you incinerate," she whispered, "I ache."

That smile tilted and shifted into something dangerous, his gaze so intent she thought she might spontaneously combust right then and there.

With a low growl, Airk stood from the chair and whipped her dress over her head before she could squeak. Then froze, his gaze drifting over her body, his jaw working. His gaze turned her electric, the throbbing at the core of her needing release. Needing his touch.

"The gods formed every inch of you to be perfection," he whispered.

A rare blush made its way across her skin, and his gaze lit with flame.

"Like an instrument to be played," he said. "I want to discover what sounds you make." He dropped to his knees. "Is this where I should touch?"

He trailed his finger softly over the throbbing bundle of nerves at the core of her femininity with surprising accuracy.

"Mm-hmm," was all she could manage.

Then he placed his mouth directly over where he'd touched. Not quite the right spot.

But he must've been attuned to her reactions, because he lifted his gaze, then moved his mouth. Twice. Until she sucked in sharply.

He didn't smile, but she swore his eyes lit with utter satisfaction. Through the flimsy satin material of her panties, he sucked, and all Angelika could do was grip his shoulders hard as her head dropped back, her eyes fluttering closed against the sensations obliterating her body.

Gods above, so this was what this felt like. No wonder people lost their common sense over this.

He stopped, and she mewled a protest. But he only stripped, then helped her out of her panties. The brush of his fingers spurred her on, and she frantically freed herself from her bra at the same time.

He grinned. "I want to touch you there next. But first…"

She squeaked in shock as he scooped her up so that her legs landed on his shoulders. In the same instant, he stood, and her perspective changed as she was lifted in the air. He spun and stepped into the wall, the rock at her back holding her up, surprisingly smooth and cool in contrast to the conflagration of heat threatening to consume her body.

Then his mouth was on her, and she lost herself in sensation, gave over control to the man whose touch became her everything. Hot and insistent, his tongue stabbed into her channel, only to be replaced by questing fingers that stroked and gentled and slid through her folds until he managed to slip one inside her, all as that sinful tongue trailed upward to circle the pounding nub of pure nerves.

Wet heat poured from her, slicking those fingers that grew more urgent, more confident, that plunged and owned and claimed. Fascinated, she watched him. Watched his mouth on her body, watched the satisfaction turn his eyes bluer as she rolled her hips, chasing the sensations pouring through her.

"Airk," she begged.

In a move of incredible shifter speed, he stepped back so that she dropped, but he caught her, bringing them both to the ground so that she was straddling his kneeling form. In front of the fireplace with her back facing the flames, she was surrounded. Caught between death and life and the beast between her legs. His shaft pressed into her, pulsed against her.

"What you do to me. Heavens and hells," he said. Almost an accusation, but she let that go as he gripped her hips, lifting her up and positioning himself at her entrance. "Is this right?" he asked.

Though from the way he held her with such confidence, she never would have guessed he needed to ask.

She nodded. "Slowly," she said.

Not taking his gaze from hers for a second, he worked his body into hers a little at a time, watching her face and stopping when she needed. Never had she been so glad that Airk seemed to read her like a book.

His chest moved with each heavy inhale and exhale, and she knew the pace was killing him, but his patience bore out. Heat and pressure filled her in torturously slow increments. As though he was afraid to hurt her. Except the expression in his eyes was one she couldn't interpret.

Possession—not unexpected from a dragon shifter. Desire, which only fed her own. But something else. Something that had her lips parting on a gasp. Almost as though he was seeing her, truly seeing her, for the first time.

He settled her fully onto his cock, every inch inside her, filling her, stretching her. She experimentally clenched her internal muscles around him and smiled as a grunt ripped from his throat. His heavy breaths matched hers.

"Do that again," he whispered. Begged.

She smiled and did as he asked. "Does it feel good?"

"I think this must be what heaven feels like." He guided his hands up over her hips, across her belly, to cup her jutting breasts.

He flicked a thumb over her nipple, and she whimpered, clenching around him involuntarily this time.

Airk tipped his head, studying her with a sly gleam in his eyes. "I think you like that. I like it, too."

He did it again, and they both grunted as her inner walls contracted with the contact. "What if I..." He leaned forward and drew an already eagerly tight nipple into his mouth, then sucked, and together they groaned. Then groaned again as she couldn't stop from rolling her hips.

"More?" he asked.

"Yes." *Gods, yes.*

He sucked, shooting sparks from her nipples through her core to light up the juncture of her thighs. She rolled her hips, more this time, sliding up and down that pulsing, hot shaft, slowly at first as she adjusted and figured out the best ways to move. The ways that hit all those luscious nerves the right way.

They set a rhythm, sensation building with each slide of her body, each pulse of his shaft, electric and real. But gradually, their bodies turned frantic, sweat-slicked and building with pressure.

"Fuck," Airk muttered, and suddenly she found herself flipped so that she was laying with her back on a rug made of some kind of soft animal fur, the fire to her left and her lover between her thighs.

He took her lips in a long, drugging kiss, then pulled back, gazing into her eyes. "Don't look away," he said. "I need to know you're real."

Her heart contracted around the words—lonely words, haunting words—and she nodded.

With an incredible gentleness that only pushed her more into that haze of sensual bliss, he took both her hands, lacing their fingers together and pressing them into the rug on either side of her head.

Then he moved, a glorious, controlled thrust.

Her lips parted around a gasp. At this angle, he was so deep inside her she didn't know where she began and he ended. Damn, this man was a fast learner.

He thrust harder, his face tightening, skin over his cheekbones flaring red, flames in his eyes glowing white. Then thrust again. Still controlled.

"You won't break me," she whispered. "Let go."

Something seemed to snap in him, and he went wild over her, pumping his hips hard. Their moans of pleasure joined and rose, filling the room as that pressure reached a breaking point, and together they tipped over into bliss. Airk never looked away, watching her as she tumbled over that precipice with a cry that seemed to drag him over with her, swelling inside her. He shouted as hot spurts poured into her body.

No need to worry about pregnancy, something they both had to will into existence.

As they came down from the high, he stayed inside her, still partially erect. He cradled her in his arms and traced the contours of her face with a finger, as she had with him earlier.

"You are beautiful when we do that," he said.

Angelika gave him a sleepy grin. "Any trouble with your dragon?"

His low chuckle lit her up from the inside. "No. He is smugly content at the moment."

"Then I guess we can call this experiment a success."

Neither of them had experience, but they'd definitely figured things out quickly together. And he'd held his dragon inside, which was huge.

Airk dropped his head to her shoulder, and she couldn't be sure, but she thought he might have placed a soft kiss there, which wasn't an agreement. But she hoped...maybe this moved them a step closer. This wasn't about mating for politics anymore. Maybe it never had been. Not really. This was simply wanting to be with him.

CHAPTER TEN

Airk pulled himself out of a deep and remarkably dreamless slumber gradually. As though the darkness was trying to hold him back. Hold him under.

He pushed upward, swimming toward consciousness until finally his vision cleared. Only to reveal Angelika, curled into him, her white-blond hair spread over the pillow in the room where he'd moved them.

After.

Perhaps we should mate, in that case. That's what he'd thought when she'd called their "experiment" a success. Only he'd swallowed back the words, not ready to give them to her, despite the way he'd already publicly claimed her. Those words had been gut instinct, half him and half his dragon, and a mistake even as he uttered them. He wouldn't say yes until he was sure.

The hardest part was more and more of him wanted that. Wanted to give them both that. His dragon wanted it, too.

Maybe it could work.

Even now, contentment filled his chest. An emotion he hadn't felt in he couldn't remember how long. The sensation sat uncomfortably with him, though. A content man might be one slow to act. Slow to realize danger was near.

Like his father.

And Airk was the most dangerous thing in Angelika's life except, perhaps, Pytheios.

Even so, he reached out to trail a finger over her cheek, savoring the softness of her, the perfect bow of her lips. She smiled at his touch, and his chest tightened at the sight. He'd made her smile. Him. Despite everything he was.

Maybe he could make her smile more. His cock, already half hard when he'd woken with her scent winding in his senses, throbbed and swelled at the images in his head. More things he wanted to do to her...with her. Airk levered up on an elbow and reached to shake her gently awake, then stopped, his hand midair, horror freezing every muscle in his body and every thought in his head.

Because wrapped around her middle, like a boa constrictor, was a dragon tail.

His fucking dragon tail.

The spikes hadn't appeared yet, and it wasn't as large as if he was in his full form. Only partially shifted, he realized. He'd heard of the most powerful dragon shifters being able to shift only a part of themselves, but those were men in control. And he was *not*. He'd never seen his body this way. Ever. The pure white scales glittered at him—mocking, threatening.

Airk swallowed, holding still, and reached for the creature inside him. Tried to force the shift, cage the animal that he couldn't risk releasing.

Only, in direct response to the attempt, that tail, which was part of him but not, curled more tightly around Angelika.

She hummed, the sound of contentment lodging inside his heart like a shard of ice. This woman, whom he'd fooled himself into thinking maybe he could mate, had no idea what kind of danger she was in. None.

Don't hurt her.

It did not escape him that he was talking to the darker side of himself. Gods, how could he have been so selfishly blind? So damned wrong in his thinking to believe he could have her. Have anyone. Even for a second.

Let her go. Please. Now he was reduced to begging.

The tail tightened again, and Angelika frowned a little in her sleep, a small murmur of protest passing her lips.

Fuck.

He couldn't let himself panic. Panic would get him nowhere. Panic was when he lost even more control and the dragon took over. Exactly what the beast in him wanted.

Airk closed his eyes and took a deep breath, seeking that state between waking and sleeping where he and his dragon were one. Not a battle of wills but an agreement. Here, he was closest to his animal side—the closest he could allow himself to get without tumbling over.

Rather than demand or push or even coax, he waited. Waited for his animal to do the right thing. The only way he'd survived those cells was because his dragon hadn't shifted. The bars of dragonsteel would have shredded them if they'd tried it. His creature side had recognized the danger. On his own.

You don't want to hurt her, Airk attempted.

They both liked this woman. His dragon found her spunky and funny, and Airk…Airk found her a lot of things.

Slowly…so slowly Airk was almost ready to give up…his tail untensed and slowly unwound from Angelika, sort of turning her over as it did, turning her away from him. Then, the shimmers and waves of a shift appeared around him, and, with even more reluctance, his dragon voluntarily caged itself back inside his body and mind.

But Airk knew what this meant.

That had been too damn close. Taken too long and needed too much effort. His dragon couldn't be trusted around Angelika. Ever.

Mating her was out. Fucking was out, too.

A growl rippled in his mind, but he had the beast locked down now that he was fully in control. He would never risk this again.

Careful not to disturb the precious, untouchable sleeping woman in the bed, Airk allowed himself one moment of harsh regret, one moment of weakness, a terrible ache taking up residence in his chest as he let his gaze trace the curve of her back exposed as the sheet had slipped aside.

He'd thought he needed strength and fire in a mate and briefly wondered if maybe he had found it in Skylar when she'd appeared in his prison. But he'd been wrong about that. So wrong.

He needed... *Gods, Angelika.*

Shattered—there was no other word for it—Airk shook his head and stepped away.

He didn't need anything or anyone, because his life was doomed no matter what way he looked at it. All he could do was take that fucker Pytheios down with him when he went. He'd been out of his mind to consider, even for a millisecond, taking a mate into this living hell with him.

Letting her go, he gathered his clothes and left her sleeping. Then he went back to the mirror to wait for Meira to get in touch.

• • •

Angelika smiled and stretched like a contented tiger in the sun, her body languorous and still lushly replete after last night. Wow, had she drawn the lucky card in the deck. Being bound to Airk would be no hardship whatsoever. For a man who'd been locked up a hell of a long time, he sure knew how to use his tongue, among other things.

"Wake up." His low rumble set her smiling wider.

That must've been what pulled her from sleep. She had a vague idea he'd been calling her name a while now.

Peeling her eyes open, she discovered an empty bed in front of her face and frowned. He had just spoken, hadn't he? Levering up on an elbow, uncaring of the way the sheets slipped, she glanced over her shoulder to find him crouched beside the bed, fully dressed. Given the alert look in his eyes, he'd been awake for some time.

"Something wrong?" she asked.

"Meira's here."

Here? With a gasp, she flung back the sheets and hopped out of the bed.

"God's teeth, Angelika," Airk muttered, glancing away, jaw going tight.

She paused in a mad dash to find her clothes, which had been strewn haphazardly around last night, to frown at him again. "Nothing you haven't seen and touched," she pointed out, though a little warily. Something in his demeanor was off.

"All three of your sisters, plus their mates, are currently standing in the next room."

That was why he was acting weird? She plopped her hands on her hips, torn between wanting to smack him in the head for being prissy about this and wanting to run out and make sure her sisters were unharmed. The fact that all of them were here was not a good sign, but at least she knew they were still alive.

"This better not be that you're embarrassed you slept with me," she warned.

Airk shook his head, which only mollified her slightly, because the next second he walked out of the room.

What just happened?

In a decent imitation of a tornado sucking stuff up, she got dressed in record time and was out the door.

Her sisters stood there, eyes so wide they looked like startled animals. Right. Because they probably heard that conversation and no doubt could smell last night's activities on her. Their mates, on the other hand, appeared less than pleased.

Only she was too happy to see her sisters unharmed to be embarrassed or argue about it.

At Skylar's not-so-subtle thumbs-up, she grinned and walked straight into their arms. "You're okay?" she asked, her head buried in Meira's hair while her arms stretched to wrap around Kasia and Skylar.

"We're fine," Meira assured her.

"Mostly," Skylar muttered.

Angelika stepped back, casting a practiced nurse's gaze down each of them, and they did appear unharmed. "What does mostly mean?"

The three glanced at each other, and Angelika braced herself for bad news. "Ararat and Store Skagastølstind have fallen."

Disbelief clanged through her like a ringing gong, sending her ears buzzing and a wave of dizziness with the sound. *Both* the gold and black mountains? How was that even possible?

"The hells you say," Airk snarled from where he stood off to the side.

All three kings bristled at that tone being directed at their queens. All three queens rolled their eyes.

"Slow your roll, Tarzan," Skylar sniped at Ladon.

At the same time, Kasia addressed Brand. "I'm fine, you overblown firepit."

Meira just quietly raised her eyebrows at Samael, who shrugged, unapologetic.

"How?" Airk asked—demanded, more like—ignoring the byplay between the mated pairs.

"A simultaneous hit," Brand said. His golden eyes had gone a flat tawny yellow, a sure sign of his anger and a promise of retribution. He'd been a mercenary before taking the throne, and Angelika had no doubt the Rogue King's next plan would involve blood. "The White Clan struck the gold mountain while the Green Clan struck the black."

"We weren't able to get everyone out," Samael added, grim to the point that a shiver chased itself down her spine, raising the hairs on her neck.

Samael was a fighter. A warrior born and bred. Actually, all three of her brothers-by-blood were, one way or another. Only Brand was holding onto the Gold Clan by the tips of his dragon claws—this wouldn't help. Samael at least had his clan's loyalty and trust. His job, before he was crowned king, was as a warrior protecting the previous king. Still, if Pytheios's allies had managed to force him out, especially after they'd failed before, it had to be bad.

"What's the situation now?" Airk asked.

"We are all crammed into Ben Nevis," Ladon supplied.

Angelika shook her head. "Well…they'd be stupid to attack us there. With those kinds of numbers gathered in one place, it'd be suicide to try it."

"Pytheios won't attack," Airk said. "Not yet."

All three of the other men frowned.

"You sound certain," Samael said.

Airk crossed his arms, feet planted wide. "He knows your numbers and the size of the mountain. He'll either wait for your people to starve because there's not enough food for everyone"—a brutal, long process—"or for dragon-shifter nature to intervene."

"Infighting," Brand spat. He already dealt with that enough.

Airk gave a sharp nod. "Exactly. Let you implode, then come in when you're at your weakest."

Silence swept the room.

"How do you know this?" Ladon asked.

Airk shrugged. "I know Pytheios. His signature is to let others do the dirty work, use an enemy's strength as a weakness, and strike only when it's guaranteed to benefit him. This is not difficult to work out."

"What do we do?" Angelika asked. They couldn't let this bastard win. Not this way.

Brand glanced around the room. "Where are we, anyway?"

"Mönkh Saridag, the southernmost mountain of the White Clan," another male voice said from the hallway.

The other man's sudden appearance had three of the four men in the room crouched and glaring, along with Skylar and Kasia. Meira simply stepped closer to Samael.

Ignoring her sisters and their mates, Angelika crossed the room and slipped her hand through the crook of the older man's elbow, turning to face the room calmly. "This is Belyy. We are in his mountain, and he is on our side."

CHAPTER ELEVEN

Airk stood in a corner, listening. As soon as Angelika had explained everything, the room had sat in tense silence for a solid minute.

She looked from face to face. "I think Airk and I should go to Kamen."

All three kings jerked upright, eyes flaming. "The headquarters for the White Clan?" Ladon demanded. "Why?"

Angelika sat forward, serious, and yet Airk caught a hint of that hopefulness she never seemed to shake in the way she held herself. Almost eager. Too much so. He glanced at her sisters. Didn't they see it?

"Because," Angelika said in what sounded like a careful voice to him. "With allies here, what if we can form an alliance with them, too? What if—"

"No," Airk said.

She tossed an irritated frown toward his corner. "Hear me out."

He shot her a hard glare. "I refuse to go with you."

The hurt in her eyes—like a flash of lightning in a night sky, blinding and then gone—about took his knees out from under him. But all he had to do was picture his dragon tail wrapped around her, threatening to crush her, and he hardened his heart to the small pain he might give her now.

"That's not what you said last night," she pointed out. In front of her family.

He ignored the looks. "I have altered my thoughts. It is too dangerous."

Angelika's gaze narrowed. "For you or for me?"

He returned her stare unblinkingly.

Angelika's eyes flared, and he swore, for the space of a hummingbird's heartbeat, that white flame sparked in those glacial depths. But the phantom was gone so fast, it could have been a trick of the lighting. Besides, it made no sense.

Angelika held no fire. They'd already proven that.

"Then I'll go alone." She turned away from him as if that answered that question.

"The fuck you will." The words snarled from his throat before he thought to utter them, cutting off all three of her sisters and their mates. Belyy watched silently, clearly reserving judgment.

Despite the way everyone else looked askance at his unusual show of emotion, she merely shot him an unimpressed glance over her shoulder. "You said you're out. You don't get a vote here."

Airk's dragon snarled so loud in his head, the other dragons in the room must've sensed it, because they each tensed one at a time, turning their bodies so that they faced the predator in the room.

The threat. Exactly what he'd always be.

The tension ratcheted up another ten notches, but apparently Angelika was either oblivious or ignored it. After an assessing pause, she stalked across the floor, right into his space. "May I speak to you in private?" she asked in a low, tight voice.

She didn't wait for him to say anything. Just turned and expected him to follow. Which he did, jaw aching with the way he was clenching it. Did she take him into the room they'd shared on purpose? Because he could still smell her—smell them—in here. Damned if his traitorous body didn't send every ounce of blood straight to his cock.

Hells.

"I don't know what is going on with you," she said quietly as she slowly turned to face him. "One minute, you're in my bed and mating is finally a real possibility. The next, you can hardly stand to look at me."

"That is not true." He mentally grimaced. Words were popping out without his permission, but he couldn't stand the edge of hurt beneath the veneer of calm she was projecting.

Angelika crossed her arms. "Then what is true? I'd love to know."

Hells. "Last night we were not sure of the situation with our clans. Now we are. With White and Green so clearly siding with Pytheios, the risk is too high."

She glanced away, everything about her appearing...brittle. Did she really care that much? "It's worth the risk," she insisted, not looking at him.

"Not with me along, it is not."

Angelika opened her mouth as she looked back at him, then paused, her gaze seeming to take in something in his expression, which he kept carefully blank.

"Not with you..." she said, eyes narrowing as she worked things out in her head. "Why not?"

"The danger," he repeated again.

Her lips flattened, but the compassion softening her expression was harder to ignore. "Try again."

"I am dangerous, dammit. I woke up this morning partially shifted—"

The last thing he expected was for delight to flare in her eyes. Almost as though melting, her body let go of the tension, and Angelika crowded into his space, hand on his arm, lips curving into the softest smile. "That's wonderful."

He jerked back, ignoring her frown. "No."

"You shifted partially and still maintained control. That's an incredible first step—"

"I was *not* in control," he snapped.

Gods, why was he even telling her this? Despite not knowing her for much time, he was more than convinced that Angelika couldn't walk away from a wounded creature. And that's exactly what he was to her. Wounded. Broken.

Sure enough, rather than fear, her gaze narrowed with speculative interest and a hint of concern. "I wasn't murdered in my sleep by a feral dragon. That sounds like control to me."

His beast snarled at that description from her lips, the sound rumbling up Airk's throat.

Her eyes widened, but she pressed on. "I'd say you figured it out."

Airk shook his head. "I am not a bird with a broken wing that you help nurse to health, Angelika."

"I know that."

"No. You think you can fix me. I see it in your eyes right now."

"Fixing you is not what I want," she uttered in a dust-dry voice.

"Semantics," he growled. Why couldn't she see this was only going to get worse?

Angelika glanced away, hands going to her hips as she thought for a moment before turning her gaze back to him, watching him with those eyes that seemed to see past the guards he put up for everyone else.

"I can't do this without you," she said quietly. "You know that."

Airk tried not to tense at the words, the tone. If she had fought, railed, or yelled, he could have stayed strong against that. But this quiet kind of pleading...

Gods, this woman would be his undoing, and he was terrified, down to the depths of his scarred soul, that he would be her destruction.

"This is important," she continued.

"I know that."

She nodded. "More than anything else, maybe." She stepped closer. Not touching, not in his space yet, but her delicate human scent wound around him. "More than me. The risk is acceptable."

"I cannot mate you."

The woman who'd shared pleasure with him last night, who, even as he fought against the pull she had for him, he wanted to throw on the bed and bury his face between her legs and watch as she shattered under his mouth... That woman turned ice cold, her eyes suddenly the warmest thing about her. So unlike her that it made him hurt in places he didn't know existed inside him.

"Fine," she said. Not angry, just firmly resigned. "Mating is back off the table."

What? No.

The knee-jerk reaction lined up exactly with his dragon suddenly thrashing inside him, sending pounding pain through his mind, his skin rippling with iridescent scales. Airk shoved all of it—the dragon and his own needs—into a dark fucking hole and buried it.

"Fine." A new word for him, but it got to the heart of his frustration fairly well.

With a nod as though things had been decided, she marched from the room to the others waiting outside. Airk followed more reluctantly.

He walked in right in time to hear Angelika announce, "We need a witch or warlock to perform a binding spell."

"Fuck that." This from Brand.

"I'm *not* asking," Angelika shot at the gold dragon. "This man has given us his loyalty." She waved at Belyy.

"And you wish him to prove it with a binding oath?" Brand wasn't letting this go, despite Kasia wrapping a hand around his wrist.

"Yes."

Airk had to give it to her—Angelika wasn't afraid of anything. It would get her killed one day if she wasn't careful. He couldn't be around to witness that. It would destroy him.

Ladon growled. "You don't know—"

Meira sighed. "She *does* know."

"Mother told us all about it," Kasia said.

"Do we know of anyone we'd trust?" Skylar looked between the men.

"You're going to let her do this?" Ladon demanded of his mate, flinging an arm in Angelika's direction. A nerve near Ladon's scar visibly twitched, a sure sign the Blood King was upset.

"*You* try stopping her," Skylar said. Not that she sounded happy about it.

Ladon turned on Angelika. "I thought you were supposed to be the easygoing one."

"I am. But that doesn't make me a pushover." The smile she turned on Ladon made Airk want to shove the guy aside—pure sunshine, and part of him wanted to keep it for himself. Only for himself.

A small, resigned growl of sound had them all turning to Brand. "I don't know of a specific mage, but I know someone who probably can make a recommendation."

· · ·

One phone call from Brand, and now Angelika was staring at two people. A man and woman, clearly a mated pair, though mating was different for witches.

That in and of itself wasn't extraordinary. What had struck her speechless was the fact that they arrived only five minutes later. Silently appearing. No rush of wind like a mage who could teleport, and this mountain, like all other dragon-shifter locations, had been warded against teleportation in general.

So how had they gotten in?

"I know you," Ladon said slowly, studying the man closely.

He received a nod of greeting. "Alasdair Blakesley, head of the Covens' Syndicate."

A warlock. Extremely powerful to head the group that governed all mages in the world at such a young age. Early to mid-thirties at most and handsome with it—raven-black hair and blue eyes that seemed to stray to the woman he arrived with more often than not.

"This is my wife, Delilah."

She nodded.

No one asked what she was, which was considered rude. She was dressed in a pristine white pantsuit, and her black hair was pinned in an elegant chignon at the nape of her neck. Her demeanor might cause one to assume she was the less dangerous of the two, but Angelika got the sense that, if anything, Delilah was the more powerful. And not necessarily a witch.

"Which of you wishes a binding oath performed?" Delilah asked.

"I do." Angelika stepped forward.

Richly dark eyes turned her way, assessing and yet unthreatening. "You understand what you ask?"

"Yes."

"These oaths can act unpredictably," Delilah warned.

Again.

"I'm well aware."

"Very well. Let me understand what you wish the oath to be."

"*You* will be performing it?" Airk asked, glancing between Delilah and Alasdair.

The woman's smile could be in the dictionary next to the word *enigmatic*. "I'm more familiar with these particular...spells."

So she was a witch? Or not? "How do you know Brand?"

The question slipped out. That darn curiosity cat-killing thing she had.

Delilah's eyes slid in Brand's direction, and she smiled primly. "I offer all my clients and contractors privacy and discretion."

Which meant she wouldn't answer for him. Angelika's estimation of this woman went up a few notches.

Delilah turned her gaze to Angelika. "Who will be involved?"

"This man." Angelika indicated Belyy with a wave. "And others."

"Others?" Kasia frowned.

"You said nothing about multiple binding spells," Skylar snapped. "I don't like this."

"One spell," Angelika said, her voice indicating this was no big deal even though she knew full well it was. But she was determined. "Multiple people."

"I'll have them summoned," Belyy said and hurried away before anyone else could argue.

"While he's doing that," Delilah said, her gaze on the man's departing back, "why don't you explain exactly what you want to happen and why?"

Thirty minutes later, the people who'd come yesterday stood in the room, tension evident in rigid shoulders and fisted hands, surrounded by the kings and queens who had been their enemies not even twenty-four hours before.

"How do you do this? Bring people together this way?" Airk muttered to Angelika under his breath. "You are a miracle worker."

She tossed him an easy grin she wasn't entirely feeling, a flock of prehistoric-sized butterflies taking off in her tummy. At Delilah's beckoning, she moved to the center of the circle the woman had formed with those men and the one woman in the ranks.

Airk wasn't going to join her. She wouldn't let him. Not with the risk of what it might trigger in his dragon. Not with his rejection ringing in her ears. Despite what they'd shared, he wasn't even willing to try to fight for her—for them—and the dull anguish that had left in her heart went beyond chemistry or political alliances.

When this became about her and him, and not the rest, she wasn't sure.

"Ready?" the sorceress, or whatever Delilah was—it still wasn't clear—asked. "Last chance to change your mind."

"This is necessary." No hesitation. Angelika was sure of the need for this action, even if it backfired on her. Desperate times and all that. Deep down, she knew this was the right path, even if where it ultimately led remained shrouded in darkness.

"All right." Delilah nodded. "Hands up."

She'd already walked those participating through what had to happen. Each person standing around Angelika lifted a hand, holding it palm facing her.

Here we go.

• • •

As she stood at the center of the circle, Angelika looked as ethereal and as fragile as she was, yet strong as dragonsteel. The woman, Delilah, started chanting, and immediately a familiar electric buzz of magic filled the air.

A string of ancient words passed her lips, known to Airk only because of the one friend he had had on the inside. Nathair had taught him the oldest language in existence—that of angels...and demons. Airk jerked at the shock of recognition, fisting his hands to keep from stopping her immediately.

What in the hells was this woman?

Raising their own voices, those in the circle, including Angelika, repeated the words with her. Over and over.

The words wound around him and through him, penetrating, becoming part of him. The chant took up space inside his head, crowding in there with his dragon. Pounding. Airk found his lips moving with Angelika's lips, though no sound came from him.

Then she gasped.

Her eyes flared wide, gaze landing on him, and he lurched forward a step only to stumble to a halt as she started to glow. Not the others, still chanting. Just Angelika. Bright lights of all colors of the rainbow came from every part of her, illuminating her as though she were her namesake—an angel in every sense of the word.

"Keep going," Alasdair called as others stumbled over words, including Angelika. "Don't stop until it's finished."

Angelika's lips started to move again, but she didn't take her gaze from him. The words, still a part of him in the strangest way, only grew louder in his head, more insistent, more frantic. The light coming from Angelika intensified, turning near blinding, and yet somehow he could still see her eyes, wide in her face.

And she was terrified.

Airk was across the room before deciding to move.

"No!" Delilah called.

But he didn't stop, moving between two of the men in the circle, he stepped right into the woman who scared him more than just about anything in this world. He took her face in his hands. Gods, she was shaking.

"Do you still want this?" he asked.

She nodded.

"Then keep going."

Holding her gaze, he spoke the words with her. One after another until the sounds blurred together, the beat primal, pumping to the heavy, unfettered beat of his heart.

The glow around her encompassed him, folded around him, like being pulled inside her embrace last night, and he never looked away, never stopped. Then, with a sudden flare, white heat lanced through the flesh on the back of his hand between his thumb and forefinger.

He'd hardly grunted in reaction when everything stopped.

Silence fell over the room, so loud it was practically deafening, and he had to blink a few times, clearing his gaze after the brightness.

"What just happened?" he was vaguely aware of one of her sisters asking, worry in her voice.

"Fuck-a-doodle-doo," Brand muttered.

"What?" That was Ladon.

Airk finally raised his gaze from Angelika, though he didn't release his hold on her. "What?" he echoed the blue king's demand.

"My king's mark," Tovar said, awe and something else in his voice. "It's changed."

He held up his hand, and sure enough, a new symbol—no longer that of Volos—graced the flesh there.

Airk jerked his own hand up and stared at an identical symbol, now stark against his own skin. A new mark of loyalty where before there had been none.

The change hadn't come with the usual searing pain, either. The sigil was not Brand's or Ladon's or Samael's, as they'd expected. The intricate twisting and turning lines were the same as those that had once graced his hand as a child, and his father's hand, and his mother's…

He traced the familiar shape, connected to this symbol more now than he'd been as a boy, the tug of loyalty and another emotion a physical presence in his chest.

The mark of the Amon family.

Angelika's family.

CHAPTER TWELVE

"I guess that answers the question about if they are the true phoenixes," someone in the room—Tovar, maybe—muttered.

Angelika swallowed, unable to draw her gaze away from the tattoo-like symbol now magically emblazoned on Airk's hand as though it had always been part of him. Her mother used to draw that exact symbol, doodle it absentmindedly wherever she went. In the dirt, even, before paper and ink or pencil were readily available. The sign of Serefina's dead mate, which had never shown on the back of her own neck because their bond hadn't solidified before Pytheios had killed Zilant.

The same soul-deep sadness struck Angelika now at the sight of it. "Mama," she whispered.

Gods, she hoped her parents had found each other at last in the afterlife.

"But which Amon is the one to follow?" someone else asked.

"The one you just pledged your oath to." Airk's low snarl of words pulled her gaze up to his face to find his eyes trained on her.

Only that couldn't be right.

"But I'm not—" She swallowed again. Had she bound these people to a dormant phoenix...to a human who could do no more than talk people round to her way of thinking? "I'm not—"

This was a disaster.

Airk searched her gaze. "Breathe," he whispered, just for her.

"I'm not—" She hadn't meant to bind them to her in this way. Only check their loyalty so trust could be established. Not as ruler to subject. This wasn't how this was supposed to happen.

Airk reached for her hand and placed it over his heart, the steady *thump, thump, thump* palpable against her palm. "Breathe," he said again and inhaled. The same way she'd done to help calm his dragon.

The kindness of that simple act, from this man in particular, knocked her back to normal. She sucked in deep, let it out, then turned to Delilah. "Why do they bear my father's mark?"

Delilah pursed her lips, then glanced to her husband, Alasdair, who tipped his head in what might have been a shrug or maybe more a, "You be the one to tell her."

"Best guess..." Delilah said, "is it's *your* mark."

"But wouldn't her mark be a combination of our father and mother?" Kasia asked.

Unlike human mates, who took on their mate's mark at the back of their neck, phoenixes were known to meld the two family crests into a new pattern. They'd never gotten to see what the Amon and Hanyu crests would look like combined, but Kasia was right. Kasia's mark was a blend of Brand's and their parents'. Skylar, the same way with Ladon's. And Meira's, too, with Samael's.

Mine should be a blend as well.

Delilah shrugged. "Magic is...mysterious." Her lips tipped up. "Since her phoenix side is dormant, perhaps her only magical connection is with her father."

Ouch.

With a wince, Angelika dropped her head forward, wishing her hair wasn't still up in that damn braid crown so that she could use the fall of it to hide what those words did to her insides. The stark pain of losing her mother ripped through her all over again, leaving her heart beaten and bloody. She may look like her father, but her mother's blood was in her, too. She knew it. But the longer she went without her, without powers, the further away her mother felt.

A gentle hand landed on the nape of her neck. Airk again.

She turned her head slightly, leaning into the pressure of his hold, trying to absorb his silent strength. Because, damn it all, she needed it right then. She hated that she did, and at the same time appreciated that small gesture more than she could say. If anything, she wanted to turn into him and bury her face in his chest. But she feared suddenly that he wouldn't let her. Reject her in front of all these people and add to the sense that she was alone—truly alone—in this world.

She lifted her head slowly, careful not to dislodge his hand. "We should go."

They'd already explained to her newly oath-bound followers the plan of going to the headquarters of the White Clan. The seat of the king.

"Actually." Tovar stepped forward, breaking the circle around her finally, which almost gave her a reason to breathe easier. "I think you should send some of us ahead of you. Let us prepare them, get a feel for things, and turn some strategic allies to our side."

"But—"

Skylar cut her off. "It's a solid idea."

Except she'd worked herself up to going. However, even she could see, sometimes, when caution was the better part of valor. "Very well." She'd just...wait. Like always.

Her sisters all huffed visible sighs of relief, which made her lips tighten in the same instance that Airk's hand did. He didn't like their reaction, either? Funny. He probably would dislike this next part as much as her own flesh and blood would. "While we wait for word, I suggest we seek out other allies."

"The Green Clan will never break with Pytheios," Ladon warned. "Red and green have the longest running alliance of our kind."

She waved that off. "I'm not talking about dragons."

For the first time since performing the oath, she wanted to laugh, because every dragon shifter in the room's expression turned dour. That sucking-on-lemons metaphor had never been so apt, because that was exactly what they looked like.

"We handle dragon problems internally," Belyy said in a voice that brooked no compromise.

Angelika snorted. "Maybe if you'd gotten help from outside, you could have fixed all this centuries ago."

Every dragon back went steel-rod straight at that, but she didn't have time to coddle the shifters' sensitive pride any longer. What she was suggesting was true, and they could use all the help they could get. Even if they got every dragon from all four clans—Black, Blue, Gold, and White—on the same side, Pytheios still had his witch. Rhiamon had proven to be his not-so-secret weapon and a hell of a lot more dangerous than any had dreamed.

"What kind of help?" Tavor asked, the first to let go of his vanity, though the lemon-sucking expression remained.

She looked to her sisters, a question in her eyes, knowing exactly what she was asking them to do. Because she would be doing the same.

Skylar could go speak with the rogue dragons in the colonies who'd kept her safe. Those men definitely had an axe to grind with the current leadership. Meira could speak with the gargoyles. As deliberately solitary and hidden as they were, they were the least likely to join this fight, but the answer to any question never asked would always be no.

They had to try.

Kasia had had their hellhound, Maul, for safety—their father reincarnate. He was gone now, so Kasia didn't have anyone to ask, but Brand, who'd been a mercenary with connections before he became king, did. Look at Delilah and Alasdair.

Meanwhile, Angelika would go to the headquarters for the Federation of Packs, where the small pack of wolf shifters who'd given her shelter—who'd become her friends—now hid. If Pytheios won this war, they would never be safe, either. She hated it...putting more people she cared about at risk, but she had to ask.

Slowly, both Skylar and Meira nodded. Kasia, meanwhile, swung her gaze to Brand. "Hershel?" she questioned.

The towering King of the Gold Clan's jaw worked, but he also gave a single, jerking nod. "I'll ask."

"Thank you," Angelika said. Then turned to Delilah and Alasdair. "You have a stake in this, too, I'm afraid."

A tiny frown pulled at Alasdair's brows. "You're referring to the red king's witch?"

Delilah, however, closed her catlike eyes, seeming to focus, her mouth then compressing. "It's worse than we thought," she murmured to him.

Beyond a tiny twitch at the edge of his jaw, Alasdair didn't visibly react. "How bad?"

"I can't see her," Delilah said, opening her eyes to look at her husband, still calm but something else, too. Worried. "I mean not at all. Nothing. As though she doesn't exist."

"So pretty damn bad," he muttered.

"Kasia can fill you in," Angelika said. She turned to the people who'd pledged their loyalty to her. "I'm not sure how long this is going to take me. You know what to do, here and elsewhere."

Belyy and Tovar both nodded, though Tovar's eyes remained trained on Airk when he did.

Right. Plan in place. Time to go. "Meira?"

She didn't need to specify to her sister what she was asking. Meira simply walked over to the mirror she and their sisters had come through, igniting into flame as she walked.

"I can't get you inside," Meira said, speaking of the Federation's home base. And she should know, as she was the one who'd sent Jedd and the rest of Angelika's wolves there recently. "Only nearby. But they have sentries posted all around it. You head into the mountains southeast from where I send you, and they'll pick you up eventually."

And hopefully not kill them before they asked questions.

"I should—"

She shot Airk a glare. "If you say you should go alone, I'm leaving you here to wait for me."

He stared at her long enough that a tiny bit of regret for snapping like that had her wrinkling her nose. She wasn't a snapper. Not usually.

When he caught the small gesture, he shook his head. Though he didn't smile, a spark of humor turned his eyes bluer. "I was going to suggest I stay here. I think the wolves would be more inclined to listen to you without a dragon around putting their fur up."

"Oh." His show of confidence in her also made her want to wrap her arms around him and kiss the man.

"We need a dragon representative," she said. "And I need a bodyguard."

He didn't accept that right away, though, searching her expression. "Maybe someone who can shift—"

"No," she cut him off. "You."

"Why?" he asked.

Good question. The answer had mostly to do with suddenly feeling fairly certain that separation from him might kick off an anxiety attack. That was new. She'd never been prone to those, but already her chest was tightening.

She latched on to the first solid reason her brain could come up with. "Your story as someone directly impacted by Pytheios, but who still insists on fighting him anyway, is compelling. You're also not part of the leadership that let things slip to this point."

She leaned around him to look at the others. "No offense." She straightened, paused, then leaned over again. "Actually, not sorry. That's the truth. Now you're doing something, though, so…good for you."

She meant it kindly, but it came out more Skylar than her.

A choked sound from Airk might have been a laugh, but when she straightened again to look at him, his expression told her he was still on the fence. "Please," she implored.

His gaze settled and blanked at the same time, but even so, she sensed steadiness more than anything. "I will come."

Relief whooshed through her—way more than was probably warranted.

"Good." She turned to Meira, and the reflection in the mirror changed, showing a narrow alleyway between pristine white plaster-sided buildings.

"The closest I can get you is the town of Victoria at the foothills of the mountains," Meira said.

No one needed to question where they were going. The Federation didn't bother hiding from other supernaturals the way they did from humans. For a little over a century now, the wolves had been headquartered in the Făgăraș Mountains, the southern part of the Carpathian range where it ran through Romania. Obviously, there were no mirrors in the forest, and Angelika would rather not use the reflection of a pond, which Meira could do if the day was still enough, and arrive wet, but...

"Is there no reflection inside the castle to use?" Angelika asked.

Meira shook her head. "They've covered all their mirrors since... me."

In other words, Angelika's wolves had shared Meira's powers, and the wisely wary wolves took pains to keep them out.

"That does not bode well for us," Airk muttered, apparently reaching the same conclusion.

Stretching her lips into a smile meant to project confidence took more effort than usual, thanks to more nerves fluttering in her gut. "I guess I'll have to be extra persuasive."

Another choked sound from the man at her side. One that could have been a snort of derision or of sympathy for the wolves. She wasn't sure which and didn't get a chance to check, because Airk didn't wait for her, stepping right through the portal Meira had created between reflections.

Blowing a kiss to her visibly worried sisters, she followed, and immediately the side window of a storefront in the middle of a quaint Romanian town was all she could see as Meira cut off her power.

They'd have to contact Meira the usual way, via modern technology, when they were ready to leave. Until then, they were on their own.

"Thank you," she said to the broad back of the silent man with her.

He glanced over his shoulder, dark brows pulling together

slightly. "For what?"

For getting me through that, and for being here with me now.

He stilled as she stepped into him, a hand on his chest as she went up on tiptoe and pressed her lips to his cheek. "You know what," she whispered, the stubble of a day's growth of surprisingly black whiskers prickling her lips.

She dropped to flat feet, the warmth of him under her palm penetrating, the cherry-and-smoke scent of him wrapping around her almost protectively. An emotion she couldn't possibly hope to interpret flashed at her, there then gone. Still, he hesitated, and she waited, wondering for a brief second what he would do.

But he turned away. "Where are we?"

"Transylvania."

His shoulders went rigid, and, without moving beyond that small tell, she got the impression he was ready to fight the next thing to round the corner. "Vampires—"

"No." She shook her head. "The bloodsuckers abandoned this region after it became popular following the publication of Bram Stoker's supposedly fictional book, *Dracula*, in 1897. Apparently, all the vampires around here were being hunted by frightened humans and decided to go elsewhere. The wolf shifters took advantage and moved right in."

Including requisitioning an abandoned castle.

"Smart."

She pointed at a peak in the distance, one Jedd had made her memorize pictures of long before their falling out, just in case something happened. "That's where we're going. We hike from here until the wolves find us and take us the rest of the way."

Airk stared at the mountain, expression turning broody. "You had better be right about them."

Angelika patted his arm even as she hid her own trepidation. Bleidd, Jedd, and the others from their pack would never harm her. But a random wolf sentry who didn't know her was a different ball of trouble.

I hope I'm right, too.

. . .

Airk leaned against the trunk of the piney tree they'd taken shelter under for the night, the bark rough poking through the thin layer of his shirt a vague irritation.

Night.

This was a bad idea, coming here at this hour. Not just because of the chill in the air, but night was when all the worst of the supernatural creatures that walked this planet decided to come out. Hopefully, the wolf shifters' presence in the region scared off any truly bad ones.

Still, the forest was a welcome change after so long sleeping against stone. Anything different was good. He tipped his gaze to the skies.

The room where he'd been held in the dungeons of Everest was built inside the peak of the hollowed-out mountain. The precipice. Generations before him had hewn those walls from the very mountain itself, turning it hard as diamonds, strong enough to continue to support the weight and designed to allow those inside an unimpeded view of what lay outside.

Any being standing outside saw only the rock, snow, and ice of the most massive mountain on the planet. The mountain was so huge, they didn't really worry about discovery by the humans determined to scale it. But putting the dungeon at the top...that was the perfect prison to torture dragon shifters. A view of skies where they could look but not touch.

Where Airk had never soared and never would.

This view of the sky here was also different. No more ice and snow. A different angle of the stars and evergreen branches overhead. Even a different feel—the sharp scent of the trees and musky earth, the wind rustling the leaves and needles for the forest, a new bite of cold that didn't affect him.

And the clacking of teeth.

Angelika leaned against the other side of the tree, arms wrapped around her middle, hands stuffed under her armpits, and her teeth chattering so hard she could pass for a woodpecker hammering away at hard bark.

He clenched his own teeth until the molars scraped against each other and his jaw locked. "Come here," he demanded.

"I'm fine," came her voice from around the other side. Not stubborn like Skylar would have sounded, or Kasia's sarcasm, or even Meira's softness. Angelika was honestly trying not to be a bother. What was she trying to prove? That she wasn't frail? That she could do this?

Sure enough, a second later she said, "Aren't the stars amazing?"

As if that could distract him from the clatter of bone on bone. What if she caught a sickness and died because she was determined not to use his natural warmth?

"I have seen better." He had, too. He'd lived in the highest place on earth, with no light pollution, a thing he'd learned of recently. On clear nights, he felt as though he could touch the cold light of the stars. Swim through the Milky Way stretched out overhead.

"So have I," he caught the faint murmur. Then a huff. "I didn't expect it to be this *cold*. It's summertime, for goodness' sake."

Given that his personal experience to measure such things against was one of the harshest places on earth, Airk didn't comment on that. Instead, he pushed to his feet, moved around the tree, and bodily lifted her up, then sat back down where she'd been, back against the trunk and Angelika cradled in his lap. He wrapped his arms around her, cringing at the way her body was shaking like an aspen leaf in a windstorm, strung so tight he could probably use her muscles to shoot arrows.

"Doesn't this break your rules?" she asked.

"Rules?"

"*Don't touch Angelika.* I'm pretty sure after giving me the most incredible orgasms, the next morning, that's what you decided."

She wasn't wrong. He said nothing.

"Don't you hate it when I'm right?" she teased.

No. It made him want to touch her more, if anything.

She shifted against him, burrowing her head between his chin and shoulder, cold little nose digging against the skin of his neck. Something inside his chest squeezed hard. Probably his dragon.

"I guess my sisters would kill you if I died from exposure on this trip."

He wouldn't like it much, either. "They could try."

"Although…" she continued as though he hadn't just dropped a subtle challenge to her family between them. "You know a terrific way to warm up is to…move around. Encourage circulation and all that."

He frowned. "You want to keep walking?" They had been traveling by foot, over rough terrain for much of it, all day. "We need rest." Or she did.

"True. Hmm…"

He waited for whatever came next. He'd started to pick up on the fact that when Angelika was worried, or rattled, or trying to be brave, was when she tended to come up with…ideas.

"I've been told fucking is a great way to get the blood pumping."

Holy shit.

Yes, his dragon growled in his head, more than enthusiastic about that idea. *Mine.*

Not ours, though. The word his animal side used was distinctly possessive and singular. Almost as though, given Airk's reaction this morning, the dragon side of him had decided Airk wasn't part of the deal anymore.

Dammit.

With Angelika's sunshine scent wending round him, her body against his, the softness of her hair tickling her jaw, Airk was already locked in a battle of wills with the beast inside and his own desires. Blood pumped through his body, swelling his already semi-hard cock to pulsing, painful life.

Holy hells. What do I do now?

Let go of her and move back to the other side of the tree. That was what he should do. Or say no. The word should have burst from him, but his mouth refused to form around it. And he didn't remove himself from her. "Better that we keep our clothes on for warmth," he muttered.

Her raspy chuckle, the sexiest damn sound in the world, was close to his undoing. "I'm sure we could get creative."

Fuck. He dropped his head back against the tree with a painful *thump* and squeezed his eyes shut.

Images—lusty, sensual, beastly images of what he'd do to her— bombarded his mind, and he couldn't even say they were from his dragon. Because, all the hells and heavens be damned, he *wanted* her.

One time had not been nearly enough.

Now he was picturing what he'd do to her—with her—in graphic, sensory-filled, brutal detail. He'd lift her from his lap and place her on her hands and knees where he could lower her pants just enough. Then, releasing his cock from his own pants, he'd surge inside the tight, hot, wet heart of her. Pound into her until the forest was filled with her cries of desire.

He tried to put a stop to the thoughts, but his mind was already far down that road. He kept going.

Nathair had brought him more than just books about combat. There'd also been rare tomes, and among those had been the *Kama Sutra*, though Airk doubted Nathair had read that one. But memories of some of the pages suddenly took on a whole new meaning as he pictured himself and Angelika in all those positions. Sexual positions drawn in titillating detail that he'd beat off to in his cell—his only form of release—now sent ideas and even more ideas slamming into him.

Her skin glowing in the moonlight. To have him push his thick cock inside her while he used his hands to stimulate other erogenous zones? He wanted to lay claim to every part of her. Leave his seed everywhere until she was his in no uncertain terms.

Even then, he wouldn't be done.

He'd sit, back against the tree like he was now, and have her straddle him, ride him. Have her take her own pleasure from his body while he watched her come and come and come. Fill her body so full of him until they wouldn't know where he ended and she began. Hells, if he could do that, there were so many ways he could take her, trap her, trap them both, in a sexual, beautiful haze and have the unique pleasure of having her come all over him. Over, and over, and over.

It might be decades before he let them up for air. The kind of prison he'd never want to escape.

A low, feminine moan yanked him out of his own head, out of those fantasies so real he almost cried out at the loss, only to freeze solid to find his hands down her pants, fingers buried in her slick heat and thumb pressing against that bundle of nerves that seemed to be the key to her pleasure.

Fuck!

"Don't stop," Angelika begged on another moan, shifting her hips to get him moving again.

Gods, what had he done? How had he—

She shifted positions in his lap, back to his chest, legs on either side of his, spreading her legs wider, and Airk clamped his eyes shut even as he was bombarded by everything that was Angelika. The musky, luscious scent of her desire hit him like a thunderclap, and he couldn't stop himself. Didn't want to stop himself.

"Fuck," he said. Then said it again.

"Airk?"

He hated the uncertainty in her voice and that he'd put it there, almost more than he adored the feel of her. Closing his eyes, he locked down the beast inside him, pushing him so deep he couldn't be part of this, then moved his hands.

The catch in her breathing, the way she relaxed against him—he would have smiled if he wasn't using every part of his control to give her this pleasure while holding the worst of himself in check.

Gods, he hoped he was touching her right. Exploring her slick folds by touch alone was fascinating, and he kept losing himself in that. But at the same time, he returned to anything that made her breathing hitch, and that seemed to be working.

"Inside me," she begged. Urged.

Happy to obey, he slipped one, then two fingers into her tightness. Pumping his fingers slowly in and out of her, he flicked with his thumb at that spot slightly above, a bundled nub that made her squirm, and she shuddered, pressing into his hand.

Yes. Fuck my fingers.

She undulated her hips, and the action pressed her ass into his pulsing cock, which was jutting straight up, trapped between his stomach and her body. Airk grunted.

She must've caught what caused the sound, because she did it again. This time, he couldn't hold back a low groan.

"I hit a spot, huh?" The smile in her voice was an invitation to play.

One he wanted to accept so much, his chest burned with it. But he couldn't. Dammit, he couldn't. He'd finish what he'd unwittingly started, they'd sleep, and then they'd find those damn wolves and get this journey over with.

He pressed harder, faster, building the pleasure inside her. Pleasure that spilled from her lips in uninhibited sounds that wrapped around his dick and squeezed. At the same time, she kept moving her ass, rolling her hips so that she rubbed his erection— hells, throttled it—as she rode his fingers until they were both panting, both mindless, both reaching for the pinnacle.

A tiny flutter of her inside walls was his only warning. Then Angelika slammed back into his body, head flinging to land on his shoulder, mouth open around a cry of completion and greedy pussy clamping around his hand as she writhed and pulsed with release.

In the same instant, her release tipped him over and he exploded, jets of come pumping from his body.

Seed that should be inside her. Dammit.

He hadn't even realized that could happen without direct stimulation. Reality brought him down from the high as harshly as a punch to the throat, but he tried not to do that to her, too. Not to drag her down with him.

Seemingly unaware of his reaction, Angelika took her time drifting back to reality, replete and languorous against him. And he held her, selfishly, as long as she let him.

The best and most horrible torture.

When she sighed—a sound of contentment that made his own chest ache—he pulled his hand out of her pants, rearranging both their clothing. Nothing he could do about the sticky dampness in his. He'd have to live with it. Then he pulled her around sideways in his lap and into him, her head lolling against his shoulder.

"See?" she murmured in a pleased little voice. "I told you we could get creative."

Airk squeezed his eyes shut, trying not to stiffen at the happiness she radiated. Because nothing had changed, except that now he knew even fantasies about her were dangerous to indulge.

"Angelika Amon." A deep voice resonated from the woods about fifty yards to their right.

Airk tensed, a warning growl ripping from his throat as he searched the trees. The distinct earthy scent of a wolf floated to him on the night breeze. They'd approached downwind. Damn the gods. He'd been so wrapped up in the woman in his lap, in chasing the small amount of indulgence he'd ever had in life, and he had failed to protect her. Failed to know danger lurked closely.

Had the damn wolves gotten an eyeful? He knew they'd had to have heard what had just gone on. A private show. Did they beat off to it?

Strange satisfaction ripped through him at that. At least they'd know she was his.

In the next instant, he shoved that possessive instinct in the same hole he'd locked his dragon in. She would *never* be his.

The woman who was the source of all his problems, meanwhile, oblivious to his internal struggle, pushed out of his arms to her feet. "I'm Angelika Amon."

CHAPTER THIRTEEN

Well, that was...whatever it was.

Angelika tried not to think about how hard she'd come with only Airk's hands down her pants, or the fact that no way could the wolves not have at least heard. She hadn't exactly been trying to be quiet. Even now, her body was still buzzing from the aftereffects, and she didn't even want to think about how they could smell her desire.

Airk, meanwhile, stalked through the woods at her side, not even turning his head once to check on her. She'd like to pretend he was too busy watching all the shifters around them—after the first sentry, they'd picked up another, then another, until six trailed before and behind—but she was pretty sure he was just avoiding her gaze.

Like last time.

As soon as she got him alone, they were going to have a chat, because either he was into her or he wasn't, but this back and forth needed to stop. After all, she'd been teasing with her comments about getting creative. *He* was the one who'd trailed those provocative fingers over her skin, brushing her breasts with the backs of his knuckles, then inching up her shirt to tease the sensitive skin of her belly before pushing lower. As though compelled.

Best to stop thinking about it, or she might spontaneously orgasm off the memory alone.

The castle chose that moment to rise up out of the dark, and Angelika paused, mouth open. Dragons hid inside their impressive mountains, but nothing from the outside gave a person warning.

This...this was different.

Built into the side of the mountain, the structure blended with the crags and spires and valleys of the rock almost as though the rock itself had built it, pushed it out of its own body. Difficult to tell in the dark, but to her it appeared as though some parts were crumbling while others had been added to recently. Either way, she almost expected the first vampire himself to come flying over the top in the moonlight. Or maybe a rush of bats.

No vampires here, though. Not anymore.

A howl went up off to her right, and Airk paused to listen and assess. At least he didn't growl. She'd thought the sentry might pee himself earlier when he'd...errr...come upon them.

Gods, she hoped her sisters never heard about that.

A second howl sounded in front of them, followed by a third to the left. Basically, an alarm network.

"This way," one of their escorts said and pulled back a curtain of vines leading down a dark hole. Angelika paused only long enough to check with Airk. His vision in the dark would be light-years better than hers. So would his other senses.

Shock skittered through her as he took her hand, pulling her behind him as though using his body to shield her, then stepped into the darkness.

His hand wrapped around hers was pure strength, totally steady. To help keep her balance, she placed the palm of her other hand flat against his back, syncing her steps to his so she didn't trip them both. Her rock in the dark.

Without her sight, beyond a very vague ambiance to allow her to walk, impressions hit her all at once: the cooler, dank air; sounds of dripping; and the mineral taste of humidity on her tongue. This might be a cave or an ancient tunnel formed into the bedrock of the mountain itself. Either way, it seemed to be leading them into the castle.

Hopefully not the dungeons.

Even then, she had faith that her friends wouldn't allow her to remain there long. Airk, being a dragon shifter, was another matter.

Their guide stopped ahead of them, and Airk pulled her to a stop behind him. Practically up against him. The man was a mass of contradictions. Fuck her but don't talk to her after. Bring her the most shattering pleasure, ignore her, then protect her. Put himself between her and whatever happened next.

The guide banged on what looked like a wall to her in the dim. A second later, a crack of light appeared and widened as what now was clearly a door was swung open. Angelika peeked around Airk's bulk, and he tightened his hand on hers in a nonverbal protest. But she smiled at the man she found standing there.

"About time you came to your senses and took us up on our invitation," Bleidd said, totally expressionless.

The leader of the pack she'd been sent to, the older wolf and her mother had had an understanding, though he'd never told Angelika what or how that understanding came to be. Still, the familiarity of his tall, lanky form, deep gray shadowed eyes, and his beard—dark gray with lighter, almost silvery stripes in the hair at his chin, which matched his coloring in wolf form—made her relax. Her shoulders, which had been up around her ears without her even noticing, dropped.

"It's good to see you, too," she said with a grin. She wanted to hug her friend, but with all the sentries around, not to mention the warning light in his eyes, she held back.

He glanced from her to Airk. "I don't remember inviting dragons, though," he said, mouth under his trim beard flattening.

"She insisted," Airk said, just deadpan enough to make her wonder.

Was that... Was he making an actual joke? While confronted with predatory shifters not his kind, even.

My, my, my. We have progress.

Bleidd grunted what might have been a laugh, eyeing Airk with a light in his eyes that looked suspiciously like respect, or maybe commiseration, since he knew her well. Difficult to tell, backlit as he was. "Follow me."

She went to move around Airk, but he didn't let go of her hand, sort of tugging her back to him so that they walked side by side, their escorts falling in line behind them as they traveled through a long, narrow hall. They were clearly now inside the castle, because the walls and even the rounded ceiling over their heads were formed from thick rectangular stones rather than the smooth continuous rock of a cave.

Eventually they turned into an even narrower alcove that housed a medieval-looking winding staircase that reminded her of sections of Ben Nevis. While most of that dragon mountain had been styled after the more ornate French castles, felt even through the general air of neglect after centuries of their wealth being stripped, older parts had a more medieval feel like this one. Definitely a castle.

Up and up and up they wound, passing a few entrances that would take them to a landing or maybe another floor, but they kept going until finally Bleidd peeled off into a hallway. To fit his shoulders through the opening, Airk had to turn sideways and duck like a contortionist. White dragons tended to be taller than most, though not as broad as gold dragons like Brand, who were the biggest of the bunch on average.

This area of the castle was more ornate. Almost as though the vampires had not only abandoned it but taken nothing with them when they went. The original décor seemed to remain, giving one the sense that the building hadn't been touched by centuries of time—rich tapestries, coats of armor, iron weapons on the walls, and she even spotted a room lit up in myriad colors thanks to intricate stained glass windows.

Definitely not dungeons, so that was something.

"In here," Bleidd said.

He opened a thick wooden door and ushered them into a room with a single piece of furniture—a glass-and-steel table, a modern monstrosity that felt so incongruous after the ancient hallway, Angelika even paused.

A conference room rather than a cell. She could work with that.

Bleidd came in with them, turning at the door to address the sentry who'd found them in the woods. "Tell Madrigan we're ready."

The sentry gave a sharp nod, then flicked his gaze to Angelika. "And Jedd?" he asked.

Jedd didn't know she was here? She tried not to wince. She'd been trying hard not to anticipate what his reaction would be, particularly to her showing up with Airk in tow.

After a telling pause, Bleidd nodded, then closed the door.

As he turned slowly on his heel, his face broke into a broad grin, and he opened his arms wide. With a sigh, Angelika walked right into a strong, all-encompassing bear hug. "We missed you," Bleidd said, his voice a rumble against her.

"Me, too."

She really meant it.

Several years living with the pack, being protected by them, getting to know them and love them, trying to fight with them even when they wouldn't let her—they might not be blood, but they were her community, her extended family. More so than the dragons, even. The fire breathers hadn't even known who she was until recently.

"As happy as I am to see you..." Bleidd stepped back, his expression turning serious. "Why are you here?"

For a second, Angelika debated not getting into the details with Bleidd, waiting for the leader, or maybe leaders, he'd no doubt summoned to join them. But if this was going to work, she needed Bleidd on her side. "My dragons need allies."

Bleidd rocked back on his heels in the closest thing to shock she'd ever seen from the calm wolf. Answering surprise sparked in her chest. Did he really think she'd changed her mind and chosen to come here to stay with them? To take them up on their offer of a permanent place in the pack? To take Jedd up on his offer to mate?

Well...shit. Maybe she should have thought of that. She'd break her friend's heart all over again.

The door handle turning had her stiffening, readying herself for the confrontation with her friend. Only the man who stepped inside wasn't Jedd.

This had to be the leader of the Federation of Packs.

Taller than Bleidd, and broader, too, he could almost pass for a dragon shifter in human form. Except his features were more pointed, sharper, and his body leaner. Onyx-black hair, skin a light olive shade, and eyes the color of jade in the sun—she'd bet he was also striking in wolf form.

"My name is Madrigan," the man said in a thick accent Angelika guessed hailed originally from eastern Europe, maybe even from this region of what was now Romania. "I am the head of the Federation."

No specific title.

The small detail got lost as a soft but dangerous warning growl came from the corner of the room where Airk had tucked himself.

Madrigan's gaze snapped to him, though he didn't otherwise move.

"You are *not* a wolf shifter," Airk stated, low and certain. "You are something else."

Madrigan, however, didn't bristle. He didn't even change expression, though she thought maybe a hint of surprised respect flitted over his features. "True."

A non–wolf shifter was leading the worldwide federation of them? How was that possible?

What are you? The question bubbled up, but she swallowed it back. Asking that was considered rude, and she needed to start on the right foot with this man.

"What are you?" Airk asked.

So much for the right foot.

Before Madrigan could reply, Airk raised his head as though scenting the wind. "Canine of some sort. Powerful. Ancient."

Still no visible reaction from the leader. "You have a good nose. Most don't pick up on the difference."

Airk crossed his arms and waited for his answer. Beside her, Bleidd didn't move, but the tension rolled off him all the same. Or maybe the way he subtly scooted so that he was between her and both men was a sign. One of the strongest men she knew was nervous? Why? Was Madrigan dangerous?

Madrigan tipped his head slowly, jade eyes glinting. "I am a berserker."

She blinked rapidly, not expecting that answer. "Really?" She didn't tamp down on her interest fast enough, and it came out in her voice.

Luckily, the man didn't take offense, sending her a smile that might have been amused if it weren't so stiff. "Really."

The ancient species was said to be extinct, or so the stories went. Longer than phoenixes had been gone. Almost two thousand years without a sighting. Legends now. Even more than phoenixes had been.

"That's not possible," Airk said. "Berserkers are—"

"Choose your words wisely," Madrigan warned.

Airk's lips pressed together, but he gave a sharp nod, a show of respect from one apex predator to another. "All my readings would indicate that a berserker is even more dangerous than a feral dragon. How are you not a threat to others?"

Actually, the tiny bit Mama had told them about his kind had been the same. The children of Odin's immortal wolves Geri and Freki, berserkers were thought to be ancient warriors who fought in a trance-like fury. Supposedly the first werewolves and then, later, wolf shifters had descended from this ancient race, their blood diluted by the eons and by mixing with humans.

Madrigan's lips quirked. "We are a thing hideous to behold... but only if we scent blood and battle."

Which meant what? They really went into a frenzy? "How much blood, exactly?" Angelika wondered.

That actually pulled a small smile from the man. "It's not just blood on its own, but the combination of that scent along with adrenaline and the pheromones released by rage."

Rage triggered them?

"Seems dangerous to be around shifters in that case," Airk commented. She nodded, thinking the exact same thing.

Madrigan shrugged.

"Actually," Angelika murmured, offering the man a small smile, ignoring how Airk's jaw popped. "That's exactly the kind of warrior we need."

To give him credit, Madrigan's only response to that was a slight raise to his thick brows. "You may regret thinking that," he said. "But I'm intrigued now. Why have you come here, if not for asylum, little firebird?"

The glance he shot Bleidd, who'd stood silently back during the introductions, wasn't angry, and yet at the same time it carried a hint of accusation. Her old friend shrugged, then flicked a glance at Airk as though saying, "I thought that's what this was about until he showed up with her."

Showed up with his hand down her pants, finger-fucking her into a glorious orgasm, no less. At least they'd left that bit out in the commentary.

Angelika drew herself to her full—though, compared to these men, rather dainty—height, gaze steady on the berserker's. "The dragon shifters need your help."

Madrigan stared for all of two heartbeats before he threw his head back and laughed. Not a harsh bark but a full-bellied laugh that took him several moments to curtail while she glared.

"Why is that funny?" she demanded when his laugh was finally reduced to chuckles.

"Dragons asking wolves for help is fucking hilarious, princess."

That pulled her up a bit short, and her own sense of humor, as well as her knowledge from the wolves' side about the way dragon shifters thought of them, kicked in. He wasn't wrong. Her lips started to twitch. A glance at Airk showed him stone-faced, which only made her want to giggle. But for him she managed to swallow it down, instead saying, "That should tell you what kind of shit we are in now."

That sobered the room right up.

"We?" Madrigan questioned slowly. "I believe you are the unmated phoenix, unless things have changed." Another glance at Airk.

She wouldn't lie to her allies the same way she wouldn't lie to the dragons. "I am not mated."

I'm not even a phoenix. I'm nothing.

"You're not mated?" another male voice, a familiar voice, queried softly from behind her in a voice edged in painful hope.

Angelika whirled around to find Jedd standing in the open doorway.

Hazel eyes wary, her one-time friend didn't come closer. He also looked...thinner, maybe. Reduced somehow. Jedd's Spanish ancestry still showed through in swarthy skin and darker coloring, not to mention the aura of a warrior. Even his black hair screamed "no funny business," cut military close, a tad longer on top. She used to tease him by saying the way it stood straight up made him look like a fuzzy teddy bear that needed a cuddle.

She didn't dare tease him now. "I'm not mated *yet*," she said. The "yet" gentle but deliberate. She couldn't let him get any ideas or give that hope soil to grow in. That wouldn't be fair to him.

The way his strong jaw tightened slightly at the word, he caught her meaning. Her warning. "Why are you here, Angelika?" he asked, harder and harsher than a moment ago.

"For help," she said simply, trying to be gentle with it. "For allies."

Jedd glanced at Airk, and she almost expected a growl from that corner. None came, but a muscle in Jedd's jaw started to tick. "*We* don't need allies," he stated in a rough voice she'd only heard from him those days before the wolf pack left her with the dragons. Without another glance at her, he turned and left the room, closing the door quietly behind him.

· · ·

Airk caught Angelika's wince and the way she glanced at Bleidd.

"Give him a day," the older wolf shifter advised.

She nodded.

"He is wrong about not needing allies," Airk said.

Madrigan's gaze narrowed on Airk, and the dragon inside him tried to break out of the dark hole he had him stuffed down. Even the air was more electric around this man, the ancient, wild magic running through his veins turning to sizzling ozone in Airk's nose. Lightning in a bottle. Fucking dangerous to be anywhere near, especially for Airk.

"I don't believe we've been introduced," Madrigan said.

No mistaking the severity underlying the veneer of politeness. Airk considered him for a brief second. "But you know who I am anyway."

Not a question.

Was that another flash of amusement in the ancient wolf's eyes? "I do. Making a gambit for the throne of the White Clan?"

"No."

The categorical, if brief, denial set Madigan's glossy eyebrows winging. "What else are people to believe when you are personally... attending to...one of the phoenixes?"

Airk stilled. Was *attending to* a euphemism for what he'd done with her in the forest? Because that topic was off-limits. Angelika's wince and the way color flared into her cheeks only pissed him off more, because she'd caught it, too.

When Airk didn't respond, Madrigan shrugged. "So what is your role here?"

Rather than continue to answer questions this man clearly already knew the answers to, Airk pushed back. "If you think, after taking down the Blue, Gold, and Black Clans, that Pytheios will not come for wolf shifters when he's done with dragons, you are delusional."

Bleidd stiffened.

Madrigan cocked his head. "He has no reason to come for the wolves—"

Airk held up one hand, ticking the points off on his fingers. "Your headquarters is located directly between the dragon strongholds in

Everest and Ararat. Dragons already think less of other shifters, but especially wolves. Your rather newly formed Federation is a personal strength that will be seen as a threat. And Pytheios will have wiped out a good portion of the people who do all the work within the clans. Workers that societies build on, cannot function without, and take for granted—plumbing, sewage, food services, childcare. Infrastructure. He will need to replace those losses—"

That finally got a visceral response from the berserker, whose hands balled into fists at his side and lips curled into a sneer. "If that rotting fuck thinks he can enslave my people—"

"He may or may not succeed, but many will die in the fight."

Madrigan's stare turned rock hard as he worked through the likelihood of that happening and the impacts in his head. The man was too ancient and too much a leader, given his position now, not to have already thought of this. Had he already made alliances with other shifters? Bears, maybe? Lions? Coyotes? Hyenas? Tigers? Or perhaps he'd gone outside the shifter community to other supernaturals?

"And your kings would be different?" Disbelief coated the words, making them sticky. Making them harder to argue with.

"Yes."

"Why would I believe you?"

"Because of her." Airk nodded toward Angelika.

She startled, though she didn't move. He could still see it in her somehow. Did she doubt him? Or doubt herself as a reason worth mentioning? Didn't she know what she inspired? How those white dragons all fell under her spell? Believed in her? Hells, pledged themselves to her in such a way they were bound for life?

"Me *and* my sisters," she qualified.

Airk stared, waiting for her to shift her gaze his way so he could shake his head. Angelika alone was enough. But she didn't or wouldn't. She kept her focus trained on the berserker.

"Phoenixes," Madrigan mused. "They'll bring their kings to heel."

Before a growl could rip up his throat, Angelika made a sound that was close enough. "My sisters and their mates are *partners*," she insisted. "Not...dogs with masters."

The pause said she'd been deliberate with that word choice.

"Good for them." Madrigan's voice was pure sarcasm.

Angelika ignored it—deliberately, Airk would bet—shooting the man a suddenly placid smile that seemed indestructible. One Airk was closely familiar with. "Yes," she said. "We all think so."

As though she'd taken the wolf's words as sincere.

Madrigan's tiny frown said her response threw him, but Angelika didn't give him a chance to recover. "My brothers-by-blood are good men. Fair men. They want peace. They want Pytheios gone. And that is all. Maybe this is a chance for the Federation to start a *new* relationship with dragons. We can be powerful allies, rather than distant acquaintances at best."

Acquaintances was putting it mildly. Enemies wasn't quite right. A wary standoff was probably closer. No love lost between the species, for certain, and that had been true since before Airk's incarceration.

Madrigan blew out a long breath, gaze sliding to Bleidd, who had remained silent. Then back to Angelika. "I assume you wish for me to speak with these kings and their phoenixes?"

Instantly, her body vibrated, though not visibly. Almost as though he was so attuned to her, he could sense it on the air. Could the others feel that? Excitement. Hope. The woman was incorrigible.

"That would be best," was all she said.

Madrigan nodded, then addressed Bleidd. "Help her set it up via the most secure channels we have."

"Of course."

"I'll wait to address the Federation leaders until after I meet with the kings."

He gave Airk a curt nod, then took Angelika's hand and offered a courtly bow over it, even clicking his heels. That should have been the end of it, but the berserker looked up, a light in his green eyes that sent tension stringing through Airk's spine.

"Possibly the best way to solidify any kind of allyship between our people would be through mating."

CHAPTER FOURTEEN

Well, *that* was a twist Angelika hadn't seen coming. A mating proposal from a creature even more ancient than dragons. "Errr..."

The thing was, aligning with a powerful man like Madrigan made sense. Especially if dragon kings were out of the question, which they were for the moment. She didn't dare glance anywhere near Airk's corner. Plus, there was Jedd to consider. Technically, as far as wolves went, he had first dibs.

Oh my gods. Dibs. What is wrong with me?

Still, this entire scenario brought up a sticky question. Jedd was her friend and would only ever be that to her, but if she was going to make a mating of convenience, a friend was better than a stranger. Except, given Jedd's feelings compared to her own, doing so would be utterly unfair to him. Madrigan, meanwhile, would be under no delusion as to her reasons for the union.

But suddenly the thought of mating for convenience when Airk was who she wanted—

Angelika cut that thought off at the knees. "Certainly an option worth considering."

The berserker smiled. One that reached his eyes. She liked that about him and smiled back.

"Please do," he urged, then stood, nodded at Bleidd, and left the room.

The older wolf blew out a long breath. "That went better than expected."

Angelika raised her eyebrows. "Oh?"

"He's…unpredictable."

Unpredictable? Or unstable? "So, you're saying don't get my hopes up about the alliance?"

His expression turned uneasy. "The council will decide, but Madrigan can be…compelling…when he wants to. Likely they'll go the direction he sways them."

Terrific. Hopefully his swaying them wasn't tied solely to that offer of mating.

"Come on," Bleidd said, holding out a hand to her.

Airk followed silently as Bleidd led her to a room like the war rooms in every dragon mountain she'd been in—all technology, monitors, and sensors. A message was sent to Ladon via a backchannel system, setting a date and time and specific mirror for Meira to do her thing. Her method was the safest to communicate by as no one could trace or intercept the signal.

Given that it was still the middle of the night, Angelika didn't expect to hear back until morning. Bleidd obviously didn't, either, because next he led them through more labyrinthine medieval halls until they got to what felt like a more modern wing of the castle with higher ceilings and décor from more recent centuries.

"This is our pack's hall," he said, stopping in what appeared to be a cozy living space set up with couches, lamps, and a thick Persian rug. A kitchen was pointed out down one hall and living quarters down another. "Don't venture beyond this point into the castle without one of us escorting you."

She nodded. Airk said nothing, as usual.

Then Bleidd took them to a bedroom. He paused at the door, taking in both their faces. "I'd give you separate rooms, but—"

"I'm not leaving her," Airk stated. Calm but unequivocal.

The sentiment wasn't a surprise, but the fact that he'd subject himself to being alone with her again was.

Bleidd closed the door behind them after pointing out the en suite bathroom, the fact that some clothes had been put in here for them, that they could help themselves to breakfast in the kitchen in the morning, and that he'd come get them for the meeting with Angelika's sisters.

"I'll take the floor," Airk said. Not looking at her again.

Angelika was too tired to argue by now. "Okay."

She went into the bathroom, grateful to find an unused toothbrush still in the package. She brushed her teeth and washed up as best she could. When she came out, Airk slipped past her, closing the door behind him without a word.

Shaking her head, she took a second to pull the blanket from the bed and lay it out on the floor, folded like a sleeping bag, adding a pillow at one end. Then she pulled a T-shirt and shorts out of the armoire, dressed quickly, and slipped between the sheets on the bed.

Impossible to relax, though.

Even her human ears picked up the faint sounds of Airk moving around the bathroom, washing up. Then a soft *click*, and she held her breath, resisting looking around.

He stood there in unmoving silence for a long moment. Too long. What was he doing?

Giving up—patience never did overrule her curious side—she lifted her head to find him staring at the makeshift bed she'd made for him. "Do you not use a blanket?" she asked.

She'd thought of that but figured he could choose what to use.

His jaw worked. "I learned to sleep on a rock slab with no…"

"No pillows or blankets?"

He shook his head.

The small action sent an answering ache through her. An ache for a boy who learned to sleep without even human comforts like a pillow. Treated no better than an animal. He must have felt so… alone. "Do you use a bed now?"

Now that he was out and had a choice. Maybe he'd grown so used to the rock that he preferred the floor? They'd used a bed when they slept together after their first time, but that could have been his way of taking care of her.

His shrug could've meant anything.

"You won't hurt my feelings if you don't use those," she said.

Another beat of silence. What would he do if she got up and wrapped her arms around him? Urged him to bed and snuggled into him? Not for sex, but for a little warmth and companionship.

Except she'd promised herself that she'd stop all that. Leave him be. For her sake as much as his now.

Angelika dropped her head to her own pillow, staring at the wall illuminated by the light from the bathroom. "Goodnight, Airk," she said.

"Goodnight," he said after another long pause.

She closed her eyes as the soft shuffle of a blanket reached her ears.

• • •

"Angel-baby!"

A man Airk recognized, stocky with ruddy skin and russet-colored hair, except for the white streak at one temple, jumped up from one of the couches in the common living area and rushed Angelika. At the same time, three other men with him perked up, grinning from ear to ear.

Airk gripped the corner of the wall where the hallway met the living area, letting the granite bricks dig into his palms. Either that or decapitate the man who dared to swoop Angelika off her feet, spinning her in circles before setting her back down. Except then the dick proceeded to lay a big, sloppy kiss right on her lips.

The growl that ripped out of him froze every creature in the room. At least twenty of them in total.

Angelika rolled her eyes without looking at him. "Ignore him, Rafe. He's fine."

The red-haired wolf shifter didn't seem to agree. Very deliberately, he took his hands off her and stepped back. "I don't think he is," he said, not taking his gaze off Airk.

Every other eye in the room also trained on him. *Terrific. Way to make friends, Airk.*

Which was such an Angelika thing to think, he almost heard the words in her voice.

Gods, the way this woman was wending her way into his life—body, mind, and spirit—he should run. Last night he'd almost reversed his position—again—and accepted that damn mating proposal hanging between them. Not because the berserker had offered, which had sent Airk's dragon into the closest thing to a panic the animal side of him got.

No. Instead, he'd lost his shit over the bed she'd made him.

He made her come. Twice. Ignored her afterward. Twice. But despite all that, there she went, making him a soft place to sleep. Fuck.

"I am fine," he said. Although his voice was still dragon. He swallowed, forcing himself to find that place of numbness. "I am fine," he repeated, sounding more normal.

The wolves in the room visibly relaxed and turned back to Angelika. The other three men who'd appeared the most delighted got to their feet to hug her, though each cast him a wary glance as they did.

"We knew you'd come to your senses." A man with black hair, blacker eyes, and deeply sable skin gave her a half-cocked grin. "After all, who could deny our awesomeness."

Angelika laughed. "Not me, Hunter. I wouldn't dare. The awesomeness is too great."

"Are you staying?" the youngest of the group—blond hair, pale gray eyes, and paler skin—asked, an eager light in his eyes. Not juvenile. Also not bothering to hide his mooning expression.

"I wish I could, Rigel." Angelika reached over to give his arm a squeeze, and the adoration only increased.

"It's not fair to ask her that," the other man snapped. Sandy brown hair, lightly tanned, and a pretty face marred only by a previously broken nose, he cast a glare in Airk's direction, as though he were directly responsible for Angelika's not being able to stay with them. Or was that a general hatred for dragons putting that hard light in the man's eyes?

"Cairn," Angelika said his name in a soft voice, more pleading than warning.

Cairn pulled his gaze back to her.

The Rafe fellow grinned suddenly, though he didn't try to hug her again. "Damn it's good to see you again."

She chuckled. "It hasn't been *that* long."

"When one of our pack isn't here, we all feel it," Rigel insisted.

The pack? They'd accepted her into their ranks officially?

A similarly youthful woman crossed the room and hugged Angelika before curling into Rigel's side, a tad possessive, though Airk knew she had no reason to be jealous. Anyone could see with Rigel it was more a case of heroine worship than puppy love. "We missed you, is what they're saying."

"I missed you, too," Angelika said, no longer teasing.

A pulse of something reached for him, as though her emotions were tangible. Sadness. A deep sadness he was more than familiar with. She truly missed these people.

As Airk watched, the rest of the wolves in the room moved into a circle around her, almost the same way they would if attacked by other predators, when they would put a child or cub at the center of a grouping for protection. The act was so obviously one of welcoming one of their own back that even his dragon didn't protest this time. If anything, both Airk's human and animal halves watched from the outside with the strangest urge to be…included. Angelika seemed to inspire this kind of personal connection and loyalty wherever she went.

The circle broke up, and everyone returned to seats throughout the room, and he found himself able to breathe again. Angelika cast him a querying glance. Airk crossed his arms and leaned against the wall. He wasn't moving. A signal she clearly understood, because she shook her head and sat down. Facing him, at least, so he could read her expressive face.

"Tell me everything I've missed," she urged.

Which got the discussion rolling. As though they'd been waiting for the chance to share with her, mostly about the wolves and what they'd been doing since they'd parted from her. Airk had to admit, the way Angelika listened and the questions she asked, she was frankly interested. Interested and invested in each as a person and a friend. No wonder people fell in love with her.

The soft tread of footfall behind him had Airk sniffing the air, then relaxing. Not Jedd or Madrigan.

"Ready?" Bleidd asked, prowling into the room.

Angelika stopped mid-chuckle to look at the alpha wolf, sighed, then got to her feet. "We'll catch up more later," she promised.

Airk came off his wall, and together they followed Bleidd from the room. It didn't escape Airk's attention that Jedd never made an appearance. No doubt Angelika noticed as well, though she kept her thoughts on the matter to herself.

Airk had seen the way the wolf shifter looked at her, watched her, when they'd been in Ben Nevis together, and that had been before she'd told him that the wolf wanted to mate her.

Eventually they stepped into a room that had clearly once been the music room of the castle. Given the way all the instruments—a piano, a harp, and something else piano-like but smaller—were covered in white sheets, he guessed wolf shifters had no interest in the space. Surprising that vampires had, though. Or maybe this castle had originally been human? Still, the ornately carved wood paneling depicting cherubs frolicking through nature gave the room an oddly dark and light feel all at the same time.

In the center of the room, someone had set up a mirror.

Bronze with similar spring images—leaves and flowers and whatnot—carved and molded into the metal with a chubby-cheeked cupid right at the top aiming his arrow down on those looking into the glass. Airk narrowed his eyes at the thing. Was that a play on the Narcissus and Echo mythology, making the looker in the glass fall in love with their own reflection?

"Princess." Madrigan strolled into the room as though he hadn't a care in the world.

Except the casual attitude belied leashed power. One whiff of the berserker, and Airk's dragon turned instantly alert, ready to challenge the man, growling low in Airk's head, the sound reverberating as though his skull were a belfry.

The berserker went straight for Angelika, which didn't help Airk any, bowing over her hand the way he had the night before when taking his leave.

He straightened with a smile. "Did you think about my offer?"

"I did," she said with an answering one, white-blue eyes glinting with an amusement Airk didn't understand.

What could possibly be amusing about an offer of mating?

Airk curled his hands into fists until his nails, though cut short, dug into his palms, drawing blood.

Madrigan searched her eyes for a moment before sighing. "Still considering, I see. That's acceptable. After this long, I've learned to be a patient man."

The berserker turned, and Airk didn't miss the significant glance at his own hands, which were still fisted. The bastard smelled the blood and wanted him to know it.

But Airk had learned patience, too. He didn't move, didn't uncurl his fists, and didn't look away.

"Is there something we should be concerned about?" a female voice interrupted.

Meira stood in the reflection of the gilded mirror, amusement visible in curiously raised eyebrows and a small smirk. Beside her, Samael's dark eyes twinkled with a similar humor but edged with a cunning assessment.

Behind her, Skylar rolled her eyes. "Alphas."

Which made Ladon growl, only to get an elbow to the ribs for it.

Kasia, however, didn't smile, frowning instead as she glanced between Madrigan, Airk, and Angelika. Brand must've picked up on her reaction, because he smoothed a hand down her back in a suspiciously soothing action.

Angelika ignored her sisters and took over as though none of that had happened, performing a quick round of introductions.

"Madrigan is the leader of the Federation," she ended. "And a berserker."

"The fuck you say," Ladon snapped, not in irritation but instead pure distrust.

Brand said nothing, but he did the stony, pissed thing with his face that meant he wasn't happy. About the same response that Airk had the day before.

Samael, meanwhile, crossed his arms, gaze narrowing but speculative. "We should listen to him."

"Why, exactly?" Brand snarled.

"Because the wolves wouldn't have let us see him and know what he was unless they were showing us a sign of trust."

Madrigan stepped closer to the mirror, ignoring the kings as his gaze moved searchingly from sister to sister. Then he dropped his head forward, as though the weight of whatever he was thinking had become too much for him.

"When you've lived as long as I have, you begin to think you've seen it all. That nothing could surprise you ever again." He murmured the words, more to himself than to the people listening and watching with a variation of confusion or suspicion.

Then he lifted his head, and in the same motion he dropped to one knee. "I pledge my loyalty to the phoenixes of the house of Amon."

Beside him, Angelika squeaked a gasp.

In the mirror, every person in the room stilled, then each couple glanced at each other, no doubt communicating between themselves using the special connection mates had.

"Why would you do that now?" Angelika asked. "We haven't discussed anything yet."

Madrigan's smile was this side of self-deprecating, and he rose to his feet, addressing her directly. "I may not have known your parents, but I knew your grandmother and her mate. And the phoenix before that. And the one before that."

Holy hells.

The berserker glanced at each of the sisters, lingering longest on Skylar with her deeply black hair...the same coloring as their grandmother. Almost an exact image of her, actually. Because Airk had known that phoenix, too.

Hells, her final prediction both saved his life...and ruined it.

"There is no denying, looking at you, what blood runs through your veins," Madrigan said. "I've already discussed with Bleidd how he came to harbor one of you and what he witnessed while under the dragon kings' protection." He nodded at the men in the mirror. "I had to see with my own eyes."

"*I* wasn't proof enough?" Angelika drew her shoulders back stiffly, an emotion flashing in her eyes that Airk could only guess at. But the way his chest tightened, he had a feeling he knew. That lesser-than belief, as though she was somehow unworthy, the one she tried to hide from everyone, had struck again, he would hazard.

Madrigan didn't seem to take in the hurt she was hiding behind a thin veneer of curiosity. "I apologize. I needed to see you all together to be certain. After all, Pytheios claims to have a phoenix as well."

Given several blinks from the others, they caught the "claims" in that sentence the same as he did. Did the berserker know something they didn't?

Angelika let out a long breath. "Well...that was easier than I anticipated."

Madrigan chuckled. No one else did.

Glancing in Airk's direction, Angelika raised her eyebrows in question, as though to say, "What now?"

He shrugged. This was her plan. He was along as a witness and dubious bodyguard.

"We should go to the white dragons now," she decided.

"*No.*"

The snarled word had everyone turning to find Jedd standing in the back corner, just inside the door, his gaze trained on Angelika, whose expression spasmed with something close to pain.

After a second, she cleared her throat. "Please discuss next steps with everyone while Jedd and I talk."

Airk remained stock-still. As still as Everest on a clear, cold night between storms, and trying to root his feet into the plush carpet. Either that or roar his rejection of that idea.

Madrigan clearly didn't like it any better than Airk, expression turning edgy, lips curled in a sneer. "Of…course." His words belied the displeasure in his eyes.

"Thank you." Casting a furtive little glance in Airk's direction, she moved across the room, following the wolf shifter into the hallway without a word.

"How serious is it?" Madrigan demanded of Bleidd, whose head was turned, staring at the closed door they'd left through.

"He asked to mate her."

"*What?*" This from Skylar, Kasia's own exclamation blending with her sister's. Only Meira appeared unsurprised.

"She said no?" Madrigan asked slowly, tone musing.

"She wanted someone else." Bleidd turned back to the room, looking directly at Airk.

Fuck.

Fuck on so many levels. But mostly because his dragon wanted him to beat both the wolf and the berserker back from the prize he had set his heart on. Claimed. Despite Airk's human half rejecting the idea.

Either man would be better for her than he ever would. Solidifying an alliance with the wolves and dragons, providing her protection. Even turning her. Unlike dragon shifters, with wolves all it took was a bite. No sign the human could handle the fire, no fated mates. Just choice. At least then she wouldn't be so frailly human, her life span so…curtailed.

Which meant that, either man she chose, Angelika would be better off.

I should walk away now. Take himself off the board of players.

CHAPTER FIFTEEN

A ngelika didn't say anything to Jedd. Not until he'd led them far away from the room housing the dragon shifter she wanted, her sisters, their kings, the closest thing to a father figure she'd had in her life, and the berserker who'd made an offer to mate her. Having all of them listening in was awkward at best—and a guaranteed blowup from someone at worst—so she was glad that he took them somewhere private.

Back to Jedd's room, apparently, in a different corridor off the pack's common area.

He closed the door behind her as she took in the space. Not unlike the one she and Airk had shared last night. Taking a deep breath, she turned to face him.

Putting aside the tension, she searched the lines and crags of his face, more haggard than she remembered. "You look—"

"Don't."

She buttoned her lips closed and waited.

"I thought…" He stopped and blew out a long breath through his nose, hazel eyes intent on hers, though he didn't come near her.

"I'd hoped that after a little time apart, you'd realize…" He stopped again and ran his hand over the buzz cut of his hair, the sound rasping in the silence.

"I wish I had."

He flinched at that. "I know. I could see it yesterday. I could see it in all your texts."

He hadn't answered any of those. Had she just made it worse for him? "I didn't want to—"

"You didn't. I needed the space."

"You're one of the best men I've ever known."

His lips crooked slightly. "That doesn't make me feel any better. When is the mating, anyway?"

She would never lie to Jedd. He'd been a true friend to her since the moment she'd arrived. "He said no."

A couple times, but the last one was…painful.

Airk meant it. He might want her body, but he would never let himself want more than that. Hells, he resented the shit out of wanting that much. She could see it.

Pleading wasn't in her nature. Pushing where she wasn't wanted wasn't, either. Stating what she wanted for herself, yes. Begging, hard no. Him wanting only her body wasn't good enough for her. So Airk was off the table, but at the same time, she didn't love Jedd enough to mate. She knew that much, too.

Jedd frowned. "Why the fuck would he say no?"

Angelika huffed a laugh at the question, loving her friend all the more for being baffled that Airk could turn her down. "He thinks he's too dangerous to be around me."

Jedd straightened, suddenly very much the warrior he was. "He's right."

Angelika shrugged, not wanting to argue about it.

He stared at her a long, quiet moment, and she waited. Waited for whatever he was working out in his mind.

"I've missed you, Angie."

She bit her lip against a sudden, unexpected sting of tears. "Me, too."

They'd spent almost every day for the last few years attached at the hip. At first with him as a bodyguard, assigned by Bleidd. Other than her sisters, and now maybe Airk—despite his not wanting to—no one knew her better.

Jedd's lips twisted. "I'll always love you," he said, almost like a warning.

She waited.

"But if the only way to have you in my life is as my friend...I'll take it."

Her stomach knotted and gnarled around itself, because the last thing she wanted was to put him in a position where he ended up hurt. But at the same time, she'd hoped...in the most selfish of ways... "Are you sure?"

He gave a curt nod and opened his arms.

Letting out a pent-up breath of her own, Angelika walked right into him and absorbed the hug he gave her with closed eyes. "Are you really, really sure?" she mumbled into his chest. Asking again because she needed to. Because she knew this was his decision, but maybe accepting wasn't being fair to him, either. "I wouldn't hurt you for the world—"

"I'm sure."

She'd give him the respect to make that choice without questioning him further.

Jedd took her by the hand and led her to the small settee in the corner, a delicate-looking one that creaked under his size. "Fill me in. Because you need a plan if you don't want to end up dead."

Angelika tried to be quick. By the time they made it back to the room, Madrigan seemed to be finishing up with her sisters and the kings. He turned with a smile that didn't reach his eyes. "All settled?" he asked.

She let Jedd nod.

Airk, meanwhile, stared straight through her.

Angelika's ever-optimistic heart shriveled a little bit more.

He should be with her to talk to the white dragons at their headquarters, because of his story and who he was. They needed to see him and understand what happened. But after that, regardless of the outcome and no matter what was going on with the war, she'd let him go. To be an assassin, to go rogue, whatever he decided.

Decision made, she tipped up her chin and walked straight to Madrigan.

A move Jedd, at least, was braced for because they'd already discussed it. She would consider the berserker's offer more seriously. If she couldn't have Airk, mating elsewhere for the political alliance was still worth considering. Jedd's heart was too involved. Madrigan's wasn't, which would put the mating on equal footing.

"I must go," she said.

Madrigan tipped his head, searching her eyes. "I know. Your sisters explained."

She hesitated. How the heck was she supposed to lead into something like this? Especially with the particular audience she was dealing with.

"Maybe after your trip, we could get to know each other a little better?" he suggested.

Angelika wasn't sure if she was breathing a sigh of relief that he'd handled that for her or sucking in the bravery needed to go through with it. "I would like that."

Abruptly, Airk stepped closer, though nowhere near touching. "Are you ready?"

Madrigan's smile turned…mischievous was the only word that came close. Then suddenly he leaned down and placed a chaste kiss at the corner of her mouth, but to Airk it would look like a lingering caress.

"Seems you have some decisions to make, Angelika Amon."

Angelika huffed a surprised laugh. Whatever this man was, he had sworn loyalty to her sisters, pledged the Federation of Packs as an ally to dragons, and offered her a place of safety and leadership at his side. Not to mention harboring what she suspected might be a wicked sense of humor. Maybe he was more worth considering than she'd convinced herself of already.

"Some lucky girl should snap you up," she whispered back.

And earned a laconic shrug. "That girl *could* be you," he pointed out in a wry voice.

Time would tell. Following her heart, granted with a good dash of revenge and logic, had gotten her only so far.

Rather than give an answer, she kissed his cheek. Then turned to Airk, who might as well have been one of Meira's gargoyle friends, carved from stone. Together they stepped through the mirror to where her sisters and mates waited in Ben Nevis.

Thanks to time zones making it almost bedtime there by now, she and Airk both took time to eat, shower, and change—this time into something appropriate for a princess and a man with royal blood in his veins.

A feminine power suit in navy with a pencil skirt. The jacket showed off some cleavage, was belted, and ended in a ruffle, no blouse underneath. And her shoes were pure boss bitch, shiny and cream-colored with peep toes three-inch heels. Not really her style, but she'd live with it for what they needed to get done.

Airk, meanwhile, had refused to wear a full suit. Instead, he'd gone with the suit pants, an ultrafine button-down shirt, and a vest that only highlighted the power of his shoulders and back. Her lady parts pulsed several beats at the sight, and damned if he didn't still, then lift his head slightly as though scenting her reaction.

Which he probably could. Damn it.

Well after dark in Scotland, after another round of hugs and quietly spoken words, Meira once again lit her fire and opened a portal to a reflection halfway around the world.

"The others who've pledged their loyalty are already there," her sister said.

"Let's hope they've laid the groundwork well," Angelika said. They could be walking into a fight, and she needed to be mentally ready for that.

"Let us hope they do not decapitate us the second we show our faces," Airk muttered, apparently thinking the same.

On that pleasant thought, she nodded at Meira. In seconds, the portal was opened, and they looked through the reflection at the headquarters of the White Clan.

The mountain that would have been her childhood home, had both her parents lived and ruled as they should have.

The room Meira had selected to send them to was basic. An empty conference room with a glass wall, one that was supposed to be near the room used by the current temporary ruler and Volos's Curia Regis for their daily meetings. Not only that, but inside information provided by the men already marked with her family crest told them that the king and his council met every morning right at this hour.

Perfect timing.

Before Angelika could step through, a spark suddenly jumped out of the mirror. Glowing red-gold, it hopped across the stone floor of Meira's room, like embers coming off a forger's hammer.

Frowning, she glanced at Meira. "Was that you?"

Her sister's identical frown turning more and more confused told her enough. "I don't think so."

The answer came not a second later, as a line of sparks and embers appeared in the upper right corner. Then the line of fire crawled down the glass, almost as though eating away the mirror before them. The further down the reflection it moved, the more another reflection was revealed. Like peeling away a sticker or label to show something else underneath.

Impossible to determine what, until a viciously handsome, vomit-inducing visage appeared in the space cleared. Red-brown eyes alight with fire, high cheekbones, warm golden skin perfect and glowing with health, and hair as black as onyx.

Pytheios.

No longer rotting. Entirely whole. And smug as a son of a bitch.

"I see the gang's all here," he murmured in a voice slick as snail snot and coated in ash. No matter the improvement in his outward appearance, his voice remained the same.

The line of embers crept lower and farther out, revealing his witch, Rhiamon, behind him, white curls floating up around her face and eyes inky pools as she worked her magic, making this happen.

"Now where could you be going?" Pytheios mused.

In a move that she didn't see coming, Airk grabbed Angelika's hand, yanked her through the portion of the reflection still showing the White Clan's conference room, then turned and smashed the wall of glass. All the reflections disappeared in a resounding, shattering crash.

. . .

F uck.
Airk was starting to understand why that was Brand Astarot's favorite word. All the kings', come to think on it. But that one word encompassed a plethora of situations.

"I guess we just announced our presence with authority," Angelika muttered at his side.

"He came for *you*," he said and winced. Leashing the growl coming from his dragon took more effort than it should have. The thing was rioting inside him.

"I know." No reaction from her.

"He can take over Meira's reflections."

She cringed at that. "Yeah. That's a problem."

"We have no idea if he saw where she sent us."

"Then we'd better work fast."

Before he could stop her, she stepped through the gap left by the wall he'd smashed, her shoes crunching on the shattered glass, and out into a corridor beyond. The space looked like a human business more than anything, with several rows of cubes backing up to a wall of glass-sided conference rooms of varying sizes, though no one occupied the area. Angelika rushed a few doors down toward the room where the Curia Regis was supposed to be meeting, only to pull up short as men and women spilled out into the same hallway, no doubt on alert after the violence of their arrival.

"What the seven hells?" A man old enough that his face sagged around the jowls, skin spotted by age, snarled.

Airk sprinted for Angelika.

But Angelika addressed that man directly, not so much as hesitating as she kept moving straight for him. "Mös?" she queried. "My name is Angelika Amon. I am the daughter of Zilant Amon and Serefina Hanyu, sister to the phoenixes, sister-by-blood to the kings of the Blue, Black, and Gold Clans."

"I know who you are," the older man who had been King Volos's

Beta snapped.

Airk stopped her with a hand on her arm before she could chest bump the dragon shifter, but she refused to let him put himself bodily between them. She bent a look so full of hatred on the white dragon shifter, Airk jerked in shock to see such an emotion on her delicate, usually kind and smiling features.

"Then you know I have come to take my family's throne back," she stated in a hard, cold voice so unlike Angelika, another jolt shook him.

This was *not* the plan. She was supposed to be negotiating.

Her chin went up, every inch of her imperial, ice-chip eyes trained on the leader's face. "Step down now and help me, and maybe I will spare your life."

Fuck.

Except the Beta, rather than killing her then and there, considered her in silence. "Loyalty to the Amon family is no longer mine to give you."

Not boasting, more like...tired.

Angelika wasn't expecting that, either. She frowned. "What?"

The smile that ghosted across Mös's features only made him appear older. "Your new followers are loyal, my dear. And convincing."

If anything, Angelika appeared shaken. "I don't understand."

Mös sucked at his teeth. "I'm saying you're too late."

"What the fuck does that mean?" Airk demanded.

A flickered glance in his direction wavered, then held. "Gods above. You are the exact balance of your parents, boy."

A moment of recognition. A moment of acknowledgment, then the Beta was back to Angelika.

"Someone else got here before you." Bitterness coated the words in filth.

"How...adorable." The low rumble came from the dark behind the gathered council members. "Thinking you had any right to the throne." The body of cowards parted like the biblical Red Sea to reveal a man Airk had met before.

In his dungeon.

Brock Hagan.

Airk knew *all* about this man. The son of Uther Hagan, the dragon Pytheios had put on the Gold Clan's throne after Brand's own family were all murdered. Uther had stood there and watched with glee as Pytheios had killed Airk's parents. Helped, even. Of all the kings, the one most culpable for following that rotting-souled red prick. His son Brock now claimed Brand was the usurper and the gold throne was his by right. More than that, though. Pytheios had declared this man to be his own legal son and heir.

Brock, like Brand, was massive, a wall of muscle. His dark bronze eyes, which could almost pass for a black dragon's, were trained on Angelika, glinting with savage satisfaction.

"After I claim this remaining phoenix," Brock said, "I shall rule over two clans—both Gold and White—bowing only to the High King himself."

Pure instinct crashed through Airk in a conflagration of flame and fury.

With a roar that came from some unholy place within him, he rushed the man. Plowing his shoulder into Brock's gut, Airk drove his legs. Astonishment at the violence and speed of his action, perhaps, stayed the gold dragon's reaction, allowing Airk to propel them both through the council's larger conference room, chairs flying in their wake, and straight through the window that looked out into the mountain-high atrium.

With a splintering of glass, they burst through, and then gravity yanked them both down.

Except Brock could shift and fly.

Airk couldn't.

CHAPTER SIXTEEN

Angelika wasn't sure if the screams in her head actually made it out of her throat or not. She sprinted after Airk, who'd moved with inhuman, even un-dragon-like speeds—more like a vampire than anything.

The dragon shifters beat her to the broken window and were already staring downward by the time she got there. Pushing her way through bodies with frantic hands, she leaned over, careful to avoid the jagged edges of the knee-high ledge left by the remaining wall. But she couldn't see him. No plummeting bodies, no dragon wings. Nothing but a tall chasm—a chamber, really—not round but shaped with the ins and outs of the mountain itself.

Mös happened to be standing beside her. Without thinking, she clutched his arm. "Where'd they go?"

Please, gods, don't let him be dead.

The Beta's answer didn't help, though. "Brock shifted and took Airk outside."

Outside. Oh gods. To what? Rend him into pieces in front of anyone who cared to watch? She jerked her head around, looking over the shocked faces of the men and women with her. Someone had to stop him, but no one was following.

"Get me out there," she ordered.

Mös frowned, white-blue gaze scanning her face. "It's not safe."

"I don't care."

Something that might have been anger rippled over his features. "I won't sign my death warrant with Pytheios by helping you now."

Cowards. Fucking cowards. All of them.

"The rest of you abandoned Airk once, but I won't. Not ever."

But she could see in the Beta's face that he wasn't going to budge. Which meant she'd have to force his hand.

"You want to keep me safe to hand me over to your new leader? Fine. Then you'd better be fast."

Before he had time to do more than frown in confusion, she vaulted the low wall, throwing herself into the abyss, turning onto her back in the air—thankful she'd gone with Skylar to learn to skydive, because *whoa*—so that she could see the horror twisting his face as she fell away.

For a heartbeat, she regretted the rash move as he didn't budge. But then it worked. Mös pitched himself after her, shifting with remarkable speed. She wasn't even halfway down to the atrium floor before he caught up to her, snatching her up in his massive talons, careful not to slice her with the edges of claws built to rend through diamond-hard dragon scales.

This was not how she'd pictured any of this visit going. That was for damn sure.

Angelika turned in his grasp and wrapped herself around one digit, watching where they went. Mös didn't stop their headlong plummet until the last moment, flaring his wings and shooting them over the tops of shops and the marketplace that took up the base of the mountain, similar to the Ben Nevis setup. Then out across the hanger and training area before bursting into pristine blue skies surrounding a mountain bounded by more mountains.

Angelika didn't bother with her surroundings, though. Instead, she was busy searching all around her, everywhere not blocked by the clotted-cream-colored dragon carrying her, searching for Brock and Airk. Brock, mostly, who would be bigger. Based on his eyes, he'd be a gold so dark he might look like antiqued bronze. In these skies, he should be easy to spot.

Please don't have already killed him.

Below them, more white dragons poured from the mountain. The Curia Regis had followed. Maybe others.

"Tell them to find Brock," she yelled at the Beta. "Get Airk away from him—"

A sound that she'd never in her life heard screeched from somewhere out in front of her, lower to the ground. A sound of pure agony ripped from the throat of a man.

"There." Mös's voice sounded in her head as he tipped his wings. "On the ground."

Wind rushed around her, stealing any further sounds she might have caught as she searched the ground in that direction. She couldn't see anything other than trees and mountain below until a patch of dark brown started to move. What was vaguely difficult to make out at first transformed gradually in her sight into wings, then a tail, until finally Brock lifted off from the ground.

"Do you see Airk?" she asked Mös.

"No." Pause. *"Seven hells."* He tipped his wings, turning them back toward the entrance, away from where Brock and Airk were.

"Wait!" Angelika tried to turn in his grasp, but he tightened around her, not letting her move. "Where are you going? Airk—"

"Dead. Brock is coming for you, and I'm not getting caught between a dragon and his prize."

Dead? Airk was...dead?

Angelika stilled in Mös's talon, eyes closing tight against the detonation of sorrow that hit her heart so hard she thought it might stop beating altogether. "Are you sure?" The question came out small.

"I didn't see him, but there'd be no other reason Brock would leave him."

The old dragon was right. Angelika dropped her forehead against the leathery digit she was wrapped around, breathing through her nose, trying to keep her head even as everything inside her was splintering, shattering with cataclysmic force. This was too much. Too many sacrifices. How could she do this without Airk beside her, keeping her out of trouble while she dragged him headlong into it?

Mös landing on the outcropping that turned into the large indoor platform jerked her out of her agony, if only for a second. She needed to take Brock down. She couldn't be taken. She'd fix that first, then mourn when the danger was past.

Released by Mös, she stepped back on shaky legs and lifted her gaze. "Please," she begged.

Scaled brows drew down over one large dragon eye facing her.

"You'll have the backing of my sisters and their kings. Three clans behind you. Don't let him have me, and you have my word."

The white dragon shook his head, but there had been a smidge of hesitation.

"Do you really want a gold dragon on your throne? Is that what is best for this clan?"

The eye she could see went hard, then lit with the fires of fury. Suddenly Mös pivoted, wings out, blocking her from Brock's view, and blasted a challenge at the gold dragon now visible in the skies. At the same time, more white dragons landed or appeared from behind her, lining up on the Beta's right and left and behind her, surrounding them both. All with wings out, presenting a united front.

Airk. I wish you could see your kin. They only needed a chance. Even Mös.

She'd done nothing to earn this loyalty beyond being who she was and the promise she'd made, but she vowed that she would in that moment. Even without Airk.

A notion that wrapped around her heart like a clamp, and the fates were turning the screws tighter and tighter.

"Where are you, little firebird?" Brock's voice sounded in her head.

Angelika shifted closer to Mös's leg, trying to stay out of sight, listening for Brock flying overhead as he searched for her under the veil of dragon wings.

A shadow filtered through, passing close by. The white dragons held their positions. Brock would have to have a death wish to try to get her out from under them.

"She's mine." He was speaking to all the dragons now. *"Release her to me, and maybe I'll convince the High King to let you live—"*

A new horrendous sound shattered the stillness, coming from below them down the side of the mountain—agony and terror and fury.

Angelika's heart jump-started as though she'd been shocked back to life.

Airk.

He was alive...and no longer human.

...

The sound of Airk's dragon blasted from his body on a wall of anguish and fury. Because he'd heard. Lying on the ground, out cold, Airk's dragon had still heard Brock's claim. The gold dragon was going for Angelika.

And Airk's dragon responded, wresting control from an unconscious Airk, the violence of it yanking him out of the void and right into pain. He flipped over to his hands and knees, vomiting blood. Brock had cut him, but the shifting of his body was holding the injury together with scales and somehow healing him faster, making it the least of his problems.

The shimmering of his vision, the glitter of pure white scales, told him that much.

Airk closed his eyes, not breathing steadily, not focusing on holding his control, none of that. Fuck all that. He could die on the ground in a pathetic human heap, leaving Angelika with people he didn't trust for protection from what was coming for her. Or he could use the only weapon at his disposal.

Himself.

With another heave, blood pouring from his mouth, he gave in. Ceded control and let his dragon take over. Rip from his body like a cannon shot.

He'd seen other dragons shift before. Theirs came on in a silent rush that didn't appear painful. His soul should stay in place as his physical form shifted around his essence—everything human about him, including his clothes, should be absorbed into his new shape.

But this...this was like being flash heated in fire, forged by agony. As though his dragon was shredding his way out of the human half of himself. Another roar clawed its way from his throat as he grew to massive proportions, his perspective adjusting so rapidly his vision blurred. Already on all fours, he felt his claws gouge long marks in the mountainside as his talons curled and fisted with the torment of the change.

Eyes open now, his perspective changed, allowing him to see over the tops of the trees. His sight sharpened, and he could make out details of the dragons protecting Angelika miles away and the bronze bastard overhead. Rage blasted through every single nerve ending, and Airk lost himself to the dragon, any part of him still human melding into the beast.

All emotion, all control.

He unfurled the wings tucked against his back, and before the full transformation had completed, he launched himself into the air. He'd never flown a day in his life, but the dragon took to the air like he'd been born there.

Not yet fully shifted, he finished the details as he flew—scales both malleable and hard as diamonds, so white they glinted opalescent in the sunlight with all the colors of the rainbow, long tail trailing behind him like a rudder, razor-sharp teeth, spiked ridges along his back.

In this form, his sense of smell honed to a greater degree, and Angelika's sunlight-warmed scent drew him, but the next scent hit—smoke and bitter ale—and his dragon zeroed in on the dragon threatening her life.

No one touched Angelika. No one.

Brock was already coming for him. Flying straight at him with murder in his eyes. Airk's dragon blasted a challenge and flew faster.

Matched one on one, a white dragon should be no opponent

for gold, who were brutishly large and good only for pulverizing, while white dragons, who were longer and leaner, were pretty flyers who could go longer distances. More than that, Airk was untrained and untried.

But Brock didn't count on dealing with a feral fucking dragon.

They clashed with a boom that rang out through the skies, but Airk's dragon was smarter than he'd given the creature side of him credit for. From deep inside, he watched in fascinated horror as, rather than attempt to take the gold dragon down in his turf of the sky, Airk's dragon pulled in his wings and turned himself into dead weight.

Brock's attack turned from beating against Airk to mortally wound to trying, at first, to slow them down, then trying to let go. Except, while the gold dragon had been distracted with blood lust and then survival, Airk's dragon had wrapped his tail around Brock's like a dog could wind a leash around its human's legs.

Brock thrashed and beat at him, trying to get to Airk's underbelly or his gizzard, where the scales were easier to slice open. But Airk had been beaten before. Even in his human form, he knew how to self-protect. Apparently, his dragon had paid attention, curling in on himself to present only the spiked back, and the gold dragon couldn't land a blow.

The problem was, Airk's dragon was so determined to kill Brock, he was blocking other instincts for self-preservation. Airk could feel the creature letting go and readying himself to ride this to the ground.

Seven hells. He'd kill them. The rage would kill them both.

Flip over, Airk willed his animal half.

Nothing.

The ground was rushing at them. They had seconds at most.

Flip. Over. He was yelling now at the creature he'd become.

Still no response.

If you flip and survive, you can rip into this fucker. Leave a message for any dragon who ever thinks to come after her.

His dragon snarled in his head, and Airk couldn't tell it even heard until the last moment, ground screaming up at them, when it stuck out a wing that caught the wind and whipped them over so hard his long neck twisted harshly, pain splintering down his back. Even flaring his own wings and Brock's already out, they hit the ground with bone-crushing force, and Airk feared the split in his human body might open up from the impact, spilling his guts all over the place.

But his dragon was too enraged to fear anything.

Before they'd even finished plowing into the ground, he reared back, then tore into Brock in an attack both violent and vicious. And out of control. He shredded through the gold dragon's scales until he exposed skin, then went at him with teeth and talons, rending bone and meat from body until the pulp in front of him wasn't even identifiable as a once-living creature.

And all Airk could do was watch from inside.

A shadow passed overhead, near enough that Airk's dragon simultaneously snarled and cowered, blocking his kill with tail and wings and body like a bird of prey.

We're dead.

They'd be labeled feral and a danger to all around them, killed on sight. And maybe that needed to happen.

"Oh my gods, Airk." Angelika's voice penetrated both for him and his dragon, and his dragon jerked his head up, almost frantically searching for her, only to find her clasped in Mös's talons in the sky, like a bird in a cage, staring down at them.

Not in horror, of course, because this was Angelika. Airk wasn't remotely surprised by the combination of compassion and fascination reflected in her features, her white-blue eyes wide. He should be frustrated with that kind of reaction, but fuck if he wasn't rigid with the tension of need. Instantly.

His dragon felt exactly the same, though.

"Stay away!" Airk shouted at her.

"Put me down," she said, but not to him—to the Beta.

The older dragon hovered in the air, not lowering as she'd asked.

Airk's dragon growled a warning to the man. Airk growled his own warning—to Angelika. His creature could kill her without blinking. She needed to stay away. Far away.

Except his dragon growled again, this time leaving his kill to posture.

"If you don't want him to do the same to you," Angelika said, still addressing the dragon holding her, "I suggest you set me down."

With visible reluctance, Mös did so, maintaining a healthy distance from Airk. But Angelika threw personal safety to the wind and, as soon as her feet touched the ground, ran his direction, stumbling over the rocks and through the trees in her haste.

"Stay back!" he yelled at her again, trying to use telepathic communication, but his dragon was blocking him.

Meanwhile, his dragon stood still, muscles quivering, breath blowing heavily in and out of his nostrils. Airk couldn't get a read on him—bloodlust and frenzy? Or the need to be near her? Both were equally possible.

Don't hurt her.

His dragon ignored him because Angelika had reached an outcropping of rock, standing out from the trees like a damned pedestal, as though the mountain was raising her to him. Airk's dragon lowered his head, and her eyes grew wide as he neared.

"Please don't eat me," she whispered.

Now she decided to be scared? But his dragon, though still trembling, stopped just short of touching her.

"Airk, gods." She reached out a tentative hand and put it to his snout, and his dragon actually leaned into her touch. "You're alive. Are you hurt?"

The damn animal might've purred, except Angelika suddenly gasped, making it jerk back.

Then, with zero warning, she burst into brilliant, red-gold flames.

CHAPTER SEVENTEEN

"Holy smokes!" Angelika yelped as everything about her flared in an inferno of fire.

Her vision immediately took on a reddish-gold haze. She lifted her arms, staring at the way the hypnotizing flames danced and glided over her skin. Over her clothes. Over everything. She wasn't burning, but she was covered in it, the warmth penetrating, seeping into her blood only to spark there.

An answering lance of desire shot through her with each pound of her heart, sending all the best parts of her tingling and pulsing with each rush.

Like Kasia.

She jerked her gaze to Airk's. *Is it finally happening? Am I getting my powers?*

Only...the fire wasn't going away. It was getting hotter.

"Um...Airk?" She shook a hand, only to have the flames leap higher as though she'd added oxygen to the mix and made it worse. The heat at the tips of her fingers and her ears started to singe. "Airk?" Definitely panic in her voice now.

Kasia's flare-ups had calmed with Brand giving her a great big orgasm every time, apparently. If Airk wasn't currently a massive dragon, Angelika might not have had a problem with that.

The dragon before her was staring at her with his head turned, one giant eye filled with what appeared to be concern.

"I need *him*," she told the creature.

The dragon snorted once, which told her he understood what she was asking for. In the same instant, the heat stepped up a degree or a hundred. Holding in a wince, she lifted her hand again to find the flames turning blue. At a small whimper from her throat, the dragon snorted again, this time sounding almost afraid. Then, with a flap of his wings, scooped her up and flew away.

"Don't follow us." That was Airk's voice but not. Rougher, angrier. Directed to the dragons on the ground.

Only several looked as though they weren't okay with that. Angelika stayed them with a hand. She'd have to trust Airk in this, even as a dragon. If he wanted to hurt her, he would have already.

She buttoned her lips around more whimpers and almost expected her fingertips to start blistering with the intensity of the heat by now. She even tried rubbing her hands against her clothes to snuff out the flames, but that did nothing.

Luckily, Airk didn't go far. Only enough away that the other dragons were around the side of the mountain. Then he landed, setting her on a rock, where her flames couldn't set the surrounding trees ablaze quite so easily.

With a suddenness that astounded her, the shimmering lines—like watching a mirage—that indicated a shift encased him. Only the dragon didn't change. Not immediately.

The concentration of her own fire, forgotten for a mere moment, made itself felt, the pain receptors in her nerves making her believe it was crawling up her hands to her wrists now. "Airk, hurry."

The dragon tipped his head back and roared even as his size decreased. Even as his scales turned to human skin and clothes, as his bones realigned so he was standing on two feet instead of all fours. Even as the sound of his roar turned human, Airk battled his way back to control.

The shimmers stopped, and he pitched forward, hands on his knees, breathing hard. But he didn't stay that way. He jerked up and ran at her. "What can I do?"

What was she supposed to say to that? *I need a big O right now?*

She wasn't even sure this was the same as it had been for Kasia. Her sister's fire had also come with migraines and visions, neither of which was happening.

Airk reached for her, circling her wrist with his hand, and suddenly—as fast as she went up like a Roman candle—the flames doused.

All she could do was squeak her shock before raising her hands in front of her face. The tips of her fingers were pink, like a sunburn, but that was the worst of it. Much better than what her imagination was painting.

"Are you hurt?" he demanded.

She jerked her gaze to his, only to stumble into a different kind of shock. The kind that left her mind reeling and her body, still tingling from the effect of her flames, lit up.

Because he was looking at her... Gods, the way he was looking at her.

"Phoenix?" he asked, the word abrupt, sharp.

Angelika swallowed down a sudden surge of sadness and shook her head. Because she...knew.

She just knew.

Disappointment on more than one level threatened to sink her. But she refused to drown. The fire might not mean phoenix, but it meant something else. Something more helpful to her than human. "Dragon sign."

His eyes flared, then settled. "Because of *me*."

Then his mouth was on hers, demanding and untamed, like the creature he'd just subdued.

Angelika didn't hesitate, throwing herself into the kiss, reveling in it. He wasn't holding himself back anymore...and holy hells, he had been before. There was more than a reluctant sort of desire in his touch. Now there was purpose, claiming.

Those last three words of his were enough for her.

That her sign had shown itself because of him—she knew what that meant. His voice hadn't held blame or bitterness or concern, like she might have expected. Because many dragons believed that dragon sign—small clues like the scent of smoke, going up in flames, or shifting smaller parts of the body, all of which a human woman destined to mate a dragon shifter could show—was more easily triggered by the man fated to be her mate.

Those three words of his had been supremely satisfied and harshly possessive at the same time.

His lips on hers now, his hands sweeping the contours of her body with both abandonment and possessive relish, told her she was right, and her heart told her she wanted this, wanted him, like she'd never wanted anything in her life.

"Tell me no now if you want me to stop," he ground out against her lips, like he wasn't even able to lift his head to speak the words.

"Don't stop." She wrapped a hand around his neck as if to hold him to her.

"Thank the gods."

Then his hands were at the three silk-covered buttons holding the top of her suit together. Except they were tiny, and it took less than a blink of fumbling with his larger fingers for him to growl with frustration, then rip it open with a *pop-pop-pop*.

Angelika would've chuckled at his haste if his face hadn't suddenly gone all intense as he gazed at her bared skin. "I wondered if you had anything on under this."

She didn't. But he had? "You hardly looked at me."

"I looked enough." His expression spasmed, almost with pain. "I am always looking at you," he said, quieter. Reverent.

He traced a finger down the valley between her breasts, then groaned. Banding an arm behind her waist, he bent her backward and set his lips to her breast, sucking so hard her clit throbbed in immediate reaction, beating to the pulse of his mouth on her.

Angelika speared her hands through his shorn hair, holding on, her gaze glued to the sight of his skin against hers, his mouth on her body. She might combust all over again right here.

"Gods," he rumbled against her. "You taste of ambrosia. There were times when I was not sure if you were temptation or torture."

She couldn't help the smile curving her lips, because her dragon was not a talker, so those words meant more than he knew. "I seem to remember you liked the taste of other parts of me, too."

The man did a full-body shudder against her. Without her feeling more than a *whoosh* of a breeze, her skirt and undies were gone and she was laid down on top of her clothes and his torn shirt. Before she could gasp at the speed with which that happened, he was on his knees, her legs up on his shoulders, mouth set to the vibrating, slick core of her.

He licked right through her folds. Not experimentally, like before. Not hesitant, either. This was a claiming. And when she tossed her head back and arched into the touch, he did it again. Then again. He didn't let up until she was a whimpering, hot mess. Not until her breathing started to hitch did he slow.

She took a deep breath, relaxing into the way he was lapping at her. "You're a...fast study," she panted.

She felt Airk's smile against her flesh before he speared that questing tongue inside her. His groan of pleasure might as well have been a vibrator, hitting her just the right way.

With zero warning, her body tipped right over the edge. Her legs clamped around his head, and a shout of pleasure punched out of her, hands clawing at his hair as she came hard, riding his mouth and tongue.

He didn't give her a chance to float down lightly, though, playing with her through every shuddering wave of pleasure. In a single, aggressive, *hot as fuck* move, he slid two thick fingers inside her.

"This feels like a dream," he said. And Angelika could hear in his voice even more than the words that this time he was letting himself feel beyond the physical. His next words gutted her. "I do not want to wake up in my cell, alone, without you."

"You will never be alone again," she promised. And meant it.

With another groan, he set his mouth to her swollen clit, sucking and sucking and sucking as he moved his fingers inside her.

As though he were a man driven.

Or a dragon shifter finally letting himself be what and who he was. Because this moment went beyond desire. This was...feral, primal, and yet went deeper than that. Gods, she was into it.

At first, she could hardly stand the sensitivity, her hands kneading into his scalp and tiny cries pouring from her throat, but at the same time she didn't want it to end.

But then...

"Airk." His name tripped off her lips as the tension of desire gripped her again, building in her already languid muscles, building in her womb, building in the lines of her body.

He lifted his head, his lips covered in her juices, white-blue eyes so like hers aflame. "Say that again."

Angelika tipped her head, through the haze of her own need seeing a deeper one inside of him.

She smiled and traced the lines of his lips. "Airk Azdajah."

He shuddered. "I never thought to love the sound of my name. So many years, it was a tool of my enemies."

Angelika cupped his face, lightly tugging at him so that he crawled up her body until she could press her lips to his and taste herself on him. "Airk," she whispered. Then another kiss. "Airk." Another. "Airk." Then pulled back, looking him seriously in the eyes. "*My* Airk," she said, the words a deliberate choice.

His eyes flared with that same soul-deep satisfaction from earlier, and he buried his face in the crook of her neck. At the same time, his hands left her to frantically divest himself of his pants. Only he was too impatient, just getting them to his knees. He suddenly reared back, up on his knees between her legs. His hand went to his cock, squeezing and stroking, the swollen head turning more purple with each stroke.

Needing to be part of this, Angelika batted his hand away and replaced it with her own, watching in fascination as her smaller fingers worked him. Silky hot skin over a steel rod, jutting from his body. Precum leaked out of the tip, and, curious, she brushed her thumb through it. He jerked in her grasp.

"I need to make you mine, Angelika Amon."

"Yes."

That was all they both needed. Airk laid her back down, laying between her splayed legs and positioning himself at her eager entrance. Then, in one strong yet beautifully gentle stroke, he entered her body.

"Fuck," he muttered.

He shuddered above her, breathing harshly as though trying to hold himself back. "This is right," she whispered.

Then, like before when he finally let go, he was pounding into her as though a dam had broken, and he was flooding her with everything he'd wanted. But this time, his gaze on her held a thousand emotions. And she reveled in every out-of-control thrust, his fervor only feeding her own. Her body slid into a hazy space where she was all feeling, all senses, all pleasure, and nothing else was important except the man in her arms.

Airk growled. "I want all of you."

Yes.

Angelika tipped her head back and watched him, watched his face as he took her, as he built the pleasure they were reaching for together. All those angles were harsh and striking, his gaze on her almost adoring.

"You are the most beautiful thing I've ever seen," she whispered.

His face spasmed with something that might have been tenderness. "Gods, more," Airk growled again.

The slap of his driven thrusts blended with the sounds of their harsh breathing. Pressure at the other entrance back there had Angelika gasping and looking over her shoulder.

Airk flicked her a glance full of questions, and she nodded, wanting more, too. More of him. She wanted him to claim every single part of her body and had every intention of doing the same to him in a thousand different mind-blowing, pleasurable ways.

Expression a cruel study of sensual need, he pressed a finger inside that un-breached place, pushing past the natural barrier as she breathed out and in. He gave her a second to adjust, then started pumping his hand in time to his hips. Angelika couldn't stop the loud moan that stuttered from her. Full. She felt so full of him.

As though he was in every part of her.

Airk smiled, his chest rising and falling, and she could have stared at that for the rest of her life happily.

An emotion rippled over his features too fast to catch. "I am going to put my fire in you, and I want to watch your eyes when I do."

She nodded frantically, undulating her hips. "Make me your mate," she demanded.

Then kissed him. A kiss that he couldn't doubt was her claiming him for hers. He'd held her off until now. She'd almost given up, despite knowing that they were right together. It hadn't been one look. Not instant. It had been more like...gravity that kept reaching for her when she neared his orbit until she got tangled up.

Seeing what he'd gone through and the way he still struggled. Wanting to help him through that, even though he wouldn't let *anyone* help him. The few times they'd talked had only made her want to know more. Know him.

Now here she was.

Airk grinned against her kiss but didn't break it as he lifted her by the hips and slid into her body until she was once again gloriously full of everything he was. He guided her but let her set the pace, forehead to hers as though the connection of their souls was even more important than what they were doing with their bodies now.

When they were both breathing heavy and the sparkling, tingling hint of an oncoming orgasm rippled through her, he inhaled long and hard, a sound coming from his chest that sounded like a forge bellows, stoking his fire.

Then Airk stilled, every damn part of him.

Long enough that Angelika drew back, searching his face with a frown. Then her lips parted on a silent gasp as his skin rippled with white scales.

Suddenly, with his hands at her hips, he yanked her right off him, setting her on her ass on the forest floor. Then he jerked to standing, stumbling back a few steps as though she'd suddenly grown horns and a tail. And she whimpered as his face crumpled, then hardened.

"Don't—"

She reached a hand toward him, but she was too late. The shift overtook him too fast. In seconds a massive, brilliant white dragon stood over her. Airk's chest heaved and he shook his head once. Twice.

Then he spread his wings, though they trembled as though he was fighting himself. With a blast of wind from the downdraft, he leaped into the air, swiftly disappearing over the trees.

Leaving her alone. Unclaimed and unmated.

CHAPTER EIGHTEEN

Gods, how could I be so stupid?
He'd been able to wrestle the shift back from his dragon, taking control, and the thing had been good with Angelika. Gentle for what he was. And the fact that she'd lit on fire, and he believed—gods, he'd believed with everything in his soul that it was because of him. All those reasons made him think he could do this.

Could make her his. Claim her. Mate her.

Airk could still smell Angelika all over him as he forced his dragon to fly away from her. Unfortunately, so could the beast half of him, and it was sending him over the edge. Frantic to get back to her.

Inside his own mind, his own body, the two parts of his soul battled each other. The violent clash raging internally meant he was jerking around in the sky as control over their flight juddered back and forth between human and dragon.

But at the end of claiming her, the animal part of him had wanted to be the one to fill their mate with fire, to turn her. He'd started to shift while Airk's cock had been buried, hilt deep, inside Angelika. The damn monster could have rent her in half if he'd succeeded before Airk had been able to tear them away.

He'd tried to run, but the shift had come on too fast.

You could have killed her! he shouted at his creature half as he mentally and physically dragged them farther and farther away from where he'd left Angelika.

But the dragon was too far gone to listen, roaring and thrashing and fighting to get back and finish what they started. What he'd promised them both.

If that split in his gut hadn't opened up with all the other things, it very well might now. Or that's how it felt—as though he was being torn and slashed open from the insides.

Airk did the only thing he could. He tried to force the shift midair. Back to human.

Nothing happened.

Which left him with one option. The thing he hated most about what Pytheios had forced him to become. A mental exercise Nathair had taught him to do as a boy. Pytheios's witch had spelled the dungeons to turn off any visitor's powers, but his dragon wasn't a power. He was the dragon, and the dragon was him. So Nathair had taught him how the magic of his creature came from his mind.

As fast as he could, Airk mentally bricked a wall in his mind. He reinforced it with dragonsteel. Blocking his dragon off, like he'd been forced to do in that fucking cell for centuries, he held him there and again willed himself to change. The shimmering lines before his eyes told him when he got it.

Then he was falling.

Behind those bricked-in, shored-up, steel-enforced mental walls, his dragon roared with the thunder of a wild creature, hatred for everything Airk was spewing from inside him. But Airk didn't let up.

At the last second, mountainside rushing up at him, his dragon made one last wild grab, wings manifesting and beating down hard enough that they didn't pound into the ground, killing them both. Instead, they struck and rolled a few feet, coming to rest in a small clearing on a bed of pine needles, laying with his pants still down around his ankles, the way they had been when he shifted and flown away.

Sun shone down on them, warming his skin, and somewhere nearby a bird tweeted, as though the world was oblivious to the struggle happening within him. Airk placed the last brick in his mind, shutting off his dragon, and the wings disappeared. So did the roar. Chest heaving, he dropped his head back against the ground, eyes clenched closed. He hated himself for what he'd just done. His dragon half hadn't known better.

This, none of it, had ever been his fault.

But thanks to Airk—thanks to reaching for Angelika like he had, believing even for a second that she was fated to be his, letting his dragon think that, too, even believe maybe they could exist together, then having to take both her and freedom away from his dragon again—he'd driven his creature the rest of the way to uncontrollable.

Too far gone to save. All rage, and gods speed to anyone who might encounter him.

Airk could never let him loose again.

And Angelika clearly was a trigger.

He brought his hands up over his face. "Fuck."

Airk didn't get up right away, needing to spend more time shoring up the walls inside his mind. Plus, his body, with his dragon so shut down, apparently healed more slowly, and the gash across his belly was still pink and slightly raw. The fact that he hadn't busted open earlier was a blasted miracle.

What the hells was I thinking?

The answer was, he wasn't. Instinct and need and a woman destined to drive him to distraction had led to a moment of pure selfish action.

Now he laid here like the useless lump he was and gathered his control more and more around him like the tattered rags of the poor woman who'd been his longest cellmate in Everest. A witch who'd spoken out against Rhiamon, Pytheios's favorite pet.

Speaking of which…

Airk grinned suddenly, though his heart wasn't fully into it.

His dragon had been good for something. They'd taken out that golden fucker that the High King had officially decreed as his heir. Pytheios wasn't going to be happy about that at all. Tempting to bring him the news personally, along with Brock's ashes.

A death sentence if he did it, but maybe he was always meant to die at the king's hands. That prophecy would be some comfort if that happened.

He winced. After all, he had a decent idea of what he was going to return to when he went back to the mountain.

What do you expect? You left Angelika unmated and alone on the side of the mountain.

Airk jerked to sitting as that realization penetrated his own self-imposed exile. He'd left her alone and *exposed*, and the only way back was to climb a mountain in a skirt and heels.

Gods be damned.

In an instant, he was on his feet, shucking up his pants and sprinting half naked over the mountainside to where he'd left her. Only he skidded to a halt in the spot. He knew he was in the right place because the combined scents of their skin and sex lingered in the air. Plus…she'd folded his fucking shirt and left it there neatly on a rock for him.

Which was exactly something Angelika would do.

Guilt plunged a dagger through his own personal regrets. He was a bloody menace and the worst thing possible for her, and here she was, folding his clothes as if she was trying to take care of him.

Pulling his shirt on, though the thing was in tatters, he followed the sunshine scent of her until it stopped suddenly. Someone had come to get her, it seemed. A new dagger—this one of worry—plunged through his chest, and he sprinted back to the entrance into the mountain.

Only to climb over the lip of rock to encounter a wall of white dragons.

They got one whiff of him and bared their teeth. *"Hold."*

He wasn't sure which of the sentries spoke. Didn't care. "Is the phoenix inside?" he demanded.

"Name?"

In other words, this one had no idea who he was and had been given orders not to let anyone in. The mountain had to be on lockdown.

"Airk Azdajah. I arrived with Angelika Amon. Is she safe?"

Silence greeted his announcement, but he didn't mistake it for ignoring him or not hearing him. No doubt the five dragons were checking among themselves and probably with their own leaders. These were military-trained men. No doubt they'd reported to someone who needed to be consulted as well.

Airk crossed his arms and stared them down, waiting in silence.

Finally, one lifted a wing, giving him a human-sized space to pass between them. "The phoenix is inside. She left word to bring you to her *if* you returned."

Airk refused to show any reaction, especially to that "if."

A man who was vaguely familiar stood at the backside of the sentries, Airk assumed to take him to Angelika. Older, the man's long hair, rather than white, was starkly black but thinning, exposing the oddly freckled skin of his skull. A clean-shaven face was creased with lines of age across lightly bronzed skin, and his hands, when he beckoned Airk closer, were gnarled and equally spotted as his scalp.

But instead of turning to lead Airk through the mountain, the man stood still, cloudy gaze sweeping Airk's form.

"My god. It *is* you."

While the rest of him had aged at a hideously faster rate than should be possible, his voice hadn't changed at all, sparking recognition that sent disbelief crawling down Airk's neck.

Not actual blood kin, this man had been the son of one of Airk's family's attendants. Workers paid handsomely for taking care of them and their property and their children. But Jordy had become one of his father's best friends and most trusted confidants. One of Zilant Amon's, too. The fuzzy memories of boyhood reminded him of thousands of small moments with this man and his own family that he'd forgotten. Could this be him, though?

"Do you remember me?" Jordy asked slowly.

"Uncle Jordy?"

The smile that was his answer looked…weary. "No one's called me uncle in ages."

No doubt. "Probably because I was the only one who dared."

Jordy had been a remarkable and feared debater who could back up his words with fighting skills.

"You always were fearless."

Airk's huff lacked any true amusement. "Everest beat that out of me over time."

The older man closed his eyes on a spasm of emotion, then hooked a hand around the back of Airk's neck and tugged him into a tight embrace. Airk remained stiff against him, unable to let himself accept any kind of pity. Still resentful that no one had come for him.

No one.

"Gods above, boy, I thought you were dead all this time." Airk jerked in his embrace, but Jordy didn't let go of him. "If I'd known, I would have burned down that entire godsforsaken mountain to get to you."

Airk swallowed, breathing through the tangle of emotions rising inside him like a mass of striking cobras. "Why did everyone think I was dead?"

Jordy sighed and pulled back. "Come with me. I'll tell you everything."

"Angelika—"

"Gathered with the Curia Regis. I asked to be informed when you returned." His lips took on a bitter twist. "I still have some friends in this mountain. I'll take you to her after we talk."

What did he mean by "*some* friends?" The Jordy he knew might not be of a royal, or even upper-class, bloodline like Airk was, but he was well-respected and well-liked by everyone who knew him. Given his position in the Azdajah household, that would have been a good majority of the dragons in this mountain.

Airk hesitated, thinking through not only that but the fact that making Angelika wait longer wasn't going to win him any forgiveness. Except forgiveness might only muddy the waters. Distance was better.

"Fine."

In a gesture so Jordy that Airk's memory almost took him to

his knees, the other man bowed his head. The move was partly a mimic of other attendants who could lean toward obsequiousness, but with his own slightly sarcastic twist. He used to make Airk laugh as a boy when he'd do it to dragons who were full of their own importance, or to Airk's own father when he got snarly. The only man Jordy never dared use that gesture on was Angelika's father, King Zilant.

If Airk had had no fear, he'd learned it partly from this man.

In silence, they walked through the training area and to a human-sized door off to one side that led into a smaller corridor. Not far down, they made it to a bank of elevators.

"When did they put these in?" Airk wondered.

"About fifty years ago. A…gift…from Pytheios. For our loyalty."

Of course. Because the White and Green Clans had been the Rotting King's most loyal supporters. The Blue Clans, on the other hand, didn't have anything nearly so helpful or modern in their mountains. Instead, their wealth had been slowly stripped. The Gold, too, though in different ways. Harder ways for the people to see. The Black Clan hadn't given Pytheios the excuse to do the same.

"I don't want to know for what," Airk said.

"No," Jordy muttered. "You don't."

They said nothing else until Jordy let him into a small, one-room efficiency apartment. One located on such a low floor, it didn't even have a perch or a window. "Tea?" Jordy asked, moving to a wall that apparently was a small kitchen with a single counter, a sink, a microwave, and a hot plate. The refrigerator wouldn't hold more than a day or two worth of food. The rest of the room was similarly basic.

Airk frowned, looking around. "Why are you living here?"

Jordy paused in the process of filling a kettle with water from a tap connected to a series of exposed pipes. "It's only me these days."

Another frown. "Your family?"

That brought bushy white brows up. "I was an only child, and my parents died when you still knew me, boy."

Airk shook his head. "I didn't remember."

"Your father's family kept me around out of kindness and gratefulness for my parents, who'd served the Azdajah happily and well for centuries."

It's only me. The words pinged around inside Airk's head. "You never mated?"

"No." Jordy didn't still this time, and he didn't turn from the hot plate where he'd set the kettle to boil, either.

That explained the aging. He must've hit that point in life that not having a mate meant his aging process started to speed up.

More silence as Jordy made them tea, then sat them down at a small kitchen table with two mismatched chairs, as there was no other seating in the room besides the single twin-sized mattress on the floor.

But the teacup was thin porcelain with pink flowers and old enough that, at a guess, this was one of the few personal things Jordy had kept of his life before. The delicate thing felt as though it might disintegrate in Airk's grip, so he handled it carefully, sipping at watery tea.

Over the lip of his cup, Jordy studied Airk's face. "You are a blend of your parents. No doubt about that."

"Pytheios enjoyed pointing that out as well, whenever he happened to be in the dungeons where I was kept."

Jordy put his teacup down with a clatter. "So it is true. You were his prisoner."

Bitterness seeped into Airk's blood, turning him rancid. He also put his cup down. "After he murdered King Zilant and my parents, plus the High King Hanyu and his phoenix before my eyes. Yes. He held me."

Jordy glanced away from the accusation no doubt shining in Airk's eyes. "I always wondered."

"And yet you did nothing."

"Not much I could do. Your household was disbanded, all who served the Azdajahs scattered to other households, or other mountains, if they could find work at all."

Airk frowned. "Why wouldn't they?"

"Thanks to the story Pytheios convinced all of our kind was the truth."

Airk had learned bits and pieces through the years. More since he gained his freedom, but mostly about the Amons and Hanyus. Nothing about his own family. "What story was that?"

"According to him, on that day, Serefina and Zilant tried to mate, but she'd chosen the wrong man, and her fire consumed the white king."

"I'd heard that much." All lies.

Jordy nodded slowly. "What you might not be aware of is this. Pytheios told only the White Clan's Curia Regis that your father, in his rage at his friend and king's death, went ballistic, slaughtering Serefina and her parents—the High King and the mother phoenix—as well as a few others, before Pytheios was able to stop him by killing him. Your mother died with her mate."

Airk sat back with a thump that the rickety chair protested with a creak of plastic and some kind of cheap metal. He stared into nothing. "And me?"

He didn't have to look up to see Jordy swallow...he heard it. "He said you tried to stop your father, and in his blind rage, he killed you, too."

Airk closed his eyes on a wave of grief so hollow and broken, he had to lean forward, elbows on his knees, to breathe through it. Even caged in the mental walls he'd built around his dragon, that soul-deep part of him cried out and the sound, the *devastation*, rattled his bones.

That lying bastard of a red king tried to destroy their rulers—and worse, the phoenixes, the line of inheritance for High King—and his family, all for what? Power? To keep the seat of High King with the Red Clan? To prevent Zilant's more progressive ideas from being tried out?

"That's not quite how it happened," he muttered at the plastic-looking tabletop.

"You're proof enough of that, boy."

Airk huffed a bitter laugh, then frowned and raised his gaze.

"You are right. I *am* proof." More so than the existence of Angelika and her sisters, possibly. Because while their parentage was still questioned by many dragons, he'd grown up in this mountain. His family had been a staple here for millennia. And to his clan, his face was indisputable.

Was that why Mös had looked at him that way when he and Angelika had arrived? Not because of Angelika, but because of Airk? Hadn't the Beta known the truth all along? Or had he also been misled?

Taking a deep breath, Airk laid out the truth of what had happened that terrible night—what happened to him for ages following, which mostly consisted of his sitting in that fucking cell alone, his escape with Skylar, and his time with the Blue and Black Clans since then.

Jordy listened, his expression growing steadily angrier. "Gods above, boy," he said when Airk finished his tale. "If people knew—"

His old friend was right. His people needed to know. "I'm going to tell them. Show them."

First, though, he needed to learn what Mös's part in any of this was. If he had been deceived, like most everyone else, they needed him. And if that was true, the Beta likely already understood the need to show his people Airk as proof, but Angelika needed to know, too. She'd probably already guessed—or at least her instincts had been accurate. After all, offering to mate him was an extreme measure and one that made more sense now that he could see the impact his existence made on just one man who'd known him and his family. Jordy looked ready to cut the false High King's throat himself.

Airk surged to his feet, determination sending his muscles rigid. "Take me to Angelika and Mös."

CHAPTER NINETEEN

The knock at the door was tentative, and the tension riding Angelika's shoulders turned to a dip of disappointment, because Airk wouldn't knock like that. The way he'd flown away from her, she wasn't even sure if he ever would come back. He might be out there, fighting his own dragon right now.

Everything in her wanted to follow. To help him. But she couldn't.

There's nothing you can do, so focus on what you can.

Which was discussing with Mös and the rest of Curia Regis—as well as the men sworn to her who had been released from the dungeons, where they'd been put on Brock's orders—what their next steps needed to be.

"Jordy?" Mös asked, looking over her shoulder at whoever had entered through the door behind her. The Beta's brows lowered in what appeared to be confusion as he addressed the newcomer.

"Did you know the truth?" A gravelly voice had her turning in her seat. "Did Volos?"

Angelika startled at the sight of not one unknown man but an unknown man...and Airk.

Relief punched out of her in a sharp breath. He'd gained control, and he'd come back. Thank the gods.

Irritation kicked in hard on the heels of stark relief.

Airk may have returned, but he wasn't looking at her, his gaze on Mös. She scowled at the man, willing him to feel the lash of her ire, which was heating up by the second. He was supposed to have been brought directly to her. She'd been *worried,* damn him. As in "couldn't concentrate because her mind was on him" worried. And here he was…human, healthy apparently, and accompanied by a strange man she didn't know, demanding answers to vague questions.

"What truth?" Mös asked. "There are many truths and many lies out there." But the tenor of his voice wasn't confidence. It belied trepidation.

Angelika slowly turned to face him as well.

"You were not surprised to see me when Angelika and I arrived," Airk said.

The Beta tapped a gnarled finger on the metal tabletop. "Of course not. My people had already informed me of your existence."

Her people, he meant.

"So you did not know that I was alive until they told you?" Airk pushed.

Mös's eyes narrowed. The man was clearly not used to being questioned. "I did not. Like everyone else, I was told you were killed in the tragedy that took so many lives. I had no cause to believe otherwise."

Angelika sat forward, studying the man closely, trying to discern what it was about that speech that bothered her. It would be really nice right now to have Meira's empathic abilities. Not that her sister could see lies or truths, but she could read emotions. "Were you ever told that Pytheios was the one who killed them?" she asked.

Mös cut his glacial gaze to her, jaw going tight. "No."

"Or that Airk was still alive?" she pressed.

His gaze slid to the man standing behind her, but this time his complexion paled ever so slightly. "No."

"And to your knowledge, Volos was also similarly misled?" the older man called Jordy pushed.

"The king always acted as though he believed the story Pytheios gave everyone." Mös glanced away. "He never gave me any indication that anything different had happened."

Angelika turned to see Airk's reaction. Did he believe the Beta?

His lips pulled back, baring his teeth. "If I find out you have fed me lies—"

A low growl ripped from Mös's throat, and he surged to his feet, leaning fisted hands on the table. "You'll what?" he spat. "Turn your feral dragon loose on me? By rights I should have you put down and put out of your misery."

The tension in the room ratcheted up a hundredfold, blanketing Angelika as every other dragon shifter in the room growled as well, flames lighting up eyes to dance and sparkle against the walls. She couldn't tell who was on whose side, though.

"Touch him, and any deal with me is done," she said quietly.

The room seemed to lurch to a halt, so still she almost wondered if hearts were still beating.

Airk, meanwhile, didn't get angry or acknowledge what she said. He went bone-chillingly cold. Not a flame in sight. He remained focused on Mös, and Mös alone. "My dragon, that you disparage so easily, is what he is because *your* High King, the man who fed you lies—lies you believed because you wanted power—locked me in a cage for five hundred fucking long years."

The flickering of firelight died down as dragon's eyes banked, shoulders and fists eased, and guilt or horror or both oozed through them. But Airk wasn't done.

"Perhaps I should ask Angelika to do the same to you." He cut his gaze to each man in turn. "All of you. Lock you up for centuries in a cage where your creature cannot ever be released. We will see how you come out the other side."

Dragons weren't naturally accepting of challenges like that, and Angelika held her breath, waiting for someone to make a move.

A relieved sort of surprise skimmed through her as each and every man and woman in the room eventually lowered his or her gaze, some even ducking their heads in shame.

"When we take this to the clan, we show them *me*," Airk said in a voice that brooked no refusal. "I will tell them my story. Not only am I living proof, I am a living witness of what happened the day we lost *two* kings, the phoenix, her mother, and my parents."

Silence.

Airk drew himself up to his full, imposing height. "And I dare you to kill me. Pytheios himself did not try because the phoenix's mother, with her last dying breath, predicted that the man who killed me, or ordered me killed, would be a pile of ash shortly after."

Astonishment slammed through her on razor-sharp breaths. Her grandmother had said that about him? But that had been after she'd passed her powers to Angelika's mother. She shouldn't have been able to predict anything. But apparently Pytheios had believed her. That was why Airk had been imprisoned instead of killed? Gods. She hadn't known.

She wanted to cross the room to his side, sneak her hand in his, and simply be with him. He was always so alone. Even now. He was strong enough to weather that isolation, but he didn't have to be.

Angelika dropped her gaze to her folded hands. "I think you'd better tell them what *did* happen that day," she said quietly. "Everything."

An hour later, several faces in the room had turned green. Two of the council members had had to leave, probably to throw up. The rest were grim, resigned, or a combination of the two.

"We didn't know." Mös wasn't posturing anymore, the anger torn from him by the truth of Airk's ruthless words. "I swear we didn't know."

"You did not once question Pytheios? About that or any of his decisions down the line?" Airk demanded.

Mös took a deep breath. "Volos was more than happy to be placed on the throne, and Pytheios is the one who put him there."

"What happened to Volos?" Airk asked.

The Beta actually flinched. "He went to Everest on business. We were told old age claimed his life there."

"Did they return his ashes?"

"No."

She glanced at Airk and knew without having to voice it aloud that he was thinking the same thing she was. They should ask Ladon if his spy within Everest knew what had happened to the previous King of the White Clan.

Mös's fingers curled into a fist on the table. "But we had our answer from Pytheios about our new king."

Angelika raised her eyebrows and waited.

"That's why Brock was here. Not for you. Yesterday, Brock arrived to inform us that Pytheios had decided to place him on the throne."

Holy hells. She'd guessed right about that? Pytheios had seriously thought he could put a gold dragon on the white throne and they'd go along with it? She'd only been posturing when she'd threatened Mös with that earlier. Had Pytheios turned so arrogant, so narcissistic, that he couldn't see the error of that decision?

She closed her eyes. Of course he had. Because dragon shifters had gone along with everything else, so why should he suspect they'd balk at this? But this new revelation also meant these men's decision to follow her had nothing to do with her and everything to do with the lesser of two evils. The false High King had crossed the line one too many times, it seemed.

The question was, could she trust these people to remain loyal? She'd have to for now. She couldn't track down Delilah and ask her to perform the same oath of loyalty for an entire clan. At some point, trust needed to happen.

"Do we know when Brock was supposed to report in to Pytheios next?" Airk asked.

No one did.

Okay. They needed to act fast, then, before the red king learned what had happened here. "What is the best way to introduce Airk and me to the rest of the clan?" Angelika asked.

Discussing that took another few hours, by the end of which Angelika was starting to hit a wall, exhaustion scraping at her. And Airk still wasn't looking at her.

"I think we have a plan," she said, pushing to her feet and barely avoiding yawning and stretching. Food had been brought in while they talked. What she needed now was a bed.

"One last item..." Mös said.

She held in a sigh. Because sitting here trying to be both polite and political was hard enough. But sitting here being ignored by the man who had almost tried to turn her and then effectively ignored her...her slow-burn temper was at a boil by now. Combine that with tired and heartsore after listening to Airk's story, and she needed alone time.

"Yes?" she asked when Mös hesitated.

"What do we call you?"

Angelika blinked. "Call me?"

"Yes? Are you our king and queen, now that you're mated?" He glanced between her and Airk. "Is that your intention?"

Oh gods. Of course they thought that when Airk flew off with her something monumental had happened. Yes, she'd come back alone, but smelling of sex that their heightened senses no doubt caught.

"We aren't mated," she said, not looking at him.

The exchange of looks in the room was a mix of reactions. Mostly disbelief.

"But—"

Even Mös didn't seem to know what to ask next.

Angelika was so far from wanting to address this right now. "I showed dragon sign, and I will mate. I'll figure out the who...soon. I've had an offer from the leader of the wolf shifters as well."

The murmur of angry voices, fully a protest, rose up like a swarm of wasps knocked from their nests.

"As allies, they might be worth considering," she said firmly. "But my place is with dragons."

The swarm settled.

"Until we take Pytheios down, let's not worry about queens and kings. We do this together." She paused, waiting for any arguments. They hadn't been shy about speaking up so far, but none came. "Lovely. Can someone take me to a bedroom, please?"

"Jordy." Mös addressed the older man Airk had arrived with.

"Take them to the Azdajahs' previous quarters."

"I'll find my own way," Airk said. "In a moment."

Sending her off alone with Jordy, apparently. Good. She'd have a chance to calm down and decide what was best for *her* moving forward.

Jordy had a kind smile and was sweetly quiet as he escorted her to elevators that dropped them a few levels down. The rooms where he led her had clearly not been used in years, though she couldn't tell if the suite had been stripped down to bare essentials or pilfered or both. No decorations remained anywhere, but furniture was covered in sheets as though awaiting the owner's return.

Only they never did. "Oh, Airk," she whispered.

"Take any room you want," Jordy said. "While the furniture is old, it works. And the rooms have at least been updated with plumbing and bathrooms and such."

She nodded.

"Is there anything else you need?"

"A mirror. A large one."

Without hesitating, Jordy left her where she stood to move down a hallway within the suite, disappearing into the room at the far end, then returning a few seconds later. "The one originally found in here is gone. An overly fancy thing someone no doubt had their greedy eyes on." He wrinkled his nose in derisive judgment. "Not your style, anyway, I would dare to bet."

"I should hope not," she agreed with a small smile.

He chuckled. "I'll make sure you have one by tonight."

"Thank you."

Jordy turned to leave but paused at the door, gaze skating over her face. "The little boy I knew is still inside him."

She had no idea what to say to that, so she waited.

The older man took a deep breath. "He waited five hundred years to get out. Maybe all he needs…*all* he needs…is someone willing to wait as long for him."

Her heart squeezed hard, as though put in screws that twisted and twisted. They'd been so close before the shift had started to overtake him.

"I know," she said softly. And gods knew she wanted to wait. "But I don't know how long I have."

Phoenixes were similar to dragons in that they aged at a similar rate to humans through infancy and adolescence, slowing more and more as they hit their late teens and twenties. She and her sisters were five hundred years old but appeared no more than twenty-five or twenty-six.

But unlike dragons, their seeming immortality was tied to their mother's powers and magic in some mysterious way. Now that her mother had died, handing her power over to her daughters—all except for her—Angelika had no idea what to expect. Best guess was that she was human now, and would age like a human, until she was turned into a dragon shifter.

If that happened…

"I don't even know if I have a hundred years, let alone five hundred in me."

Jordy opened his mouth to respond, then seemed to think better of it. With an understanding nod, he closed the door behind him.

Angelika stared at the thick, old-fashioned wooden thing, then closed her eyes and blew out a breath, long and even, letting go of the tension still riding her.

Or trying to.

"Are you unwell?"

She snapped her eyes open to find Airk standing in front of the door. Damn silent dragon shifters. Mental note to make all the hinges in her home squeak if she mated one.

"You tell me."

Any concern in his eyes cooled. "I came to tell you that we can't mate."

What would he do if she threw something at his head? But she was too…tired. Even for that. Exhaustion, the kind that was of the heart and soul more than the body, dragged at her. The memory of all those words he'd spoken while he drove their pleasure higher, words that had filled her so full of happiness she could have flown, now added to the weight. "If I didn't already understand that from you flying off, you not looking at me that entire meeting clued me in."

Airk took a step forward, as though to argue, but suddenly a terrible sound—like the screaming of a thwarted siren—slammed through Angelika's mind. Inside her head, and yet she still slapped her hands over her ears in a useless attempt to shut it out.

"What's happening?" she tried to yell over the noise, but Airk's eyes were closed, his face a study of concentration as white scales rippled over and over and over across his skin and his face only to switch back to human just as fast. The noise was driving his dragon forward, and the man was holding it back through sheer, teeth-gritted will.

She didn't dare try to touch him or call to him again.

As fast as the noise started, though, it stopped. Not to return to normal. More like her ears were plugged, plunging her into her own silent bubble.

"My people," a familiar, smoke-laden voice clanged in her head. "This is your High King speaking."

• • •

Pytheios stared into his witch's cold face as he spoke to dragon shifters everywhere. He knew her magic was working to transmit his message because the few gathered in the room had cried out when she started her spell, then relaxed when Rhiamon had nodded at him to begin speaking. His was the only dragon shifter mind on the entire planet that she wasn't touching, somehow tapping into their telepathic communication.

He didn't question his witch's growing powers. Or fear them. She'd need to be disposed of quickly once his throne was assured, but he was certain she remained under his control for now.

Although, she might cause her own demise at the rate she was going, which would work out just as well for him.

Ever since he'd killed Merikh—sacrificed their weakling of a son to bring Rhiamon back from the dead—her powers had visibly been taking a toll on her. She was even paler now than she had been a week ago, skin almost translucent, showing the blood pumping through her veins in time to her heart. Her white curls hung in greasy clumps around her face as though she hadn't showered in weeks. And her eyes...

Before her death and resurrection, when she used her magic and only then, her jewel-green eyes would turn solid black with silver pupils and the black would appear to leach into the skin surrounding. Now her eyes were never their previous color, and the shadows leaching into her skin had spread, almost a mask across her face and temples, draining down into her cheeks. Perhaps death had filled her with such power, she could no longer disguise it behind human eyes.

She was deteriorating with it. However, he needed her too much to dispose of her yet, so he'd handle with care.

Especially when she was touching him, as she was now, her hands clasping his like manacles, nails digging into the undersides of his fingers. He ignored the small discomfort. Even if she were to draw blood, his newly mated and restored body would heal.

"As my power grows," he continued speaking to his people, "I am able to reach you all. Yet another proof that I am who I was always meant to be. Your High King. Now blessed by my phoenix mate."

Heat shot through his hands, coming from Rhiamon, and he almost jerked away, but he wasn't done with his message.

He'd explained to her the plan with Tisiphone and how he didn't love the girl. She was merely a means to an end. He'd thought Rhiamon had accepted the necessary steps he'd taken. Perhaps not.

"There are still dragon shifters who resist the truth that is staring them in their treacherous faces. I have shown you my newly healed body. I have introduced you to the true phoenix and successfully mated her. Yet still you fight me."

He paused, letting those words sink in.

"Now I am pleased to announce that our lovely phoenix savior is with child. With *my* child."

On cue, as they'd discussed previously, he released one of Rhiamon's hands to hold his out to Tisiphone, who stood nearby. Visibly wary of the witch, his new mate neared his side and took his outstretched hand. Their people wouldn't see her, but they would be able to hear her.

"Tell them, my heart," he murmured in the most loving voice he could muster, hiding a wince at another flare of heat from Rhiamon.

After a glance at the woman making this happen, Tisiphone's chin came up, a self-satisfied smile gracing her lovely lips. "My people, I am thrilled and blessed to announce to you that the next generation of phoenixes will be born six months from now. A girl, perfect and healthy, to carry on the legacy reinstated after five centuries of drought. May the beauty and luck of my phoenix ancestry remain with dragon shifters always."

With a nod of satisfaction, he released her hand, turning back to Rhiamon to finish his own message. "To those of you still resisting, I say walk away from your false alliances and declare your loyalty to me if no other rightful king steps forward in your clan. At the end of the era, you don't want to find you've chosen the wrong side."

Again he paused, letting that thought linger. Then his lip curled as he was unable to quite contain the soul-deep rage that any single dragon, let alone clans, had moved against him. "And make no mistake: to stand against the High King and his phoenix is to stand on the side of death. Stand with me now or know that I'm coming for you. No mercy will be given to any dragon who doesn't bear the right mark on their hand."

On that declaration, Rhiamon released his hands, cutting off the magic without even a blink of struggle. He studied her impassive face closely. Difficult to ascertain her emotions with those eyes. The power she wielded… Yes, he would do well to eliminate her soon.

All he needed was to take down the traitor kings, the phoenixes dragons had *never* needed in the first place, and their pathetically blind followers.

• • •

The bubble that kept Pytheios's voice in Airk's head shared space only with the raging of Airk's dragon, who was battering at the mental walls that he'd built around him after that misstep with Angelika. The creature hadn't broken through yet, but the false High King's voice sent him into fits so violent, Airk's entire body shook with the agony of it, shards of pain splintering through his mind, his bones, his blood, his gut.

Then, as suddenly as it started, the bubble popped and normal sound resumed, Pytheios no longer in his head.

But Airk remained still and silent, eyes closed, wishing for the first time since his release that he was back in his dragonsteel cage. His dragon had only tested those bars once, and they had sliced them both so badly it had taken Airk a full month to heal from the damage. After that, the threat of killing them both had helped to keep the beast inside him leashed.

Now that they were free, the two halves of his soul were pitted in a never-ending battle.

"Airk." Angelika was at least smart enough to stay on the other side of the room.

He didn't open his eyes. "I cannot," he said in a voice that was all smoke and lingering rage. "We will kill you, and I could not live with that."

So saying, he turned and, using every sense except sight, left the room. Only to almost walk over Jordy, who was hauling a massive wood-trimmed mirror down the human-sized hallway to Airk's family's old rooms.

"What are you doing?" Airk demanded, his dragon still very much in his voice.

Jordy flinched but only a little. "The phoenix asked for a mirror."
Damn it, Angelika.

He spun on his foot, stomping right back to her door, and let himself in. Again. Because she still hadn't locked the damn door behind him. The woman needed to learn to be more careful.

The room was empty. However, the sound of her voice led him into the bedroom that had been his as a child. He paused at the door to find her with her back to him, angrily yanking sheets off the furniture and muttering into a large phone-like device he hadn't seen.

"Dragon shifters. My sisters can have them. I give up, Jedd."

Jedd? The first thing she'd done was call the wolf shifter who wanted her?

Jealousy clawed its way up Airk's back, tightening each muscle along the way. Not just jealousy—possessiveness and a tidal wave of an urge to be the one she went to with her problems. Not Jedd. Except Airk was the problem she was discussing.

Angelika snorted a laugh at something Jedd said. "Give me a nice fuzzy bunny shifter with a gut and a sweet attitude any damn day."

Angelika was swearing, which told him even more than the frustrated words that she was at the end of a tether.

"A pain in my ass. Since the day he showed up in Ben Nevis." She paused, listening to whatever that damn wolf had to say.

"I don't think so."

Another pause.

"You think I took one look at him and that was it?"

Everything inside Airk stilled at those words, his heart taking a nosedive for the soles of his feet.

She shook her head adamantly, listened a little longer, then sighed. "I'm too tired to think about this right now." Another pause. "I'll be in touch tomorrow with more."

With that, she hung up and tossed the phone onto a chair, going back to making the bed.

One corner of the sheet got hung up on the leg of the chair she was uncovering, and she gave the most adorable little growl. "I'm *way* too old to believe in..." She grabbed the sheet with both hands and gave a harder yank with each word. "Love. At. First. Sight."

Love. Gods above. Didn't she know he was the last person she should give her love to?

The sheet didn't give, but apparently she'd had enough. She stopped yanking, plunked her hands on her hips, and tipped her head back, appearing to glare at the ceiling, or perhaps talking to it.

"I was supposed to be pretending to be a wolf, but did I leave him alone? Nope. Then I sort of propose, and he says no. Should have left it at that. But did I?" She shook her head and went back to her tugging. "Nope. I kept hoping, like an idiot. Isn't the definition of insanity doing the same thing over and over and expecting a different outcome? I should have known better."

Her voice cracked on that last word, and Airk fisted his hands to keep himself from going to her. There was no way he could fix this, and he should just stay away, but gods, she suddenly appeared so…small.

"I always was the reckless one. People think it's Skylar, but it's me." Angelika finally yanked the sheet off what had been a big velvet-covered rocking chair his mother used to read books to him in. He'd forgotten about that chair and had to close his eyes against the sudden swelling of memories that hit with the force of a dragon's mace-like tail to the head.

A soft sound had him opening his eyes again, though, to see Angelika had flopped into it, leg hooked over the low arm of the chair. She dropped her head against the softly cushioned back and took a deep breath. "All right, Angelika Amon. Put on your big-girl panties and admit you were wrong. Time to let him go."

No.

The knee-jerk reaction was his dragon…but him, too.

She wasn't done, though, her tone now like she was giving herself a mental kick in the ass and bolstering pep talk all at the same time. "Pick a different dragon. Anyone will do. You're a phoenix, so the fire won't kill you. Hopefully. But being a dragon is better than being human—"

"No!" The word was out of him before he even thought it. Spewing out on a wave of possessiveness, but also heartbreak and the need to keep her safe. He'd made her get to this point. His brokenness was breaking her, too.

Angelika was on her feet in an instant, shock turning to a brave glare, her chin tipping up, anger in every line of her body. Except her eyes, which were begging him not to put her through any more.

He'd tried. Gods knew he'd tried. "Do not dare to give yourself to just anyone," he ordered. "I will not let you."

She crossed her arms, wariness changing to fury in her narrowed eyes. "You forfeited your right to have any say in this."

"You cannot—"

"I'll do what I have to in order to survive and to take out my family's killer. Unlike you, I don't run from my problems, Airk. I face them."

"You think I run away?" He threw the words at her, his own anger and frustration rising to meet hers. "I am trying to *protect* you."

She picked up a small pillow from the chair and hurled it at his head. "I didn't ask you to."

Airk ducked, which only seemed to make her angrier, and she searched the room for more ammunition, but it was all still covered up. So she took off her shoe.

"Gods above, Angelika, what do you want me to do?"

Angelika stopped, hand raised to fling the shoe at his head, and stared at him a long beat before slowly lowering it. "I don't know." She dropped her gaze to the shoe in her hand and shook her head, more at herself, it seemed. "Not this, though."

Damn. There was no answer here. He wouldn't risk hurting her, let alone her life.

Angelika sighed. "It's time to let you go."

The pain that shot through him at her soft, determined words came close to what had gone through him the day he'd lost his parents and been locked up in his cage. His dragon railed and clawed and roared, and…gods, he had to get out of here. Now.

"Promise me you will not mate rashly," he threw at her.

Then he walked from the room. Hells, he practically bolted. He pulled up at the sight of Jordy in the foyer still messing around with the mirror and paused only long enough to address his old friend. "I need you to stay with her. I will stay at your place."

Jordy didn't so much as blink. "I'll keep her safe, my lord."

Airk trusted that he would. "And cover that fucking mirror."

Then he stalked from the suite for the second time before he did something rash himself. Like go back and push his fire into her.

CHAPTER TWENTY

The second Pytheios's voice had sounded in Kasia's mind and she'd realized Brand was hearing it, too, she'd known what would happen next. Her mate took every threat personally and seemed to only calm when he'd sunk himself inside her and they both visited the heavens together.

Not that Brand ever missed an opportunity to claim her body— her, either, for that matter—but after an incident like that, their lovemaking tended to turn more…intense. Almost as though he needed to prove to himself that the Rotting King hadn't snatched yet another loved one from his arms.

Her big, scary dragon-shifter mate didn't disappoint, either. Buried inside her, eyes aflame with golden light, hands wrapped possessively in her long hair, and a harshly beautiful sort of demand tightening his features. His earthy, wood and smoke scent surrounded her, which only turned her on more.

"Kasia." Command laced the single word.

Ecstasy exploded inside her, and all around her their bed went up in flames, coming from them both. As she pulsed, Brand's cock grew thick inside her, and he threw his head back, shouting as her pleasure tipped him over into the abyss of his own.

In the midst of the pleasure, he put his mouth to hers. "I'm yours," he groaned against her lips. "Always."

The words swept her along, tumbling her over into a second

orgasm simply on the strength of her love for this man, entirely caught up in the magic of what they had together.

As happened sometimes since the night they mated, her ability to have visions intertwined with her release. With each crest of the most incredible pleasure unexpectedly came a different flash— pristinely clear, with audible sounds and vivid colors. Vision after vision. She didn't try to watch them or keep them in her mind, instead focusing on Brand's face and the sensations flowing through her body. The beautiful completion in his eyes as they shared the intense climax. Riding it to its end, until they'd wrung every nuance they could from the joining.

Brand collapsed over her, chest heaving, and she relished the weight of his body on hers, his still semi-hard length inside her. Closing her eyes, she gave herself permission to just be with him. She could review those visions after they'd had this first. This moment where their souls settled together, entwined and replete.

The only time she ever saw her mate truly content.

As their breathing slowed, Brand kissed the side of her neck, then her cheek, and lifted his head to pin her with eyes still molten gold but no longer flaming.

"What did you see?" he demanded.

Kasia's lips twitched, and she turned in his arms, feathering her fingers through his shorter hair. When they'd met, he'd worn the dirty blond locks on the long side to cover the mark on his neck, but since becoming king, he'd decided to display that family symbol with pride.

"I should've known you'd notice," she murmured.

"Nothing about you escapes me, princess." He wrapped a lock of hair around his finger and tugged her closer to lay a sweet, swift kiss on her lips. "So...the vision?"

"I don't know, lizard boy. I was a little distracted with an orgasm or two, so I didn't pay much attention."

The smug satisfaction that curled his lips was probably worth bonking him on the head for his arrogance, but she was too sated and happy to bother. Instead, she closed her eyes and let go, her fire coming up and over them both.

"Can you see?" she asked.

Only recently had Brand started being able to watch the visions with her if she included him in her fire. Best guess was he used the link all mates shared once they were bonded, though the ways in which mates used that link differed by couple.

"Yes." His voice reached her as though far away, down a tunnel.

Several scenes came on all at once, and deliberately she slowed them down, taking the time to inspect each one.

A vision of Meira in labor, strawberry blond curls plastered to her head as she breathed through her labor pains. Samael at her side, holding her hand, looking overwhelmed. "Almost there," someone was saying. "One last push."

Before Kasia could assure herself everything would be fine, the image changed. To one she'd seen before. A man inside a cell high in the mountains. So high the sky was more black than blue. He sat on a long stone bench and stared out at the stars. Airk. She knew that now. Sitting with his elbows on his knees, hands in his hair. Shorter hair, though, not long like when he was actually held.

Gods. Was she seeing the past or the future? If Pytheios captured him and put him back in that cage, Kasia wasn't sure Airk would survive that. His mind or his dragon might break.

The next vision came, a flash of Airk and Angelika, fingers of one hand laced together, staring at each other in a kind of wonder. "My mate," Airk whispered. "It worked."

What worked? Angelika was dormant. What did that mean?

Then, finally, an image that sent the fear of all seven hells through her like the hammering cut of a broadsword. A swarm of dragons—red and green—descending over a mountain. But the image disappeared before she could see more than the tips of rocks, not enough to identify the location. Then Pytheios—so much younger-looking than she'd ever seen, harshly handsome with it—walking through a room with no identifiable details. A massive room inside the mountain, maybe, but again it could be any dragon-shifter lair. Then the vision shifted, showing him approaching what appeared to be a handful of white dragons. All she could see were their feet lined up in a row as though guarding an entrance.

"Bow to me now or die," Pytheios ordered.

With a gasp, Kasia's eyes flew open, the flames turning to smoke as they died, only to encounter Brand's grim expression. He'd seen it all, too.

"He's going to take the White Clan's mountain," he said.

Fear for her sister curled Kasia's hands around his biceps. "We have to warn Angelika."

. . .

"My lady?"

The lights turned on, and Angelika blinked out of what hadn't been a great sleep anyway. She sighed. "Jordy. I've asked you repeatedly to call me Angelika."

"Yes, milady."

She shook her head. But mid-shake he was already across the room, handing her an armful of clothing. "You need to get dressed."

The urgency in his voice finally penetrated her sleep-fogged brain. Without hesitating, she was up and moving into the bathroom to change.

"What's wrong?" she asked Jordy through the cracked door. She stripped off the men's T-shirt Jordy had scrounged her up to sleep in and started to dress in black slacks and a white silk blouse with a collar the 1980s would be proud of.

"I wasn't told," he called over the screen at her. "Only that you had an urgent communication."

Communication?

Angelika's fingers paused on the last button of the blouse, mind spinning over who might be trying. Only a handful knew she was here. Not even that. Her sisters and their mates, and the wolves plus the dozen or so white dragons she'd met with yesterday, except they wouldn't be calling her for a "communication," which left her sisters or maybe the wolves.

That was it.

Any of them contacting her off schedule here was very bad.

"Has Airk been notified?"

"Yes, milady. He will meet you there."

Angelika had to ignore the spiked pit in her stomach that he wasn't here right now. She'd gotten accustomed to having him around, at her side, in such a short time.

So get unaccustomed quick.

Finished dressing, she twisted her hair into a topknot. The best she could do with such short notice. Then she motioned Jordy to lead the way, pausing only in the foyer as something struck her as odd. "Why is there a sheet over the mirror?"

"Orders from young Airk."

She winced, calling herself all sorts of fool. No wonder Meira hadn't tried to reach her that way. The same reason Airk wanted it covered. Pytheios's earlier trick with the mirrors. Airk was still protecting her. Hells, even his rejection was a form of protection.

She knew that. Loved him a little bit for it, even. At least she would if it wasn't getting in the way of them being together.

With a nod, they hurried on through the labyrinthine halls, back to the room next door to the one Airk had smashed through the windows with Brock. A smaller conference room.

As soon as she walked in, she found Airk, Belyy, Tovar, and Mös waiting. Mös hit a switch on the wall, and the glass turned opaque. At his nod, Tovar tapped a few keys on a keyboard, and the single, small TV screen was suddenly filled with all three of her sisters and their mates.

No relief in their faces, though, as they saw she was all right and safely with white dragons. She hadn't even had a chance to inform them of the success allying with their father's clan yet, given that the specific date and time they'd arranged was later today. But their expressions told her that this call wasn't about that.

"I've had a vision." Kasia didn't even bother with a hello.

"Pytheios is coming for the White Clan."

"Fuck," one of the men in the room muttered. Not Airk. He stayed silent.

"Do you think he already knows about Brock Hagan's death?" That was Tovar asking Mös.

All three of Angelika's brothers-by-blood snapped to attention. But Brand was the one who prowled forward, tucking Kasia behind him so he could shove his face in the camera. "Hagan is dead?" he demanded.

Angelika nodded. "He came for the throne. He was here when we arrived—"

Airk cut her off. "*I* killed him."

"Remind me to shake your hand next time we meet in person," Brand said. Though the snarl in his voice made him sound angry, the light in his eyes was clearly relief and ultimate satisfaction.

Airk nodded.

"How do you know they're coming?" Mös asked.

"Who the hell are you?" Ladon snapped back.

"Our ally. He was Volos's Beta." Angelika stopped them all from posturing with a firm insertion, then turned to her sister. "What did you see, Kas?"

Kasia gently moved the bulk of Brand's body behind her so that she was once again visible on the screen. "A swarm of red and green dragons over a mountain. Then Pytheios landing and confronting a line of white dragons, telling them to swear allegiance or die."

"Which mountain?" Mös leaned forward, flaming gaze sending eerie white shadows dancing over his face.

Kasia grimaced. "I couldn't see enough details. I'm sorry I can't give you more to go on."

"How long?" Airk demanded.

"I don't know." Kasia shook her head. "Hours, days, months. There was nothing to indicate time."

"Forewarned is forearmed," Angelika said, repeating words their mother had said so often it had become a family joke until the day the red king showed up and killed her.

Angelika swung around to face her new allies. "We need to move up our timeline."

They'd planned to introduce her and Airk to the clan in groups, starting with the leadership. They couldn't wait to stretch that out in the gradual approach now.

Mös gave a jerking nod. "I'll announce a mountain-wide meeting. Best be for..." He checked his phone for the time. "For later this evening to give us time to get the word to everyone. In the meantime, I'll heighten security and start procedures to lock down all White Clan mountains."

With a nod, she spun back to the display. "Thank you for the warning—"

"Don't hang up." Kasia rushed to cut her off. "There's something I need to tell you and Airk together. Alone."

"If you think I'm leaving—"

Mös cut off his words at a growl from Airk, but Angelika put a hand on his arm. "You can stay," she said. "We need you."

He stared at her long and hard. After all, he was following her more out of hatred for Pytheios than any loyalty to her. But finally he nodded. Jordy, Belyy, and Tovar left the room. Out of some kind of respect, she suspected, Mös moved to the back of the room. A silent observer.

Angelika faced the screen. "What else?"

She braced herself for all manner of bad news.

Kasia took a deep breath. "You two were mated in one of my flashes. I think."

• • •

Airk had to shake his head to clear it of the triumphant roar of his dragon. "What?"

"I believe she just said we mated," Angelika offered. Instead of smug, though, she sounded as befuddled as he felt. Nor was she looking at him, keeping her focus on her sisters.

His dragon wanted to pick their little phoenix up and go make that a fact instead of a vision right this instant. Airk fisted his hands, holding the mental walls around his creature half, needing to be sure…

"What do you mean, you think?" he asked.

Kasia hummed in her throat, her icy eyes, so like Angelika's, going unfocused. He'd seen her access her visions enough to know that's what she was doing.

Kasia detailed what she'd seen, then blinked as though coming back into herself. "Do you know what that might mean?" she asked. "What worked? Have your powers manifested?" The last she asked of Angelika.

But the woman beside him seemed thunderstruck, eyes wide and unseeing, mouth opening and closing.

"Angelika?" Meira prompted.

"Fuck me," Angelika muttered, the swear word on her lips jarring.

She dropped her gaze, staring at the ground, still unseeing, as though working through that. Then she sort of tipped her head sideways, as though assessing his own reaction while not looking at him.

"I've shown dragon sign," she told her siblings. Then raised her gaze to look at her sisters. "That has to be it."

Airk breathed out through his nose, slow and controlled as Kasia's words repeated through his mind.

It worked. It worked. It worked.

That's what Kasia said. Could he mate Angelika successfully, without his dragon killing her? Not for him—for her. Then the White Clan would be even more likely to accept her as their queen. But more than that, she'd be less vulnerable. No longer human and frail with it. She'd be able to hold her own.

And she'd be mine.

His dragon rumbled a low, satisfied growl of possession and agreement all mixed together.

"You're sure?" Skylar demanded.

Angelika seemed to come out of her stupor. "I'm sure. I went up in flames that didn't burn me. But no phoenix lines. No hint of anything except dragon sign."

I can turn her safely, without my dragon killing her.

Finally, the realization sank in fully. He'd seen enough of Kasia's visions come true in the short time he'd been around the sisters to not question it. Sometimes the interpretation was wrong, but the visions always came to be.

Gods, please let her be right about this one.

Because for once in his life, he wasn't going to question this gift. This blessing.

"I am afraid you must excuse us," he said to all of them and no one in particular.

Every man on the screen grinned, or some variation of it, and all of her sisters frowned. He didn't bother to turn off the call as he grabbed her by the hand and tugged her out the door, ignoring the man still in the corner of the room.

Two steps down the hall, Angelika dug her heels in, jerking them to a halt. "What do you think you're doing?"

Airk leveled a hard, semi-confused stare on her. It seemed obvious to him. "What do you think?"

Only instead of any positive emotion she might have given him, particularly given the way she'd been pushing for this, she scowled, blue gaze flashing. "Excuse me? Now that you know for sure it's going to work, you're ready to fuck me and put your fire in me?"

Of course she'd see it that way, stubborn woman. Airk stepped into her, hands slipping into her hair, dislodging whatever she'd used to pin it up, the white tresses falling about her shoulders as he shoved his face right in hers. "No. Now that I know I will not *kill* you, I cannot...not do this."

Some of the anger leached out of her, her shoulders easing, but she was still scowling. "You didn't trust in us, but one word from my sister's vision, and it's all okay?"

"I did not trust *me*." How could she not see this? "Do you not understand? Killing you would be the same as killing a butterfly or a unicorn—something so pure and precious, it would have destroyed what I have left of my soul."

Angelika settled at that, searching his gaze. "You were afraid?"

She asked the question as though she'd thought him incapable of the emotion. "I was terrified. But knowing it can work safely..."

The tip of her pink tongue flashed out, wetting her lips. "Why?"

Oddly, now that he had his hands on her and wasn't fighting his dragon anymore, the creature was...calm...inside him. "Why what?" he asked, searching her gaze.

"Is this only to turn me?"

"Yes..." She tried to tug out of his grip, and he stepped closer. "And no."

She gave her head a tiny shake, the silk of her hair tangling more in his fingers with the gesture.

"I want you to be safe and able to take your rightful place among your father's people. *Our* people," he said. "So yes, for those reasons."

Her eyebrows twitched down, clearly not loving that.

"For you," he said. "Not for them. Because this is what *you* want."

The eyebrows eased, only slightly. "Mating is for hundreds of years. You're willing to tie yourself to me for centuries, for a lifetime, just to give me what I want?"

Airk released a slow breath and lowered his head until his lips hovered over hers. "Be mine," he whispered, holding her gaze. "That is what *I* want."

The hitch in her breathing was his only hint that she liked what she heard. "You want me?" she asked, also whispering. Airk's lips tilted. A full smile that still felt rusty after centuries without a reason to use it. "Did you not hear a word I said during that first disastrous mating attempt?"

A laugh punched from her. "Nothing is obvious with you, Airk Azdajah." The smile tipping her lips was tremulous.

She was right. He hadn't been fair to her, even as that was what he'd been trying to be. He searched her eyes. Had all that back-and-forth ruined the relationship for her? "Will you mate me, Angelika Amon?" He grimaced. "It will not be easy for you. I do not like to talk. I do not know how to be around people. Touch can be difficult for me. My dragon even more so. I may be more liability than boon, but I will protect you with every—"

Angelika placed one finger over his lips, stopping him. "Yes."

Airk and his dragon both stilled. "Yes?"

Her slow smile was the most beautiful thing he'd ever seen. "Yes," she said again, then grinned, eyes dancing. "But please hurry before you change your mind again."

Happiness had been a part of his life once. He remembered laughing and playing as a boy, the sound of his parents tucking him in at night, the murmur of content in his home. But the emotion almost sideswiped him now. Forget walking at a human pace. He swept her up into his arms and sprinted through the mountain to his family's rooms. The place he'd grown up. Claiming his mate here seemed...right. As though they were reawakening these rooms together with hope and a new, fresh start.

He didn't take her to his childhood room, though. Instead he took her to the larger suite that would have been his when he'd reached maturity. Only, the second he stepped into the room, he found it not covered in sheets and unused, but pristinely and newly cleaned with fresh sheets on the bed. As though it had been ready and waiting for them. It even had a vase of roses, pink, and smelled of the flowers, though Angelika's sun-warmed scent filled him full.

Slowly, gently, he lowered her feet to the ground, staring into her upturned face, so trusting. "We need to take this...slowly."

Just because the vision said they'd be successful one day didn't mean today was that day. The last time they tried this, his dragon tried to get involved.

"I can do that," she whispered. Angelika traced her fingers over his face—his jaw, his lips, his neck.

A new burning in his chest told him he might not be able to. But her safety came first, so he forced himself to calm as much as he was able, though his cock was as hard as a steel mace and throbbing already.

"Is this okay?" she whispered. In her eyes he could see a tumble of fascination that reflected his own. They'd done this before, but that reaction only seemed to grow with each new contact. But also in those ice-blue eyes lay a sort of quiet fear. Regret squeezed his heart. He had put that in her.

"If I died in your arms," he said, "it would be a good death."

She shook her head, though she was smiling. "No talk of death. This is a first step to a new *life*. Yes?"

He hoped so, but he wouldn't make that promise, either.

Instead, he brushed a finger lightly across her delicate collarbone, then traced the V neckline of her blouse down to the first button, undoing it slowly, then the next, until he bared the upper swell of her breasts encased in lace, which he stopped to trace as well. Her breathing increased, and gods' teeth he liked that. Liked affecting her that way.

Hooking a finger in the material of her bra, he dragged it down until one rosy-tipped breast spilled into his hand. Her nipple was already swollen, pressing into his palm. Out of curiosity, just to see if she liked it, he squeezed at the tip, and her gasp shot straight to his already straining cock.

She liked it. So did he.

Fascination overtook him, focusing him on that one reaction and dragging it from her again. He rolled the nub between his fingers, and she moaned. A shudder charged through him at the sound. The angels and cherubim had nothing on pleasure from Angelika's lips.

"Hold me," she whispered.

On a groan, he hooked one arm around her waist and dragged her against him, burying his face in her neck, inhaling the floral scent of her. He rubbed his cheek against hers, the sound of his stubble against her soft skin somehow perfect. Everything about her a flawless foil to him.

"You are so beautiful," he whispered in her ear.

"I think we've been here before, sir," she sighed back.

Then she stepped away. He let her go, arms dropping to his sides, and hungrily watched as she unbuttoned the rest of her blouse, promises he desperately wanted to reach for there in her eyes as she slowly, unselfconsciously undressed before him. Not looking away from each precious inch of skin she revealed, Airk stripped as well. Maybe a little faster, though. He was naked long before the last item of her clothing hit the floor.

He took her in, standing before him in a way that no other man would ever see. Not if they valued their life. He'd heard tales of the Greek goddess Aphrodite, of the beauty of Helen of Troy, of the Amazons, and of Cleopatra, the Queen of Egypt, and he didn't imagine a single one could hold a candle to the ethereal siren standing before him. His dragon pressed against the walls containing him, but Airk wouldn't release the creature from his mental bonds until he needed their fire.

"Gods, Angelika. How am I supposed to stay in control when you look at me that way?"

His siren smiled, frosty eyes heated, needy. "What way?"

"Like you want me to—"

"I do." Her smile turned even more fiery. "I want your hands on me, Airk. Your mouth. I want you inside me, possessing me. And I want to do the same to you."

She moved toward him, every step a sinuous, delicate glide that left his mouth dry. "I want us to reach that paradise together. Often."

So did he, gods save him. But first they had to make it over this huge hurdle.

"What do you want?" she whispered.

"To see my family's mark on you." The words were out before he even thought the thought, and he jolted with the realization that the need had been there all along. He'd just never let himself reach for it.

Angelika tipped her head, tenderness shining at him. "Let's make that happen."

Holding out a hand, she beckoned him to follow as she backed up to the bed. When her calves hit it, she climbed up, still facing him, sliding back, her smile encouraging. Then she splayed her legs open, showing him paradise.

On a groan, Airk crawled across the bed to cover her body with his weight and claim her lips in long, deep, drugging kisses, losing himself in the taste of her, the feel of her silky, petite body against his. Airk touched her everywhere, his hands gliding and dipping and pausing to tease—her legs, her belly, her breasts, before losing himself in the triangle of curls at the juncture of her thighs.

She was slick and hot, ready for him.

He wanted to linger and explore every part of her, but the way his dragon was seeking release, seeking their mate, waiting might make his control slip.

"I'm going to join us now," he murmured against her lips.

"Hells yes," she moaned back, and he couldn't stop the chuckle that echoed in his chest. Didn't want to stop it, because that happiness was inside him again. Just a spark, but the warmth was all he needed.

CHAPTER TWENTY-ONE

Angelika held her breath as her lover aligned himself to her body, then pressed inside. Slowly, slowly…gods, so slowly she wanted to scream and savor at the same time.

His muscles locked and trembled above her as he controlled the thrust so tightly, pressing, pressing, until his cock filled her to the hilt, stretching her and yet familiar now in the best way.

Any second, Angelika expected Airk to come to his senses and pull away. Or run away. Again. But maybe just knowing that he could do this without killing her had given him permission to relax.

He stopped suddenly, breathing hard, eyes locked to hers as he visibly struggled for control, his white-blue eyes turning dragon for a flash.

Maybe not.

Angelika took his face in her hands, staring deeply into his eyes, seeing the man but addressing the creature buried inside. "You have to let Airk do this, with your help, if you want me to belong to you both."

Was she getting through? Could the dragon even fathom her words, let alone understand and act?

Airk blew out a long breath, then the ridges of his muscles gave a little. "He likes your voice."

Moving restlessly against him, Angelika grinned. "That's great… but right now I really need your fire inside me."

A rare blush surged into her cheeks at her boldness, and Airk's eyes twinkled, even as his gaze turned more intense, searing her with a look. He obeyed the demand and dragged his hips back, almost as slowly as he'd entered her, before pressing inside again in that masterly, controlled manner.

"Faster," Angelika demanded and moaned at the same time, using her feet against the backs of his legs to try to hurry him up.

"No."

She gave a tiny *grrrr* of frustration, even as her body sang with the sensations his total, controlled possession was building inside her.

Airk's smile turned predatorial.

He continued to torture them both with the slow surge and retreat. No wonder this man had withstood the years in captivity. If control was a superpower, he was the most dominant man on the damn planet.

A spark of her naturally teasing nature struck, and Angelika started trying ways to tip that control over the edge. Not much. Not enough to let the dragon out. Just a little.

She ran her hands up over the backs of his legs, squeezing an ass that was pure muscle. His smile turned almost taunting, and she had a feeling he was well aware what she was attempting. Not that she gave up. Next, she trailed her foot up the back of his leg, adjusting her position, seating him more deeply as he pressed forward.

That drew a small grunt from them both.

"I know what you are doing," he whispered.

She shot him her most innocent, wide-eyed look, even batting eyelashes. "I'm getting thoroughly fucked."

The color that surged into his cheeks at that told her he liked those words. He liked them a lot.

To prove her point, she clenched her inner muscles around him as he dragged his cock out.

That drew a full-on groan from him, and he reared up over her, the sound of fire stoking in his chest unmistakable.

Finally.

"If you still want this, open your mouth." A command, stark, harsh, and uncompromising, even as he gave her a choice.

As if she'd change her mind. Clenching her inner muscles around him again, she did as he asked, opening wide.

On a growl that was pure dragon, his eyes lighting on fire as his chest glowed from within, Airk lunged at her. His kiss, when it came, was exacting, ravaging, and still in utter control. Heat poured into her mouth, not burning, only adding to the heat consuming her body from his touch.

His fire stopped suddenly, and he buried his face in her neck, going eerily still.

"Airk?" she murmured.

She feathered a soothing hand over his shoulders, his back.

On a roar, he lifted his head, staring down at her with worry clouding his eyes, watching her closely.

"Stay with me," he begged harshly. Almost a plea.

Had it suddenly occurred to him that, if she was only a human with dragon sign, that she wasn't a phoenix? Which meant that, if he wasn't her fated mate, he could kill her with his fire. She had no fire to mate him with, which she'd always assumed was what protected a phoenix from dying. Gave them the choice of mates.

Hadn't he realized?

Because she'd known that the second she'd recognized what her dragon sign was. Known and accepted the risk. Immediately. No question.

But the heat inside her wasn't burning, wasn't eating away at her insides. If anything, it only latched on to the bliss coursing through her veins, heightening her pleasure.

Angelika's eyes went wide. "If you want to join me in this orgasm…" A shiver racked her from head to toe. "You'd better get going."

The relief that poured through him melted over his face and his shoulders, only to pour blood into his cock, thickening her inside him.

"Thank the gods," he muttered.

. . .

Desire, pleasure, and relief apparently combined with an elemental sort of possession in a way that turned to pure, incandescent pleasure.

Airk let go of the last of his fears—the first being producing fire without releasing his dragon, and the second watching Angelika burn to death in his fire. Neither had happened. She was his now. Theirs.

And he intended to give himself to her fully. He was hers. Forever.

Rearing back onto his knees, he clamped his hands around her thighs, lifting her bottom up, and held her there as he pounded into her. Her body was wet and hot and tight around him, grasping at his cock with the most delicious drag as he surged in and out of her.

He stared into her beautiful face, accepting her total trust, the passion seizing her features as she moaned around her pleasure, feeding his. For once, he didn't need to be in control. Falling forward, he gathered her into his arms and kissed her, over and over, in time to his body as he built their combined pleasure higher and higher.

"Airk?" Wonder laced his name, and he knew she was close.

A tingling gathered at the base of his spine so intense his body felt electrified. He let go of the final mental barrier, dropping those walls he'd built around his dragon, and together, on a shout of total completion, they poured a new kind of fire into her, for the first time in memory acting as one.

Angelika bore down on him and tossed her head back on a scream of ecstasy, her orgasm dragging his own pleasure out, and Airk shouted to the skies as sensation sizzled through his body and streams of his essence poured into his mate's body. His dragon pressed harder, roaring in his head and sending another wave of fire into Angelika, whose breath hitched. Then she cried out again, a second orgasm ripping through her so hard, her body milked his with a stranglehold until every last ounce of him coated her womb.

Only then did they slow. Sweat-slicked and breathing hard, he buried his face in her neck, reaching for control again.

But he didn't need to. His dragon was…oddly content…inside him.

He clutched her more tightly to him, suddenly wanting to claim her again, just to watch her face as she tumbled over into that abyss of sensation, to taste more of her, feel more of her. But that would come later.

She was his, now and forever.

Gently, he moved them so that they lay on their sides facing each other. Taking a deep breath, Angelika twined her fingers with his, then lifted eyes glowing with hope and an undeniable happiness to meet his gaze.

He sucked in sharply at the look in those eyes. Ages ago, he'd given up all hope of having this. Having a mate.

"My mate," he whispered the word, his dragon humming with satisfaction inside his head. "It worked."

Her lips drew into a smile precious with happiness. "Just like Kasia said."

Airk dropped his forehead to hers. "Thank the gods."

"See?" she teased. "If you had just accepted my good sense when I brought this up the first time, we could have saved a lot of time and angst."

Airk grunted at that.

"In fact, I think we should make it a rule that you listen to me from now on."

He huffed a laugh, shaking his head. His little mate was incorrigible, but then, that had always been part of what drew him to her.

Angelika bit her lip, staring at him as though he'd grown two heads.

"What?" he asked.

"I've never seen you so…"

Happy. Relaxed. Free. He grimaced. "It probably will not last. I am pretty sure my nature is not this."

Hmmm… She didn't seem too bothered by that fact. "I think I have a good sense of the man I mated."

She did, too, even when no one else wanted to get close enough to try.

"We need to work on your self-preservation skills," he murmured.

Angelika's grin might have lit up the entire room. "What do I need those for? I'm a dragon now."

He grunted. "Not yet."

Not until the bond snapped into place and his family's mark seared into the skin at the nape of her neck. Bonding could take seconds for some, years for others. The mysterious connection was something dragons didn't question or try to explain. They just accepted it and waited.

A new kind of tension filled him, tightening the strands of his muscles one by one, first across his shoulders, then down his back, his arms.

A new kind of worry.

Keeping her safe was always a concern, and until that bond, he was determined to never leave her side. But once she could shift, the new problem was making sure nothing happened to *him*. Because if he died, the bond would drag her into the grave right after him.

Fuck. What was I thinking?

He'd permanently bound her to a man who couldn't shift. Shouldn't ever shift again. Which meant he needed to be more careful than ever with himself.

"Stop," Angelika mumbled, voice turning sleepy.

"Stop what?"

"Remember…I can hear when you're overthinking. Probably a bad habit from being locked in a cell with nothing else to do. All bad things about protecting me from you or from myself, probably." She flung a leg over his, plastering her delectable body even closer, and burrowed her head under his chin. "You can just stop."

For once, surrounded by her sunshine scent and her heat with her in his arms, Airk was inclined to agree. He'd probably wake up tomorrow with a thousand regrets and even more worries.

Something he'd never seen coming.

He'd never, ever seen *her* coming, even when he'd always seen her.

He snuggled her closer. "Stealthy."

"What was that?"

"You. You are stealthy." He closed his eyes. "Snuck under my skin and into my life even while I was looking."

A soft chuckle tickled his chin. "Good thing for you. If you haven't heard, I'm quite the catch."

"Because you are a phoenix?" He shook his head, then had to reach up to pull a gossamer strand of hair off his face. "I do not care about that. Never did."

"Ah. So you mated me for my body, then?"

He couldn't help his smile even as he shook his head. "Sleep."

She seemed to settle, and his heart tried to stop altogether at the sense that this was beyond right.

After a beat of silence: "Do you think they'll accept us?" she asked in a small voice he'd never heard from his brave mate.

"Accept us?"

"The White Clan? As leaders, I mean."

Airk had zero intention of stepping into any kind of leadership position. Not without being able to shift. But Angelika... "They will love you," he said. "Everyone does."

She mumbled something into his chest that might have been, "Not everyone."

What was that supposed to mean? "Hmmm?"

"Nothing."

He didn't believe her, but he was familiar with that tone by now. She had no intention of telling him. "Are you going to sleep now?"

She shrugged. "I'm not sleepy."

Airk slowly opened his eyes, not really taking in the rock wall across the room. "Oh? What are you?"

A small silence greeted his question. "Um...maybe we should try that mating thing again. Just to be sure it took."

Now a slow smile crept across his mouth. "I do not want to

wear you out."

"No chance of that."

Airk lifted his head to stare down into sparkling eyes. Then flipped them in the bed so that he was on his back and she was seated across him, straddling him, the long, already achingly hard shaft of his cock pressed right into the hot, slick core of her.

Her eyes went wide, and she laughed. "I guess I'm not the only one not tired."

Airk tucked his hands behind his head, thoroughly enjoying the view.

Her eyebrows shot up. "What are you doing?"

His smile was slow as his mind flipped through the *Kama Sutra* book Nathair had brought him and all the things he wanted to try. "I'm letting you play," he said.

Confusion darkened her eyes to sky blue, brows lowering.

So he gripped her hips, lifted her up, and impaled her on his rigid cock, almost coming then and there at the stark moan that ripped from her. Then, seated deeply inside her, he let go. "Play, little mate." A command.

Angelika's eyes widened, comprehension dawning.

For a split second, he wondered if she would balk. The swift color flooding her cheeks told him she might. He waited. Patience, learned patience—finally a fucking virtue.

Then her eyes narrowed, a spark of challenge in them, her lips tilting. She undulated her hips, and Airk smiled, then hung on for the ride.

CHAPTER TWENTY-TWO

Angelika wasn't sure who was more nervous: her or Airk. Rather than meet with individuals and smaller groups of the clan, gradually spreading the word of their coming here and the switch in allegiances, the imminent attack on the mountain meant a single clan-wide introduction. At least to those in this mountain, who accounted for approximately 65 percent of her father's people.

Jordy had brought a small throng of people to their suite this morning, all of whom had been sworn to secrecy until this announcement was made. They'd spent hours—no joke—primping her and spilling her into a dress that she would have guessed was designed specifically for a phoenix when she first saw it.

Made of some white floaty material, the long skirt had hidden slits almost to her waist that parted to reveal long lengths of leg when she walked. But the bodice was what struck her as the most appropriate. The material had been cut to look like feathers over her breasts, leaving a deep V bare to her navel. The same wing design on the back attached cape-like swaths that trailed behind her. Her face had been made up with glittering, pearlescent shimmer around her eyes and temples in a subtle winged pattern.

To top it off, her white-blond hair was pulled back into an elegant ponytail with a hard part down the middle. Over that, they'd placed a delicate diadem—more like a chain—of white and pale blue diamonds. A single strand traced the part in her hair, with two strands to either side, all connecting at her forehead, where a looped pattern formed.

Looking in the mirror, she had been put in mind of elves and fairies, elusive and even more secretive than dragon shifters. Otherworldly.

Not her.

"Where did you get this so quickly?" she'd asked the man who seemed to be in charge of the group helping her.

The sadness in his smile was her first warning, but his words still sliced like razor blades. "This is what your mother would have worn when her bond with King Zilant solidified and she was crowned Queen and he High King."

"Oh." She swallowed hard.

Her helper had offered a kindly smile. "You may have the look of your father, but you are willowy, like your mother. This was custom made for her, and it fits you like a glove, though we had to shorten the hem a bit."

Tears burned at that. She was told so often that she was a reflection of her father, who she'd only ever known as a hellhound, and even then, none of them had truly known who Maul was until the end. The end she hadn't been there for.

But never her mother.

"Now, now. No crying, or I'll have to start all over." Her helper had rushed over with a tissue, blotting carefully.

Angelika had huffed a laugh. "I wouldn't want to ruin all that. You're a miracle worker and a true artist."

He'd smiled. "When you have a canvas this lovely, it's easy enough."

A low rumble of a growl had come from the corner of the room where Airk sat. He'd been ready in less than an hour, and, despite the protests of everyone else, had stalked into the room where she was being made up, grumbling about the constraints of his suit and this being a ridiculous parade of folderol.

They'd put him in a three-piece suit of a shiny gray that almost appeared silver, white pearl buttons, and a pale blue tie that matched her own headdress—or they'd tried to put him in it, anyway. He'd refused the jacket, and damned if she hadn't always had a thing for a guy in a formal vest with the sleeves rolled up.

The man drying her tears had frozen at Airk's rumbled warning, then, very carefully, pulled his hands away from her.

"Stop that," Angelika mouthed at him.

Even though she knew he couldn't. A newly mated dragon male was possibly the most dangerous creature on earth—instinct and his creature driving him to a possessive kind of protectiveness. Oddly, a huge turn-on, and she hoped they couldn't see how her nipples peaked at the sound. Sure enough, his gaze drifted down her body to the evidence of her reaction.

He merely shrugged, offering no apology. And was that a smile?

He'd be unbearable for a while, she understood, and despite thinking of herself as an independent, modern woman, shivers of anticipation for the next time they were alone tiptoed up her spine.

His gaze sharpened, spearing her as though he'd read her thoughts.

Jordy had ushered her helpers out at that point, leaving Airk and Angelika alone. Her mate had stayed seated, but his gaze had traveled over her in the most delicious way, heating her up from the inside out.

"Do you know what that dress makes me want to do to you?"

She'd swallowed hard, but for a different reason this time. Because now that they'd mated, it was almost as if Airk had finally given himself permission to just be with her. Holding nothing but his dragon in check. Even that seemed…easier…though difficult to tell in only a few hours.

She shook her head.

"It makes me want to lift your skirt, bend you over that table…" He glanced at the piece of furniture in question. "And fill you full of my fire all over again."

Her heart beat a rapid tattoo that he no doubt could hear perfectly clear. He'd already done so twice more through the night and once again this morning.

That lack of experience thing only seemed to make for more fun as they both tested new touches, explored each other with abandon, and generally went with whatever felt good. Really good. For instance, she now knew that he shuddered every time she licked between his balls. Who knew such a small touch could set him off that way? And he'd figured out that her riding him gave him ample access to all sorts of parts of her. That orgasm had come harder than the others.

What might they learn this time?

She'd moved to the table in question and placed her palms on it, feet spread, then glanced at him over her shoulder, promises in her eyes. Temptation parting her lips. "Like this?"

Color flared over his cheekbones, and he'd grunted as though in pain. "When we get back."

"Now." She batted her eyes.

His hands fisted around his crossed leg. "Jordy will be back to escort us any moment."

"Then you'd better lock the door."

He moved so fast she hardly saw the blur of him. In seconds he was up, door locked, his pants down around his knees and her dress rucked up to her waist. Fingers delving deep, he'd tested her to find her ready.

"Fuck."

Their coupling had been harsh and hard, fast and furious. And beautiful.

Afterward, he'd insisted on cleaning her with a washcloth before lowering her dress. "They will smell me on you. Smell what we did," he warned almost apologetically.

"Let them."

The primitive flare of satisfaction in his eyes might have led to round two, except Jordy knocked at the door at that moment.

Actually, he might have earlier, and they didn't hear him.

Now here they were, standing in the shadowy room that led out onto a balcony that reminded her of videos of British royals at

Buckingham Palace in London waving to the masses after some splendidly opulent occasion or other. Similarly, this balcony looked out over the large common area at the center of the "town," packed so tightly with white dragon shifters all Angelika saw was one big blur of faces and colors of clothing.

No sound, though. They remained eerily silent as Mös made his announcements.

Probably shock because of finding out so much—the wrongful death of Zilant Amon, Serefina's escape and her children, Pytheios's hand in everything, the death of Volos now in question, Brock being named king, his death, and now the arrival of Airk and Angelika both, with all the implications.

Rough day to be a white dragon shifter. Pity settled around the need to help them if they would let her.

As Mös got to Zilant's wrongful death, he introduced Airk, who shared the same story he had with the leaders. The silence turned heavier, angrier. Though she couldn't tell now who it was aimed at. Themselves? Their leaders? Pytheios? Or even Airk, if they didn't believe him? Probably a little of all of the above. She needed to be ready for that.

"One of the phoenixes—the daughters of King Zilant Amon and Serefina Hanyu," Mös announced, "has come to us willingly, offering to devote herself to the clan of her father, if we will have her."

That announcement, at least, pulled an audible inhalation from the listeners. Not a gasp, necessarily. Almost like taking a breath before the impact of a hit they could see coming.

Mös turned, and Angelika found her legs were weighted with lead. Nerves were never a problem for her usually, but this was… important. She needed her father's people to accept her.

A glance at Airk showed him watching her in that intense way of his, concern drawing his dark brows down. Almost as though he could sense her panic, his lips turned up in a barely there smile. Just for her.

The encouragement tables had neatly turned.

Something seemed to jump-start her nervous system and force

her limbs to function. Stepping forward, she moved until she stood slightly ahead of both men on the platform, looking out over the sea of faces. Those closest she could see more clearly, and an array of emotions reflected back to her—stoic nothingness, hostility, awe, curiosity...even relief on a few.

Meira had done this once, facing an introduction to the Black Clan. How had her poor, quiet sister, blessed with empathic abilities, survived under the scrutiny and weight and judgment?

Drawing back her shoulders, Angelika forced a new surge through herself—stone-cold determination. If Meira could do this, so could she. Taking a deep breath, Angelika started to speak the words they'd agreed on yesterday in that meeting but paused before the first sound passed her lips. A memorized speech wasn't going to do the job.

They needed to see her heart.

"For five hundred years, my mother hid us away, keeping us safe from a man who misled us all. Giving us the time to mature, to be ready to meet our mates and take our places among our people."

She swallowed, now realizing who she looked out on. "If my parents had lived, I would have known you. Grown up with you. Celebrated with you. Cheered with you. Fought beside you."

Nothing from those watching.

She tipped her head up, closing her eyes. "As a little girl I used to close my eyes and picture what my life would have been, and I like to think, with the blessings my phoenix mother would have brought to this clan and all dragon shifters, that it would have been a good life. Happy and well cared for. For all of us."

Angelika opened her eyes. "But that future, that life, was stolen from me. Stolen from you, as well. All we can do now is move forward with what has been given to us."

That determination coursing through her coalesced in her belly, a rock of fortitude on which to build. "I offer myself to you. Not as a leader or a ruler. I offer myself in any capacity that this clan needs to find that future again. To take back what was stolen. I offer my sisters and all the powers of my phoenix family. I offer my sisters' mates and an alliance with their clans. And…" She turned and held her hand out to Airk. They hadn't discussed this, and she hoped like hells she was doing the right thing. "I pledge my life and these offerings by making myself one of you permanently, by taking a white dragon shifter as a mate."

• • •

Airk stared out over the crowd, inspecting every single face, and his dragon coiled inside him, stoking their fire. Most reactions were benign. But, almost as though a spotlight fell on each individual with a harsher reaction, he picked out glittering flame-filled eyes. Gazes full of a starving sort of fury and uglier emotions—blame, suspicion, even retribution.

For him? For her? He didn't care. They were a threat.

Angelika was still speaking, her face an open book of guileless obliviousness. She didn't see the menaces out there among the people she was pledging herself to, or maybe she didn't want to see. But he couldn't get her off this platform where she was vulnerable fast enough.

Deliberately, he stepped closer to her, taking the hand she'd offered in one and settling his other hand at the small of her back, which earned him a sideways glance.

Luckily, she was winding down. "I know this is a massive decision, and one every dragon must make for himself, herself, and for your families. My door is open to anyone who wishes to discuss it. No one—" She tilted her chin down, turning earnest but also deadly serious. "Absolutely *no one* will be punished or thought less of if you decide to leave."

Behind him, Mös gave a soft growl that no one else below probably heard. They hadn't talked about that at all during their meeting.

With a final nod, Angelika turned away. Turned her back on predators who could move at incredible speeds and snap her neck in an instant if they wished. Not only that, she paused there, looking him dead in the eyes, and Airk's lips flattened as he realized that she knew exactly what she was doing and why.

She was offering trust. Foolishly.

He added a conversation about risking her damn life to the list of things they would be talking about next.

Finally, she raised her hand in a courtly gesture he hadn't seen in ages. Airk moved quickly to offer his arm for her to lightly place her hand on. Despite his dragon driving him to pick her up and run, they walked sedately off the platform and back inside.

As soon as they were out of view, he looked at Mös, Belyy, and the others. "We need to get her somewhere safe."

"No." Angelika's answer was soft but firm.

This time a growl did rip from him, and for once he was in perfect accord with his dragon. "You did not see some of those faces. Flaming eyes giving away their emotions—"

"I saw."

Fuck. Of course she did. Stubborn mate. "They want you dead, or me dead, or both. Both is more likely."

"I know."

"Then there is no way—"

Angelika put a hand to his cheek, soothing, her gaze full of a thousand unsaid words—regret, apology, but also determination. "That's exactly why I need to be seen among the people. Immediately. Hiding will only make those already against us question us louder."

Airk's body seized with trepidation. "What do you mean, among the people?"

"Exactly that." She looked over his shoulder at Belyy. "I want those who bear my family mark with me."

"As protection?" Belyy asked slowly.

She shook her head. "As witnesses. They need to hear your stories, too."

After a pause, Belyy dipped his head in a half nod, half bow.

She lifted her gaze to Airk, her hand still cupping his jaw. "Can you keep control?" she asked, searching his gaze.

In other words, she was doing this, with or without him.

"I will have to," he said, voice guttural now. "There is no way I will let you do this alone."

Her smile was resigned, but then she wrinkled her nose. "I'm just as scared for you as I am for me," she said. "But I know this is the only way to gain their trust. And without trust…" She shrugged.

Gods, he'd mated the rashest, bravest, most selfless woman he'd ever known. Both heavens and hells on earth, because he might die of terror before he reached old age if she was going to put them in situations like this all the time. "How did I get the selfless one?"

Angelika grinned, but her next words stole his breath. "I want babies," she leaned forward to whisper. "Your babies. But first we have to make our world safe for them."

The image of her, belly swollen with *his* child, was as cruel as a gunshot and as beautiful as a dream. And damned if now he didn't want to pick her up, carry her back to their chambers, and fill her full of his seed, willing it to take root in her womb.

"You may be the death of me, Angelika Amon," he muttered with a shake of his head.

"Angelika Azdajah," she corrected.

He closed his eyes at the sound of her name that way, but his lips twisted. If she could be selfless, then so could he. "Your father's line has no male dragons to carry on the name."

"Neither does yours, other than you," she pointed out.

"My father wasn't king."

She blew out a breath. "I guess we're both stubborn." He lifted an eyebrow at that, and she huffed a soft laugh. "Let us figure out names later. First, I want to change, and then we will go on a little walk."

Half an hour later, both of them dressed in pants called jeans and plain white T-shirts, she led them out into what most dragon mountains considered to be the heart of the community. At the base of the atrium inside the hollowed-out mountain was what essentially acted as a town hub.

Airk paused at the sight.

He'd grown up here in his early years. Played in these streets. And in his cell, when he had nothing to do, he pictured every building, every detail, every paved cobblestone of this place. In his imagination, he would wander in and out of the shops and businesses. Other than his parents' faces, this was the memory he'd held on to most. Maybe because he'd always felt…safe…here as a child. A place of wonder and his people.

Home.

And it hadn't changed. Not in five hundred years.

Well…not much. The first two or three levels had always been businesses of all types—restaurants, shops, a bookstore, grocers, even a nail salon and a barber. Some of the shops were different since he'd been here last, he could see already—the buildings still mostly original but updated. And the area was more brightly lit than before. Gone were torches and streetlamps, replaced by the more modern trick of lighting the dragons used inside their mountains, bringing the day into the would-be darkness.

Unlike Ben Nevis, which was set up more like a main street with a single thoroughfare, Kamen was more like a village inside castle walls. The architecture was modeled after human innovations over centuries, seen in the archways, domes, and towers of Byzantine styles, but combined with the open-and-closed spaces more often seen in Chinese buildings. However, everything here was white. Pure white walls.

Nathair had once shown him pictures in a book about Greece, and the white buildings of Santorini had reminded him a little of home. But those structures were simpler. These were ornate. Carvings of dragons crusted in pearls and opals and white diamonds, symbols of their people, their kings, the ruling houses, turrets with intricate carvings. The city of Kamen sparkled.

A scent struck him—chamomile, the small daisies that grew all over this mountain, aromatic, fruity, and floral. Combined with the scents of rock and the slightly smoky scent of dragons, the smells dragged him into memory after memory.

I am home.

He lowered his gaze to find Angelika turned and waiting, a compassionate sort of understanding in her eyes. She reached out a hand to him. "Show me what you missed most," she said.

He stared. "Did I speak my thoughts?"

She shook her head. "No. But I think I caught them anyway."

He blew out a harsh breath. How could he ever deserve this woman?

Stepping forward, he wrapped his hand around her smaller one, and together they moved into the first building.

A tea shop, of all things.

The proprietor and all his customers looked up, then gasped. One even sank into a deep bow. "My lady," they murmured.

"Please don't stand on ceremony for me," Angelika said with a wave of her hand and an infectious grin.

The one in the bow rose, and the others lifted gazes that had been lowered. Airk stared at them all, unsmiling, searching for any evidence that these people were those who might harm her.

Angelika, however, appeared completely relaxed, her smile one of open friendliness. "I grew up on stories my mother told me of this place. She used to talk about this shop and how my father loved the piroshki here."

The proprietor, a man not much younger than Airk, changed so rapidly from wariness to a warm gratification it would have been funny if Airk wasn't busy wrestling with a memory long forgotten, her words bringing it back.

"That is so kind to say," the man was saying. "My mother ran this establishment when Zilant was king. She would be so gratified to hear that he loved it." Then his gaze swung to Airk. "I remember you, though you were a boy. Older than me."

Airk nodded slowly. "I used to come here with my mother." He smiled, suddenly hearing her voice in his head. A voice that had faded with time long ago. "She would say that more business could be done over a good meal with two women than a hundred men in a stuffy room debating."

The way Angelika's hand tightened around his, Airk knew she

understood what that memory meant to him. Not his mother's last screams, which he'd heard in nightmares for a hundred years after her death, and sometimes even still. But a fond moment.

"Your mother was a smart woman. And kind. I always liked her because she'd bring me candies." The proprietor took a breath. "What can I get you?"

Angelika turned to the glassed-in case displaying an array of baked goodies, her face suddenly giving him an idea of how she would have looked as a little girl—cherubic and eager.

"Hmmmm…" She pondered. "What's your most popular—"

"For the High King!" a rough male voice boomed out.

CHAPTER TWENTY-THREE

A blur moving faster than Angelika's vision could track bolted from the back of the tea shop straight for her.

Before she could so much as open her mouth to shout, Airk was between them, one hand wrapped around the attacker's throat, lifting him off his feet. The man swung like a pendulum for a moment, thanks to his own momentum, then came to a dangle. Feet thrashed, and his face turned purple as he garbled and glared.

A growl ripped from Airk's throat so fearsome that every single dragon in the room flinched. So did Angelika. The man, smarter than first impressions might indicate, went utterly still, eyes bugging out as he stared at a newly mated dragon in full protection mode. One who could easily go wild. Airk had not held that part of his history back when he'd been introduced. This guy was lucky he hadn't already been gutted. Or worse.

What would I feel if that had happened?

Nothing. This man made his choice. But did feeling nothing make her a horrible person? Or maybe more dragon than she realized?

"Who sent you?" Airk demanded in a voice so unlike his own, she knew the beast was speaking more than the man.

Her assailant moved his mouth, but only a mangled noise came out.

Gently, Angelika laid a hand on Airk's arm, and his muscles

jumped and twitched under her touch.

"Airk," she said softly.

Slowly, after a long hesitation, he turned his head, his eyes fully dragon, flames of white sparking at her, lighting up the sharp angles of his face in a harsh glow.

But no ire for her. If anything, his features softened slightly.

"Don't kill him," she said. Not yet, at least.

In the same instant, two men burst into the room, clearly guards alerted to the danger. They pulled up sharply at the little scene, looking between Airk and the man and her, then exchanged a glance.

Which almost made her laugh, because they were clearly floundering. *Bet they didn't train for this in dragon school.* Now was not the time for humor, though.

Hoping her mate was more in control than he looked, she cleared her throat and addressed the guards in a firm voice. "Take this man away to be interrogated. Do not harm him, though."

They glanced at her, then warily at Airk, obviously not thrilled with the idea of taking a kill away from a pissed-off alpha. How the shifter he held hadn't passed out from lack of air at this point, she had no idea.

"Airk?" she asked. "Please."

Only because she was touching him did she feel the shudder that ran through his body. Then he blinked, and suddenly his eyes were human again. His hand opened, almost as though some invisible force cranked the fingers out of their clench, and the man dropped to the floor in a heap, still breathing, though rasping. Warily, trying to stay as far from Airk as they could, the two guards took an arm each and dragged her attacker away.

Airk's chest heaved—up, down, up, down—as he stared into space. She didn't move. Watching and waiting. Then he angled his head, addressing her without looking. "That could have gone so much worse."

"I'm safe. So are you. And we can get answers we need," she said, keeping her voice slow and steady.

His muscles were still tight beneath her hand. He was hating this, and she hated putting him through it. "I can't let this stop me. This is important," she whispered.

And he closed his eyes, fighting more than just his instinct as a mate. Then, finally he straightened and gave a small nod.

Slipping her hand in his, because deep down she was more shaken than she was letting on, Angelika turned back to the room. "I apologize for that," she said. "Was anything broken? Everyone unharmed?"

Which got her open-mouthed stares of shock.

Dragons really were more fragile than what the creatures shifted into would lead one to believe. Once they'd made sure everything was set to rights, they'd sampled some of the goods, then continued on. After the tea shop was a seamstress, then a grocer, several clothing stores, a leather-goods shop, and along the way they were stopped several times by random groups wanting to meet the phoenix.

No more attacks.

No one even dared look at Airk, let alone approach him, whether because of who he was or because of what he'd done in the tea shop, she wasn't sure. She gritted her teeth over it every single time all the same. Acceptance would be a slow process. After seeing his treatment in the other clans, she'd known that already. All the same, maybe she'd hoped that his own clan would be more welcoming.

And…unfortunately, they didn't have that kind of time.

Airk didn't loosen up until they made it back to their suite hours later. He walked in behind her, bolted the door, then stalked past her to the kitchen, where he opened a bottle of vodka and took a long swig.

Eyebrows lifting, Angelika moved into the room as well, giving him time to decide what his reaction was going to be. After hearing about her sisters' mates and their possessiveness and protective instincts, she expected another marathon round of orgasms. Looked forward to it, even. They just had to get past the Tarzan-and-Jane instinct first.

Pretending she wasn't hyperaware of his every move, she instead focused on the baskets and bundles that had magically appeared all over the suite. Gift baskets, it appeared. Food, clothing, books, bath oils. Some necessities, some just for fun. One of which was where he'd got the vodka.

See? she wanted to say, *not everyone is angry.* Some clearly were ready to believe.

Idly, she picked up a small box wrapped more simply than all the others, in brown paper tied with twine. She unwrapped it and lifted the lid, expecting some small bauble—homemade, perhaps, given the wrapping.

With a scream, she dropped the box, her hand going to her mouth.

Airk was across the room in an instant, box off the floor and in his hand. If she could have saved him from seeing what was inside, she would.

A doll, crudely made and without a face, but with long white-blond hair and orange-and-red wings of fire. Her, clearly. But this doll had been gutted, with real entrails—of a rat or some other small rodent, probably—hanging out of her.

Unfortunately, despite wanting to minimize the impact on Airk, the reaction set in. Everything from today—those bloodthirsty faces in the crowd, the attack in the tea shop, and now this—hit her hard.

"Airk," she whispered.

Her mate's expression was pure rage as he lifted his head, but the second he got a good look at her, the rage fell away, replaced by a combination of panic and tenderness. Emotions he would never have shown her, or maybe never allowed himself, even a week ago.

He dropped the box and had her in his arms in an instant. Sweeping her feet off the ground, he carried her to their bedroom, where he sat on the side of the bed, her across his lap. She curled into him and breathed him in, listening to the steady beat of his heart.

And tried her damnedest to forget what she just saw.

After several long minutes of him running a soothing hand down her hair and back, Angelika relaxed into him. "That sucked," she muttered.

Airk sighed against her. "Yet you are going to go out there again tomorrow anyway?"

She nodded. "And the next day, and the next, and the next after that. However long it takes, I'm going to convince them all. Win them all."

With a small growl, he laid his cheek against the top of her head. "I would argue that it is a losing battle, but I more than anyone know how convincing you can be."

She huffed a laugh, a tenderness she'd never expected for herself with her mate welling up inside her. "Look at how well that turned out for you." She poked him in the chest with the tip of one finger.

Airk grinned. She felt it all the way through her soul. Gods, this man.

...

Pytheios strode purposefully through Everest toward the massive room where all his warriors gathered. He pulled on a pair of supple leather gloves as he walked. Even his people's respect as he passed by was deeper, more gratifying, as though he suddenly commanded their attention.

He needed to drain those fucking phoenixes and steal immortality from their souls. But for that, first, he had to win this war—*without* killing the three mated kings until after he'd sucked their mates dry.

Starting today.

In a darkened tunnel, his private entrance to the training room, he stopped beside the man who had to be held up by two others, head lolling between his shoulders.

Purposely, Pytheios had what remained of Jakkobah poured into one of his fancy, collarless silk suits. He'd chosen a deeply red one that made the Stoat appear even paler than usual. Hard to do, given the man was near albino. Although the effects of torture probably accounted for his appearance more than the color of his clothing.

With satisfaction, Pytheios tugged at the jacket, resituating it more squarely on a frame that had turned even bonier. "You know what to do."

This traitor was going to pretend that he'd escaped and gather Pytheios's prizes together in one spot for easy plucking. That was the deal they'd made to stop the torture.

Jakkobah lifted pale eyes that had popped so many vessels the whites were now red with blood. The Stoat's gaze hardly seemed to register the world around him, but then he mumbled out an answer. "I will ask for the kings and their phoenixes to be brought to me."

Pytheios nodded. "Don't move from where Rhiamon puts you."

"I don't think that will be a problem," Jakkobah slurred.

He wasn't wrong. The man couldn't stand without help. Both his Achilles tendons being sliced open so many times they never healed properly had assured that.

Next Pytheios moved to stand before the cloaked woman who was off to the side, as though she didn't want to be near others. Or perhaps they didn't want to be near her. "My love," he murmured and feathered the back of his fingers over her skin, trying not to show his revulsion at the paper-thin texture and the way it moved under his touch as though not attached to the bone and muscle below.

Rhiamon lifted those eerie eyes—voids inside the sockets of her skull. "Merikh?" she asked, tapping one of her fingernails against the side of her thigh, the only indication that she wasn't as serene as she appeared.

"Soon, my love. Once this war is won, we will bring him back from the depths of death together." The only promise he knew would bind her to his will. "We need the phoenixes for that."

A lie, because he had no intention of using the firebirds' powers to resurrect his pathetic excuse for a son, but as more incentive for the mother.

Rhiamon nodded.

"Let's go get them."

He turned and continued the rest of the way down the tunnel. The instant he appeared in the war room, every soldier at his command—a massive army of red and green dragons—already lined up in rank and file, hit the floor, going to one knee, heads bowed. He'd pulled all his forces away from every mountain except Everest for this. For today. They'd done so quickly, ready to strike before the other kings got wind of his movements.

"Rise," he commanded, then strode to his generals. "Are we ready?"

King Fraener of the Green Clan, the most loyal of his allies, stepped forward. "Yes, my king."

Pytheios nodded, satisfied. When he'd tried to take the Black Clan, he'd made the mistake of ignoring how the phoenixes' powers allowed them to move large groups quickly, which meant he had faced not one clan but three.

He was ready for that this time. In more than one way.

Turning, he glanced over his shoulder into the darkness where his witch waited. He nodded. The last time they'd tried this, she'd sent them to a field well away from where they would attack. From there, they had shifted and coordinated.

This time, he had a different tactic in mind.

He bent his gaze to the floor and waited for Rhiamon's magic to strike. A white mist crept from the tunnel, and his men, the lesser-trained of his warriors—after all, he'd had to fill in his lost ranks with bodies—shifted on their feet but held position. They'd been told how this would work.

The mist slunk across the smooth rock floor of the cavern, polished by thousands of steps, both human and dragon, over the ages. It grew thicker, denser, until it obscured his feet. Then, like a room filling with water, the mist began to rise.

Like last time, the strangest sensation of losing himself in an otherworldly realm, one where his senses—all of them—were turned off, came over him as the white closed over his head. His mind told him he should at least smell clouds, the combination of ozone and water, or feel the droplets condensing against his clothes and skin.

Hear the breathing or feel the body warmth of the men at his side.

But nothing. She encased them all in...nothing.

There wasn't even the sense of having moved, as though his feet were still on solid ground. Until, with an abruptness that sent shock lancing through his body, the ground disappeared, and gravity yanked his body down hard and fast.

As agreed, Rhiamon had dropped them over the top of their target, high enough that he and his men would all have time to shift before they hit the ground. She landed them sideways from how they'd be standing so each unit was stacked on top of the other in the air, allowing them to shift in waves to give them space.

Pytheios, at the top, shifted immediately, then flared his wings and hovered, giving his men time to do their jobs.

Surprise was on their side. If his plan worked, they should infiltrate the mountain before most of the dragons inside had a chance to shift, let alone defend.

Sure enough, the swarm of red and green dragons, in all their vibrant, glorious colors, quickly took out the sentries outside the mountain. Then they poured inside. The chaos and cacophony of battle reached his ears. Then screams joined the sounds only shifters with their enhanced senses would pick up on.

"Don't come yet, my king," King Fraener's voice sounded in his head.

He narrowed his eyes but stayed where he hovered in the skies. Patience was a virtue when warranted. He waited.

And waited.

And waited.

This was not how this was supposed to go. They had the greater numbers, surprise on their side, and his witch.

What the fuck was taking so long?

Suddenly, all sound cut off. In the air, Pytheios cocked his head, listening.

"We have the phoenixes cornered."

Smug satisfaction rolled through him. As planned.

"Hold them there," Pytheios shot back.

Finally, he could end this all right here and now. Finally, he'd make dragons whole, taking the powers that should have rightfully been theirs, setting his people free of the sway phoenixes held over them.

Pytheios dove, weaving in and out of his men posted outside to keep any strays from escaping. Landing on the flat outcropping of rock, he shifted as he strode inside the Blue Clan's only remaining mountain of Ben Nevis, where he'd already driven the Gold and Black Clans.

At the back of the massive cavern, he found five white dragons— likely those who had pledged themselves to Skylar Ormarr—shifted and standing in a line, their wings flared wide, facing off against several of his own men.

From his lower vantage point, now that he was human, he could see Jakkobah on the ground with three of the four phoenixes kneeling over him, the three kings standing beside them, grim as fuck.

And they should be.

But Pytheios frowned. "Where is the fourth phoenix?" he demanded softly, so he couldn't be heard, as he came alongside Fraener, still a dragon of a camouflage green that always reminded Pytheios of dog shit.

"Only the three showed, my king."

Fuck.

He needed all four. He was sure of that. But perhaps he could drain the last one later. She'd be easier to capture than the others, anyway, without a mate to worry about. Pytheios strode inside and addressed himself to the white dragons protecting their precious good-luck charms. Fools.

"Bow to me now, and maybe I won't kill you." He wouldn't ask again.

"Meira?" Kasia asked her sister.

"I can't," came the answer. "She's taken over the reflections."

Pytheios didn't bother to hide his smile. Rhiamon had turned off the bitch's use of reflections to teleport. No getting out that way.

A low growl emitted from Ladon, whose entire face was lit with the blue of the flames in his eyes. "Skylar—"

Then, before Pytheios's very eyes, every single one of them disappeared. Pytheios's satisfied smile froze on his face before dying a swift death.

"What the fuck just happened?" he demanded.

No one answered at first. Pytheios stared at the space where his prizes had been a second before. Jakkobah had been with them, and now he and the white dragons were gone, too.

"Report," he demanded.

"My king," Fraener said. *"The mountain is…empty of all except those we killed."*

Shock rocked him to his core. Either the phoenixes had grown in power, or they'd been warned. Either way, he'd lost them. Again.

A roar thundered up his throat and out into the sky as he shifted with a swiftness that rode the edge of pain. "Where did they go? Get me answers now!"

CHAPTER TWENTY-FOUR

Determined not to be scared off by the previous attack on her, Angelika had set herself to walking among her father's people every day.

My people.

The underground city here was a large one. Larger even than Ben Nevis, which was a smaller mountain. Regardless, the size meant it would take some time to visit everywhere. But at least the word had spread. Fewer shocked faces greeted her when she showed up, though they still stared. Fewer bowed and curtsied, word seeming to have also gone round that she didn't require such tributes.

No more attacks. She was pretty sure no one wanted to test Airk again.

That wasn't what she wanted for him, though. To lead by fear. Not here, with these people who had once been friends. A place he had felt safe as a child. But for now, they had to use the tools the gods and fates had granted them, and his reputation definitely fell under that category.

This particular shop was no hardship to visit, at least. Angelika ran a finger down the soft wisps of silk hanging on a rack. "This looks like Givenchy couture."

The man running the shop smiled at a woman who might be his sister or his mate, Angelika wasn't sure. "It is," he said. "In addition to my own designs, I am able to replicate human designs for our people."

At a fraction of the cost, no doubt. "I always wanted to dress like Audrey Hepburn in *Sabrina*."

The man lit up. "One of my favorite fashion film moments."

Angelika tried not to blink. She'd grown up on the "outside" among humans. Spent centuries of life participating in the changes wrought on societies, living and absorbing them all in real time. The invention of and the rise of motion pictures was possibly one of her favorite developments. Although air-conditioning in hundred-degree-plus Kansas summers might just beat that out. Still, it often surprised her when dragons talked of more modern inventions. She had to remember that they didn't live in strict isolation, though they stayed fairly separate from humans. Mates were found among humans, and they helped introduce changes in language, technology, and so forth over time.

Airk, meanwhile, was a complete blank. Because he *had* been forced to live in isolation. She snuck her hand into his. "*Sabrina* is a movie from the 1950s," she explained. "We can watch it together, sometime—"

The abrupt and unmistakable sound of screams—hundreds of them—struck hard and fast, coming from outside.

Angelika ran for the door. Airk got there ahead of her, slamming his hand against the wood so she couldn't tug it open. At the same time, he wrapped his other hand around her wrist as though anchoring her to him before she could do something rash like... like rush out into the street.

Which was exactly what she'd been about to do.

"Wait," he demanded.

Heart pounding, she still recognized the common sense in the demand and nodded.

Pulling away from the door, he cut his gaze to Tovar, on escort detail with them today. The other man ran outside without another question. Waiting for him was Angelika's own personal hell. The wails of terror outside diminished slowly but still washed over her until she wanted to cover her ears against the sound. Instead, she focused on her mate. On his eyes. The strength of his shoulders. Not that Airk went unaffected. A muscle ticked in the side of his jaw as he looked steadily back at her.

The door jerked open before she saw the flash of movement of Tovar's approach. "Angelika needs to come. Now."

"Why?" Airk demanded.

"Her sisters—"

She didn't wait for more, pushing past Tovar and sprinting out into the streets. Chaos reigned as the people who lived in the mountain rushed to implement the safety protocols all dragons drilled, battening down the hatches. Weaving in and out of the press of bodies, she tried to move toward the sounds still coming from what she realized was the hangar and training room all dragon mountains touted.

"Excuse me," she muttered as she avoided a shoulder to the face.

A growl behind her sounded half a beat before she was swept up in Airk's arms. "Everybody move," he bellowed, and immediately a path cleared before them.

He took off at a sprint, the walls and faces blurring around her as he ran them toward the shouts and cries.

Toward her sisters.

The second they made it through the smaller tunnel leading into the cavern, Angelika gasped. Because there were at least a thousand dragons in the room. Blue. Gold. Black. All of them in some state of shock, panic, or injury.

"Oh my gods. What happened?" she breathed, heart squeezing hard as she tried to force her mind to make sense of it all.

Airk's fingers flexed against her hip where he held her—not shock but support, she vaguely identified. "Over there," he said, then took off again.

She clung to his neck, the nurse in her wanting to stop him and put her medical training to use helping those visibly bleeding and worse. More than one dead body lay on the ground, most with someone keening over their loved one, grief contorting their features.

Meira had to be miserably blocking her empathic powers with

everything in her pure little soul.

I should be helping. But she needed to see her sisters before she could hope to do any good.

Their faces suddenly appeared between the throng of people, and Angelika almost tried to climb Airk to get a better view.

"Meira!" she yelled.

Strawberry blond curls flared out as her sister spun, her gaze searching for Angelika. Airk ran the last bit, and before she could even ask, she was on her feet, her arms wrapped around Meira's neck.

"You're okay," Angelika said. Then said it again, because she needed convincing.

Meira nodded, then took a deep breath before she crumpled in Angelika's arms, tears coming hard and fast. "My power wouldn't—"

But the words choked off.

"Where are Kas and—"

From the ground where they were kneeling over someone, Kasia and Skylar also leaped up, closing around her, and Angelika closed her eyes on a sigh of stark relief. They were unharmed. Thank the gods.

"How did you get here?" Because there wasn't a reflection big enough.

"Kasia and I used our combined teleportation powers," Skylar said. "We've been practicing ever since the attack on the Black and Gold Clans drove us all together."

Angelika knew what they were talking about. Kasia could take anyone with her, but only a short distance. Skylar could send anyone a very long distance, not including herself. If they worked together, they could combine the effect. They must've gotten amazing at it to get all these people here so fast.

"What happened?" she asked.

"My vision was wrong," Kasia said, bitterness in every word. Her sister's extra pale face hardened with anger. "*I* was wrong."

Wrong? Her vision? Which one?

Skylar squeezed Kasia's shoulder as they all broke apart. "He wasn't coming here," she said. "Pytheios attacked Ben Nevis."

Gods above.

Angelika, still holding Meira, turned her head, looking around at the carnage and the devastation the rotting red king had wrought. Families uprooted and ripped apart. He'd brought this down on three clans—half his kingdom—like a child throwing a tantrum because someone took his favorite toy away.

Why was he so hells-bent on being High King?

She met Airk's gaze over her sister's heads and drew strength from the anger and determination swirling in his otherwise stoic eyes.

Her mate would not let this stand. Neither would she.

"I have to help," Angelika said to Airk as much as her sisters.

"The infirmary can't hold this many people," Tovar said from behind her, and again she allowed her gaze to roam over the room, now professional, assessing.

"Set up triage here," she ordered. "I want the critically wounded in the south corner. Send the Healers to them. I'll be here for more minor treatment. I'll need equipment."

Tovar blinked at her, and she had to remind herself that not everyone knew all of her story yet. "I'm a nurse," she said.

Whatever emotion flashed in his eyes, it disappeared in the next blink. Then he was gone, obeying her orders. Her sisters and their mates immediately started moving through the room, spreading the word, helping sort and move those who needed moving.

Angelika knelt over the nearest body to her. A man who might've passed for a white dragon, except for the tint of red in his hair. Physical traits of all sorts were common among dragons, regardless of clan, thanks to the human mates, but there was something familiar about this man.

"Who is this?" she asked.

"Jakkobah." Ladon, nearest to her, was the one to answer.

She blinked again. "Your informant?"

Ladon's jaw tightened. "Yes. He's been tortured, I think. Can you help him?"

Her training kicked in, shutting down her shock. First, she checked Jakkobah's pulse, finding it weak, thready. At the same time, she listened to his breathing. His chest was moving, but his lips were a bluish hue, and a slight whistle was coming from somewhere on each inhalation.

Immediately, she ripped open the ornately embroidered silk overcoat he was wearing and hissed between her teeth. Not only had the man clearly been starved, but he'd been beaten. Severely and often enough that one set of injuries hadn't had time to heal before the next round was doled out.

He could survive that, though, now that he wasn't being reinjured.

But someone had pierced his lungs multiple times, shoved some kind of metal tubing down the hole and let his body's accelerated healing seal the skin around it so that with every inhalation most of the air entering his lungs whistled out of the tubes, blood and spittle coming up with the air.

Those tubes would have to come out, but in surgery. Not here on the floor. With them grown into the surrounding tissue all the way through, probably, removal would be tricky. Her first priority was his ability to breathe until then.

"I need something to plug these tubes," she said.

After that, she didn't look up, focused first on Jakkobah, then on each new case, each new person as they came to her. Mös stopped by at some point to inform her of what was being done from a logistics standpoint, shutting the massive doors that closed in this space from the outside. Bringing in all their scouts and guards. Arranging for all the new arrivals to at least have blankets or sheets to sleep with. Almost four full clans within these walls were thousands more than this mountain was built and stocked to accommodate.

She'd agreed to all his suggestions, giving him full control over the mountain at least until the chaos died down and she wasn't needed in here anymore. At some point, each sister checked in, Meira bringing her food and forcing her to stop and eat.

Airk, however, didn't leave her side. He helped. Lifting people, moving them, holding pieces together for her to bind. But he was never more than twenty feet away.

Over time, more people were brought to her rather than fewer. The Healers—those dragons with the universal donor blood type—were relatively rare. Most clans had a handful. Usually one, maybe two, stayed with the king. Others were assigned to other mountains or to the Alliance or Enforcer teams in each of the colonies. Unfortunately, because healing required them to give blood to heal those in need, after a while, they had to rest and regenerate more blood or they risked their own health.

Most of the Healers also had medical training, though, and they worked side by side. She didn't know how long. Hours and hours. Through the night. Until her brain had to take an extra beat to process each word spoken to her, each request made, and her body felt like little lead weights had been sewn into her skin, making her moves sluggish.

Each sister then started to try to convince her to stop. To rest.

"I'll rest when no one needs me," she'd insisted, not stopping what she was doing.

Airk didn't ask, though. He watched her with flat-lipped intensity. Not disapproval. More like reluctant support.

More food and coffee were shoved at her as she went along, until finally…finally…the last patient had been seen to.

"That's it," one of the Healers said when she looked for the next person. A blue dragon. She thought maybe his name was Fallon, but her brain was too fuzzy to be sure.

She slowly blinked. "All of them?" she asked when his words finally penetrated.

He nodded. Then, "Well done, my lady."

She shook her head. "It wasn't just me."

The way the Healer glanced nervously over her shoulder told her Airk was standing there, though she didn't need that hint because the hairs on her nape stood up. With a sigh, she turned and wrapped her arms around his neck, sinking into him, eyes closing of their own accord.

"Are you going to sleep now?" he asked into the top of her hair.

She huffed a laugh. "Yup."

Somehow, with his arm around her waist, she managed to walk all the way back to their suite. Though she was so exhausted she hardly had any recollection of the journey once she was there. He managed to get her to brush her teeth and change into another oversize T-shirt. Then they were slipping between cool sheets and he was wrapping his body around her like a protective barrier.

"You are incredible," he whispered.

With a smile and a sigh, her body let go, relaxing into instant, blissfully deep sleep.

. . .

A tiny puff of air against his arm wasn't the first Airk had felt. Probably the fifth in the last hour or so. He'd hoped, when he'd felt Angelika stir against him, that she'd go right back to sleep. After how hard she'd worked, her body needed the rest.

But she was awake.

Awake and brooding if those tiny, noiseless sighs were any indication.

Curling his arm around her waist, he settled her into the curving crook of his body and set his chin on top of her head. He didn't ask her to talk about it. Too many people, since he'd gotten out of his prison, had wanted him to talk through his troubles. It never helped. But he let her know he was there.

Her sigh this time was audible.

"We can't support almost four clans' worth of people in a single mountain," she pointed out.

He was right. She'd been brooding.

"No we cannot," he agreed.

"All those people…" She breathed in, her ribs lifting his arm with the movement. "It happened so fast."

"It did." He'd talked with the other kings, and their own shock at the speed of the attack had been evident in hard, glassy eyes and hands that involuntarily curled into fists.

"It's a miracle my sisters got them out. Especially with Meira's power shut off."

After a second of quiet, Angelika scooted around, twisting over to face him, frosty eyes solemn in a way that told him she was deep in her head. "Is it hopeless?"

Hearing that question from her lips, from the one person who had never given up on him...Airk's heart spasmed.

Blowing out his own breath, he lifted a hand to smooth her white-blond hair back from her face. "That is what Pytheios does," he said eventually. "He makes you believe giving up and letting him have what he wants is the only choice. That it will save lives. That it will keep the peace."

Angelika listened, gaze searching his.

Anchoring himself on the feel of her in his arms, he didn't fight the emotions. The fury, the need to quit, give up, the urge to end his own life.

"He might even convince you that he is right." When he'd been younger, he'd been more easily led astray, more desperate to be set free. "I found myself wanting to believe that Pytheios had been justified. Forgetting who my parents were. Who Zilant was. What *good* even looked and acted like." He shook his head.

"How?" she asked. No judgment. Simply trying to understand.

Airk didn't answer right away, giving her question serious consideration. "Pytheios believes in what he is doing. He is convinced that dragons relying on a phoenix to bring us peace, or luck, or dictate who rules is wrong. He believes our kind are strong enough not to need another species." His lips twisted. "He believes this so strongly, he is willing to sacrifice anyone who gets in his way. He is sure he is doing this *for* his people, whether they understand it or not. That his actions and decisions, even the most difficult ones, are all about what true leaders do."

"But..."

Airk's lips quirked. "But then I remembered that, historically, our people's peace and prosperity was always greatest when a phoenix mated a High King, and worst when a phoenix could not be found for whatever reason. Also how my father always said that leaders should never hide their actions from the people. Every action, every decision should be in the open. Pytheios only works in the shadows, concealing his true actions behind lies and sycophants."

Angelika remained quiet for a moment, then, "You're incredible, too," she said. Repeating his own words back to him. "I hope you realize that."

Her words stilled his bones. His soul. Incredible wasn't exactly high on his list of words he'd use to describe himself. Broken. Cast aside. Forgotten. Those were more accurate.

She pressed a hand over his heart. "I'm serious. That you could hold on to your hope, after so long..." She shook her head, then inched closer and pressed her lips softly to his. "The rest of us have no right to give up in the face of what true determination looks like."

Like him?

"I was not hopeful all of that time," he reminded her.

She smiled, the spark returning to her eyes, and inched even closer, winding her arms around his neck, pressing her breasts against him in the most distracting manner. "But you held on, and that's what matters," she whispered.

Airk's body stirred with her so close, plastered down his front, her fresh-air-and-summer scent filling his lungs, her warmth and her smile right there for him alone. But giving in to his needs could wait. "You should rest."

This was about her. Her needs.

"You know what would really help me rest?"

The way she wiggled against him had him squeezing his eyes shut, muscles tensing against the urge to roll her under him. "What?"

A long pause had him opening his eyes again.

"If you make love to me." She grinned, the beauty of the way her face lit up for him threatening to steal his heart and never give it back.

"*That* is not restful," he pointed out.

Why was he arguing with her?

"It is afterward," she shot right back. Then rolled her hips against him, pressing into the hardness of his already pulsing erection.

There *were* all those *Kama Sutra* positions he wanted to try, not to mention the fact that he could finally…let go…with her. Entirely.

Airk growled and rolled her beneath him like he'd wanted to anyway. "You do make an excellent argument."

Which earned him a giggle, the sound shooting straight to his groin. One that quickly disappeared as he claimed his mate's mouth in a kiss meant to banish all the doubts, all the fears. Even if only for a short while.

In one swift move, he swept the oversize T-shirt over her head. Leaning on one elbow, he trailed his fingers over the curve of her neck, her collarbone, between her breasts to her belly. "Gods, you're so…soft."

Fascination blended with need as he took his time exploring by touch alone. Desire ratcheted higher at the sight of his hand against her skin and the way her muscles would flutter and jump under his touch. He teased a particular spot at her hip, then, curious, leaned down to feather his lips, his tongue, over the sensitive flesh, and smiled when she groaned.

He did it again, nipping at her hip with his teeth, and she shuddered.

"Does that feel good?" He truly wanted to know.

"Mmmm," she sort of hummed. "Want me to show you?"

"Yes."

Almost of one accord, they rolled so that she leaned over him. Only she didn't immediately show him. Instead, she kissed him, taking her time, teasing with soft brushes, until he speared a hand through her hair and deepened the kiss, entwining their tongues, sucking at her lower lip.

"Whoa." She pulled away finally, breathing heavily. Staring at him with desire flushing her features, her hair tousled from his hands. Sexiest damn thing he'd ever seen.

Now he understood why Ladon stared at Skylar like she was an obsession. Because she was. And he was for her, too. Airk could see that much in the way Angelika's gaze skated over him as possessively as he ever did with her.

Which only made his cock harden to steel.

With a smile, Angelika scooted lower, pausing to kiss and nip her way down his body. She stopped when her head was level with his hip and traced the dip and swell of the muscles and bones forming the V there with the softest brush of a fingertip. Sure enough, his muscles jumped at the touch, as though they couldn't take the pleasure.

With a low chuckle of satisfaction, she leaned over and used her lips, her teeth, her tongue, and damned if he wasn't groaning the way she had at the same touch.

Eventually, she lifted her head, pinning him with eyes aglow. "What's the verdict?"

"It feels good."

She smiled. "Yes, it does." Then, before he could fathom what she was up to, she moved the tiny bit needed and sucked his cock into her mouth, going only halfway down.

"Fuck," he groaned, hands back in her hair, lifting the tresses away so he could watch, fascinated by the sight of those lush lips wrapped around him.

"More?" she asked, her warm breath whispering over his straining hard-on.

"I am supposed to be taking care of you."

"Mmm. But if it's what I want, too…" She took him in her mouth again, and he couldn't stop himself from holding her still while he thrust, in long, controlled slides in and out of her perfect mouth.

But he only let the desire build so much before he stopped her, pulling her away. Before she could protest, he was off the bed, swooping her up only to set her on her feet. He dropped to his knees before her, using his hands to gently spread her legs wider.

The first swipe of his tongue was…heaven. He wasn't sure which was better, her taste or the sound of her moaning his name.

He lifted his head, pinning her with a commanding look. "You may *not* come," he told her. An order.

A fantasy he'd been playing in his head for a while and could now give full rein to.

Surprise and a small flash of defiance lit her eyes. He slid a single finger inside her and didn't look away as he fucked her with it. "Trust me," he said, meaning it.

Gods, he meant it because she could, and he'd never thought that possible.

After only the barest hesitation, she nodded.

Smiling, he placed his lips over her clit, playing her with his mouth and using his fingers until she was whimpering and so close. The fluttering against his fingers told him that much.

Moving fast again, he got up on his feet. He spun her around, clasping her to him, her back to his chest, and whispered in her ear. "In one of Nathair's books, I read about this position that is supposed to encourage female orgasm. I would like to attempt this with you. Yes?"

"Gods, yes," she breathed.

"Good." Pressing his hand to her spine, he pressed until she bent over in half at the waist. "Reach your hands up toward me," he demanded.

She did without question, and he clasped her by the wrists so that she could do the same, anchoring them together. This would allow him to hold her upright while he…

Fuck.

Airk took a long moment to enjoy the view. The pale globes of her ass spread so that he could see her pretty nether parts, glistening and ready for him.

"Ready?" he said.

"Yes."

Muscles already straining with the need to possess her, he positioned his throbbing cock at her entrance and pressed inside, filling her, strangled by her.

"Oh my gods, Airk," she whimpered.

"Hold on," he warned. Then reared back and thrust back in, hard, sinking deep until he filled her to the hilt.

The sound that came from her was somewhere between a moan and a scream.

"Keep going?"

"If you stop, I'll kill you," she told him.

Grinning from ear to ear, he didn't stop. The pace he set was brutal on purpose. Partly because the sounds of pleasure pouring from her drove him to it, but also because, in the back of his head, the idea lingered of wringing her body with pleasure to the point that she could let go of her worries, if only for a few hours, and sleep. He'd exhaust her with orgasms.

"Oh." Her body rippled around his cock.

Deliberately, Airk used his dragon speed, increasing his thrusts.

"Oh. Oh. Oh, gods!" She clamped down hard on him, her orgasm tipping him into his own pleasure with a loud bellow as he continued to thrust in and out of her body.

Only he wasn't done.

As both of their orgasms waned, he had her on the bed, his mouth back on her, fingers inside her, playing with her. And he didn't stop until her breathing picked up in time to his mouth, and her hips started to undulate, chasing the touch.

That telltale flutter hit his fingers, and he latched his mouth around her clit, that nub of nerves that seemed to be the button to set her off. He sucked. Hard.

And she screamed.

Her legs clamped around his head as he sucked her through not one but two more orgasms, the second one softer, shorter, but no less potent, if the sounds of her pleasure were any indication.

He stopped when she involuntarily jumped at the touch of his tongue, turning too sensitive to handle more.

Smiling in a way he hadn't in years—fuck, in centuries—Airk crawled back up her body to pull her into the curve of his own in such a way that he surrounded her but could allow his gaze to linger on her face.

I do not deserve her. This.

For once in his life, he pushed the thought away, buried it in the dark hole where he usually stuck his dragon. Time enough tomorrow for worries.

Angelika tried to open her eyes, the lids fluttering, and smiled as their gazes connected. "I like that position," she murmured.

Slurred, more like, but he chuckled anyway. "Sleep, my mate."

Almost as though she'd obeyed an order, Angelika went limp in his arms, snuggling her head under his chin. "You too, mate."

CHAPTER TWENTY-FIVE

Angelika's eyes popped open as she went from deep sleep to wide awake with a disorienting jolt.

"What?" Airk mumbled in the sexiest, sleep-laden low voice. Her body shivered in immediate, stark reaction.

But what woke her was too urgent to stop and indulge first. "Kasia wasn't wrong."

Rather than waffle or ask what she meant, his pale blue eyes opened, trained on her face, instantly alert. "How so?"

"Her vision." She shook her head—how had they not guessed sooner? "She wasn't wrong. He's coming here next."

Airk's thick, dark brows drew down over his eyes. "How would he know to come here?"

"Brock."

The truth of her realization settled in his own expression.

She laid it out anyway. "These are all guesses, but Brock was sent here specifically and probably should have checked in by now and hasn't. Because my sisters had to go somewhere, and now this place is suspicious. Because Pytheios has been a step ahead of us all along. Take your pick."

After a long beat, his eyes hardened to frosty flame. "I think you are correct."

They needed to get everyone out of this mountain and somewhere Pytheios wouldn't think to look. Now.

Without another word, they were both up, hurrying to the bathroom to shower and dress. Not together, because even with the urgency that would be distracting. She went first. As they traded, Airk told her, "I called Jordy. He is gathering your sisters and our councils together. Here."

For privacy? Good call. While these rooms had some updates, they weren't exactly comfortable. Hells, they were lucky to have running hot water.

She was tempted to kiss him, but they didn't have time. In short order, they dressed. As she braided her wet hair to get it out of her way, she could hear Airk letting the others in. When she emerged, it was to find the living area of their suite filled to the brim. Not just her sisters and their mates, Mös, Belyy, Tovar and the other council members of her father's clan, but the viceroys and guards from Ladon's, Brand's, and Samael's clans as well.

Full house.

The way the groups stood, each of the four gathered with their own in a different corner of the room, put her in mind of middle-school kids at a dance, still figuring out hormones.

"Are we waiting on anyone else?" she asked Airk.

He shook his head.

Raising her voice, she addressed the room in general. "Has everyone been introduced?"

A few nods, mostly from the kings and her sisters, along with a lot of sour faces. She shook her head, wishing that she had more time to prepare them, to show them how to work together. Something deep inside told her she could—look at where they were now, so much further than anyone had believed—but she was out of time. "Whatever past offenses, personal or otherwise, you are dealing with, if we want to survive this—if we want to take Pytheios down—then we work together. Can you do that?"

Sour blanked out, adjusting after another beat to expressions not blank but purposeful.

"What is this about?" Ladon was the one to ask.

No way to ease into this. "Kasia's vision wasn't wrong," she said.

Her sister blanched but didn't bobble. "It happened exactly as I saw it."

Angelika shook her head. "When you first told me, right after the vision happened, you said that he used different words."

Kasia frowned, gaze going fuzzy as though trying to remember. "I must have been in shock. I'm sure he said—"

"Bow to me now, or die—that's what you told me he said."

"Is it?" Kasia shook her head.

"But yesterday, he said it slightly differently. Right?"

"True…" Kasia let the word trail off as she thought through it. Then her chin came up, eyes going harder. "My visions aren't always easy to interpret, but the words used are *never* wrong."

Brand set a hand to the small of his mate's back, a gesture of support.

One Angelika appreciated, because she didn't have time to comfort them through this. "Exactly. I think your vision *was* of this mountain. We're next."

"Holy hellfire," Mös muttered, then snapped an accusing glare to her and Airk. "What have you brought down on us?"

Before Angelika could respond, Airk's snarl set every person in the room on edge as he speared the Beta with a look filled with rage and promised retribution. "You *could* be ruled by Brock right now, and that gold dragon would be ordering you to attack the Black, Gold, and Blue Clans. You think you would be any safer?"

After a long, twitchy stare down, Mös looked away first.

Not that that eased any of the tension suffocating the people in the room, at least if the set of shoulders and jaws was any indication.

"We need a plan," Angelika dropped into the stony silence. "One that he won't expect."

Skylar and Ladon exchanged a look, then glanced at Samael and Meira, then at Brand and Kasia.

"It's time," Brand said.

Time? Time for what? What plans had her sisters and their kings been making while she and Airk been off recruiting?

• • •

"Are you sure about this?" Skylar whispered as they all took their spots inside the massive hangar.

Angelika shot her a look that said to quit.

"Leave her alone," Meira said. "We've asked her already."

"But the bond... She can't shift. She's not fully dragon yet."

If ever. Angelika had survived Airk's fire, but something was missing. She could *feel* it, but she couldn't pin down what, exactly. As though the change couldn't happen. Or wouldn't. What was the point of her showing dragon sign if she was going to remain human the rest of her life? Maybe they'd done the mating wrong? But she didn't think so, and she refused to worry him with her questions.

"We're better bait if he thinks he'll get all four of us," was all she said now.

Each of their mates had expressed displeasure in this part of the plan. Loudly. Or, for Brand, lots of growling and grunting. Airk, however, had remained dead quiet.

Not punishing her with silence. More like he didn't trust himself not to lose his shit if he opened his mouth. The kiss he'd laid on her as the kings had left with everyone else had been...explosive. And desperate.

"Do what you must," he murmured against her lips. "But come back to me."

She'd loved him even more in that moment and yet hadn't told him so. Neither of them had shared that word yet. She didn't want him more distracted if she said it. For a newly mated dragon, leaving her alone in the mountain of Kamen while he and the kings took their four clans halfway across the globe had to be nothing short of torture. So she'd kept her feelings to herself.

"I'll see you soon," she whispered back.

She didn't think about how the gargoyles had said no to being part of this. Or how Hershel and the Covens' Syndicate had agreed to only limited help. No one had been able to track down the hellhounds. But they had the majority of four out of the six clans' worth of dragons. They had Enforcers from the Americas colonies. They had the wolves. And they had a plan.

Their plan had to work. It *had* to.

They didn't dare use the mirrors. Not yet. Which meant using the same interconnected method that had allowed Kasia and Skylar to get dragons out of Ben Nevis quickly. Apparently—Meira's idea— the Blue, Black, and Gold Clans had been drilling all their dragons to group together in specific, relatively protected places throughout Ben Nevis. As soon as the attack hit, fighters had kept Pytheios's forces distracted while Kasia and Skylar used their combined versions of teleportation to go from group to group, sending them to Angelika in Kamen. They'd waited for their attackers to herd the fighters into a single group together so that they were able to get them out in one shot.

Such an action had drained both of her sisters terribly, but blood transfusions from their mates had brought them back to full ability. All of which had been used again, getting every soul in this mountain to a new location.

A secret location nowhere on this side of the world.

Alaskan wilderness. Genius move.

Angelika glanced at the five white dragons who'd insisted on remaining behind to guard them. Two who had made an oath to Skylar a while back, plus Belyy, Tovar, and Jordy.

Kasia had been the one to convince Angelika to allow it in the end. "My vision," she'd said. "They're in it."

Now she and her sisters were together and, mostly, alone for possibly the first time since their mother's death.

With a sigh, she laid her head on Meira's shoulder. "How's mini-you doing?"

She felt more than saw her sister's smile. "I felt him move for the first time last week."

"What?" Kasia demanded on a squeal. "Why didn't you say?"

Meira shrugged. "We were...busy."

"Not too busy for baby stuff," Skylar insisted, tapping Meira's foot with her own.

Meira's deep breath moved Angelika's head up and down.

"What did it feel like?" Angelika asked.

"Like…tiny bubbles."

"It was gas." Skylar's eye roll was in her voice.

Angelika reached across Meira and flicked her arm for that, and Skylar actually pretended to jump. "Hey."

Meira chuckled. "It wasn't gas. I'd thought, a few times before, that I was feeling the baby, but I wasn't. This was…different."

Another deep breath, and Meira's hand crept over her belly in a protective gesture as ancient and instinctual as motherhood.

"What did Samael say about you staying behind?" Angelika asked her.

"I think he would rather have remained here with me."

A massive understatement, no doubt.

Skylar's sarcastic snort said she thought so, too. "I believe Kasia threatening him with fucked-up, world-ending paradoxes if we didn't match her vision was the only thing that made him go."

"Made them all go," Kasia tagged on. "Those lizard brains are definitely all instinct when it comes to their mates. But it's kind of cute."

They all chuckled over that.

"I heard that," one of the white dragons called out in the dark.

Which only made them laugh harder.

Gods, it felt so good to be with her sisters again. Angelika's smile slipped into a frown. "After this is over—"

"Please let this be the end of it," Skylar muttered.

They all nodded.

"Anyway, after this is over, we'll be apart."

They were all quiet for a second, contemplating what that life might look like. Apart, yes, but safe. And settled. No more running. No more hiding.

They'd be living among dragon shifters, who tended to be ruled by their passions and had difficulty letting go of the past, especially past grievances. She wasn't naive enough to believe there'd be no more fighting. But still…no one coming for her or her sisters all the time would be a refreshing change.

"Do you remember that time…" She paused to think. "I want to say we were about seventeen or eighteen years old. Europeans—and therefore dragons—had discovered the 'new world' existed, and Skylar got the bright idea that we should get ourselves over there somehow. That distance would make it harder for Pytheios to find us."

Skylar leaned forward. "Uh…and I was right."

Angelika grinned. "Not for another few hundred years, Sky. Anyway, Mama was trying to explain how we'd have to travel with humans, and that they weren't just letting anyone go, and all the dangers. Weather, provisions going bad, months cooped up on the ship, the possibility of being caught between two warring human factions on the seas. But especially that it would be unsafe for women traveling alone in general. And Skylar said—"

Kasia straightened suddenly. "That's right. She said, 'We'll build our own ship.' Oh my gods, I'd forgotten that."

Meira hid a grin behind her hand, and Skylar scowled at them all.

"Is this going somewhere?" she demanded.

"Well, Mama, of course, said no, but you decided we would do it anyway and surprise her. You were so sure of yourself and managed to convince the rest of us to go along. And Kasia went to check the price of ships."

Kasia frowned slowly. "No. That wasn't me. That was you."

Angelika shook her head. "Don't you remember? You had to run away—"

Her sister winced. "From those ruffians trying to steal my purse."

"Who's laughing now?" Skylar crowed.

Angelika chuckled at Kasia's embarrassed frown. "Anyway, while we didn't get our own ship and sail off right away, we did beat most settlers to it eventually. It took more planning and more time than we anticipated, but we got there."

They smiled at one another. Those years before dragons finally started coming over in big enough numbers for them to worry about had been some of their happiest. No looking over their shoulders constantly. They'd found friends and shelter with the native inhabitants. They'd lived full lives.

Not lives without danger or sorrow or hard times. Living as long as they did meant a lot of goodbyes and seeing friends and loved ones pass on to the afterlife. But there was a difference between living and simply surviving. The same as the difference between raw cocoa powder and milk chocolate.

"My point is, we can do damn near anything when we do it together."

After a beat, Skylar wrapped her hand around Angelika's and squeezed, then took Kasia's on her other side, and Meira slipped hers into Angelika's. They sat there together in silence. Just being together. Waiting for the man they'd always been waiting for.

To find them. To try to kill them.

It ended now. It had to.

...

Airk sat on the stone floor, back against the rough wall of the cave and legs splayed out in front of him. Along with Ladon, Samael, and Brand, he waited in the smaller space where a single mirror had been positioned. A mirror that only reflected themselves back.

They weren't sure if Meira would be able to use it to communicate once the attack on Kamen came, but they had to try.

Skylar was the one who'd come up with this spot. Or, more particularly, she'd reached out to a contact in the colonies. A black dragon shifter—Rune Abaddon—who'd been rogue for the last few decades but had been reinstated to his team of Enforcers very recently. A situation that apparently involved taking down the leaders of the Alliance, whom the old kings had set to govern dragons in the Americas. An act that should have marked them as traitors and yet didn't. Something about taking out Pytheios's lackeys.

Airk had no idea what to think of that.

However, Skylar trusted the man implicitly. Her mother had sent her to Rune for protection when she died. Meira and Samael, whom Rune had helped in a separate incident only a few months ago, did, too. So, for that matter, did Brand, who'd interacted with the black dragon as well as his Enforcer team, the Huracáns, soon before he'd found Kasia. Airk trusted Angelika's family, so here they were in a mountain in the wilderness of Alaska. A raw mountain, unexcavated or made for dragons. One they didn't all fit in. Which meant most of their people were camped out in the forests around it.

Exposed.

And ready to fight.

He slid a searching glance toward the other three men in the room. Their connections with their mates, through the bonds already in place, meant they could feel them. Gods, what he wouldn't give to feel Angelika right now. Still, not one of the dragon kings had so much as twitched. He had to take it on faith that they would know if something bad happened.

"Ladon?"

Airk glanced briefly at Arden, Ladon's sister, standing in the entrance to the small cavern where he sat, only to return his gaze to the mirror.

"Yes?" Ladon asked.

"The red dragon named Jakkobah is awake, and he wants to speak with the kings."

Fuck. "Bring him here," Airk said.

Out of the corner of his eye, he caught her wince. "He can't be moved yet."

"Then it will have to wait," Brand growled.

Airk nodded. No way in hells was he not going to be here if Angelika suddenly needed him.

"He insists it is urgent. Turn more hearts to our side," Arden said. "Particularly white dragons."

Airk stiffened at that before glancing at Ladon. Jakkobah had been *his* informant, after all. The blue king's face could've been carved from rock as he stared back, and Airk knew what they were all thinking.

Of the three of them, Airk was the liability. Unable to shift. If their phoenixes needed them, the other three would be better equipped to do something about it. More than that, he could picture Angelika if she were here. She would volunteer or urge him to. He knew it.

"I will go," Airk said finally, though his dragon snarled at the idea.

Ladon jerked his head. "He may only speak with me."

They'd deal with that if it happened. "Do you trust him?"

"Yes."

"Do you trust *me*?" Airk asked next.

"Yes." No hesitation.

Airk tried damn hard not to be surprised by that. Angelika was the only one, other than Skylar to a certain extent, who'd shown that kind of faith in him since his release.

"Is there anything that would make this man trust me?" he managed to get out of his own head to ask.

"Aniferes," Ladon said.

The word slid with sour recognition through him, but Airk only raised his eyebrows.

Ladon shrugged. "Our code word. One he made up so only he would recognize it."

"Actually...that word was made up by another." By Nathair. The one who had kept him educated. The one who, in the end, helped him and Skylar escape.

Aniferes was "Serefina" spelled backward.

A word they'd come up with to mean hope and hold on. Nathair would never entirely turn his back on his brother. His hope was in Pytheios, not against him. But he hadn't agreed with what the red king had done to Airk, either.

Airk pushed to his feet. "If I am not back before the attack comes, tell Angelika…" Gods, what message could he leave that was enough?

But Brand was the one to nod. "We'll tell her."

He searched the faces of the three men in front of him. The only ones who might understand. With an answering nod, he strode out of the door with Arden.

All those still healing from injury had been set up deep inside the mountain, where fewer lives might be risked protecting them if the battle found its way here. Airk hadn't left the mirrored room since they arrived, so he followed as Arden let the way through pitch-black twists and turns leading deeper into the ground. He jerked to a halt at the sight of what appeared to be a massive boulder blocking their way. Only the texture of the rock was…off.

"Is that a…"

"Cave troll," Arden affirmed. "He came with Rune Abaddon's team of Enforcers who knew of this place. Apparently, this was the troll's mountain until recently."

Arden patted a pattern on the creature's back, or maybe its knee. Suddenly, the boulder shifted out of the way, uncurling from what appeared to be a deep sleep.

He blinked at Airk as he passed through. Or at least appeared to. Difficult to discern, given the crunched-up arrangement of features making a face. For his part, Airk refused to turn his back on the massive, gray-skinned beast. The thing had to be close to fifteen feet tall and looked to be made of rock, dust coating its leathery skin and facial features hidden in a face made up of crags and crevices.

"You new dragon," the troll said in a voice that was low but surprisingly smooth. Slow and even, like time itself.

How was one supposed to greet a cave troll? He settled for introducing himself. "Airk Azdajah."

"White dragon?"

Not really a question, but Airk nodded anyway.

The troll grunted. "Me called Vilsinn."

"Pleasure," Airk said. He eyed Vilsinn warily, waiting for any sign of aggression.

When the troll meekly stared back, Airk glanced around, searching for any signs that this might be a carnivorous one of its kind. Most trolls were vegetarians, but a few got a taste for human blood, and that was it for them. At least he didn't see human bones scattered about the chamber.

"Me protect Airk while in this place," Vilsinn said. "Protect *everyone* in here."

Airk pulled his gaze back to the troll and caught the implication. If he hurt anyone in this space under the troll's protection, Vilsinn wouldn't hesitate to kill him. "Fair enough."

That earned him a slow bob of the head before the troll rolled, with the creak of leather and a sort of grinding sound, into a ball and tucked himself back into the doorway he'd been blocking, looking, suddenly, like any other boulder. Airk would be checking all the other boulders a little more closely in the future.

But he didn't have time to waste, turning to find Arden waiting for him. Even deeper into the mountain, Arden led him to a tiny alcove where the man named Jakkobah was laid out on the ground. Reed, Arden's soon-to-be mate—news Angelika had squealed over when she'd been informed shortly before everyone left Kamen—was there, grim faced as Airk entered. If Reed had expected his own king, he didn't show any sign of it. A Healer was also in the room, sitting on the floor beside Jakkobah, tubes hooked up to draw blood from him into the Stoat's arm.

The Healer—one Airk recognized from his helping with all the injured the day before, a man with black hair and bright blue eyes—glanced up. "I'm almost finished."

Airk nodded. "I'm Airk."

"Fallon."

"With Ladon's people?"

"At the moment. I was an Enforcer with the Huracán team until a few years ago. Finn, their alpha, is my brother. Rune is a friend. But Ladon needed my services more."

Another nod. An Enforcer with the same group that had set

them up with this mountain? They'd take all the fighters they could get.

Finally, Fallon finished his work—not that Jakkobah looked any better for it, but he'd always been naturally pale. As soon as they were alone, Airk knelt beside the man he'd always believed to be Pytheios's faithful right hand. Hells, he'd probably jerked the king off when the man was too decrepit to do it himself.

"You have one minute to convince me that I should not snap your neck."

Jakkobah blinked his pale eyes at him. "I believe the cave troll would have issues with that threat."

He wasn't wrong. "Fifty seconds."

"If I could have gotten you out of Everest sooner, I would."

"You did not get me out. Not good enough."

"Every attempt to kill Pytheios resulted in the death of the person I sent to deliver it. I covered my tracks well, but losing a man who could tell all the clans the truth of what happened to our kings and phoenixes...there was no way that wouldn't blow back on me."

Airk considered those words. Pytheios always was steps ahead of everyone else, and he would no doubt eventually learn who was behind Airk's escape.

Nathair. What had happened to his friend?

"Who do you think encouraged Nathair to befriend you?" Jakkobah asked next, as though reading his mind.

That snapped Airk's brows down. "What do you mean?"

"A long play." Jakkobah's lips quirked. "A bit of what American football fans call a Hail Mary. Nathair's loyalty to his brother was ingrained, but I had hoped that if time allowed a friendship to develop between the two of you, eventually he might be the key to your freedom. So I encouraged him to visit you from time to time." Satisfaction pulled at the man's angular features. "I was right."

Airk battled his dragon, who raged inside him, because that still wasn't good enough. This man had hidden behind others all while protecting himself. Even if he had worked against Pytheios, it hadn't been nearly enough.

Then Jakkobah's choice of words penetrated, dread thudding inside him like boulders down a mountainside. "You said *was*?"

Pale red eyebrows lifted in question.

"You said Nathair's loyalty *was* ingrained."

An emotion passed over the red shifter's features that looked a hell of a lot like regret and guilt. "Pytheios executed him before my very eyes."

The hit came out of nowhere, and yet he'd seen it. He should have known. Airk bowed his head, breathing hard through the thunder of emotions lashing at him with the news. His friend. His sweet, kind, brilliant friend. His only friend for centuries. Nathair was dead.

At Pytheios's hands. His own brother. "Why was he killed?"

Jakkobah hesitated, as though he was weighing the cost of telling the truth.

"Why?" Airk snapped.

"For his part in your escape. Pytheios found proof of it and killed Nathair in front of me...to loosen my tongue during interrogation."

The truth. A truth that could bring Airk's fury down on Jakkobah, and the Stoat knew it. Which meant he was being honest.

Hands fisted so hard his nails drew blood, Airk closed his eyes against his own grief and searched for the ability to see beyond personal retribution and use this man for what he could do to help the cause. The way Angelika would. "Aniferes."

Jakkobah didn't react, but something told Airk that he'd relaxed with that word.

"Ah." The Stoat seemed unsurprised. "I see we've been speaking with Ladon Ormarr."

"And Nathair. *He* told me that word."

"Who do you think told it to him?"

Airk blew out a long breath on a half growl. Either he trusted him or he didn't. If Jakkobah had information to share, he would, at the very least, listen. "You wanted to speak with me?"

"With a king." He cocked his head in a motion that reminded Airk of a bird. "That's not you."

"And yet, I am who came to listen."

"True." The Stoat paused, calculations going on behind his eyes. Then Jakkobah slipped a small metal device into Airk's hand.

Looking at it, he knew from being around Meira that it had something to do with modern-day computers. "What's this?"

"Proof that Pytheios's phoenix is a female-born white dragon shifter who was made into a phoenix by his witch."

Airk almost pulverized the small device as his hands clamped around it. "What kind of proof?"

"Video footage of the magic performed to make it so."

Seven hells. "How did you get this?"

"As soon as the tech was good enough, I spent years setting up secret cameras throughout Everest. There's more on there, but Pytheios's false phoenix... That's what you need to bring him down."

"Why did you not tell us sooner?" Airk's voice descended to a growl.

Jakkobah simply lifted a bored eyebrow. "I was unconscious, dear boy. And you are wasting time."

He was right.

Airk surged to his feet, pausing at the door to look over his shoulder at the heap of bones that was a dragon shifter lying on the floor. "Thank you."

Jakkobah's eyes flared briefly, and the man actually hesitated a beat before finally giving a nod.

Airk left him there, rushing back to the kings. They could share this with those gathered here, bolster the truth with those fighting for them. But even more important was reaching the dragons not yet on their side. Meira was their best bet to get this information out to everyone else. Preferably before the fighting started.

The question was: How could they get this to her?

CHAPTER TWENTY-SIX

Angelika sat cross-legged on the floor, stuffing her face with a sandwich that one of their guards had put together for everyone for dinner. Which felt normal. Or at least normal adjacent.

So when Meira's spine snapped steel-rod straight, her gaze going sort of hazy, it took Angelika a solid ten seconds to stop chewing before she could ask, "What's wrong?"

But Meira didn't speak. She just spun around, facing one of the hundreds of mirrors they'd placed all over the mountain—inside and outside. Immediately, the image changed, showing Samael in a small cavern, almost impossible to see in the dark, lips pressed together in a grim line and dark eyes glittering with flame. Behind him, Ladon and Brand stood back, equally grim.

"Meira," Skylar snapped. "You weren't supposed to—"

"I called her," Samael cut her sister off. "It's important."

The mates stared at each other a long moment. Were they speaking in their minds? Angelika didn't care. She was too busy searching the room for Airk.

But he wasn't there.

Before she could ask where her mate was, Meira shoved her hand through the mirror and took something from Samael before pulling back out and shutting off her power. The transition back to their own reflections was so abrupt, Angelika let out a sharp breath.

"What did he give you?" she asked.

But Meira didn't answer. She grabbed for the nearest device, a laptop, the only one she'd brought down here with her. Plugging whatever he'd given her into it, she started up what appeared to be a video, and they all gathered around her to watch what seemed to be some sort of surveillance feed, black and white, a tad grainy and from above and at an angle. But what was clear on the screen were four figures. Pytheios. Jakkobah. Tisiphone. And the witch, Rhiamon.

Tisiphone lay on a slab. As they watched, Rhiamon raised her hands, and some kind of material—dirt, maybe?—rose from a small cylindrical container at the foot of the slab.

"Is that an urn?" Kasia broke the silence hanging over them.

No one answered. On the screen, the particles floated in the air, coalescing over Tisiphone's body in a thin layer, appearing to form to her shape, though it was difficult to tell from the angle and distance.

Angelika frowned, familiarity tickling her mind. "Is that…?"

"Oh my gods," Kasia whispered. "Please, no."

"Those are ashes," Skylar said, her voice dropping low, almost a dragon's growl of anger.

Horror wrapped around Angelika's heart and squeezed so hard she couldn't breathe. "He couldn't. Could he?" Angelika choked out.

Again, no answer.

They were all probably too terrified to voice it. Because if they knew anything about Pytheios, it was that there was no line he would not cross. Meira didn't speak, staring hard at the screen, but her hands were shaking, making the image bounce around. And no wonder. She'd been the one to discover their mother's ashes had disappeared from the place where she'd died. That lonely, empty field behind their house in Kansas.

No one said it, but they were all thinking it.

If Pytheios had fucking *made* a phoenix…

The floating layer of ash—that had to be what they were looking at—suddenly started to glow, as though turning to embers. Brighter and brighter, they sank down over Tisiphone, absorbing into her skin and lighting her up.

The girl opened her mouth on a scream that they couldn't hear as they watched, the feed having no sound. Her body bowed and contorted in visible excruciating pain, face crumpling and grimacing. Meira made a whimpering sound, hands shaking harder, and Angelika pulled the computer from her sister's unresisting grip to hold it up for them all...

Suddenly, Tisiphone went dead still, collapsing on the slab like a rag doll shaken too hard by an overeager dog, head lolling, white-blond hair so like Angelika's mussed and spilling over the sides of the stone she lay on. Angelika leaned closer, as though she could physically get a better look in the room, studying the girl.

Was her chest even moving? Had they killed her?

Tisiphone remained that way, but the witch's arms were still raised, her mouth moving, hair raising and falling as though a breeze circled the indoor space. She was definitely still going...chanting something.

Then Tisiphone jackknifed to sitting on a visible gasp for air, mouth wide open and eyes wild. But after that initial violent reawakening, she settled, sitting quietly. She held her arms out in front of her, seeming to study her own skin. After a second, faint lines started to become visible on the grainy feed. Swirling, fine lines that glowed like the hottest ember, forming the pattern of delicate feathers.

"Oh my gods," Kasia said again, this time with a distinct waver in her voice.

"Fuck," Skylar spat. "That rat bastard just—"

Meira's head dropped forward, as though she couldn't handle the weight of the truth, and Angelika set the device on the floor to wrap an arm around her.

"He used our mother's ashes to make Tisiphone a phoenix." Angelika said what no one else would.

She didn't need to be touching Meira to sense the flinch, visible, like a tic. Her sister took a deep breath, then another, then raised her head, expression rock hard. "I need to get to the communication room."

"No." Skylar jerked to her feet. "Separating is a bad idea."

Meira's chin jutted out, determination written all over her. "All dragon shifters need to see this. I can try to do that, but only from my setup in my rooms at Ararat. It could make a difference."

"Not given where most of them are right now," Angelika pointed out. "After. We can't risk it."

"No. Now." Meira remained adamant, chin jutting out. "They'll find a way to show them. Or I will. But if it changes the minds of some who are still on the fence, it's worth it before the fight."

"The risk—"

"Then you all come with me."

Angelika tilted her head, meeting Skylar's gaze over Meira's shoulder. After a second, Skylar gave a jerking nod.

Together, they stood. "Follow us," Angelika ordered the dragons on guard duty.

Without hesitation, they marched after her and her sisters. Because Meira was right. This could make a huge difference to every dragon who believed Pytheios was supposed to be High King because of his supposed phoenix.

• • •

Airk's first stop after Jakkobah had been the kings. After scrounging up a computer, they'd watched what was on the metal item the Stoat had provided, their silence turning heavier by the second.

"Fuck me," Brand had muttered when it was over.

"I don't think I can show that to Meira," Samael had said. "In her condition, she shouldn't get that upset."

Ladon had stood in stoic silence, jaw clenched, staring at the image paused on the screen.

"We have to find a way to show this to everyone," Airk had insisted. "They have to know."

That's when Ladon had clapped a hand on Samael's shoulder.

"Meira's our best method to get this message out. Not just to the people here—to shifters everywhere. We don't have a witch, but Meira has the best chance."

Samael had shaken his head, then shaken it again, clearly not thrilled with the way of things. "In that case, I'll take Meira to Ararat myself. Her setup there is the best way to get it out."

Brand had given a sharp shake of his head. "We need you here—"

He'd stopped as Samael's eyes flared with black flame, and the gold king snapped his mouth shut. Airk hadn't blamed him. With Meira pregnant, the black dragon king's protective instincts had to be screaming at him.

But in the end, they'd convinced Samael to give Meira the video but remain here in Alaska.

At the same time, they'd hurried to set up for what they hoped she could do next, and she'd come through.

She'd set that video up to broadcast in every way possible to dragons across the world. To the war rooms and communication rooms in the mountains, bypassing network security to hit TVs in the mountains, too using the humans' emergency broadcast spectrum limited only to dragon shifters' personal devices—who knew where she got those lists—to push the video to them individually. And probably many other ways he could hardly fathom after so long in his dungeon.

But where he and his allies were in Alaska, they didn't have TVs or war rooms, and their personal devices didn't work. So they'd loaded the original file onto a bunch of laptops.

Now Airk stood on an outcropping of rock, showing his own people the proof. White dragon shifters, all in their human forms, spread out through the trees of the forest below him. He held up a borrowed computer, playing the video for them at the same time that Meira was broadcasting it all those ways.

He wasn't the only one showing this. Brand, Ladon, Samael, but also Jordy and Tovar; Finn Conleth, who was the lead Enforcer of his team; Ladon's men Asher and Reid; and several others had gone to show this to their people simultaneously.

With dragon shifters' heightened senses of both sight and hearing, they could all take it in perfectly fine regardless of how far back they stood from him. The silence that hung over every person gathered throughout the mountainside was the same as had hung over the kings when they'd played this earlier.

"I recognize her," someone said in the crowd. "She grew up in the Unnamed Mountain."

Airk stiffened at that. The same mountain where he'd pulled that unclaimed dragon mate from their dungeon? Where they'd attacked before he'd opened his mouth?

"You don't recognize her," another voice shouted the denial. "This is a fake. Anyone could have made this video."

A grumble—half in agreement, half unswayed—spread through the crowd like slow-moving thunder coming from a distance.

Belyy, at his side, stepped forward, and silence fell over them again. "*I* knew her personally. She is no phoenix." He grimaced. "Or she wasn't, until..." He waved a hand at the screen.

The man couldn't even bring himself to say what that witch had done to her.

Then Mös, also standing with him, turned his head, studying Airk. The speculative gleam in his eyes had Airk frowning, the sensation of something coming at him that he didn't want crawling over his skin.

The ex-Beta turned back to face their clan. "There is only one dragon we can trust. If those in leadership weren't in on it, they were oblivious to it, which is almost worse. Myself included. But this man—"

He clapped a hand on Airk's shoulder. Only through sheer will did Airk not growl at the touch, his dragon curling inside him like a striking snake.

Unaware or undeterred, Mös continued. "I believe that the gods saved this man so that he could step up to rule when the time was right. He endured what he did—*all* that he did—to come out pure on the other side. Untainted. Worthy."

A murmuring passed through the crowd. Not anger but… agreement.

Fuck.

Angelika should be here for this. He was the last man anyone should be promoting to rule. Airk started shaking his head.

"Not only that, but Airk Azdajah is mated to a true phoenix, the daughter of our previous king. He is the son of Zilant's beta, already in line for the throne."

"No," Airk stated. Unequivocally.

Mös's neck cracked he snapped his head around so hard, a scowl descending. "What do you mean, no?"

Airk was tempted to stare the man down. The word *no* held the same definition in all languages. But he could practically hear Angelika's voice in his head telling him to work with Mös, try to make him understand. These were their people.

Fuck again.

He faced the gathered crowd rather than Mös. "In captivity, I had to contain my dragon. That side of me is feral. Cannot be released. I would not be right as your king if I cannot lead you in the skies."

"You took down that gold dragon!" someone shouted from the back.

"Like a true king," Mös stated, nodding. "He killed Brock Hagan, protecting you, his people, from the man Pytheios wanted to put on *our* throne."

All supportive words. Building faith in Airk. Even so, there was still something in the way he was acting that set Airk's teeth on edge. Something…wrong.

"King Airk Azdajah," a new voice cried out.

"King Airk," other voices took up the call.

Fisting his hands at his sides, he pushed against the instinct to shut down. An instinct driven by years of having to hold everything inside himself, never giving Pytheios the satisfaction of a reaction of any kind. But that kind of reaction now wouldn't fix this or stop this. This was getting out of hand. What the hells was he supposed to do? What could he possibly say to turn this rising tide?

He was not their king and never could be.

Airk held up a hand, and silence settled over those who had once been his people. "After what you have been through, you deserve a king who is whole, at one with his dragon side. I am *not* that man."

"You owe us this," Mös snapped.

"I *owe* you?" Airk's growl was a low rumble of sound that stilled the other man.

Even a predator knew when the larger threat had decided to focus on them. The Beta blinked rapidly. "You are mated to the phoenix who has pledged herself to this clan. You are next in line for the throne by blood right. You have even more against Pytheios than we do. This is *your* war, son. Fight it or get the hells out."

The dragon way. If you weren't useful, you were cut loose. "I am *not* your son," Airk snarled. "And Angelika does not need a king to lead this clan. She can do it herself."

A flash of emotion brightened Mös's eyes, like a sun flare. Also an emotion that Airk recognized—pure triumph.

"We will only ever follow a dragon shifter as our ruler," Mös stated, utterly controlled.

Realization struck too late, like a gong rung after dessert had already been served. *That* was what this was about. Discrediting both Airk and Angelika as the true leaders for the white clan. Clever fucking bastard.

Airk folded his arms, staring the older man down. "That thinking is what landed you with Pytheios in the first place."

"You're right."

Airk frowned. Where was this going?

Mös's tipped lips sent tension spiraling through his bones. The man was too smug, and Airk wasn't practiced in the art of perception and politics. "But we were…I was…guilty only of ignorance. Perhaps the White Clan is better served remaining apart, out from under any High King at all."

Airk's brows snapped down. "The hells you say."

Mös shrugged. "The ins and outs of what brought us all to

this point are so convoluted, it isn't worth looking for blame or retribution. I have to think about what is best for *my* people. Something you clearly aren't prepared to sacrifice to do."

My people, not our. Because Airk was and always would be the outsider, from the day Pytheios had shoved him in that cell in Everest.

"And what is best for *our* people?"

"Staying out of it." Without further ado, Mös turned to face the gathered clan. "If you agree with me, come with me now."

About half of the people turned to follow. The others shifted uncomfortably on their feet, restless and unsure, a low murmur of discussion growing louder and louder.

"Coward." Airk spat the word at the Beta's back.

Mös quietened, though he didn't look over his shoulder. "You don't know what I've done for this clan," he said, still without moving.

"If it involved walking away, turning your back, ignoring the signs, or looking the other way, then *this* moment, right now—this is your chance to redeem yourself. Be a true leader and stay."

Mös whipped around, the wrath on his face turning into a snarl of ugliness. "A *true* leader, as you say, is one who makes the hard decisions."

"This is one of those decisions."

"A true leader protects his people. First, last, and always."

"If you think leaving now means Pytheios will not come for you, you are sorely mistaken. And if your plan is to wait and see who wins, then come crawling back, like the snake I suspect you are... If it is us, we will not take you. If it is Pytheios..." Airk's lips curled at the name. "Then you deserve what you get."

"Do you hear him?" Mös boomed out. "He's aligned himself with the other clans and not with his own people. Not truly. How can we trust him?"

Another round of grumbling rose from the people.

Airk wasn't about to debate semantics. He didn't have time for this shit. Either they stayed and believed, or they didn't. "Make your own choices. I have a rotting king to defeat."

...

Angelika settled back in the cavern in Kamen after her sister's stunt with the video. Gods, it sucked not being with the clans to see how that was taken. Had it made a difference? It had to have, right?

"It made a difference," Kasia was the one to murmur.

Skylar glanced away. Meira offered a small smile. Angelika could only sit there and hope.

"Making the same mistake twice isn't something I do," a smooth, beautiful voice poured from the darkness of the cavern beyond.

Angelika froze, staring at Meira. She wasn't even sure what she did next, moving on instinct. All she knew as that all four of them were on their feet in a heartbeat, facing the direction Pytheios's voice had come from, though they couldn't see him yet.

"I tracked your signal here." That voice slid and curled around them like a snake. "Quite a move, sharing that video. Jakkobah's gift to you, I assume? I wonder how he got it past me?"

None of them answered.

"No matter. Truth is harder to prove than you would think, and I can still feel so many of my people loyal to me. So I came for you. But this time, unlike Ben Nevis, Rhiamon has learned how to get past the wards. My people have been sent directly to the heart of this mountain, rather than above it."

The white dragons with them shifted, forming a line between them and Pytheios, though Angelika still couldn't see where he was.

At the move, a chuckle bounced off the rock walls and crawled down her spine. "I'll tell you the same thing I did last time," he said. "Bow to me now, or die."

The darkness stirred, and out of the shadows emerged a human figure—Pytheios himself. Alone.

"What was that no-mistakes thing again?" Skylar jeered.

Then glanced at Meira, but their sister shook her head.

"Can't get those reflections to work for you again?" Pytheios's voice was a satisfied purr.

"Plan B," Kasia whispered.

Which basically meant getting out of here...or pretending to.

The white dragons before them, already prepared for what that phrase meant, shifted back to human and hurried to them. Together, Kasia and Skylar were meant to use their powers to teleport them all elsewhere, though not to where the others waited. Not yet.

Except Skylar shoved and Kasia touched...then nothing happened. They were still in Kamen.

"Oh dear," the red king taunted. "Can't use those powers, either?"

That's when panic started to creep in, heat crawling up her nerves, flooding her logic. They'd determined that the witch was turning off Meira's powers somehow, but now she'd gotten to Kasia and Skylar, too? How?

Gods, the second part of this plan better work, or they'd have no way out of here.

"My king, no one is here."

Angelika blinked at the voice in her head.

Pytheios's reaction, however, was...nothing. Not even a twitch. Her sisters didn't react, either. Had they heard that, too? Or was she the only one?

Angelika tried to take in her sisters' faces surreptitiously, but they were all focused on the king and only him.

"Keep him talking," a new voice sounded in her mind.

A feminine voice, and Angelika almost gasped at the sound, barely managing to swallow it down in a rush of relief.

Delilah was here. The second part of this plan was going to work.

Hopefully. Unless Rhiamon shut the witch—or whatever Delilah was—and her warlock husband, Alasdair, down, too. But they didn't know she was coming, so there was a chance.

"What's the plan here?" Angelika asked Pytheios, projecting as much bravado as she could. "Kill us in front of witnesses?"

He sneered, then held out a hand. Out of the dark, the figure of a woman, not much younger than they, appeared, sidling up to her king.

Beautiful and willowy, she reminded Angelika of Meira's stature, with Kasia's direct gaze and Skylar's stubbornly tilted chin, all with Angelika's coloring.

Tisiphone.

My mother's ashes are inside her. They are the reason she's a phoenix. Even in death, Pytheios couldn't leave their poor mother in peace.

But was that this girl's fault? What if she was as much of a victim as anyone else here?

Skylar, Kasia, and Angelika all looked to Meira, who was focused now on the false phoenix, studying her, reaching out with her empathic ability, unless Rhiamon shut that down, too. After a second, she closed her eyes, chin dropping to her chest. "She wants to be here. Wants us dead. Wants to be queen," she whispered. "I'm sure of it."

Angelika hadn't needed the words. Meira's disappointment was palpable. They'd all hoped to save Tisiphone from this monster, but apparently she was right where she wanted to be.

Which made her just as much of a monster.

Tisiphone opened her mouth, but before she could speak, a woman appeared beside Angelika. Delilah, with her raven hair perfectly coifed and in a suit and heels no less. Beside her was her mate, Alasdair.

"Quickly," Delilah said. "That witch's powers are already trying to find me."

Without hesitation, they all joined hands.

"No—" Pytheios's shout was cut off mid-word as, in the next moment all of them—including their guards—disappeared from Kamen and arrived in the chamber in the Alaskan mountain where their mates waited.

But there was no time for a reunion.

Meira spun toward the mirror while Angelika searched the room for her mate. Where was Airk?

With a flicker of Meira's flames, the mirror before them changed, showing Pytheios inside the mountain, though now with Rhiamon and Tisiphone both. But they weren't only looking for him. The image changed rapidly, moving from mirror to mirror within the White Clan's mountain, exactly as they'd set them up, searching in rapid succession.

Showing them precisely what forces Pytheios had brought with him.

"Holy hells," Ladon muttered. "Even after that video, he's still got the entire Red and Green Clans mobilized against us."

The numbers didn't lie. How could Pytheios have such a strong pull? How could people not see the truth—that this man was a liar and a charlatan, out for power alone, and didn't care who he took down as he grabbed for more and more?

"It won't take his witch long to track the trail I left for her," Delilah, still with them, warned. "We have five minutes, tops."

CHAPTER TWENTY-SEVEN

Airk did an about-face a human general would have saluted and marched back into the mountain. He paused inside the cavern entrance and glanced over his shoulder. Half of his clan was still leaving, Mös at the head of them.

Turning away, he closed his eyes against the sight. Angelika would have handled that better. He'd only achieved splitting his clan with indecision.

Two steps down the tunnel back to the kings, a voice sounded in his head—Ladon. *"Five minutes. Positions."*

Angelika.

That meant Pytheios had gone to Kamen. Did it mean the phoenixes had gotten here unharmed? They assumed Pytheios would follow.

He couldn't think of his mate now. He wasn't dead, which hopefully meant she wasn't, either.

Stuffing all those mating, alpha-male, protective instincts into a dark hole, Airk sprinted back to the mouth of the caves only to pull up short at the sight of his white dragons shifting and taking to the skies along with a tumult of blue dragons. They'd been blessed with one of those rare blue-sky days with plenty of fluffy white clouds drifting by, and his blue and white brethren who could blend in easily with one or the other had every intention of taking advantage of that fact.

Or running away. His entire clan could be deserting their posts for all he knew.

The last dragon blended in with the clouds as, with no warning or sound, red and green dragons appeared, pouring down on them from the skies as though the clouds above had burst open and instead of rain...poured out death.

Fighting the frenetic urge to go find his mate, Airk forced himself to sprint down a different tunnel, not far from where their wolf-shifter allies were already gathered. If any dragons made it into the mountain, they'd be forced to face wolf shifters in their human forms. Other than the entrance, none of the spaces here were big enough for dragons.

No use wasting the wolves outside in this fight. Dragons didn't fight on the ground if they could help it and would only burn the land-bound shifters from the skies. Better that these allies remained inside as a last line of defense.

He skidded to a stop beside two massive wolves, already shifted—Bleidd with his dark gray coloring, and Jedd a lighter gray but with a cream-colored undercarriage and piercing hazel eyes. Both massive, muscles tensed under their fur. With them stood Madrigan, intense and listening to the thunder of fighting already raging outside, nose twitching at the scents of blood and battle but not yet shifted. He'd already explained that when he let his creature go, the carnage would be massive.

He was a last resort.

Getting a cursory nod from each—all of them grim faced, ready for war—he stopped and turned to face the entrance to the mountain.

Those who couldn't fight—too young, untrained, too old, the sick, and especially all the injured from the previous attacks—were housed inside this mountain. A cave troll wasn't the only thing these fuckers would find if they tried to come inside.

Even more important, the phoenixes were supposed to remain inside, protected. Angelika was safe here, and that was the only thing keeping his dragon from running to her instead of standing to post.

A massive boom blasted down the cavern tunnel, almost seeming to rock the mountain itself.

Hells, what was going on up there?

But Airk didn't move. Instead, he focused on the sound of the wolves behind him breathing and any hint of intruders from ahead. Together, they waited.

"All those who still pledge their loyalty to me..." Pytheios's decrepit voice suddenly sounded in his head. A grind of sound his dragon wanted to claw out of his ears even if it left him maimed. *"Now is the time to show your brethren who the* true *High King is."*

. . .

L adon's muscles coiled at the sound of the rotting king in his head even as he plowed through a green dragon, shredding the thing with his claws, then discarding it. It didn't take a genius to know what was coming next. Pytheios's message was damn clear, and Ladon had just placed himself and his people, who blended in with the blues of the skies, between the red and green dragons who'd arrived below him and the white dragons above him, hiding among the clouds. The ones who were still leaderless.

Not a single king's mark on a damn hand up there. If any of the white dragons were going to turn on them, now was that time.

"Incoming!" he shouted, taking an evasive maneuver before even bothering to look up.

Half a beat later, the impacts of bodies hitting bodies sounded like grenades going off around him. And the skies, even in bright daylight, lit up with a hundred fires.

"Permission to kill." He sent the order not only to his people but to the others. *"White dragons not switching sides, hold, or we'll kill you, too."*

They couldn't tell the difference otherwise. Airk, feral or not, needed to get his ass up here, because Angelika couldn't, and this plan was already falling apart at the seams.

A swooping move took Ladon outside the fight and up into the sky, where he could get a dragon's-eye view, assess, and coordinate.

"Skylar." He shot the thought to his mate, still safe within the mountain. *"Watch your back. We have turncoats."*

No answer.

He jerked his gaze in the direction of the entrance to the caves where she hid, trying not to allow fear to creep into what he needed to be doing right now.

"Skylar?"

Nothing.

"Answer me, mate."

"I was busy slitting a throat or two, lover." The sound of her voice had him bobbling in the air in relief, and he didn't give a shit who saw him.

"Fuck, woman. You scared me."

An unimpressed snort reached him down their connection, along with an emotion something akin to rolling her eyes and laughing at the same time. *"You focus on you."*

From his phoenix, who was a fighter herself, he expected nothing less. *"Next time, kill them faster,"* he shot back.

"Ladon," his Beta's voice sounded in his head, Asher's tone a warning.

Jerking his focus from where his mate was, Ladon turned in time to find red and green dragons on the move, rising from below in greater numbers to come at his people hard.

Fuck. They were surrounded.

• • •

Jaw clenched so hard his teeth threatened to crack, Brand watched as Ladon's clan got pulverized from both sides, pinned between white dragon traitors and Pytheios's own forces. But Ladon didn't send out the signal for him.

Not yet.

He had to trust his friend and ally. But sitting on the sidelines doing fuck all had never really been his style.

From his hiding spot, over the edge of a mountain peak farther to the west, the metallic scent of blood and the burning ash of fire hit his nostrils. But he still didn't move, him and his people remaining in human form deliberately to hide their numbers, waiting. Keeping the big guns for the secondary stage of this fight.

Pytheios's voice in his head had made him want to rip out his eardrums. The words, however, had sent a cold spike through him. Keeping his back to his clan deliberately, as though he might not have heard the message, Brand waited for the first traitor to dare to turn against him, come at him.

Because, of all the allied clans, the Gold Clan was still the most torn over Brand's rightful role as king. Many had prospered under Uther Hagan's rule, and since Brand had taken over, all they'd done was fight off the red fuck who insisted on ruling. The rotting king who claimed to have a phoenix—but Meira had shown people proof. With all the ways she'd sent that video out, no way could it not have reached at least some of those with him. And no way did they keep that shit quiet.

Had Pytheios somehow missed that? Or did he know that many wouldn't believe or wouldn't care?

His only warning was a shout, but he was ready. Whipping around, he knocked the attacker out of the air and was on him in a heartbeat, jerking him to sitting by the neck.

Brand leaned closer, getting right in his face. "I thought I warned you."

His people were all free to leave of their own accord without retribution, but for anyone who came at him or anyone aligned against him, the judgment was death.

If anything, the man's bulging pale gold eyes grew larger, fear extinguishing the fire in them. "Don't—"

Too late. Brand twisted the man's head with both hands, snapping his neck with a satisfying crunch.

Letting the body drape over the rock at his feet in a heap, Brand stood and angled a look of pure alpha rage over those staring in a combination of disbelief, horror, and other emotions he didn't have any fucking time for.

Shifting just his eyes, he used the telepathic connection and the bond with his people to communicate with them and them alone.

"You were given a choice long before we got here," he said. *"Join me. Or leave."*

Kasia had been the one to convince him of that mercy. Given the way things had gone down—the murder of his entire family, and no one seeming to question why the Hagans were suddenly the rulers—he'd planned on hunting down every last fucker without his family's brand on their hands and executing them.

But Kasia had swayed him, and he'd given in. After all, many of his people could have been misled or ignorant of the truth. Benefit of the doubt and all that shit.

He'd thought that act of kingly mercy had worked, too, because while some had left, he'd let them go peacefully. Proving to all that he kept his word. Meanwhile, the rest who'd stayed…his brand marked their hands. With a frown, he dropped to a crouch over the dead man's corpse, which was already turning ashy around the edges. Picking up her hand, Brand ran his thumb over the magical marking between thumb and forefinger on the back—only to find the skin there slightly puckered.

A gods-damned tattoo. Not a true mark of loyalty.

"Kasia," he shot down the link to his mate. *"Don't trust anyone from the Gold Clan. Some are traitors."*

"Then I suggest you kill them before they make it a problem," came her immediate reply.

Gods, he loved his mate. The fates sure as fuck knew what they were doing when they blessed his undeserving ass with that woman.

Rising to his feet, Brand couldn't help the smile drawing his lips back. A nasty one, if the way the men nearest him flinched was any indication. Only one thing he could think of might work fast enough to deal with this now. Focusing on that mystical bond with his own people, he reached with his mind toward those whose brands were real, toward the magic and the loyalty that put those marks on their hands in the first place. Only then did he speak.

"If you are loyal to me, kneel now."

Immediately, hundreds of men and women peppering the mountainside dropped. Those who were true, at least. Maybe eighty or so remained standing, staring at those kneeling with confusion.

"Kill the ones still standing," he ordered.

Then he turned his back on the sounds of carnage, looking toward the dragons battling it out in the skies and waiting for his signal to join the fray.

No black dragons could be seen. Which meant Samael hadn't received his signal yet, either.

Brand prayed Ladon didn't need them for a few more minutes at least. Until his people took care of the traitors, they weren't going anywhere.

. . .

Samael gritted his teeth as blood, fire, and bone rained down from the violent melee above his head. From the ground where he and his people hid camouflaged in the shadows of the massive pine trees that blanketed these mountains, it sure as hells looked like they were losing this fight already.

Ladon's people were taking a pounding. Smart of Pytheios to cut their numbers by calling on all his traitorous followers, evening out the two sides facing each other, but also adding confusion of who to trust into the mix.

In fact, Samael had initially expected several from his own clan to turn on him.

Of the three kings standing against Pytheios, Ladon was the most secure, having been practically begged to take over long before the war. Brand was probably dealing with a lot of shit right now, his clan being the most contentious about their current ruler. But Samael…he was born common and had to fight his way up the chain of command. He wasn't even royal.

But his previous king, a good man and a good ruler, had blessed him as the heir to the throne right before his own death. That had to be the only reason no black dragon shifters were turning against him, or against their own, right now.

"Ladon?" He sent the message not only to the blue king but to Brand and Airk as well as their mates.

No answer from his ally and brother-in-blood. No signal, either.

"We are as useless as two shits down here," he muttered to himself.

Reaching down that beautiful connection between himself and Meira, he felt for his mate. She was nervous but calm, the glow of her perfect and unique, their child snug and warm in her belly. He'd never adore anything or anyone the way he did that woman.

"I love you," he sent to her.

"Don't do anything rash," came her request. Not a demand, but she knew him. She knew why he'd say that to her. *"And I love you, too."*

Spreading his wings wide, Samael launched himself into the sky with a single order shot to his own men. *"Follow!"*

In his head, Brand's voice sounded the same order to his people.

• • •

The never-ending clash of dragons was unmistakable, even from inside these damn caverns.

"Samael didn't wait for the signal," Airk informed the wolves waiting with him in the dimly lit hollowed rock.

I should be there. With my people. Killing them or fighting beside them. Either way.

Maybe the white dragons who had turned wouldn't have if they'd had a king to follow. Someone in the air with them.

But he couldn't be that, and the knowledge was tearing his insides to shreds.

"No!" A female voice crying out echoed down the cavern to where he stood.

"Get away from us, you bastard." That distinctive snarl he recognized completely. Skylar.

Airk didn't hesitate. "Stay here," he threw over his shoulder at the wolves as he took off at a dead sprint for the room where Angelika and her sisters were supposed to be waiting out the battle in safety.

He passed the body of one of their guards, throat slit. The scent of the blood indicated that had happened minutes, not seconds, before. How had he missed the sound of the scuffle?

The crackle of a familiar voice, though, had him put on a burst of speed, rounding the corner into the small "room" where Angelika stood, backed into a corner with her sisters. Airk pulled up short at the sight of Pytheios standing before them. The witch standing at his side must've teleported them inside in a blink.

"You're mine, now," Pytheios snarled.

The battle was a distraction?

Rage—both his and his dragon's—consumed Airk, burning like a flash fire through every cell of his body. A growl formed from the depths of the hells he'd lived in for centuries and crawled out of his throat, clashing with every animalistic, protective instinct and turning into an otherworldly sound.

Pytheios swung to face him, even as Rhiamon remained focused on the phoenixes.

"I *dare* you to try to kill me," Airk snarled.

He didn't wait for the bastard to spout whatever vitriol was about to come out of his mouth. He ran at him. Fast enough the red dragon king didn't have time to move. But Airk's only thought was getting him away from his mate and her sisters. Rather than go for the kill, he swung Pytheios around by the arm, then drove his legs until the man backed out of the room. For once, he and his dragon worked as one, and together they slammed Pytheios into the cavern wall. Wrapping both hands around the king's neck, Airk kept going, pounding his body in the wall over and over until a Pytheios-sized imprint formed in the rock.

And, for a microscopic second, the king's limp response, the way his head snapped back and forth with each slam, had triumph rising inside Airk.

I'll kill him now and end this.

Almost as though he'd waited until the moment that thought passed through Airk's mind, Pytheios grabbed him by both wrists, halting the slamming. Hells, halting his fight full stop. Airk fought, muscles bunching and straining, against the king's grip as the shifter pulled his arms wider and wider, forcing him into a weaker position.

Then, with no warning, Pytheios released him and slammed a fist into his gut. Airk heard the sound of his own rib snapping before the pain splintered through him.

Punctured lung.

But the agony of every breath didn't cool his fury. Airk stumbled back, paused, then launched himself at Pytheios, coming out swinging. Only with every punch he landed, no matter how jarring, the king delivered back three even harder. The succession of blows stunned Airk with the old king's speed and strength, weakening him more with every blow, slowing his return volleys.

"I may not be able to kill you, boy," Pytheios sneered, "but I can take you right to the edge."

The brutality that came next turned into a relentless barrage of pain and a blur of cavern rock as the fight took them farther and farther away from Angelika.

. . .

Angelika swallowed down the sting of bile and the urge to scream as the vicious sounds of Pytheios and Airk's fight faded away down the cavern hall. The only thing keeping her from outright terror or running after them was the knowledge that Airk was right. Because of her own grandmother's prophecy, Pytheios wouldn't dare kill her mate.

Instead, she did the only thing she could.

Focused on Rhiamon. She frowned as she took in the witch's withered appearance. Her skin had turned paler with a sickly pall, making her appear jaundiced, her eyes sunken in her skull and her body emaciated. As though the magic she wielded was sucking the very life force from her.

And maybe it was. Maybe that was the price she paid for such power.

Angelika ignored the small poke of pity for the creature in front of her. She needed to buy time. Their plan for dealing with Rhiamon depended on Delilah, who was supposed to have stopped the witch in Kamen earlier.

But apparently that hadn't happened.

"Is this really what you want?" she asked the woman.

Rhiamon's unblinking stare didn't so much as twitch. She wasn't looking *at* Angelika or any of her sisters so much as over them. Through them.

"Pytheios killed your son," Kasia tried as well. "I saw it in a vision."

Rhiamon didn't move.

Angelika flicked a glance at Meira, who shook her head. Powers still off.

"He forced you to create a phoenix to take your place at his side," Skylar prodded, her tone not pitying but disgusted.

Angelika's heart pinched at what she was about to say next. "He is replacing your son with Tisiphone's child as heir. How can you help him do such a thing?"

The witch gave the barest twitch, so fast Angelika wasn't sure if she actually saw the movement.

"I have no choice," Rhiamon whispered. "He brought me back. I am his to…control."

His to control?

"He'll have a hard time doing that from where we're sending you." Delilah's husky voice sounded from the darkness, pinging all around the small cave.

As though manifesting from thin air, the mysterious woman appeared before Rhiamon, Alasdair at her side.

Immediately, hatred clawed Rhiamon's expression into a harsh snarl that obliterated any remaining beauty. She raised her hands as though to attack, but then made a tiny sound of distress as her body froze. Her hands lowered to her sides in little jerks, as though she was fighting it.

"We can't hold her long," Delilah said almost conversationally, though from behind her, Angelika could see how the woman was starting to tremble.

Then, also from nowhere, a man appeared directly before the witch.

Tall and lanky, the older gentleman had salt-and-pepper hair—more salt than pepper—which he kept short, and a thick handlebar mustache. All that silvery hair stood out starkly against his deeply tanned, leathery skin, which spoke of countless hours in the sun, probably on a bike, because she knew who this was.

"Hershel?" Kasia's voice filled with hope and relief.

Brand's friend. Not a demon or an angel. Neither good nor evil. But ancient. An ancient spirit with incredible power. The man turned his head at Kasia's exclamation. Bright blue eyes, undimmed by time twinkled, and crinkles that Angelika could tell came from smiles easily given fanned out from the corners.

"Hey there, love," he greeted in a voice belonging to a man who must smoke a lot of cigarettes. Fire and brimstone in that voice, and yet so gentle.

"You came," Kasia whispered.

He nodded while, beside her, Meira gasped, and Angelika flicked a glance toward her sister in time to catch her flinch. "The witch is afraid," Meira whispered.

"She should be," Skylar snapped.

"I hear you've been a naughty girl," Hershel said, returning his focus to Rhiamon.

Then, he leaned forward as she jerked and trembled in her invisible bindings, desperation to get away clear even in the void of her eyes. Hershel kissed her. Placed his lips to the witch's. Her skin immediately grayed and pruned, as though his very touch was mummifying her body.

Rhiamon's eyes widened, pure fear glittering there. But then she sucked in, and for a brief moment her eyes turned human and Angelika swore she found relief there. "Kill me," Rhiamon begged.

Hershel paused, frowning in what almost appeared like pity. "For that, love," he said, "the hell I send you to won't be...so bad."

Alasdair grunted. "Work faster."

Hershel clasped his hands to either side of the witch's face, holding the touch as her body turned more and more corpse-like— shriveled, gray, and dead. He didn't stop kissing her until, finally, he lifted his head and pulled his hands and mouth away.

Angelika swallowed at the sight of Hershel's eyes gone fully, inky black. Then Hershel blinked, and his blue eyes were back to normal.

"Fuck me, she was something unnatural," he muttered.

"Are you okay?" Kasia asked, reaching for his hand.

Hershel's smile turned sad. "Whatever she was, she wasn't human anymore."

"What did you do to her?" Angelika asked.

"Sent her to the hells. Fourth level, and that was a mercy. They'll determine where her soul belongs from there."

"We can't stay," Alasdair said, grimacing apologetically. "The witch was our problem, and we took care of her. Pytheios is for dragons to deal with."

"You did more than enough," Angelika said when Skylar looked like she wanted to argue.

"We'll catch up later, love," Hershel said to Kasia. Then he was gone.

So were Alasdair and Delilah.

Before Angelika could even take a breath, Kasia and Skylar looked at each other, and she already knew exactly what they were thinking.

With their particular brands of teleportation, her sisters could fight. Angelika hadn't ever seen them in action, but they'd described it. Kasia would take them both into the air, where they would drop over dragons, touching them and teleporting them elsewhere, taking them out of the battle. Sometimes sending dragons to other places, or more often to their deaths by cutting out thousands of feet to the ground without the creature losing momentum.

Their mates were fighting now. The rage of battle could be heard even this deep into the mountain. No way were her sisters not jumping into the fray.

"Keep each other safe," Meira told them softly.

"We love you," Skylar said to them both as Kasia took her hand, and then they were gone, too.

"Angelika?"

She turned to find Meira standing beside the mirror in the room. Powers restored, she too had a job: to set up in the area where those unable to fight were hiding. If she had to, Meira would try to get them out through reflections.

Meira would be safest there with dragons, wolf shifters, and a cave troll between her and death. Angelika wasn't about to stop her. "Love you, too," was all she said.

With a smile that said the same, Meira disappeared into the glass, leaving Angelika alone in a room with only her reflection.

"How sweet," a female voice cooed from behind her.

In the reflection, a woman stepped forward, flames already dancing along her skin and in her eyes.

Flames that, as human as Angelika remained, despite her mating, she knew could kill her.

Whipping around, she faced a girl who could easily have passed as her sister. Same white-blond hair, same slender build. Eyes a deep red, now, rather than frosty blue.

"That isn't your power that you wield," Angelika informed her. Fury, rather than fear, filled her up. "It's my *mother's* power."

Tisiphone smirked. "She's dead. It's mine now."

Angelika had no way out and no way to defend herself. Tisiphone was going to use her mother's fire to kill her. She knew it as surely as she knew her own name. But at least Airk would go on without her. Because their bond hadn't snapped into place yet, he was safe from her death.

If he survived Pytheios.

Angelika took a breath and focused. Damned if she wasn't going down without a fight.

Skylar especially, but even Kasia, had taken to fighting like newborn foals to milk. But Angelika, while she hadn't loved it like Skylar had, wasn't entirely defenseless, either.

With a snarl that would do Airk proud, Angelika launched herself at the other girl.

Avoiding Tisiphone's hands and skin where the flames rippled, she punched her hard in the sternum, which backed the girl up several feet, her expression turning satisfyingly stunned. Not waiting to enjoy the moment, Angelika kept at her, hitting her next in the shoulder. Then she leaned back and kicked her square in the stomach, which made Tisiphone double over on a groan. With the other girl's balance thrown off, Angelika dropped into a crouch, and spun with one leg out, and swept that bitch right off her feet.

The other girl landed on her back, her head cracking hard against the rock and all the flames extinguishing in an instant. Before she could shake off the wind being knocked from her, Angelika was on top of her, taking her by the head with both hands.

"You think my mother left me vulnerable?" she snarled in the girl's ear. She banged the girl's head into the ground. "I promise you that I am not going to let you keep her inside of you."

Without warning—no sound or even a twitch of her body— Tisiphone disappeared. Angelika dropped the few inches to the ground with a painful thud.

"There's no way to get her out of me," Tisiphone said from behind her. But the sound of flames more than her voice had Angelika whirling with a gasp.

Right in time for the false phoenix to blast fire out of her palms straight at Angelika, who threw up her arms as though that could ward off death.

A blur of movement caught her eye at the same time, and

suddenly a wolf was between her and the fire. A gray wolf she recognized immediately. He took the brunt of the blast, his body going up in flames so fast the putrid smell of burning fur filled the small space.

"Jedd!" she screamed as more wolf shifters burst into the room.

CHAPTER TWENTY-EIGHT

L eaving the wolf shifters to deal with Tisiphone, Angelika ran to where Jedd lay on the ground, still in wolf form, and dropped to her knees beside him. She didn't dare touch him.

A sound like a whine accompanied every tortured, agonized breath her friend took. Even so, he tried to lift his head. *"Angie?"* His nickname almost broke her. *"I'll be fine."*

The nurse in her knew that was a lie.

The burns covered the entire side of his body that had taken the brunt of the impact. Charred black around the edges, and there weren't many edges. Most of his flesh was a massive open wound that looked like raw hamburger and yet white at the same time. In spots on his legs where there was less flesh, she could see bone.

Gods, the smell. In this closed environment, she couldn't escape it.

Touching him was out of the question. Infection was a massive problem with burns like these. At the same time, there was nothing she could do to help him from here—the medical equipment lay deeper within the mountain, with Meira and all the other injured.

Angelika swallowed and smiled back at him. "That was probably a bad move in hindsight," she attempted to tease.

Because the only thing she could do now was ease his pain a little. Her only hope was that the burns happened so fast and deep that the nerve endings might be numb from the shock of being severed. At least for a little bit.

The shimmering of Jedd's shift whispered about him, reflecting strangely in the dim light of the room until he lay there in his human form. Which was so much worse, because the severity of his injuries was more obvious to her now.

Jedd raised a shaking hand and placed it against her cheek, caressing her cheekbone with his thumb. "Worth it," he said in a voice gone so ragged, she couldn't deny that he'd inhaled some of those flames.

Which meant they'd be eating him alive from the inside out.

Doing her best to hide the knowledge of what was coming, Angelika leaned into his touch. "I forbid you to leave me," she whispered.

Jedd eyed her with a flash of spirit in eyes already turning cloudy and said nothing.

"*Please* don't leave me."

He wasn't her mate, but he'd been her friend. One of the best men she knew. This world would be far worse off without him in it.

Because of me.

"Would blood help?" She was technically a dragon shifter, and she'd try anything at this point.

Or…all shifters used that method, and she looked over at Bleidd, realizing for the first time that the room had gone silent. Tisiphone was gone. *Damn Mama's teleportation.* The wolves were all watching, mourning beside her, the pain in their eyes too much to take. She knew that if they thought he could be saved, they'd be carrying him to the cave troll now.

But Jedd tipped her gaze back to him and managed to shake his head. "Too…late…"

Even swallowing appeared to take him a lot of effort. He waved an ineffectual hand in the air, as though he couldn't quite control the limb, and she took it in hers, squeezing. "Jedd?"

What could she do? She had to fix this.

He seemed to understand the question in her tone. "Take down Pytheios. Keep your promises to my people."

He was saying goodbye. She shook her head, silent tears no longer staying locked inside, trickling over his fingers. "You have to help me do that," she insisted. "You're part of that alliance. That promise."

Her voice broke over that last word, and she had to try two more times to get it out.

A boom rocked them from outside the mountain, the battle raging even as he died in her arms.

Jedd's eyes started turning glassy with the onset of death, but his gaze remained steadily on her face. "I've always loved you, Angelika Amon."

Angelika's heart shattered at the truth in his voice. Gods, what had she done? He couldn't die. Not like this.

Suddenly, Jedd's face relaxed into an expression nearing contentment. "Find...peace." He was barely getting the words out now, inhaling with a whine of agony between each word. "With... your...mate."

"Not at this price." Her whisper was as wrenched as her heart.

Jedd squeezed her hand. "For...me."

Angelika squeezed her eyes shut because she understood what he was saying. To live her life for him. To love and move on and hurt and laugh and all of it...for him.

Leaning down, she put her lips near his ear. "I love you."

And she did. Not in the way she loved Airk, but in the way two souls who were always meant to be part of each other's lives loved. A bond that even death could not break.

"I...know." She heard the grin in his voice. "And...that's... enough."

As she pulled back to see it on his face, Jedd's body bowed up, as though his soul was fighting to escape the pain. Then he went limp in her arms. Chest still. Eyes unseeing.

A wail rose from inside her like no sound that had ever come from her before as she dragged him onto her lap, heedless of the blood, rocking them both back and forth as though she could will him back to life.

"Awww... That's too bad. Was he a friend?"

The sugary female voice had Angelika jerking her head up on a gasp. Through the haze of tear-clouded eyes, she recognized that Tisiphone had reappeared between her and the wolves. The woman raised her hands to blast fire at Angelika again.

A loud yelp was the last thing she heard as two rocky arms emerged from the floor below her and dragged Angelika into the wall of the mountain itself.

All vision and hearing went dark and soundless, as though someone turned off a switch, because Angelika was still wide awake. Pressure and stillness consumed her, encased her, and threatened to crush her. Fear, however, didn't factor into the sensation because she knew exactly who had her.

Meira's gargoyles.

They hadn't agreed to help in the war against Pytheios, but perhaps they were still fulfilling the promise to her mother to protect her daughters.

Technically, that should only apply to Meira, but maybe...

"I have to help them," she tried to say.

Them.

Airk. Her sisters. Her brothers-in-blood. The wolves. Her people. Even the ones misled by the rotting bastard who stood at the heart of all this carnage.

Angelika thought her mouth moved, but no sound came out, her voice only in her head, and even that she couldn't hear.

What little oxygen had been in her lungs leached away, and with it her ability to stay conscious. If she could see right now, she'd be mesmerized by black spots as she passed out, her head turning woozy.

She didn't bother to struggle. Bound by the rock, she couldn't move anyway. And she had every faith the gargoyle wouldn't let her die. He or she had just saved her from Tisiphone. She knew, without a doubt, that's what they were doing.

Suddenly, the impenetrable hardness crushing her opened around her as though the mountain spat her out. She and the gargoyle rose together from the floor of the mountain into a different chamber to the sound of stone grinding on stone, rough and raw to ears that had only been listening to silence. He'd brought her to a room filled with sunlight and an opening leading to sky outside. Sky teeming with dragons and fire.

A chaos of color.

Like a flock of birds wheeling, a squadron of black dragons, Samael in the lead, flew low over the ground, pouring flame down over a mass of white dragons on the ground. White dragons. Her people.

Gods, what had happened?

Even as she watched, a spearhead of multiple-colored dragons, headed by an onyx black dragon that wasn't Samael—Rune, maybe?—formed and burst through a swath of red and green dragons attacking blue who were clearly fighting white from above. But through the gap they made in the sky, more red and green dragons poured in. Airk and Pytheios were nowhere to be seen.

Turning, she found a male gargoyle, intimidating and fascinatingly beautiful in his way, standing in full gargoyle form, with a body carved from solid stone, wings flared wide as though he might wrap them around her at any second.

His grotesque face in this form appeared to be made from the carvings of many different beasts—the mane of a lion, head of a water buffalo, brow of a gorilla, tusks of a wild boar, legs and tail of a wolf, ears of a bat, and body of a bear. The strangest part was his eyes. Human eyes surrounded by delicate, purple-bruised skin that faded underneath the cracked rock that surrounded them.

Like a being possessed.

"Where is Meira?" he asked.

This had to be Carrick, the leader of the chimera of gargoyles who'd taken Meira in after their mother's death.

"Meira went through the glass. She's in the safest part of this mountain. Near the cave troll who protects her." Angelika pointed at the skies, where she suddenly caught sight of Brand ramming through from above like an avalanche of gold. "Can you help us?"

His face did nothing, made no twitch, no sign of emotion. "Gargoyles don't get involved."

Just like wolves didn't, and witches didn't, and every other blasted creature on this planet didn't. Except some had today. Even if only in part.

"If you think Pytheios will be satisfied with controlling only dragons, rest assured, he'll come for others next. A war with the wolves. A war with your people."

"He'd have to find us first."

"Or you could avoid the war altogether with one battle. Now."

The gargoyle merely stared at her long and hard. "Stay away from that woman, daughter of Serefina."

That's when Angelika caught it. The flash of emotion. This man had been in love with her mother. How had Meira, with her empathic abilities, missed that little tidbit? Had her mother held any returning affection for him? She'd mourned her missing mate all her life, but maybe this gargoyle had helped assuage the hurt, even if only for a short time.

Angelika put her hand over his. "My mother was lucky to have a friend in you, Carrick. Thank you for that."

A tiny pause, then he nodded. "I will watch over Meira." With the grinding of stone, he sank back into the floor.

As soon as the bulk of his body was gone, Angelika looked out and caught sight of Airk. Somehow, he and Pytheios had fought their way outside the mountain. His back was to her, short shock of white hair unmistakable, and as she watched, his head snapped back as he took a punch.

Then Pytheios, faster than she'd seen any dragon shifter in her limited time with them, rose and shifted into the massive beast he could become, bloodred scales almost grotesque in the harsh light of day. Like looking at someone's insides. He snatched Airk, still human and swaying on his feet as though a light breeze would tip him over, up in one claw and took off into the sky.

"No!" Angelika shouted.

"Pathetic," Tisiphone said from right beside her. Appearing out of nothing, unharmed and smiling. "Time for a little trip."

The other girl wrapped her hand around Angelika's wrist in a bruising grip, and suddenly sight and sound blanked out again. This time in a familiar way as they traveled the in between—that realm of nothing between space and time—to wherever Tisiphone was taking her.

• • •

Airk was holding on through sheer will alone. His own blows seemed to have barely nicked the king. Meanwhile, his own body had been beaten to the hells and back. But what concerned him more than the pain, more than the blood coating his throat and mouth and pouring from his nose, more than Pytheios flying him down the mountain, was the silence of his own dragon.

His animal half wasn't raging, wasn't clawing to be released to defend them both. It sat inside him, near the surface, watching but silent and unmoved.

Why?

A howling sounded below, coming from inside the mountain—the distinctive call of wolves. Ones who had lost a brother.

Airk managed to turn his head to see green and red dragons landing and running toward the entrance. He hoped like hells that had been a deliberate move on the part of the wolf shifters. Setting themselves up as bait to draw some of the fighting to their ground.

As the first dragons moved inside, a sound like an animal in so much pain it unleashed rage—somewhere between a wolverine and a demon—went berserk, echoing off the insides of the mountain.

And Airk, even through the haze of pain, realized exactly what that was.

Madrigan had unleashed whatever he became.

Last resort. That was supposed to be a last resort. Even after all the proof these fuckers had been shown, the loyalty to Pytheios had set them on the losing side.

We're losing.

"*Fight,*" Pytheios snarled in his head before dipping low to scrape him over treetops.

Airk curled in on himself, taking the brunt against his spine and trying to use Pytheios's talons as cover, but he refused to shift and refused to answer.

"*Fight, damn you.*"

Airk frowned at the tone in Pytheios's voice that time. Frustration. As though he was being thwarted and didn't know how to deal with that. Why was the king so angry that he wouldn't engage? Why not leave his bleeding body on the mountainside and hope someone else finished the job?

Honor.

The word whispered through his mind. Not Pytheios's honor for himself, but the perception of others. All the dragons out here could see them now. If he didn't kill Airk, he'd be branded a coward. If he killed Airk still in human form, that also made him a coward.

Neither of those acts were worthy of a High King, and the fucker was starting to realize his mistake bringing their fight out here.

Airk's dragon, still leashed inside his head, whipped his tail, nudging at Airk, as though trying to tell him something.

Maybe because the dragon half of him knew as well as Airk did that Pytheios wouldn't risk that fucking prophecy and actually kill them. But what if the king did? What if they could drive him beyond reason?

What if I can force the prophecy?

At that, the dragon in him uncurled, baring razor-sharp teeth in a smile filled with hatred and satisfaction.

He knew what his dragon wanted.

But Angelika?

Pain wrapped around his heart as though it had tangled up in barbed wire only to get shredded, and the way his dragon whined, Airk knew he felt the same.

This sacrifice was more than about them now…it was about their mate.

Angelika's perfect face planted itself in his mind's eye, her gaze sad. He would leave his mate behind broken and alone. Like her mother had been.

But she'd be alive, and Pytheios would be dead.

Trees slapped at him again, one striking just right and peeling off several layers of flesh from his back. He held in his cry of pain, like he had so many times in Everest, refusing to give this bastard any satisfaction, because he knew that, more than anything, pissed the false king off.

With a roar, Pytheios dove, talons outstretched as though he might drive Airk into the ground.

Airk didn't so much as look or flinch, staring back at the dragon's underbelly and calling on the patience that had served him well. A flash of movement caught his eye as an indigo dragon streaked toward them. Ladon. Four red dragons rose up in the king's path, cutting him off from helping.

Airk closed his eyes. He used to escape into his mind, making up stories or visiting his parents and having a conversation with them. Anything to not be mentally in the room. He did that now. Picturing Angelika the last time she'd shared his bed, all sleepily sated and smiling at him.

"*I love you,*" his imagination's version of her said in his mind.

Words they hadn't exchanged. Hadn't dared to. He had convinced himself in those moments that they didn't need to. That she was his mate, and that was all that mattered. Now...

"*I wish I could have truly heard those words from your lips,*" he told this vision of her.

Maybe...maybe the flesh-and-blood Angelika would hear. Would feel the truth of his love for her.

The ground hit hard, yanking him out of his own head, but not hard enough to kill. Damn the king.

Pytheios released him, leaving him uncomfortably draped over boulders, injured enough that every movement, every breath, hurt like a son of a bitch.

"*Hold on.*" Samael's voice pounded in his head. "*We're coming.*"

Airk didn't hold out hope, though, staying focused on his task. Through the pain, Airk pulled his lips back in a grin coated in his own blood and spittle.

"Cannot do it, can you, coward?" It took every effort to hurl those words out.

He ignored Pytheios's warning growl as he coughed, then spat out a large clot of blood. Then grinned again. "Now everyone can see how scared you are of a phoenix's prophecy. She told you the man who killed me or ordered me killed would be dead shortly after, and you can't face the odds that she was right."

"Shut up, brother," Brand voice sounded in his head, which only made Airk grin wider.

The dragons around them could hear him, and that was exactly what he wanted.

"Do it," he hissed at Pytheios between teeth clenched in pain. "Show them you don't fear a phoenix."

Even through the blood and swelling closing his eyes, Airk couldn't miss the moment Pytheios's control snapped. The moment the decision was made to kill him, so obvious in the resolve that hardened the rage in the rotting king's eyes.

The king raised his head, the rumble of fire in his belly a sign he was stoking his flames to burn him to death, but Airk refused to look away or try to escape. If he died, the prophecy meant Pytheios would soon follow. Now he looked at the bond between him and his mate not solidifying as a blessing. He wouldn't take her with him to the grave. And that was enough.

"I love you," he tried to send the thought to Angelika. He wasn't sure if she heard him. Gods, he prayed she did.

"I have a better idea, my king." A woman's voice pierced the air, even over the constant thunder of dragons battling overhead.

Airk jerked his head around to find Tisiphone standing on an outcropping a few feet away, hand clamped around Angelika's arm.

Pytheios paused, talon midair.

"Burn *his bitch* instead," the false phoenix crowed.

Time apparently didn't slow down when fear flooded your

veins. It sped up. Because the next moments seemed to happen simultaneously.

Pytheios inhaled, stoking the fire in his belly, the scales above Airk casting a red-gold glow over his vision. Tisiphone disappeared. And Angelika reached a hand toward Airk, his name forming on her lips.

Then a torrent of flame hailed down on her, obscuring his view of her. For a heartbeat, he thought he saw feathers, delicate red-and-gold feathers, through the red of the flames. But that had to be wishful thinking or his mind protecting him, because what he really saw was her eyes on him as her mouth opened in a scream. One he couldn't hear over the roar of dragon fire, but he felt to the depths of his soul.

Three screams shattered through his mind. Her sisters, wherever they were, sounded as though they were burning with her.

Pytheios didn't stop.

The flame kept going and going. As though all his rage could be absorbed by annihilating her completely.

Then, with jarring abruptness, the heat and light and sound cut off as Pytheios swallowed the flames. Even the sounds of the fighting had crumbled into silence. Screaming silence.

As the smoke cleared, Airk searched for her. Searched for his mate's body on the rock, but he couldn't see her. Ignoring the pain, though moving so fucking slowly, he pushed to his knees with a groan. He tried to get to his feet but couldn't make his body stand. So he crawled. He crawled as fast as he could push himself, leaving a smear of blood over the rock underneath, aware all the while of the king standing over him, dragon teeth bared in a cruel smile.

When he reached the boulder where Angelika had stood, all he found of his mate was a pile of ash.

CHAPTER TWENTY-NINE

The only sound that dared be heard all over the mountains was the crackle of flame. Small blazes started by dragon fire falling from above or bodies turning slowly to ash. But around Airk, only silence. Not even a breeze stirred the needles on the trees.

Or perhaps that was him alone.

Perhaps the grief of losing his mate was so immediate, so all-consuming, that the battle going on overhead was shut out.

"No!" a woman shouted, followed by another's cry, then sobs.

Kasia and Skylar, some small part of him acknowledged. Sounds that exactly matched the one his dragon was making as he stared at the pile of ashes that had been Angelika only minutes ago. And yet, the sound wouldn't come out of him. As though his dragon was protecting Airk by taking all the pain into himself.

All he felt was…numb.

"He killed her." Some random dragon shifter's voice drifted through his mind. *"The king killed a phoenix."*

"Maybe he isn't the High King," another voice whispered.

Only to be overridden by, *"Maybe she wasn't a phoenix."*

Then another voice. *"He turned her to ash in a minute. What does that mean?"*

Then another. And another. And another. Until Airk's mind was a cacophony of voices beating at him.

Vaguely, he was aware of a shadow looming overhead. A

deep chuckle scraped over him, followed by the wind of wings as Pytheios took off into the air. Where were the kings? The Enforcers? Probably in shock.

Screw them all.

"My people." Pytheios's voice was like a spike through his head. *"A true phoenix wouldn't have been touched by the flames."*

The voices went quiet. Listening.

Pytheios continued, *"I have only eradicated a liar and a charlatan from our midst."*

Angelika was dead. Airk didn't give a shit.

"I'll show you touched by flames, you rotting red bastard—" Ladon or Kasia must've gotten to Skylar before she could do something rash, because her words broke off abruptly. Airk didn't look to see why.

"We showed you who the liar is," Brand's voice boomed through him. *"That video is the truth."*

"Lies!" Pytheios hissed. *"A desperate attempt to make you doubt after what you've seen with your own eyes. Fight with me now!"*

A roar rose up from both sides, from every dragon around him. The noise only escalated as the battle overhead resumed with an impact of bodies and a conflagration of fire.

"Get into the mountain!" Samael's voice pierced the noise. Aimed at Meira, probably, though how she'd gotten out here, Airk didn't know. The panic there should have had Airk trying to help, because he could hear in the king's voice that they were losing.

But all Airk could do was kneel beside his mate.

They were mated, but he wasn't dead. He should be a pile of ash with her, following her into death.

Oh gods... She would have survived if their bond had solidified and she could shift into her dragon form. But he'd held himself back. He hadn't let himself love her as deeply as a mate deserved.

Because I am a coward.

The promise of everything he could ever want had been there in her eyes, in every touch, in the way she didn't give up on him, even when he pushed her away.

If he had only reached out and accepted it. The fates had given them the chance, with Angelika showing dragon sign and surviving his fire.

This is my fault.

She could have survived. She could still be standing here, facing down the bastard who had taken everything—everything—from them both.

My fault.

My fault.

My fault.

"I love you." The words came out of his swollen mouth so cracked, even Airk couldn't understand them.

He swallowed hard and tried again. "I love you, Angelika Amon."

The clash of dragons all around him faded away, drowned out by the numb and cold threatening to consume him.

Gods, this hurt. This was too much. More than losing his parents or his king. More than the physical pain inflicted during his incarceration. More than holding his dragon back all this time.

A rumble sounded around him, the ground shaking with it, shifting violently under his knees, but Airk braced against it and didn't look.

"Oh my gods. Airk, get out of there!" Kasia yelled.

But he refused to tear his gaze from Angelika's ashes. His body started involuntarily rocking, and the words, now that the dam had broken, spilled out of him.

"I think I have loved you from the start. Even before you approached me that night in Ben Nevis, I noticed you. How did no one else see what and who you were?"

He shook his head, still rocking, silently pleading at the same time that her soul might still hear him from the heavens. Hear these words he should have told her ages ago.

"I thought, maybe, the gods had sent me Skylar. But I knew that night when you offered to be my friend…I knew…that they had sent her to bring me to…you." He crumpled over the last word, bending in half as the pain finally penetrated the numbness and his dragon howled in his head. "I should have told you."

He leaned forward, pressing his forehead into the ashes of his mate, the closest he could get to her now. He couldn't even hold her, see her face.

"I am sorry. I will spend the rest of my life being sorry."

A tiny, wet, hot nose pressed into his cheek, and Airk lifted his head to stare straight into the red glowing eyes of a hellhound puppy.

With a grunt, Airk straightened, eyeing the creature before him, the strong scents of smoke and putrid rot filling his nostrils.

Legend held that the arrival of a hellhound portended death. Probably because they tended to kill anything that encountered them. But he knew for sure now that hellhounds embodied warriors who had unfinished business and were killed before their time—reincarnated to finish that business.

"Maul?" Kasia's voice broke over the word, closer than she had been a minute ago.

Airk stared into red glowing eyes, looking for the man who had been his king in them. Could Zilant Amon have been reincarnated again?

An image flashed in his mind, the way hellhounds communicated—that of a man with military-short hair and hazel eyes.

Even through the numbness, a tiny spike of shock broke through. Jedd.

Jedd was a hellhound now?

The black puppy—though still the size of a small horse—lowered his head to nudge Angelika's ashes with his nose, emitting a whine that wrapped Airk's pain in a layer of acid, eating holes through him. The wolf shifter had loved her, too.

A movement had him glancing past the hellhound to find three full-sized ones lined up before a massive, steaming crack in the earth. Jedd had brought reinforcements.

"Grandfather?" Meira's voice sounded from behind him, and he turned his head to find all of them—Meira, Skylar, and Kasia—

standing behind him, staring at the remains of their sister and the reincarnation of... Was one of those hellhounds the previous King of the Red Clan?

Unfinished business.

Kasia suddenly sucked in. "Are you...Brand's father?" She was staring at the largest of the death dogs.

Another surge of emotion pierced the numbness. If the kings Hanyu and Astarot were both here—two of those whose lives had been cut short by Pytheios's own hand, warriors with unfinished business—what about...

He turned his gaze to the last of the animals before him. The one staring at him hard.

"Father?" Airk croaked.

The hellhound's face spasmed with what? Pain? Regret? Pride? Then he bowed his head, flashing an image of Airk as a boy, as his father taught him hand-to-hand combat.

A slow burn ignited inside him, traveling over the pain in creeping cinders of flame, turning it into something explosive. The numbness disintegrated under a wellspring of rage. Rage...and purpose.

Angelika would want her people to live—those loyal, at least. To thrive. But Airk had nothing to live for anymore. Not without her. He was expendable.

He looked at Jedd, watching him so intently, and gave his order. "Find the false phoenix. Kill her."

Kill Pytheios's mate, and the king would die, too.

Before he could blink, Jedd disappeared with an odd popping sound, then reappeared with the white-haired woman who'd brought Angelika to her death clasped in his jaws. Her body flickered, as though she tried to teleport and it worked for a beat only to stop, returning her right back to the hellhound.

Tisiphone's eyes grew wide with fear as realization that she couldn't escape sank in, and Airk actually smiled, and he thought maybe Jedd did, too, around his grip on the woman. So did the line of hellhounds behind Jedd, drawing flapping lips back over gruesome teeth, eyes glowing brighter in the darkness of their skulls.

"A phoenix for a phoenix," Airk told Tisiphone. "Only seems fair."

At no visible sign from Jedd, the hellhounds descended on the girl, snarls ripping from their throats. Her screams pierced the air, only to cut off abruptly as they ripped into her flesh, tearing her to shreds until all that was left of her were strings of meat and skin and shards of bone in a pool of crimson blood that dripped over the boulders like a waterfall of carnage.

High overhead, a roar to rattle the heavens blasted out louder than all the fighting and fire raging around them.

Pytheios.

Only the sound wasn't the death throes of a mate whose soul was being dragged to the underworld by his connection with his other half. It was a challenge.

How was the king not dead?

"You think I didn't protect against that?" Pytheios demanded. "My witch made sure my mate's death would never take me."

Four massive hellhounds turned to face the sky almost as one unit, the military men they had been in previous lives showing in their precise movements. The growl they answered the rotting king with wasn't a warning. It was a dare.

"Watch over Angelika," Airk said to Jedd. "I'll take care of Pytheios."

Actually, fuck that. He was going to kill *everybody*.

This was why the gods had trapped him in that hellhole. Because his feral dragon was going to take down the king. Even as beaten and broken as he was, he would find a way.

Airk started his shift right there, unlocking every gate inside him, tearing down every wall he'd ever built around the wild creature trapped within his soul. The shift didn't explode from him. It came on slowly, his bones realigning with each stage in agony-rending cracks, as though his dragon was being forced to piece them both back together.

But when he was finished, while still weak, he was at least whole.

Airk beat his wings, launching into the air, careful not to disturb Angelika's resting place with the wind he created. As he lifted his gaze to search for Pytheios, though, the tiniest of movements from Tisiphone's remains caught his attention.

The roar of his dragon in his head almost pulled his focus away from what was happening, until his dragon also caught the scent, and together they looked closer, hovering and watching.

Ashes.

Sooty, feathery ashes the color of storm clouds rose and floated into the air, drawing out of the scattered bits and pieces that had been Tisiphone the same way that video had shown them rising to hover over the false phoenix's body when she was made.

A dance of death and impossibility, undisturbed by the breeze.

Gods above.

Everything inside him seized, his dragon more still than he'd ever been as they stared at what was happening before their eyes.

The deep gray cinders floated through the air to hover over Angelika's ashes, then coalesced above her. Swirling and eddying and rippling, the pieces formed into something not solid but recognizable. The familiar face of a woman. Of Serefina. She opened her mouth, lips forming a single word.

Angelika.

Even after her death, the phoenix was still fighting for her daughters.

Arms of ash formed out of the swirling mass and reached down to touch Angelika's ashes, which seemed to ripple as though they recognized her mother, and Serefina's apparition smiled.

Mother and daughter finally reunited.

The deep gray soot turned white-hot, glowing so brightly Airk's eyes ached and burned in his head until he wanted to claw his own eyes out. Around him, he could sense others looking away, unable to watch. But Airk fisted his claws, needing to see. Needing this to be real.

The combined ashes swirled and writhed like a hurricane made of pure light.

Then he saw it, and hope that he'd been holding back burst around him, as bright as the light coming from his mate.

From that molten, churning mass, a figure arose, like Aphrodite being born from the sea.

A figure so gloriously beautiful, Airk's heart threatened to burst inside him at the sight.

Angelika.

Her white-blond hair flowed around the perfection of her figure, her frosty eyes now entirely white as they shone with the power manifesting inside her. And all over her skin, unmistakable lines formed, sparkling brilliant white.

Feathers.

The mark of a phoenix.

CHAPTER THIRTY

Silence overtook the mountain and skies as though every creature on earth had come to a ragged halt. Airk wasn't sure if the silence was because shock had shut down his hearing or because all the fighting had stopped. He didn't care, either.

She's alive.

Gods, what did that mean? Was this a specter of her? Like Jedd or his father? An angel sent to finish this fight, then leave him again.

If anything, his dragon's rage escalated, turning molten in his veins, because his mate was here now. His mate, who needed Pytheios dead. But Airk wanted to go to her.

Desperation and rage tore him apart as he and his dragon battled in his mind as they always did, always at odds with each other, jerking back and forth in the air.

Angelika made the decision for them.

Her sweet, beautiful face contorted into something that reflected the heat of wrath consuming him from the inside out and sent terror lancing through both parts of him. Because his Angelika would *never* show an emotion like that.

"Angelika?" Meira, standing close by, called to her sister, reaching out a hand. Worry, not relief, wavered in her voice. No doubt the empath could feel as well as see what was going on with her sister.

Skylar apparently didn't need empathic abilities, because she pulled Meira back slowly, shielding her pregnant sister behind her, putting her body between them.

This terrifyingly beautiful creature wasn't Angelika. Not entirely.

Her body continued to glow brighter and brighter. Then, in a flash of light more brilliant than any sun flare, white flaming wings rose from behind her. Her lips curled in fury as she lifted her hands and light shot out of her. Electric strands like lightning, but ones that didn't flash then disappear. The strands connected her to every dragon, every creature around them, like a web of sizzling light, and she was the spider in the middle.

The light hit him so hard, Airk grunted with the impact. With that, a sensation of electricity ran over his nerve endings, as though he'd grabbed hold of a lightning bolt and couldn't pull away. His dragon roared as they both realized they were paralyzed. Held suspended in the air, not able to even move the muscles of their eyes. Angelika hadn't even left her sisters out of this web of paralysis.

Staring at his mate in horror, he could sense the moment she decided to do something so against her true nature the expression in her eyes shattered his heart all over again.

"This is what I died for?" she asked in a voice so soft, terror ripped through him along those electric lines. The terror of every person caught in her net.

"I died to save creatures who treat female-born as political objects or built-in nannies. Who have killed precious, vulnerable mates by manipulating the mating system to falsely give them to dragons not destined to be theirs. Who allowed this lying king, who murdered your kings and queens and two phoenixes, to reign for centuries." Her face contorted more. Twisting into something impossibly brutal. "*Centuries!*"

Her head whipped round to stare at a dragon in midair. White. Mös? Difficult to tell out of the corner of his eyes, which couldn't move.

"Either you were blind, oblivious, or in on covering things up," Angelika declared. "Either way, you are unfit to lead."

Mös's scream hit the air, his body contorting with whatever she was doing to him down that electric line.

"Or..." Angelika suddenly mused, sounding bored. Like a cat playing with a mouse when she'd already eaten her fill. "Perhaps you are unfit to *live*."

"*Angelika, stop!*" Airk shot the thought at his mate. This wasn't who she was.

Only the creature who had risen from the ashes wasn't his mate. His sweet, funny, merciful mate who everyone loved the moment they met her because they could feel that she was on their side... that she made everyone in her orbit important to her. What looked back at him from those glowing, white eyes was something wild, uncontained, and uncontrolled. All passion, all rage, all sensation, all revenge, and *nothing* of her softness.

A creature to match to his own dragon.

Mös's screams cut off, but Airk had no idea if the white dragon was dead or she'd merely stopped hurting him.

Then Angelika turned her head to look directly at Airk, brows lowering as though she were confused.

"*Can you hear me?*" he thought at her.

A slight narrowing of her eyes he took as a yes.

"*Who are you?*" Her lips didn't move, but the thought was clear inside his head.

"*I am your mate.*"

Pain skated over his nerves, as though someone dragged razors over the soft flesh under his scales, and he ground out a groan even as he tried to keep it in. But the sensation ended quickly. A warning.

"*Liar.*"

She didn't recognize him? Airk's dragon howled inside. Maybe they hadn't mated.

"*I do not lie. Not to you. Not ever.*"

She cocked her head, focusing on him in a way that he knew... he knew beyond a shadow of a doubt that her next move would involve death.

"*If you were my mate*"—he could hardly hear her over the roaring and thrashing of his dragon—*"you would have died with me."*

Airk swallowed, wanting to close his eyes, overwhelmed by anguish that he couldn't have done that, couldn't have been with her in the afterlife, even so briefly, to help her. What happened to her in those moments to make her into this? Had she been afraid? In pain? *"The bond had not solidified."*

No change in the creature watching him.

"I am Airk Azdajah, and you asked me to be your mate." He willed her to remember. Willed it with everything inside of him. *"I said no. The worst decision of my life."*

"Why would you deny your mate?"

"Because I did not deserve you and I did not want to hurt you." Was that a flicker of hesitation in her eyes? So difficult to tell around the glow. *"I gave you my fire."*

Angelika actually laughed at that, though the sound wasn't a happy one. *"A phoenix gives a dragon her fire. Not the other way around."*

"You only showed dragon sign. Gods, Angelika, remember. Remember me. Remember us."

Suddenly, that electric line tugged at him, drew him out of the air while every other creature in her thrall—all of the dragons who'd been fighting, the Enforcers, the other kings, even Pytheios—remained imprisoned and unmoving. Even her sisters, who she loved so dearly, were caught and held, forced to watch.

She pulled him down to her. At the same time, his body shifted—not of his will, but of hers, the air around him wavering, perspective changing until he was once again human and standing, held immobile by the crackling lines wrapped around his body.

Angelika's gaze skated over his features, but no recognition lit her eyes. More like she was assessing his worthiness.

"You and your dragon fight each other," she said. *"He's... untamed."*

Not feral. Odd choice of word.

But now that he wasn't in dragon form and his lips couldn't move, he couldn't communicate with her. Airk stared at her, reaching for her with his soul. Pleading with her, the real her, to come back to him. Because the phoenix in front of him was a threat. If he had to kill her...

Turn me.

That would be her proof. They were mates. He believed that in every cell of his body. Every part of his soul.

"Turn me." He tried to make his lips work, his vocal cords. But nothing moved. Nothing except his dragon, who stilled inside him, listening to Airk in a way he usually never did.

Angelika tipped her head, studying him.

"Turn me," he tried again, thinking the image at her at the same time.

His dragon rumbled in his mind, the sound one the animal side of him had never made. Never. A gentle sound. Coaxing.

Angelika's eyes widened infinitesimally.

"Turn me," Airk repeated, his dragon adding that sound again. Both of them begging her.

"You would risk that?" she asked.

Suddenly, he was released from the bonds, the electric lines dropping away from him. Airk pitched forward, hands on his knees, and inhaled, reaching for his dragon, both sides of him no longer at odds. "Yes. I am your mate," he said, lifting his head and straightening, gazing steadily back at her.

"I am your mate," he repeated when she frowned. "Look at me. *See* me. I am your mate, and you are my heart—my soul. I cannot live without you, Angelika."

His dragon rumbled that soft sound again, and Airk understood him. Understood the love in that sound.

Angelika blinked, her eyes losing the brilliant light, turning frosty blue, and suddenly she looked lost, like a little girl abandoned. But only for a flash. Then the rage was back, eyes turning even more brilliant white, painful to look directly at. "Very well."

She stepped forward, closing the distance between them, but didn't touch him. Giving him the final choice in this matter but visibly not believing this would work, her expression almost taunting.

They'd done this while joined physically already. Several times to be certain. He hoped like hells that counted toward this newest attempt. What had her sisters said? That mating worked when both believed. Both chose.

Airk shook his head. "You must choose me, Angelika. You know that."

She tipped her head again, the flaming wings behind her stretching farther out as though she was preparing to take off into the skies. "According to you, I already did," she said. "Either that is true or it isn't."

She was right.

Without hesitation, his dragon with him in every way, Airk made his choice. Stepping forward, he took her face gently in his hands and lowered his lips to hover over hers. "I love you with everything I have inside of me. Put your fire in me, Angelika Azdajah."

Her eyes flickered again, but he didn't wait, pressing his lips to hers in a kiss that he poured his emotions for this woman into. Holding nothing back. Willing her to feel the connection, the love, the perfection that she was to him. The balm to his soul. His match. His mate. As he was hers. Her partner. Her support. He hoped her everything, like she was for him.

Destined by the fates but chosen by their souls.

No sound, no movement warned him. Her lips were still beneath his one moment, then pressing back, answering him kiss for kiss. And then, heat.

Heat pouring down his throat, but also washing over him as her flames consumed him both from the inside and the outside.

But Airk didn't stop kissing her. Didn't pause to wait for death to claim him. He trusted it wouldn't. Believed in them so fully, his faith eclipsed everything. Eclipsed fear, worry, doubt, hesitation.

His dragon rumbled, but the sound wasn't afraid. It was... content.

Then fire stoked in his own belly. Not consuming, not out of control. His dragon adding their own flames to the inferno rising inside.

Airk sank into the kiss, choosing this woman all over again. Only this time with *all* of his heart. Nothing held back. Not even his dragon.

A small gasp escaped his mate.

He opened his eyes to find her staring back. Pure white fire swirled all around them, cocooning them, sheltering them from every watching eye. The fire didn't burn to kill—it burned to *transform*. To bond. To meld them together until they were one. At the same time, a line of flame started at the top of her eyes and burned down, revealing the change, returning her to him.

Her. His Angelika.

"Airk," she breathed.

He smiled, relief rushing through him in a wave of emotions so immense there were no words. No way to comprehend the enormity.

She searched his gaze as though trying to find answers there. Did she know what had happened to her? Was she aware?

"You're mine," she whispered.

"I always was," he said. "My love for you extends beyond time, beyond death, and beyond despair."

With a sob, she threw her arms around his neck, kissing him with every ounce of the joy and laughter and love that had always been at the core of who she was.

Something snapped in place inside Airk's body, like everything settling inside, followed by an instant burning sensation at the back of his neck—the mating bond solidifying as the mark of his house, or maybe her house, or both, magically recognized the bond now solid between them and seared into the skin for all to see. At the same time, the brokenness of his body washed away. Instantly gone, pain melting away, as though their mating had healed everything about him. A man made new.

Suddenly, he could *feel* Angelika—her exultation, her hope... her power. Gods, she was pure power. A miracle.

The phoenix.

The realization came hard on the heels of another. He could also feel his dragon. Not as though they were two separate beings warring within the same body. But now a part of him as much as he was part of it. One and the same.

Everything healed. Put back the way it always should have been. And yet, the most important thing in all of that was...her.

Airk pulled back. "Gods, I did not think I could love this much."

Angelika's answering smile imprinted on him, a memory he would take out and turn over every single day of his long life. Perfect, incandescent happiness. "I did," she teased, smile widening to a grin.

Airk chuckled and kissed the end of her nose. "Time to kill the one who should never have been king."

Angelika's smile didn't dim. Instead, it morphed into determination and resignation. No fear, though. And no doubt.

"You have to be the one to do it," she said.

She was right. Especially after that display of raw, untamed power within her, dragon shifters would never trust her again if she was the one to kill the king. Besides, a throne was either passed down or won through combat.

Airk nodded.

With a sigh, she released them from the fire, the flames melting away like fog blown clear by a soft breeze.

CHAPTER THIRTY-ONE

The electric strands Angelika still held tethering every living soul around the mountain remained where they were, a manifestation of her will and the power now filling her so full she buzzed with it. Her skin was alive with it. Airk was the anchor to which she tethered her humanity to keep that power from overwhelming, from taking over. Just as she was the anchor for his dragon.

They were one and the same, the two of them.

A true bonding. This was why a king mated to a phoenix was named High King. Because the partnership of their souls was what would bring the supposed luck or blessings. Together, and only together, were they truly balanced.

Angelika released her hold on her sisters and brothers-by-blood. The movement in the sky of a black, blue, and gold dragon dropping down to join their mates was something she was aware of but not focused on.

Keeping the rest of her captives tethered, Angelika adjusted so that they could move and speak but still not go anywhere. No more death. This was about Pytheios…and him alone.

"Go," she said to Airk.

The ease and peace with which he shifted nearly took her breath away. No pain. No struggle. No fear. He and his dragon were finally one.

Fully in control, he took off into the sky, the wind his wings generated beating at her. And she watched him go. Watched him nod at Samael, Brand, and Ladon as they passed one another.

Please let him be victorious.

She had faith, but nothing was written in stone, and they'd only now truly found each other. This was the final hurdle. And a man who could kill two kings and two phoenixes wasn't to be underestimated.

The second Airk hovered before the rotting king, Angelika released Pytheios from her hold.

"It's just you and me now," Airk snarled.

The red dragon pulled his lips back, baring his teeth. *"I've already bested you once, whelp. I can do it again."*

The two dragons flew at each other, the slam of their bodies booming off the mountains around them. Pytheios went for the jugular, but Airk did some kind of flipping maneuver, coming down on top of the red dragon. They were close enough to the top of a mountain that he sank his claws into Pytheios's wing and slammed the bloodred dragon into the rock face, carving a swath through the trees and rocks. Relentless.

Until Pytheios got his legs underneath him and shoved at the mountain, dislodging Airk, who flipped back but stopped himself midair. Pytheios hadn't waited, though, launching himself off the rock and right at Airk. But Airk used the king's momentum to pivot and fling him into the skies.

With a gasp, Angelika jerked several of those electric lines, pulling other dragons out of the path of the fight.

Pytheios charged again, but again Airk flung him away, this time getting in a swipe with his tail as he did.

Could everyone else see what she could see?

Airk, when he and his dragon had been at odds, had been fighting himself as much as his enemy. Trying to maintain control. But now that he and his dragon were joined, they were in control.

And a thousand times more powerful.

Pytheios had beaten Airk before because Airk had been human and holding back. Now...her mate was only waiting for the right moment. Which came with shocking speed.

Pytheios went for another swipe, but this time Airk, instead of diverting him, met him head-on. The two dragons beat at each other, relentless and fierce. Every blow that landed reverberated off the mountains. But Angelika didn't wince.

As she watched, her heart in her throat, a hand slipped into hers, and she turned her head to find Meira there. Then another hand in her other one, and on her other side she found Kasia. Skylar wrapped her arms around Angelika's waist, her chin to her shoulder. Behind them, her sisters' mates watched the battle in the sky, grim and yet confident. Did they see what she did?

A cry from all those in the air had her jerking her gaze back upward to find Airk and Pytheios plummeting to the ground, only something was wrong.

Pytheios was on top. *He* was controlling the fall, driving them downward.

Angelika sucked in sharply, clasping her sister's hands harder. "Airk," she whispered, knowing her mate would hear her.

The two thrashing dragons passed out of view behind the peak of the mountain. A second later, a crash of sound louder than thunder preceded a *whoosh* of wind that flattened trees, threw dirt everywhere, and knocked Angelika and her sisters off their feet.

The air hadn't even cleared before she struggled back to standing. "Airk," she called out.

"I'll send you."

She whipped around in time to catch Skylar's shove in the chest. Then all sound and sight blanked out for a moment before she appeared at the edge of a crater.

Dirt and debris still hung in the air, and at first she couldn't see anything. But her brothers-by-blood dropped down over the space, their wings clearing the air, blowing the dirt away...

To reveal Airk standing over Pytheios's broken, limp body, teeth sunk into his jugular but not punctured yet.

"This is our kill," his voice said in her mind. All the minds.

"Yours and mine."

He was right. Angelika took a shaky breath and released the dragons held immobile in the sky, only vaguely aware that the fighting didn't resume. Instead, they all moved to hover in the skies and watch.

Witness.

A glance at Skylar, who had arrived with her sisters, and Angelika was instantly transported to the bottom of the crater, standing on a rock near Pytheios's head.

She stared into one large red eye, filled with so much hate and fire.

"For killing my father, Zilant Amon, King of the White Clan, I judge you," she said, letting her voice ring out for everyone to hear. "For killing my mother, Serefina Hanyu, my father's mate and a phoenix, I judge you. For killing my grandparents, the King of the Red Clan and his phoenix mate, *your* rulers, I judge you. For bastardizing the witch Rhiamon's power, I judge you. For killing your own son Merikh, I judge you. For creating a false phoenix, I judge you. For stealing the lives of hellhounds and other creatures to extend your own, I judge you. For deceiving your people, I judge you."

She paused, staring at the dragon shifter who had wrought so much pain and devastation. "Do you have any last words?"

Pytheios, despite the state he was in, despite facing his own death, seemed to smile. *"I regret nothing,"* he spat at her. *"Nothing, except that I didn't kill off your entire species when I had the chance. Dragons don't need you. We are the most powerful creatures in this world, and we don't need any others determining who rules or how. I did this...all of this...for my people."*

He truly believed that. She could see it in that snakelike eye staring back at her unblinking. Unflinching.

Angelika tipped her head. "Don't you see?"

"All I see is abomination."

"What you see is your origin. Dragons came from the first phoenix. *You* are what rose from the ashes that first time." Closing her eyes, she placed her palm gently over a scale, feeling the tremble of his hate and fear. But she ignored that, knowing Airk would hold him.

"See the truth," she whispered.

And shared with him…with them all…the history that she had been shown in death before she'd risen from the ashes.

In a void of light, she'd been surrounded by her ancestors. All the phoenixes who had come before, and they'd shown her…

The first phoenix, a creature all instinct and fire, turning to ash, and from that ash arose a thousand tiny lights, like stars of all colors, which became the first dragons. And a single brighter light that became the new phoenix to guide them, temper them, and bless them.

The dragon under her hand shuddered at the vision, but she didn't stop. She showed him more.

Generations upon generations who had followed. Every so often, dragons would lose faith and rise against one another or the phoenix. Three times this had happened before. And with any wrongful death of a phoenix, the shifters would lose a part of themselves as punishment rather than the blessings they could have had.

First the split of soul, creating the possibility of feral dragons if they didn't anchor their animal to their humanity. Like Airk. Then the creation of the clans, separating brother from brother by color. Then all female-born dragons becoming sterile.

The death of Angelika's own grandmother had been what split the new life in her daughter's womb into four phoenixes. And finally, with the death of Angelika's mother, the full blessings of the first phoenix that had been buried inside Angelika were awakened by her mate.

A dragon.

"*Oh gods.*" Pytheios's voice inside her head broke. Because even the king, whose soul was as rotten as his flesh had once been, could feel the truth of what she showed him. "*What have I done?*"

A small part of Angelika ached for this man. Power had

consumed and distorted him to what he'd become. What he'd wrought. Power and a broken heart. Because she truly believed he had loved her mother, now that she could see beyond him.

"Don't worry," she whispered. "I will set it all right again."

With that, she let the fire come, pouring over her skin, over every part of her. Those flaming wings extended behind her, and, with a single touch, the king was gone.

A swift death, more merciful than his actions deserved, but to her, this was the right way to end all of the violence and fighting that his reign had brought down on her people.

She closed her eyes and held on to her fire, picturing the world of her people as the magic of those visions showed her how it had been to start.

The power inside her built and built and built, thrumming through her.

With a cry, she flung her arms out, and the light that burst from her was so radiant her sight was blinded. But she didn't stop.

Every dragon, not just here, but those all over the world, including dragon mates as yet undiscovered, became a precious glow to her. As though she could see them all, touch them all.

Heal them all.

Her body started to shake with the enormity of what she was trying to do, tears leaking from the corners of her eyes.

It was too much.

Arms came around her—softly, though, a hand cradling her head. "I am here," Airk whispered through the light.

The shaking eased as she drew on her mate's strength, still searching, seeking and finding every soul she needed to touch. Her brothers-by-blood, her sisters, and Airk were the last she reached for.

"For us all," she whispered. Knowing they would *all* hear her.

Then her power burst from her in a single, sharp wave, and darkness consumed her vision, the sound of Airk's voice calling her name growing fainter with each passing moment as she disappeared once again into oblivion and fire.

· · ·

Airk found himself holding his dying mate in his arms, surrounded in her fire but not burning with it, because he was hers now, as she was his.

Angelika had given everything. Like everyone else, he'd seen it all. Everything she had to fix…ages of betrayals, to fix consequences, to save their people.

But this time, despair didn't consume him, didn't drag him down into the pits of the seven hells. He was her mate, the binding so strong that he could still feel her, even in this form. The funny, indestructible, glorious soul he'd been blessed to walk beside in this life.

She wasn't dead…because he wasn't. His body wasn't turning the same ashy gray as hers. The fire wasn't touching his flesh.

A shadow fell over him, and Airk lifted his head to stare at the three women who dropped to their knees beside their sister.

Kasia. Skylar. Meira.

Tears poured down their cheeks, shock turning their skin pale, and a hopelessness rounding their shoulders that Airk couldn't understand.

"She's not gone," he said softly.

All three jerked their gazes to him, confusion darkening frosty eyes to a darker blue.

"What?" Meira's question trembled on her lips.

"*You* can fix this." He didn't know how he knew, but he did.

Maybe witnessing how a phoenix could pass on her powers to her child and yet still live was how he knew. He'd been there the day the red queen had passed her powers on to her own daughter, Serefina.

Realization lit Kasia and Skylar up with hope almost as radiant as Angelika had been when she'd risen before. But Meira's head dropped, her hand going to her belly, where a sleeping dragon prince lay.

Kasia wrapped her hand around Meira's. "You saw your son take the throne," she said. "He'll be dragon, not phoenix, but he'll live."

"Do you see it?" Meira asked. "What we'll become?"

Kasia shook her head, a sadness tempering the hope there. "But our grandmother lived. So will we."

Skylar, on Meira's other side, took her other hand. "And so will Angelika."

Meira turned to look over her shoulder at Samael, and Airk couldn't miss the way the King of the Black Clan swallowed. The pure fear in his eyes for his mate...and his unborn child. But he also didn't hesitate, dropping to one knee behind Meira, he placed a kiss on her lips. Unspoken words passed between them.

Ladon closed his eyes for a second, then did the same with Skylar, who put her forehead to his. Brand dropped to both knees and wrapped an arm around Kasia's waist. "I'll follow you to the grave happily, mate."

The three phoenixes didn't hesitate. Didn't wallow or take time to reconsider.

How they knew what to do, Airk had no idea. But each raised both her hands in the air and held them, palms together, fingertips spread, like a lotus flower, up to the skies.

Then, one at a time, they called forth their power—Kasia's gold fire, Skylar's blue fire, and Meira's black fire. The flames flowed over their entire bodies at first but, as he watched, gathered and crawled softly upward, moving up to gather and coalesce in the palms of their outstretched hands, as though each was holding an orb of intense, dancing power.

But the more flame they gathered, the grayer their skin became, morphing from healthy flesh to something that resembled a stone carving. A marble statue ancient peoples would have worshiped.

The last part of them to change was their eyes, and all three, in unison, tipped their heads back on a silent, final inhalation.

Then the orbs of fire still held in their hands floated, one by one, down to Angelika's body, now almost as gray as her sisters. Each orb absorbed into her unmoving heart, lighting up the organ through the layers of dying flesh and visibly absorbing into her blood, her veins turning a fiery orange.

Molten lava pulsed through her body in orange-red spurts. But nothing else happened.

Airk didn't look away from his mate. Waiting.

The soft tread of a paw preceded a shadow crossing Angelika's body, and Airk raised his head to find Jedd nosing at his mate's arm.

An image flashed in Airk's mind: an image of a shared laugh between the wolf shifter and Angelika, a moment of pure friendship. Then the tiny hellhound lifted its head to the skies and opened its mouth in a silent howl. Instead of sound, a similar orb of fire rose from the pit of his maw. Like with her sisters, the orb moved to hover over Angelika's body before sinking into her flesh and absorbing.

With a wobble, Jedd fell to his side, the red glow of his eyes dimming, then dying out entirely, leaving holes of black nothingness.

Lining up behind them, each of the other hellhounds did the same one by one. First Brand's father, who chose to share the image of Brand's first shift with his son, the pride of that moment palpable even now. Brand swallowed convulsively. "Take care of our family in the afterlife until we can join you," the gold king whispered.

Then Brand's father was gone, sending his fire into Angelika.

Then Airk's own father was there, moving to stand before him. Only instead of one image, a multitude flashed through his mind. Not their time together, but images of Airk after his parents' death. From afar, as though seen through the veil of death. Airk surviving in the dungeons, growing into a man, learning despite the hopelessness of his situation. His escape and the moments that had led him here.

His father, his mighty father, bowed before him. Then, before he could have just one more moment with his parent, the hellhound sent his fire following Jedd's and Brand's father's into Angelika, before falling dead at Airk's feet.

Only this time...this death...held peace. Not horror. Not fear. Not sorrow. Just peace.

The last hellhound, the incarnation of King Hanyu, finally stepped forward, and he stared long and hard at the figures of his four granddaughters. Then an image appeared in Airk's mind—all minds—as perfect as the day it happened.

The day their mother, Serefina, was born.

The joy, the sheer delight of a father, and now that of a proud grandfather who had been avenged, radiant in the moment.

Please let her be able to see this, he begged the gods. *To know this moment.*

Then the final hellhound gave himself over to her.

Once that last piece absorbed into her, Angelika jolted, and her heart lit up, the flash so bright Airk had to close his eyes. Only to open them and watch in utter awe as her heart pumped once. Twice. Then, as the glow of fire faded, it picked up a steady rhythm.

But none of the sisters moved.

Airk leaned forward and whispered in Angelika's ear. "Open your eyes."

And she did.

The gray ash coating her cracked with the motion and fell away to reveal healthy flesh beneath. She stared at him with new eyes. Eyes a kaleidoscope of colors, as though she was everything now. All things to her people, not just one clan.

She took in his face, then smiled, and more ash fell away as Airk's heart soared to the very heavens.

"Thank the gods," Brand breathed.

A swift glance showed Kasia, Skylar, and Meira all emerging from the ash that had coated them.

Except the sisters all turned to look at the hellhounds lying dead on the rock beside Angelika.

"I am sorry—" Airk started to whisper.

Angelika shook her head. "It's okay. Look."

All four death dogs were starting to glow. Airk hadn't been there when Maul died, but he'd heard descriptions that sounded like this. Unlike Angelika, this was not a bright, heavenly light, but red, like the hounds' eyes—eerie. Each of the bodies pulsed with the color that lifted from him like an aura before solidifying into streamers of flowing red, casting its light over everyone gathered near the hellhounds.

The streamers slipped and swirled and coalesced, forming not one image but four. Murky at first, then clearer, as each of the men who'd finally finished what had been needed of them in this life became more defined with every passing moment until they stood, hovering above the hellhounds' corpses. They gazed down at the upturned faces of their kin and friends…and smiled.

"See?" Angelika whispered. "Everything is better now."

As though they agreed with her, the figures, still smiling and gazes still trained on their loved ones, faded away.

With a rumble that shook them all, the ground from whence they'd sprung closed up, sealed tight.

A deeply contented sigh escaped Angelika, which seemed to be a signal to all of them. Each mated couple wrapped each other up in arms and lips and relief.

"My love…" Ladon's voice held wonder, not concern. "Your eyes."

Airk peered closer. Like Angelika, Skylar's eyes had changed. So had Meira's and Kasia's, each now the colors of their mates—a deep gold, brilliant blue, and onyx black.

Meira put her hand to Samael's cheek. "I'm a dragon now. We gave her everything."

"Disappointed?" Kasia asked Brand.

The gold king snorted. "No. Now I get to call you lizard girl."

Kasia groaned and rolled her eyes but also tightened her arms around Brand's neck. With sharp breaths of joy, all four couples took a moment to simply hold each other.

"Umm…" Angelika murmured into Airk's neck. "I'm *not* a dragon."

Airk pulled back, unable to keep the smile from his face. "No. You are perfect."

"Shit, brother," Ladon muttered, though his tone remained laughing. "Don't say things like that or all our mates will expect it."

"I think I'd throw up if you said something like that to me," Skylar quipped.

The sound of Angelika's soft chuckle was sheer bliss.

They'd done it. They'd defeated Pytheios. They'd all survived it. Jubilation would come. He knew that. But for now...gratefulness was all he felt.

"I hate to interrupt this little...celebration."

Airk raised his head to find Tovar, shifted and standing a respectful distance away.

His old friend raised a hand, indicating all the previously battling dragons and wolves watching in silence. "But you have some things to sort out."

EPILOGUE

Angelika stared into the mirror at a woman who was her but not her.

The eyes in particular were taking some getting used to. But today she was more not her than ever. All gussied up in a dress that had taken way more discussion than a dress should take. Everyone—her sisters, the newly established council for the White Clan, all the other clans, the designer—had an opinion.

Dressing by committee sucked.

Worth it this time, she tried to tell herself. Because this was Airk's coronation day.

It had taken months...*months*...of dealing with details and the fallout of everything that had led to Pytheios's death. Months of healing, but also decisions and new laws and reaching out to those who'd been discarded or left behind by the previous rulers. Months to take Pytheios's stash of wealth, combine it with all the clans', and redistribute equally, starting fresh. Months to start on the dreams her own father had held when he'd been prepared to become High King—for the clans to live in equality, the colonies to govern themselves, and to dissolve the mating council, giving mates the time and resources to find their mates themselves.

They'd allowed the clans to go back to their own mountains and select their leaders anew. Even the Gold, Black, and Blue Clans had done so. In the end, Brand, Ladon, and Samael had all kept their thrones, Brand doing so perhaps the biggest surprise.

Though perhaps not, after what Angelika had shown her people that day combined with the appearance of his own father at the end.

The Red Clan had chosen no one of royal blood, not entirely trusting anyone Pytheios had allowed to live who could be a political threat to his throne. Instead, taking a leaf from the Black Clan, they'd chosen a warrior with not a drop of highborn in him. The Green Clan had chosen to execute King Fraener, the only king to remain by Pytheios's side throughout the war. In his place they'd selected a female-born named Meilin, the first queen dragons had seen in millennia.

That had been a shock.

However, the reports that whatever Angelika had done that day had touched female dragons, allowing them to mate, allowing them to bear children, had come hard and fast these past months. There were even a few reports that had started months or even years before her rising from the ashes. Almost as though the promise of her coming power had started to change things even when it lay dormant inside her and split between her sisters.

Moreover, human mates had also changed, no longer showing a sign on their neck unless their specific mate's fire was used to bring it forth. No more need for second-guessing or for a mating council that could be manipulated or corrupted.

Hearts, too, had been changed that day.

Not all hearts, though.

Some of her people didn't believe or refused to let go of old ways, but many fewer than Angelika would have thought possible. There was still more to do. New systems would always have kinks to iron out. They weren't perfect by any means. Or completely safe. After all, dragon shifters were as volatile as their fire.

But they had peace. They would build from there.

This dress, however...

Angelika sighed and plucked at the skirt, making a face at herself in the mirror. They'd decided that as the mate of the man about to be crowned King of the White Clan, she should wear white.

However, as the phoenix, they wanted her to represent the other clans as well. Which had been a tricky prospect, with many of the considered gowns making her look more like a clown car exploded on a white canvas.

But they'd finally settled on this design.

The dress was a figure-hugging, white satin slip with delicate, detailed lace overlayed. Wide straps of lace over her shoulders turned into a sheer backing down to her waist. The skirt flared out from mid-thigh in layers and layers of the same lace, reminding her a bit of traditional flamenco dancers. The bottom of the skirt had been dyed in vibrant hues blending up from black at the bottom, representing all the other clans, but in a gradient that looked remarkably like flame.

The dress was absolutely gorgeous. That wasn't the problem.

The problem was her in it. Fancy was not her way. They'd curled and styled her hair down with the sides drawn back and done her makeup to lovely effect. The woman staring at her was beautiful in a way she'd never seen herself. Her sisters had always all had more color than she did. She'd seen herself as a pale version of them most of her life.

Especially when her powers had remained dormant.

But this creature looking back at her from the mirror was all color, all fire, all things. And she wasn't sure she was up for that. As *the phoenix*—the only phoenix, now—she *was* all things to dragon shifters.

"My lady?" Jordy appeared in the reflection behind her.

"Is it time?"

He shook his head. "Not quite yet. The king has...disappeared."

Disappeared. The small frown that tugged at her brows wasn't worry so much as confusion. "What do you mean?"

"He said he had something he had to do before the coronation. That it was important."

Angelika thought for a moment of his behavior leading up to this day, and realization dawned with the softness of sunlight peaking over mountaintops. Just to be sure, she closed her eyes, feeling her way down that connection that mates had.

"It's okay," she told Jordy. "I know where he is. I'll go get him."

Airk's faithful friend, now one of their closest advisors, smiled.

As soon as Jordy left the room, Angelika used the teleportation—both Kasia's and Skylar's combined inside her now—to go to the one place she should have known he'd need to see.

Everest.

Curious, she glanced around the surprisingly large chamber that housed the dungeons where Airk had spent most of his life. New dragonsteel doors to each of the eleven cells were spaced evenly around the edges of the circular room. Sunlight streamed in from the glass moonhole directly above.

Angelika closed her eyes for a moment, heartsick that this and only this had been her mate's entire world for centuries. She offered up prayers of gratitude that he had survived it, lasted long enough to get out and find her.

Taking a deep breath, she opened her eyes and strode—slippered feet almost silent on the stone floors, the *whoosh* of her dress louder in the space—to the one cell with an open door. Looking inside, she found Airk sitting on a stone slab she knew from his descriptions had been his bed, elbows on his knees and head in his hands.

Angelika didn't enter. Instead, she held out her hand, beckoning. "My love?"

Slowly, Airk's head came up, and his eyes ignited at the sight of her.

"How did you get here?" she asked, starting off with something easier to answer.

"Delilah helped me."

"I would have—"

He shook his head, though his gaze gentled. "I thought I'd get in and out while you were getting ready."

Angelika read between the lines. He'd needed to do this alone. Something she could understand.

"I *had* to come here," he said, seeming to mistake her silence for disappointment.

"I know." She held out her hand. "But this is the last time. We should only look forward from here, don't you think?"

After a long pause, almost as though he was gathering his strength to leave, Airk rose to his feet.

Dressed in a very simple black suit with a crisp white shirt, a foil to her own clothes, he looked every inch the king he was about to become. Somehow, as usual, he'd managed to get away with refusing a tie or any other accessories. Probably the growling had convinced the others to drop it and focus their efforts on her instead. Even so, her body ignited—metaphorically—at the sight of him. Gods, her mate was something else.

He took her hand and allowed her not only to lead him out of the cell, but, after one last glance around, he nodded, and she brought them right back to their bedchamber in Kamen.

With a shuddering breath, Airk wrapped his arms around her waist, drawing her back against his chest and laying his chin on the top of her head to stare at the two of them in the reflection of the mirror they stood before. "You look beautiful."

She wrinkled her nose. She did, but she'd been expecting some comment about where they'd just come from.

"Why the face?"

She raised her eyebrows at his teasing. "Are you saying my face looks funny?"

He chuckled. "You are the most beautiful thing in my world, and you know it."

She hummed a little. Who knew her mate would turn out to be a big romantic and a poet with words? He told her things like that all the time. Much to the laughing chagrin of her sisters' mates.

"Mrrow..." A tiny little sound had her looking down, and Angelika couldn't help her chuckle.

"I think *she* would prefer to be the most beautiful," she teased him.

A gift from Meira, who had informed Airk that he clearly was a cat person or hers wouldn't love him so much. The little white ball of fluff dogged his footsteps like he was her mama.

Airk just grunted, giving the kitten a mock glare even as he scooped her up gently before setting her on top of the impressive cat tower he'd bought for his new pet.

Someday, he would be an amazing father. Gods, she loved him.

"Are you ready?" he asked, turning back to Angelika.

Shouldn't she be the one asking that?

"No." She sighed. "But I'm the one who should be asking. It's *your* coronation."

An odd little twinge reached her through the connection between them. Not worry or anything bad, really. Just...odd. It had been going on the last few days, but she figured he'd tell her when he was ready.

Airk moved closer, only to frame her face with his hands, fire blazing in his eyes as his gaze skated over her features. "My miracle," he whispered.

"No pedestals." She poked a finger in his chest.

Airk grinned. "Of course not. Only endless love."

She grinned back. "I can handle that if you can."

Airk leaned forward, pressing his lips to hers. As happened every single time with them, passion flared with the simple touch. Angelika had to be the one to draw away. "It's time."

Her mate sighed, forehead to hers. "I know."

After she reapplied her lipstick, she took his arm, and together they left the small antechamber to enter the throne room in the mountain of Kamen together. Arm in arm.

Airk had insisted.

Wherever the king went, so went the queen. Usually ahead of him, he joked, forging the way.

Their clan was all gathered, dressed in their own finery, to witness this moment. Mirrors were set up all around the room, the same way they had done for Meira's wedding to King Gorgon, when Angelika had still been hiding amongst the wolves. Ages ago, it felt like now.

No more secrets. No more appointed kings. Everything done in the open.

Using the power Meira had given her, Angelika ignited her flames, no doubt making her dress appear even more remarkable. The reflections in those mirrors changed to show the other clans there to witness as well. At the front of the mirrors from the kings' seats in the mountains of Ben Nevis, Store Skagastølstind, and Ararat stood her sisters and their mates—strong, steady, and smiling at her.

In Meira's arms lay sleeping a healthy baby boy with a shock of black hair poking out above his baby blanket. Kasia, meanwhile, wasn't yet showing her own pregnancy, though Brand's protective hand around her was a dead giveaway. Behind Ladon, Arden stood with Reid, now mated and glowing with happiness. Skylar, holding on to her mate with one hand, shot Angelika a thumbs-up with the other. The rest of the mirrors showed other locations. The Enforcers and Alliances from each of the colonies in the Americas, Africa, and Australia. The wolves. The gargoyles. The witches. As usual, they hadn't been able to track down any hellhounds, though hopefully none of their loved ones remained in that form.

The ceremony was quick—also at Airk's insistence—and before she knew it, he turned to thundering applause, the newly appointed King of the White Clan. The last of the six rulers to be crowned.

Angelika breathed in both relief and pride. Their people were whole again.

Except, instead of turning to offer her his arm as they'd rehearsed, Airk raised a hand, and silence descended. "As the dragon shifter king mated to a phoenix," he boomed out for all to hear, "it is technically my right to also take my place as High King on this day."

Angelika clasped her hands before her, trying not to shift self-consciously at all the stares coming her way. They'd discussed this. Airk had decided to give up that right and make all the kings into a mutual council instead. The others had agreed.

How would their people take it, though?

"However, I believe that these past five hundred years have shown us how power lying with one man can be a dangerous thing.

An addiction, even."

A low murmur swept through the room.

Airk raised his hand again for silence. "I have conferred with all the other rulers, and we have agreed on two things."

Two? This is new. Angelika tried not to frown.

At Airk's nod, the five rulers of the other clans, with their mates at their sides—those that had mates, anyway, including her sisters—stepped through the mirrors into the throne room in Kamen with them. "The six rulers will form a council that confers and determines all laws together."

Those rulers stepped up onto the dais with Airk, turning to face their people as a unit.

Angelika smiled. *This* was right.

"And..." Airk continued. "The first act of this council is to crown our phoenix, Angelika Amon-Azdajah, as High Queen."

A loud buzzing hit her ears about then. Or maybe it was more that all rooms were buzzing with murmurings and her ears had muffled the sound because of the shock running through her system.

She even shook her head as Airk looked back at her. She hadn't asked for this.

"Our old system did not work," he continued, turning to smile at her. Speaking to her as much as to their people. "I think we all agree on that. Time for a new way. Our High Queen will not make decisions alone. All things will happen through her council of rulers. But she will be the constant. The northern star."

He turned, backing down the few steps of the dais to the floor, then dropped to one knee, head bowed. Each of the other kings and queens turned and did the same, forming a line before her, their allegiance palpable. Not a smidge of hesitation in a single one.

After a small pause, in silence, every other dragon shifter she could see rose from their seats, then kneeled in a wave of submission.

To me. Gods give me strength.

"I love you." Airk's words reached her through their connection, almost as though he'd heard her silent plea. So did his strength and his certainty that this was right. *"You can do this."*

Still she hesitated.

"You were born to do this, my love." The surety in his voice, in the frost-colored eyes he lifted to her face, melted away her qualms.

Angelika pulled her shoulders back, lifting her head high, looking out over her people as her mate's love and support washed over her. She looked at each of her sisters, happy and safe and empowered. She looked at her sisters' mates, good men each one.

Her mother and father would be proud and happy...and relieved. They were watching over them from the heavens. Angelika knew that. Knew that all her phoenix ancestors were there, too.

Angelika sent up a new plea to them—*grant me wisdom, strength, courage, and kindness to be the ruler our people need.*

The finest attributes of the four women Serefina Hanyu Amon and Zilant Amon had brought into this world.

At the slightest bow of her head, accepting the honor they were asking of her, Airk rose and approached, pulling out a delicate silver diadem from the inner pocket of his jacket. The delicate swirls of metal formed tiny little feathers and flames.

He placed it on her head, then backed up a step and bowed again, from the waist. "Gods bless our High Queen."

As one, their people rose to their feet, shouting that phrase three more times. But Angelika hardly heard them, breaking what she was sure was some sort of protocol and going up on tiptoe to kiss her mate in full view of the gods, her sisters, the kings and queens, and everyone.

"If you thought I was bossy before..." she whispered against Airk's lips.

"Maybe I should have said gods save the king," he whispered back with a chuckle and went right on kissing her.

EXCLUSIVE

BONUS CONTENT

Airk

Airk tried really fucking hard not to tense as Angelika applied the first aid that she seemed determine to give. The touching was a problem, but the way she kept talking, kept drawing him in, kept sharing things that made him want to know more…that was a much bigger problem.

"I might have no fire, no power like my sisters, but I *am* going to make a difference in this war," she said.

There. There was the side of her who'd proposed they mate. The side determined to not be shoved to the sidelines. He got it. But he didn't want her in harm's way either.

"Healing people is a way to be helpful." Didn't she see that?

"It is," she agreed. "But with the accelerated healing shifters have, I'm rarely needed in any capacity that way. Never in a lifesaving one. A Healer with a universal blood type is the one who makes a real difference around here."

Airk said nothing. She wasn't wrong.

"That's why I wanted to discuss our mating that night," she said. "It seemed like the only thing I could do to make a difference."

He shot upright, rolling over and swinging his legs to dangle off the high bed, to stare at her with that inscrutable, immovable expression of his.

Saying no the first time had physically hurt. He wasn't doing that again.

"I refuse to discuss mating with you." The words came out flat.

"I wasn't going to propose or anything," she snapped. Her chin took on a suborn tilt even as she glanced away, muttering, "Even if rejecting me wasn't very forward-thinking of you."

Don't answer her.

Get up and leave.

She ducked her head and fiddled with the bandage now dangling and loose around his leg. They sat quietly, the room thick with unspoken words as she continued to work.

And he tried damn hard to say nothing until he could get well away from her.

It didn't work. "Why do you wish to mate me?"

Her hands stilled in their work, and she blinked at his leg. "Like I said...to make a difference," she repeated. "For my family and for our people."

Not because she thought he'd be a good mate. Even just a friend? "Is that all?"

Angelika's eyebrows tried to crawl into her hair, and he hid a grimace.

"I mean," she paused. "Physically, I think we'd—"

His dragon suddenly shoved from inside, breaking the cage around him, roaring to the fore.

"No," Airk snapped. He clapped his hand over his wrist to hide the shimmer of white scales peeking through.

Only he was pretty sure she saw.

"You know, a mate would give your dragon an anchor," she pointed out.

She definitely saw.

"You could try to shift—"

"The time for that passed long ago." He was speaking slowly and quietly now, because it was taking everything he had to hold his dragon back, control balanced on a knife's edge. One slip and he'd lose everything. "If I shift, I go feral, and your sisters' mates will have to put me down. Are we finished here?"

She glanced at the bandage, which had started to unravel again, then pulled the stool closer and started rewrapping it. Again.

Fuck.

He needed to get out of here.

"Okay. Then maybe I can travel with you to help reach out to dragons from the White Clan. I'm a people person. Plus, they might be more willing to listen to both a phoenix *and* one of their royals. Maybe I'd have...er...a little more success in convincing others to our side."

"As opposed to my lack of success, I take you to mean?"

She cleared her throat. "I believe that's the third settlement that"—a longer pause this time—"wasn't interested?"

Was she babying him?

"That chased me out violently is what you meant to say."

"What if—"

"I refuse to negotiate this with you further."

The way her shoulders rounded slightly, he knew he'd hurt her with that. He couldn't let himself care.

"I didn't think we were negotiating," she said. "I was just—"

"Angelika."

Gods didn't she see how much he was struggling right now? How tempted he was? But his dragon's response to her was a problem. One of many.

"Then what's your plan?" She secured the end of the bandage and scooted back to look up at him.

She'd asked him this before.

"My plan does not concern you."

Airk shot to his feet, needing to get out of there, and she did, too...which brought them very, very close. He'd have to touch her to move her, and touching her was a very bad idea.

She lifted her chin like a dare. "Not mating you doesn't mean I don't care what happens to you. We once talked about being friends, and I would like that—"

He almost groaned. Now she brought that up? "No."

The word felt like ash in his mouth. Like poison. Like the wrong word.

Heat blanketed the room, like a roaring fire on a cold winter's night, coming from him. From his dragon. Airk locked down tight, not letting a single flame out. Not even in his eyes. A muscle in his jaw ticked with the effort.

And he knew Angelika felt it, the way she searched his expression. The way she took shallower breaths.

"I want you." The whispered words tore from her.

Angelika's eyes flared wide immediately. Why? Did she not mean those three words? They were a gut punch of furious need, lashing at him. Not just his dragon. This was him, too.

Anger joined the fire inside him and he narrowed his eyes. "Is this a new idiom I have yet to encounter?" he asked slowly, carefully.

"Er…I hope not."

He stared at her. *She wants me. Does that mean what I think it means? What I want it to mean?* "What do you want me for?"

She hesitated only ever so slightly. "Pleasure."

Another gut punch.

"Pleasure." He rolled the word around in his mouth as though it were a foreign concept.

Pleasure.

"Yes."

"You wish me to pleasure you?" Doubt layered the words.

A waft of a new scent drifted up to him, ratcheting every muscle tighter with the knowledge that just talking about this made her body respond to his.

"Yes," she admitted.

He jerked trying to take a step back—not that he could. But he also didn't look away.

Pleasure.

The heat inside him was as close to out of control as he'd ever been. She wanted him for pleasure. She wanted pleasure from him.

A riot of images—never far from his mind when it came to this woman—played out before him. Kissing those lips until they were swollen and pink, until she gazed at him through a haze of desire. Sucking the sensitive peaks of her breasts. He'd read that alone could make a woman reach orgasm. Touching her between her legs and giving her pleasure there with his mouth.

With his cock.

All the ways he could pleasure her.

She took a deep breath. "And I want to pleasure *you*."

Holy fuck.

His cock was so hard by now it ached.

"And make you laugh. And show you things about the world today and—"

His expression went blank, a small part of him dying a little with the realization of what she meant, and his arms dropped to his sides. "You pity the pathetic creature from the dungeons of Everest. Is that it?"

"No." She grabbed his hand, the soft touch of her against him more than he had the ability to resist. "This isn't pity, *dammit*. It's companionship. And...and..."

"And?" The last thing he wanted from her was pity.

"Chemistry." She flung the word at him, frustration driving her now.

He frowned. "I do not—"

Angelika went up on her tiptoes and pressed her lips to his. A soft, sweet, barely there touch.

Airk went utterly still at the contact for half a heartbeat. He'd wanted this since that day he'd talked to her outside the Ben Nevis hanger. To kiss her. To touch her.

She was soft, and sweet, and gods...

She started to pull away.

His control snapped so hard he reverberated with it, and Airk groaned at the pain of that loss but also the ache that simple touch of her lips had driven through him, like a stake to the heart. He slipped his hand under the heavy fall of her hair to urge her closer.

Angelika's arms crept up around his neck, and she pressed herself against him as their lips collided, but with such immediate need, it took them a second to line everything up right. The kiss took off from there. They melded and meshed and released and came back together with a shocking desperation that stole every logical thought from his mind.

All he could do was feel.

His first true kiss, and he was caught in the deadly force of an avalanche. He didn't have experience, but he didn't need it. Not to touch her.

This was a compulsion and yet as natural as breathing. Every tiny sound from her telling him what she liked was all he needed.

And all he wanted was…more.

He gripped her hips, pulling her harder against him. He took over, kissing her the same way a drowning man might hold onto a rope in a storm, as though she might anchor him to this world by her touch alone. She moaned into his mouth, and he swept his tongue against hers. A tiny gasp tore from her, and he did it again.

And again.

And again.

Reveling in the way she pressed into him with each touch, each sweep.

Mine, his dragon growled in his head so loud, so close to the surface, unaccustomed fear blazed through the desire, severing it.

Claim her now.

"*No.*" Airk thrust her away hard enough that she stumbled back. "This cannot happen. No kissing, or mating, or friendship," he said, ignoring the confusion, the hurt, crossing her face. "Especially not with you."

She curled in on herself, dropping her chin to her chest, which hurt as much as any lash across his chest ever had. He had to get out of here before he did something stupid like try to take that back. Cold control drove his steps, and she said nothing as he stalked from the room.

He didn't stop.

Not when the door *snick*ed shut behind him. Not when his enhanced hearing picked up the sound of her forceful breath. Not when everything inside him screamed at him to go back. To start over.

To say yes to her proposal.

ACKNOWLEDGMENTS

Dear Reader,

No matter what is going on in my life, I get to do what I love surrounded by the people I love—a blessing that I thank God for every single day. Writing and publishing a book doesn't happen without support and help from a host of incredible people.

To my fantastic, equally dragon-obsessed readers (especially my Awesome Nerds Facebook fan group!)...thank you so much for going on these journeys with me, for your kindness, your support, and generally being awesome.

Angelika and Airk's story was in my head from the moment I started the series, and finally getting to see these two come together—and everything that means in the wider world of my dragon shifters—has been the best journey. I hope you fell in love with these characters and their story as much as I did. If you have a free sec, please think about leaving a review. Also, I love to connect with my readers, so I hope you'll drop a line and say "Howdy" on any of my social media accounts!

To my editor, Heather Howland... Wow! What a journey. In the summer of 2017, we were just spit balling paranormal romance ideas. We started with a single dragon series—Inferno Rising. But we loved some other ideas as well, so we sprinkled some fairy dust on them and ended up with not one but two dragon series—Inferno Rising and Fire's Edge. Now it's 2021, four years later, and we've finished ten books, plus another four novellas in the Brimstone Inc. spinoff, eighteen awards, and, best of all, a deep friendship and partnership that I will always treasure.

To my Entangled family... Your support, your friendship, and your commitment to making incredible books have been career altering. You are awesome, amazing people who are a blast to be around and who turn out the best books. Keep doing what you do!

To my agent, Evan Marshall... For your guidance and faith in me. I can't tell you what it means to have you in my corner.

To Nicki, who has read every book, edited most of them, and been the voice of "you can do it" in my head when I lose my own... You are the best bestie a girl could ask for. Love you! And now that you're back in AU, miss you so much it hurts.

To Alyssa Day, Alexandra Ivy, Carrie Ann Ryan, Anna J. Stewart, and Kait Ballenger... Your cover quotes for these two series are appreciated more than you probably realize. I love the romance author community and the support we give one another. You'd better believe I intend to pay it forward. Thank you!

To my support team of beta readers, critique partners, writing buddies, reviewers, friends, and family—so, so many (have I mentioned how blessed I am) and every single one of you is appreciated for everything you are. As always, a thousand thanks and hugs!

To my author sisters/brothers and friends... You inspire me every day!

Finally, to my own partner in life and our beautiful kids... I don't know how it's possible, but I love you more every day. Damn, I am a lucky woman.

With love,
Abigail Owen

talk about it

Let's talk about books.

Join the conversation:

f @harlequinaustralia

♪ @hqanz

◉ @harlequinaus

harpercollins.com.au/hq

If you love reading and want to know about our
authors and titles, then let's talk about it.